FAMILY HONOR SERIES BOOK #1

sHATTERED JUSTICE

[A NOVEL]

KAREN BALL

Multnomah® Publishers *Sisters, Oregon*

SHATTERED JUSTICE
Published by Multnomah Publishers, Inc.

© 2005 by Karen Ball
International Standard Book Number: 1-59052-413-6

Cover image by Jon Bradley/Getty Images

Scripture quotations are from:
Holy Bible, New Living Translation
© 1996. Used by permission of Tyndale House Publishers, Inc.
All rights reserved.
The Living Bible (TLB)
© 1971. Used by permission of Tyndale House Publishers, Inc.
All rights reserved.
The Holy Bible, New International Version (NIV)
© 1973, 1984 by International Bible Society,
used by permission of Zondervan Publishing House
Revised Standard Version Bible (RSV) (including Apocrypha)
© 1946, 1952 by the Division of Christian Education
of the National Council of the Churches of Christ
in the United States of America

Multnomah is a trademark of Multnomah Publishers, Inc.,
and is registered in the U.S. Patent and Trademark Office.
The colophon is a trademark of Multnomah Publishers, Inc.

Printed in the United States of America

For information:
MULTNOMAH PUBLISHERS, INC.
POST OFFICE BOX 1720
SISTERS, OREGON 97759

05 06 07 08 09 10 — 10 9 8 7 6 5 4 3 2 1 0

PRAISE FOR KAREN BALL'S NOVELS

Shattered Justice

"Karen Ball speaks to the heart. Readers will fall in love with her realistic characters and gripping story line in *Shattered Justice*. A surefire hit!"—KAREN KINGSBURY, bestselling author of *One Tuesday Morning* and *Beyond Tuesday Morning*

"Whenever Karen Ball dips her writer's pen into the inkwell of real life, she grasps it with a velvet hand and crafts a story that gives readers eternal truths written on a scroll of enduring hope. These are the stories that soothe a wounded spirit and lift a weary soul."—ROBIN JONES GUNN, bestselling author of *Sisterchicks Down Under*

"*Shattered Justice* is for anyone who has ever known grief or asked God, 'Why me?' Karen Ball paints a beautiful picture of redemption and regeneration, and shows that even our suffering sometimes has a greater purpose. Keep a box of tissues handy, because you're going to need it!"—TERRI BLACKSTOCK, bestselling author of *River's Edge*

A Test of Faith

"Anyone who has ever struggled in a mother-daughter relationship will identify with *A Test of Faith*. The story is as real as the evening newspaper. It was as if I was reading about my own mother, my own daughter, and perhaps more profoundly, reading about myself."—DEBBIE MACOMBER, *New York Times* bestselling author

"As a mother of daughters, I was quickly drawn into the world of Anne and Faith. I laughed and I cried throughout *A Test of Faith*. And at the end, I thanked God for my own mother and daughters. Thank you, Karen Ball, for this beautiful and memorable story."—ROBIN LEE HATCHER, bestselling author of *Beyond the Shadows*

The Breaking Point

"*The Breaking Point* is compelling and strikingly honest. This story touches the heart and gives hope for struggling marriages. Karen Ball writes with clarity, depth, and power. It's a pleasure to recommend this engaging and memorable book."—RANDY ALCORN, bestselling author of *Safely Home*

"*The Breaking Point* is must-reading for any couple seeking God's ideal in this wonderful covenant we know as marriage."—ANGELA ELWELL HUNT, bestsellng author of *The Debt*

"Gut-wrenching in its honesty and passion, *The Breaking Point* packs a powerful message of obedience and God's healing."—BRANDILYN COLLINS, bestselling author of *Brink of Death*

"A heartfelt novel about the craggy recesses of marriage—where God does some of His best work. Karen Ball's writing is emotionally gripping and full of insight."—JAMES SCOTT BELL, bestselling author of *Breach of Promise*

∾

NOVELS BY KAREN BALL

Shattered Justice

A Test of Faith

The Breaking Point

"Bride on the Run" in the *3 Weddings and a Giggle* anthology

For my brothers, Kevin and Kirk.
It was easy to write about a strong and loving sibling
relationship because of you two. You're two of my best friends.
You guys have always been there, teasing me, encouraging me,
driving me nuts and making my life richer—and lots more fun.
Thank you for all you are. Thank you for all you've given me.
Thank you for the ways you've helped me grow in my faith.
Thanks, most of all, for loving me the way you do and for
being the best brothers ever. I love you guys.
Even when you drive me nuts. <wink!>

AUTHOR'S NOTE

I always try to make my books as accurate as possible, especially when I'm depicting something like law enforcement. However, I confess I have taken some definite liberties in this particular book. I needed Dan Justice to live and work in a rural Oregon mountain community. There was just one problem: That's not the way things work with the Jackson County Sheriff's department. Not now, anyway. Years ago, I'm told, we had deputies devoted to the more remote areas of our region. Sadly, as has happened in many states, budget cuts have cost us far too many positions in law enforcement, and our devoted sheriff and deputies are spread woefully thin. Even so, they do a great job of keeping Jackson County and the Rogue Valley a wonderful and safe place to live.

Fortunately for my story, a fictitious benefactor came along and donated funds for a test program that would bring a sheriff's deputy to live and work in my little made-up town. And while that and some other elements aren't true to life, I've done my best to be as factual as possible, whenever possible.

To that end, my sincere gratitude goes to Jackson County Deputy Michael Hermant for his patience in answering my questions regarding the ways things work in the sheriff's department. I so appreciate your kindness as you shared your time and expertise with me. Your input was invaluable. Thank you!

Trust Him when dark doubts assail thee,
Trust Him when thy strength is small,
Trust Him when to simply trust Him
Seems the hardest thing of all.
Trust Him, He is ever faithful,
Trust Him, for His will is best,
Trust Him, for the heart of Jesus
Is the only place of rest.

ANONYMOUS

∾

"Listen, O heavens, and I will speak;
hear, O earth, the words of my mouth.
Let my teaching fall like rain
and my words descend like dew,
like showers on new grass,
like abundant rain on tender plants.
I will proclaim the name of the LORD.
Oh, praise the greatness of our God!
He is the Rock, his works are perfect,
and all his ways are just.
A faithful God who does no wrong,
upright and just is he."

DEUTERONOMY 32:1–4 (NIV)

PROLOGUE

*"We are not at peace with others because we
are not at peace with ourselves, and we are not at
peace with ourselves because we are not at peace with God."*

THOMAS MERTON

*"What I always feared has happened to me.
What I dreaded has come to be. I have no peace, no quietness.
I have no rest; instead, only trouble comes."*

JOB 3:25–26

DAN JUSTICE DIDN'T KNOW WHAT WOKE HIM, WHAT pulled him from the heavy weight of drugged sleep. A sound. One that didn't belong in the empty silence of his house.

He closed his eyes. *House.* Not a home. Just an empty shell where he lived with his memories.

The sound came again. He forced his eyelids up, his vision to focus, and turned his head toward the window. A tree branch scraped against the glass, driven by pelting raindrops and a fierce wind.

A storm.

Yeah, well, why not? The weather might as well fit with the rest of his life. Dark. Raging.

Hopeless.

Bitterness burned at the back of his throat as Dan pushed his heavy limbs to a sitting position.

This was why he didn't like taking those crummy pills. Sure, they made him sleep—were the only way he slept anymore—but it took too long to shake them off.

Even longer to shake off the dreams they set loose.

Yeah. No sleep beat a night of tortured dreams. He rubbed a hand over his face. Coffee. He needed coffee.

He made his way to the kitchen, his head heavy, feeling every one of his nearly forty years. And then some. He pulled the cupboard open, reaching for the coffee…

Instead, his fingers closed around something hard. Cold. He removed it from the cupboard, holding it, studying it. It fit in his hand with deadly precision; its size belying its power. So compact…barely larger than his hand. The perfect size, which was why he'd chosen this one to put in the cupboard…when? How long ago did he do that? Decide his family needed a measure of protection in the home?

He hoped—no, prayed—they'd never need it. But he'd seen too much in his work as a sheriff's deputy. And then the threats started. So he brought it home. Put it in the cupboard. Just in case…

He made sure they knew how to use it. Showed them where the ammo was stored, in a small can that once held cocoa.

"Do it like this." Now, as he'd done then to demonstrate the moves, he flipped the top of the container open with a thumb, scooped the loaded magazine free, and slid it into place—all with a minimum of motion and sound.

He had them practice until they could perform the action with ease. Was so proud of the way they'd taken his instructions to heart, the seriousness of their study. They were ready. He made sure of that.

What a pathetic waste of time.

His fingers fisted over the gun. All his precautions, all his painstaking preparation and planning…none of it mattered. He hadn't been able to protect them. To keep them safe. All his life, he'd worked to keep people safe. To see justice done—

Justice. What a laugh. There was no justice. No right. No wrong. No innocent. No guilty.

That's just the pain talking. You don't believe that.

Believe. The laugh that sliced through the silence was hoarse, wrenched from deep in his gut. What did belief matter? Did it stop evil? Save those who deserved it? Make the guilty pay?

Hardly.

Justice was a myth. A nice little fairy tale to make children feel safe so they could sleep—

Sorrow cut as deep as any shard of glass, piercing him. No. Justice didn't exist. He'd been a fool to think it did. There was only…

His gaze lowered to the cold steel in his hand.

This. There was only this.

He shifted the gun in his hand, letting it settle into place. Nestle in his palm, supported by the finger that lay along the barrel. Single action. Semiautomatic. A masterpiece of precision. Reaching with his other hand, he gripped the barrel, slid it back, and heard the round chamber—the sound equal parts comfort and caution, allure and alarm.

One flick, one small motion, and the gun would be ready.

Ready for what? What are you doing?

He drew a deep breath. What was he doing?

A single movement, a tiny click told him the deed was done.

The safety was off.

What was he doing?

The one thing he promised he'd never do.

The one thing left that he could do.

Stop the pain.

Forever.

ONE

"A name is the blueprint of the thing we call character.
You ask, What's in a name?
I answer, Just about everything you do."
MORRIS MANDEL

"'What is your name?
For when all this comes true, we want to honor you.'"
JUDGES 13:17

GO OFF.

Dan Justice stared down at his pager. Hard. Concentrating. *Go off, darn you. Go off . . .*

"Justice, will you relax? You're drivin' me nuts!"

Dan looked at his irritated partner. "Aw, I'm sorry, man. It's just, well, you know."

Steve waved off Dan's words, then his big paw went back to rest on the cruiser's steering wheel. "Yeah, I know. But it's not like this is your first."

Dan couldn't restrain his crooked grin. "Not like it's my tenth, either."

Steve's brows arched under his hat. Though few sheriff's deputies wore the hats anymore, Steve seemed surgically attached to his. From the minute he reached the station, he didn't take it off. Dan couldn't imagine it. He loved almost

12

everything about his job as a Jackson County sheriff's deputy, except the hat. "You making fun of me, partner?"

Dan put his hands in front of him, chuckling. "Wouldn't dream of it. Any man crazy...er, *brave* enough to have ten kids has my respect and admiration."

The punch to Dan's arm was as good-natured as it was solid. "Riiight. Whatever you say, bucko. But if I've learned anything, it's that you can't sit there watchin' your watch—"

"I wasn't watching my watch."

"—*or* your beeper, thinkin' the kid's comin' any minute." Steve steered the state patrol cruiser to the highway off-ramp. "Babies show up when they're good 'n' ready. And nothin' we do will rush 'em."

Dan leaned back against the seat. "Yeah, I guess you're ri— *stop!*"

Steve slammed on the brakes. The cruiser fishtailed, then came to a screeching halt. "What?" He looked around, eyes wide, hand already reaching for the release on his seat belt. "What did you see?"

Dan took in Steve's tensed state. He was ready for action. Dan swallowed. Oh boy. Steve was not going to be happy with him.

He frowned at Dan. "What's goin' on?"

Dan offered a sheepish grin by way of apology and pointed to the side of the road. "A flower shop."

Steve's gaze narrowed, and he peered through Dan's window. "A flower shop? Did you see someone inside with a gun?"

Might as well bite the bullet and admit it. "No. Just...flowers."

Understanding was slow in coming, but Dan knew the millisecond it hit his partner. If the hard glitter in Steve's eyes hadn't signaled it, the edge to his voice certainly would have.

"Flowers. Let me see if I've got this straight." He read the sign above the door. "That's a flower shop—something, I understand, they have in abundance here in good ol' Medford, Oregon. So you yell at me to stop. For flowers."

With a sigh that came from somewhere in the basement, Steve pulled the cruiser to the curb. "You got five minutes."

Dan was out of the car in a heartbeat. He was inside the shop and at the counter in two. "Hello?"

No answer. Dan surveyed the interior of the store. Wasn't anyone working? He could almost hear precious minutes ticking away. "Hey, anyone here?"

Dan wasn't sure what he heard first—the scream or the sound of glass shattering. But the next sound was one he recognized all too well.

A gunshot.

His senses slammed into full alert, and he drew his gun as he keyed the mic at his shoulder. "Gunshots fired! Get in here, Steve!"

Vaulting the counter, Dan headed for a large set of double swinging doors, which probably led to some kind of storeroom. From the sound of things, that's where the action was. Fortunately, there were windows in the doors, so he should be able to get the lay of the land before he went in.

As he drew near the doors, he heard a loud voice. Male. Angry.

No. Furious. Like a bull moose out of control.

Pounding footsteps had Dan spinning, but he relaxed when he saw Steve coming, weapon drawn.

"I called for backup. Whaddya got?"

"One gunshot." Dan indicated the doors. "Sounds like a fight going on."

They moved to look through the windows. What Dan saw made his heart plunge. A raging man, gun in one hand, large glass vase in the other, screaming at a woman cowering against the wall. Even from the doors Dan could see her face was bruised, bleeding.

"Domestic."

Dan nodded. Domestic disturbance. *Lord, help us.* Why couldn't it have been a simple armed robbery? Crooks you could reason with, most of the time. But domestics? No way. People in these situations were flat nuts.

And dangerous.

Steve held a hand in the air then counted down with his fingers. *Three…two…one…go!*

They burst through the double doors. "Police! Freeze!"

The guy was so far gone, he didn't even hear them. He just kept screaming at the terrified woman. He threw the vase at her, and she pulled herself into a ball as it hit the concrete floor next to her, glass shards going everywhere.

The man was on her, grabbing her by the hair, jerking her to her feet. "I *told* you what I'd do to you if you ever saw him again, you stupid—"

"*Police!*" Steve's bellow practically shook the walls. "*Freeze!*"

The guy heard that. He'd have to be dead not to. He spun to face them, the weeping woman in one meaty paw, the gun in the other. "This ain't none of your business."

Steve and Dan inched closer, keeping their guns trained on the man. "You made it our business, pal, when you shot that gun off."

He shook the woman. "This is *my* store."

"Drop the gun." Dan kept his voice low and even.

"I got a permit for this gun—"

"*Drop* it! *Now!*"

He wavered. The gun started to lower.

The woman's trembling hands clawed at her hair, trying to pry her captor's fingers loose.

Stop! Dan tried to catch her eye. But it was too late.

"Jimmy—" her broken words came out on a sob—"do what they say, baby—"

Her voice was like gas on a sputtering flame. Jimmy spun, slamming the gun into her face. "Shut *up!*"

"Drop the gun, Jimmy. *Now!*"

Steve managed to keep his voice steady, but Dan knew his partner felt the same thing he did: Time was running out.

As though he sensed it too, Jimmy jerked the battered woman in front of him, clamping an arm around her neck as he pinned her against him—and pressed the barrel of the gun to her temple.

Shock sent Dan reeling as he realized the woman was pregnant. *Oh, Lord...please...* "Come on, Jimmy. Don't do this."

Jimmy pressed his cheek against the top of the woman's head, all but spitting his fury at her. "See what you did, Shelia? See what your whoring around got you?"

Desperation glistened in the woman's eyes as she looked at Dan. Her hands moved over her slightly swollen abdomen, as though to protect the child within her from what was happening. Terror held her mute, except for a pitiful whimper.

God, please! Stop this guy! You can stop him...

"Drop. The gun." There was steel in Steve's tone. If anyone could take this guy out, even hunkering behind his hostage, it was Steve. All he'd need was one opening.

And as much as Dan didn't want to see anyone die, he'd do everything he could to give Steve that opening.

Father God, give me the words. Help me save this woman. His fingers tensed on his gun. *This baby.*

He forced a friendly note into his voice. "Come on, Jimmy. It's not worth it."

At the change in Dan's tone, the man's brow crinkled.

Dan dipped his head toward Sheila. "*She's* not worth it. No woman is worth dying over, man." Should he mention the baby? Appeal to him for the baby's life?

"She *betrayed* me!"

Dan licked his dry lips. No. Keep his attention away from the baby. Too much risk. If he thought the child wasn't his... "I hear you. But she's a woman. You know how weak they are." He took one step forward. "They're not like us, you know? Not strong."

"She'll see how strong I am now."

Dan had to struggle to keep the anger out of his tone. "That's right."

"Strong enough to make her pay."

"Sure. Make her pay. Let her see what she lost." He forced a chuckle, amazed when it sounded authentic. "She had a real man with you, and she blew it. She doesn't deserve you."

"You better believe she doesn't deserve me." His tone hardened. "Or my baby."

Dan's heart sank. No escaping it now. "That's right. *Your* baby. Forget Sheila. She's nothing. But that baby, man. You gotta get it. Raise it right."

Jimmy's lip trembled. "No way they'll let me near it now."

Dan's mind scrambled to interpret. "Who? The courts?"

"They hear what I did, they'll put me away."

Bingo. "Nah, they'll understand. They're men, too. They know what it's like. They'll see you're a good man, and you'll be a good dad."

Sirens sounded just outside. Backup was here. "Hear those sirens, Jimmy?"

The man listened.

"There's an ambulance outside. They can check Sheila out. Make sure the baby's okay. Just let her go, Jimmy. Let's walk out of here together, and I'll tell 'em you were a stand-up guy when it counted."

Out of the corner of his eye, Dan saw Steve moving, angling for a shot. Dan shifted so that Jimmy had to turn his head away from Steve.

"I tried." Jimmy moved the gun away from Sheila's temple, rubbing at his eyes with the back of his hand. "I tried to be a man. Tried to make her love me."

"Sure you did. You did everything you could."

"I thought she loved me." Jimmy ground his teeth, shaking Sheila. "You said you *loved* me!"

Dan jumped in. "So she lied. What woman doesn't li—?"

"You *said* you loved me!"

The anguished wail in Jimmy's voice sent a chill ripping through Dan. "Steve! Now!"

But even as Dan cried out, he knew.

It was too late.

The next few seconds seemed to take an eternity to pass. In simultaneous motions, Jimmy pressed the gun against Sheila's temple, his finger convulsing on the trigger, and Steve took his shot. The two explosions mixed, as violent an assault on Dan's senses as what he saw in front of him.

Sheila's head jerking. Red everywhere. Her body going limp. Falling.

Jimmy's cry as the bullet struck him. His hands grasping for Sheila as he fell. Her name the word that ushered life from his body.

And then…silence.

Cold, barren silence.

Dan lowered his gun and went to feel for a pulse at Sheila's neck. But it was no use. She was gone.

The double doors burst open as police and paramedics came in. Dan moved out of the way, watching as they went to work. A touch on his shoulder drew his attention, and he saw a somber-faced Steve standing beside him.

"You did your best, Dan."

He looked to the woman on the cold, concrete floor. Too bad his best wasn't good enough.

The paramedics shook their heads.

"The baby?"

One of the paramedics looked up at Dan's hoarse inquiry. His eyes said it all. "The mother wasn't far enough along. Baby didn't have a chance."

Dan swallowed hard.

"Let it go, partner."

Dan met Steve's gaze.

"We can't save them all, Dan."

He was right. But that truth didn't do much to stop the aching knowledge, deep inside, that Dan should have been able to save this one.

∾

They were the most beautiful eyes Dan had ever seen.

Deep, endless blue. Wide open and taking everything in.

Sarah had told him they probably wouldn't stay blue. And as beautiful as they were, Dan hoped his wife was right. Hoped this little one's eyes would take on the rich brown of her mother's eyes.

The baby gurgled, and Dan's heart ached. For a moment, the image of Sheila lying lifeless on the floor—of another infant, one who never had the chance to live—haunted him.

He'd barely gotten back to the cruiser when his pager went off. Steve drove him to the hospital in record time, red lights flashing, siren blaring. Just before Dan hopped out of the car, Steve offered this bit of wisdom: "You can't let the loss get to you, partner. Go be with your wife and your new baby. Focus on life. Let death take care of itself."

Focus on life.

He was trying. He traced a finger down the baby's soft temple. "So what's it like, kiddo? Being born? There you were, all safe and warm in Mom's tummy, then bam! You're shoved out into reality."

Reality. Cold. Dismal. A world where women love the wrong men. Where children die before they have the chance to live. Where no amount of prayer can change some people's hearts.

No wonder babies screamed when they were born.

Stop it. Stop thinking about it.

Sarah was still deep asleep. Well, she deserved it. She'd worked hard. And her work had produced a miracle. That's what he needed to think about now. The tiny miracle in his arms.

Dan cupped his daughter's head, leaning close and drawing a deep breath, savoring the sweet fragrance of new life.

His daughter. A tiny gift from God.

Lord, please, help me keep her safe. Help me keep them all safe.

Sarah. Our little boy, Aaron. They're in Your hands, I know. But sometimes, Father…sometimes I get so afraid.

Dan closed his eyes, unable to stop the images of Sheila. Jimmy. The paramedics shaking their heads. *"Baby didn't have a chance."*

He cradled his infant close, felt tears slip down his cheeks. "Oh, Father, why the baby?"

Deep within him, a battle raged as despair grabbed hope by the neck and wrestled it to the ground. Pinned it. Fear rammed into peace and joy, shaking them from what Dan had always believed was rock-solid footing.

Jesus, Jesus…

The name was a prayer from the depths of his spirit.

Please, take these images away. Help me keep my eyes on You, Lord, not on the world. Help me…

The tiniest sound caught at him, and he opened his eyes, looking down. His new daughter gurgled again, bubbles of baby laughter on her pink lips. Her wobbly head moved, and she looked right at him—Dan was sure of it—and smiled.

Trapped under that blue gaze, Dan felt the battle within ease. Hope rose from the ground, brushed itself off, and raised its arms to the heavens.

Tears choked Dan again, but this time they held the sweet taste of gratitude. No, he couldn't help Sheila or her little one. But he could do everything in his power to ensure this tiny creature in his arms had a chance.

More than that. He'd ensure she had a life full of love and faith and truth.

Who is this child, Father? What shall we call her? Dan sighed, watching the baby blink as his breath caressed her face. *What's your name, little girl?*

He listened to the silence, drank in the peace that had settled over them. Leaning back in the rocker, he hummed.

At the sound of his voice, the baby's tiny hand came up, those perfect fingers reaching toward him.

Dan smiled. "You like that song? I do, too. You know, my momma used to sing it to me." He started singing it softly, letting the lyrics wash over them with their promise.

"Be not dismayed whate'er betide,
God will take care of you…"

He lifted the soft baby blanket from the arm of the chair and tucked it around his daughter.

"Beneath His wings of love abide,
God will take care of you."

Dan smoothed the soft hair. The nurses couldn't get over so much hair on a newborn.

"God will take care of you,
Through every day, o'er all the way;
He will take care of you,
God will take care of you."

His words slowed. It was as though a choir of *amen*s resounded in the heavens, washing down over the two of them. Awe shivered up Dan's spine as a certainty dawned in his heart.

God *would* take care of this child.

Of course, God watched out for all of them. For him and Sarah; for Aaron, their toddler son. But Dan had a powerful sense that she was special.

That God had given this little girl a special touch of…of…

He studied that little puckered face.

Wisdom. There was an almost ageless wisdom in those wide eyes. He cupped his daughter's face and pressed a kiss to her forehead.

"Now there's a picture I'll always remember."

Dan turned his head and smiled. "Hi, Mommy."

"So—" Sarah yawned—"any closer to a name for the little angel?"

"Funny you should ask. I do have an idea. Sort of."

Sarah pushed herself up to a sitting position. "Did you bring the names with you?"

"You think I'd dare come without them?" He pulled a fat envelope from his coat pocket and upended it on the bed. A pile of napkins tumbled out.

Sarah looked down at them. "You're sure your mom did it this way, huh?"

"And her mother before her. And *her* mother before her. 'Dedicate a baby to God—'"

"'—through a name chosen by focused prayer—'" Sarah finished the familiar family credo for him—"'that He may make Himself known in every aspect of that child's life.'" She held her hands up. "Okay, okay. Far be it from me to break with tradition. So, where were we?"

Dan peered over the baby's head at the napkins from Sarah's baby shower. Prior to the shower, his mother had asked all those attending to come with a baby name, complete with the meaning of the name. They wrote them down on the baby shower napkins, then gave them to Sarah before she left.

"You do remember how this almost ended for you, don't you?"

Dan looked at his wife. "I assume you're talking about when my parents named me?"

"Well, they did name you *Justice.*" The teasing glimmer in her eyes made him grin. "Justice Justice, now there's a name!"

He shook his head. "That's not what happened, and you know it, minx."

He'd heard the story over and over. How his mother and father had sorted through the name napkins from *their* baby shower. How his mother said to his father, "Wasn't there a name that had something to do with justice?"

Dan's father loved this part. "I stared at her like she was just this side of nuts and said, 'You think God is calling you to name our son Justice Justice?'"

"And I said," his mother always added, "'Of course not. But what was the name?'"

They looked through the napkins, then pulled one free. The name *Avidan* meant "God is just."

"I looked down at the sleeping baby in my arms," Dan's mother said, "and knew. It was perfect. Avidan."

His father's agreement never wavered. "A strong name for a strong man. We knew that's what our son would be. Strong of body, heart, and spirit. And we were right."

His parents were something else. Dan prayed he was as good a parent to his little ones. He plucked one of the napkins. "Here, this is it."

Sarah took the napkin and read it out loud. "Shannon. *Wise one.*"

"Exactly." Dan cuddled the baby.

There was such tenderness in the curve of Sarah's mouth. She laid a hand on his arm. "I like it. A lot."

Dan passed the baby to Sarah. Then he sat on the side of the bed and slid his arm around his wife and daughter. "Welcome to the world, Shannon." He hugged Sarah close. "You're going to love it here."

And as he gazed down into that face, Dan made a vow. He'd do his best to ensure that was true. To protect and shelter his wife, his children. To make their lives as happy and blessed as possible.

Your best? Better hope it's more effective than it was today.

Dan pushed the dark thought aside.

It would be. He'd make sure of it. Whatever it took, he'd make it happen.

Or his name wasn't Avidan Timothy Justice.

TWO

"We often think of great faith as something that happens spontaneously…used for a miracle or healing. However, the greatest faith of all, and the most effective, is to live day by day trusting Him."

RICK JOYNER

"I will light in your heart the lamp of understanding, which shall not be put out."

4 EZRA 14:25

TEN YEARS LATER

"I STILL DON'T SEE WHY WE CAN'T GO WITH YOU."

Dan looked up from where he was double-checking his day pack to his daughter. Or what he could see of her from behind the family room couch, where she was sprawled. One hand and one foot lay along the back of the couch, and Dan could just see the top of Shannon's head.

Sarah often said their little girl didn't have any bones in her body, and from the way she was lying there now, kind of like one of the throws draped over the back of the couch, Dan figured his wife was right.

Shannon popped her gum, her hand waving. "Well, okay, I understand why you don't want *Aaron* to go, but me? Why can't I come?"

"Shannon…"

She peered at him over the back of the couch. "I mean, it's not like you and Mom don't go out together all the time just the two of you. Man. You'd think you guys were still dating or somethin'."

"Parents dating? Heaven forbid." He didn't even try to keep the chuckle from his tone.

She pushed up to her knees and hung over the back of the couch, hands folded in entreaty. "C'mon, Daddy. Let me go with you."

"Shannon."

"You said I'm old enough to start learning how to shoot."

He crossed his arms over his chest. "And you will."

She grinned.

"Just not tomorrow."

Her grin dissolved and a pout took its place. "You're so mean."

Dan arched a brow at that but kept his tone pleasant. "Yeah, that's me. Mean ol' Dad. I mean, wow. I hardly *ever* spend time with you and Aaron. Just one night a week for family movies, and then there's that dumb reading thing we do with the Chronicles of Narnia a couple times a week. Oh, and band concerts and parades and gymnastics…" He closed the day pack. "Yessiree. Mean as they come. That's me."

A tinge of red lit Shannon's cheeks, and she developed a sudden fascination with her fingernails. Dan kept the twitch from reaching his lips. His offspring's little ploy to avoid eye contact wasn't fooling him one little bit.

"I like hiking, too, you know."

The woeful note to her tone made the twitch harder to hide. "Yes, I do know that."

She lifted those amazing eyes of hers—rich brown in color, like the finest Belgian chocolate, carbon copies of her mother's eyes—and pinned him with a soulful expression that would have done any puppy proud. "*Please*, Daddy?"

Oh, man. If she was this good at almost nine, she'd be deadly when she hit her teens. And high school? The boys wouldn't stand a chance. Steeling himself, he let his expression warn her she was pushing it.

She ignored the tacit reprimand and brought in the big guns. Her lower lip slipped out just a fraction; her long lashes batted. "Pleeeaaaase?"

"Well, since you put it that way—" Dan batted his lashes, and excitement sparked in Shannon's eyes—"No."

The spark fizzled, and her lip shot into a serious pout. "That's not *fair!*"

"What's not?"

They turned. Sarah and Aaron stood there, smiling over a large bowl of popcorn. Dan took an appreciative sniff, then went to scoop a handful of still-warm popcorn from the bowl. "Your daughter thinks it's unfair that we get to go out together. Without her."

"Ah." Sarah set the bowl on the coffee table and ruffled Shannon's hair. "Sorry, kiddo. Tonight is family time. And tomorrow is Dad's and my time."

"You remember what happens in a week, don't you?" Dan leaned on the back of the couch.

Shannon's head bobbed. "It's August first. My birthday."

"Right, and we're all going out together next weekend to celebrate."

"That's right." Sarah hugged Shannon. "And I've got a special surprise for you."

"Really?" Shannon was all smiles. She adored surprises. And Dan knew she'd love this one, big-time.

During the early years of their marriage, Dan and Sarah discovered C. S. Lewis's Chronicles of Narnia. They fell in love with the stories of children who traveled to a magical world and met Aslan, the mighty lion. It became a nightly ritual for them to cuddle up on the couch and read the books together.

Then when the children were born, they read them at bedtime as soon as first Aaron and then Shannon were old enough to follow the story. Amazing how easy it was to get the kids into bed at night when doing so held the promise of time with Aslan and his world.

Now the kids were as enamored of the series and its characters as Dan and Sarah. But Shannon had a special love for Aslan. Dan wasn't surprised. The great lion was the perfect picture of Christ. And Shannon was head over heels in love with Jesus. Had been since she was old enough to say her own prayers. So when Sarah discovered a beautiful golden lion's head pendant in a jewelry store a few months ago, it was a no-brainer. Shannon had to have it.

Sarah had the back of the pendant engraved with a special message from mother to daughter: *Shannon, See life with God's eyes. Love, Mom.*

Oh yeah. Sarah was going to score big with this one.

Twelve-year-old Aaron dropped onto the couch next to his sister. "Shove over. Man, what a couch hog."

"Moooommm!" The wail was accompanied by a swat at Aaron's arm.

What was it about siblings that made them go for the jugular at the least provocation? Dan and Sarah heard over and over from people what wonderful kids these two were, so polite and pleasant at school and church and their friends' houses…

Everywhere but home. Here they seemed bent on doing each other in.

Of course, Dan's two sisters always reminded him it had been the same with the three of them. But *his* kids should be better behaved.

"All right, you two." Dan sat between them on the couch. "To your corners."

He ignored their groans and protests, looking up at Sarah instead and patting the couch next to him. "Hey, beautiful, wanna sit by me so we can smooch?"

Sarah rewarded him with a kiss as she sat down.

"Oh, *gross!*" Shannon curled as far into her corner of the couch as she could.

"Ignore 'em." This from Aaron as he reached for the TV remote. "They're only doing it 'cuz they know it grosses us out."

"I'll have you know—" Dan plucked the remote from his son's hand—"I'd kiss your mother whether it was gross or not."

"Gee…" Sarah licked butter from the popcorn off her fingers. "Thanks, hon."

He chuckled as he flicked on the TV. "Get ready, kids. We've got a real treat in store for tonight's movie night. Something we haven't seen for a long time."

"Cool." Shannon scooted to the edge of her seat as the screen blossomed to life.

Aaron shoved one of the small pillows on the couch behind his back. "So we don't have to watch another—"

Both kids fell silent. Stared. Then: "Dad!"

Amazing. His children could wail in harmony. "Yes?" He didn't bother to look at them. He didn't need to.

"John Wayne? Again? We watched a John Wayne movie last week!"

For once Shannon didn't argue with her brother. "Yeah, and two weeks before that." The pout was once again in residence. "I thought family movie night meant we'd get to watch a movie *we* liked."

Dan settled back against the couch cushions, the bowl of popcorn on his lap, Sarah snuggled in the crook of one arm. "We like John Wayne movies."

Aaron pointed at him. "*You* like John Wayne movies."

Dan looked down at Sarah. "Do you like John Wayne movies?"

"Love 'em."

"Oh, brother!" Aaron threw his hands in the air.

Dan chomped his popcorn. "Now, let's be fair, kids. Last week was *Hatari!* That's a safari movie."

"And two weeks before that was *The Green Berets*. That's a

war movie." Sarah snagged a piece of popcorn. "But tonight—" she angled a grin at Dan, and they gave each other a high five, saying in unison: "It's a *western*!"

Dan flipped the remote into the air, pretending it was a six gun. "*Cahill, U.S. Marshal*. Yee *haw*!"

Shannon pushed back against the couch cushions. "You two are so weird."

Aaron snorted as he leaned forward and grabbed some popcorn from the bowl. "Weird doesn't even *begin* to cover it."

"Goofy."

Aaron gave his sister a thumbs-up. "Bizarro."

"Freaky."

And on it went, the two tossing words back and forth. But Dan just linked his fingers with Sarah's, not saying a word. Because for all of their complaints, he noticed as the Duke sauntered onto the scene, neither of the kids got up and left. Instead, they settled on either side of him and Sarah and prepared to suffer through the movie.

Of course, it only took a few scenes for them to be as engrossed in the story as Dan and Sarah. And when John Wayne finally saved his two sons and brought evil ol' George Kennedy to justice, Aaron and Shannon were stomping and cheering as loud as either of their parents. Louder.

"Man!" Shannon stretched, grinning at Dan as he flicked the TV off. "I'm glad that creep got dead."

"Oh, honey—"

Sarah's quiet reprimand was cut off by Aaron's snort. "Bloodthirsty little critter, aren't you?"

Shannon planted her hands on her hips. "Well? Aren't you?"

"Sure." Aaron stood. "But I'm a guy. Guys are supposed to be bloodthirsty. Right, Dad?"

By now, Dan struggled to keep a burst of laughter trapped inside. He could tell from the chagrin on his wife's features that laughter was not the proper response. He cleared his throat.

"Well, I don't think *bloodthirsty* is quite the right word, Aaron."

His son's brows arched. "Okay. Then how about out for justice. I mean, isn't that what your whole job is about? Justice? Making the bad guys pay?"

"Justice is more than just making people pay, honey." Sarah was looking at Aaron, but she nudged Dan as she spoke.

He knew she wanted him to follow her lead. Problem was, he wasn't sure he agreed with her. "Right…" Dan leaned forward. "Bad guys—" he inclined his head—"criminals, people who hurt others, need to be stopped."

"But shouldn't they suffer some kind of…you know, *consequence* for hurting people?"

Shannon joined in. "Yeah, like we get punished if we do something wrong."

"But real justice, God's justice, is about grace as much as punishment."

The kids looked at their mother, and Dan could see their minds working on that one. Well, he couldn't blame them. He was having a little trouble absorbing it, too.

"What do you mean?"

Dan wanted to echo Shannon's question. Instead, he kept his features as clear of confusion as possible and waited for Sarah's answer.

"Okay. You know everyone sins, right?"

Dan almost nodded along with the kids as they agreed. "Right."

"And you know, according to God's law, we all deserve the same punishment for those sins."

Dan was all over this one. "Death. We all deserve death."

Sarah looked at him, a half smile on her face. "Right."

"But that's why Jesus came."

Aaron flicked a glance at his sister. "Yeah, He came to die for all our sins. And when God brought Jesus back to life, we were set free."

"Exactly." Sarah patted Aaron's knee. "So Jesus' blood

washed away all our sins, past, present, and future."

Shannon frowned. "So we can do as much bad as we want now? And it's all okay?"

Dan could have told Sarah that question was coming. It only made sense. If grace covered everything, then why worry about being good? "Not quite, half-pint. God showed us grace by sending Jesus, but that's for the eternity side of things. Jesus' death on the cross and His resurrection bring us eternal life. But it doesn't take away the consequences, here and now, of our wrong actions."

Shannon pursed her lips. "But if we're forgiven…"

"We're forgiven by God, honey." Sarah leaned her elbows on her knees. "That's the grace part of God's justice. Someone had to pay the ultimate price for our sins."

"Death." Dan grinned at Aaron. Like father, like son. They had that one down pat. "Right. But Jesus paying that price didn't get rid of consequences. So if you do something wrong—"

"Like force your kids to watch a gazillion John Wayne movies?"

Dan flicked a finger at Shannon's pert nose. "Funny kid. If you do something wrong, there are consequences. No escaping it. That's where the punishment side of justice comes in. So justice is about grace *and* punishment."

Shannon chewed on that for a moment. "So, it's like, okay, so Aaron hurts me—"

"Sure, make *me* the bad guy."

Shannon ignored her brother. "So grace means I forgive him for being stupid and mean and—"

Dan put his hand out to stop Aaron's protest. "I think we get the point, Shannon."

She snickered. "Okay, fine. But it takes a while sometimes to trust people who hurt you, even after you forgive 'em. So that's the consequence he has to deal with, that I might not trust him for a while?"

Sarah hugged her. "That's right. The one who hurts you

receives grace when you forgive him. And he faces the punishment of losing your friendship for a while."

"Okay." Aaron stood again, yawning. "I think I get it." He grinned and wagged his eyebrows. "But I still like it when the *real* bad guy—" he made a face at his sister—"gets his."

Yup. Dan grinned to himself as laughter filled the room. A definite case of like father, like son.

THREE

*"Parting is all we know of heaven
and all we need of hell."*
EMILY DICKINSON

*"He was...a man of sorrows,
acquainted with bitterest grief."*
ISAIAH 53:3

"STAND ASIDE, KNAVE, OR PAY THE ULTIMATE PRICE!"

Dan crossed his arms. "You gotta be kidding me."

Sarah peeked at him from behind her hand holding an arrow nocked against the string of her bow. She hadn't drawn the bow, of course, so there was no danger.

Not unless you counted what Dan's eyes did to her heart rate. Yes indeedy. *That* was danger. And all she could say was, bring it on!

A pout tinged her features. "Come on, Dan; I got set up first. You have to let me shoot."

He hesitated, and she could almost hear the gears turning in his brain as he tried to come up with an argument that would win him first shot. But finally he surrendered, stepping aside with a heavy sigh and a gallant wave of his well-muscled arm.

"After you, my lady."

My lady. Oooo, she liked the sound of that. Even better, she liked the feel of that. Being Dan's lady.

She tossed him a kiss, then took her stance. She drew a bead on the target, pulled back the notched arrow…then let the arrow fly.

Dan slipped an arm around her waist as they followed the projectile's sure path, straight to the heart of the target they'd chosen: a thick piece of moss-covered bark leaning against a boulder.

"Perfect!"

Sarah grinned up at him. "The shot or the shooter?"

The evocative curve of those broad lips sent a shiver across her nerves. "Both."

Their mutual love of field archery had been a happy discovery early on in their dating years, back in college. Some of their best times in the nearly seventeen years they'd been married had been times just like this, where they hiked, taking turns choosing a target, then seeing who could hit it with the most speed and accuracy. A competitor to the core, Sarah loved it when she shot better than Dan—which even he admitted was most of the time. She seemed to have an uncanny eye.

At the end of the first day they shot together, Dan gave her a lopsided grin as he helped her into his Jeep. "Remind me never to make you mad at me while you're holding a bow."

She leaned forward, slid her arms around his neck, and pressed a kiss to his lips. "Even if you did, it would be okay."

His arms encircled her. "Oh, yeah?"

She nuzzled his neck. "Yeah. I'd make sure to miss all the vital organs."

Sarah chuckled at the memory.

"What are you laughing at, Mrs. Justice?"

She glanced up at her husband. The wind ruffled his thick, brown hair. She'd tried so hard to get him to wear a hat when they were out in the wilderness, but to no avail. And for once, she was glad. Slinging the bow over her shoulder, she reached up and tugged at his wind-tumbled hair. Even cut short, it was thick and soft, and she loved to comb her fingers through it.

"I'm not laughing *at* anything, Mr. Justice." Her fingers caressed the back of his neck. "I'm laughing because you make me so happy."

If he'd been a cat, he would have been purring. As it was, the low sound deep in his chest had more the rumble of a lion. Or a tiger. "Mmm. And you make me happy."

Target shooting was forgotten as he tugged her close. Her eyes drifted shut, and the feel of him flooded her senses. When he finally released her, they both were breathless. Sarah took a step back, glanced at the target, then dropped her best imitation of a curtsy.

"Next shot is yours, Sir Justice."

His grin was all male. "Indeed, wench. Step aside and watch a master at work." Dan slid an arrow from the quiver at his belt and took his stance where Sarah had been.

He nocked the arrow and drew back, his smooth motions bearing testimony to his athletic grace. Standing there, bow and arrow at the ready, he reminded Sarah of the old Robin Hood movies. Except Dan was better built than the actor in those old movies.

Sarah smiled. *Much* better built.

At six foot four, Dan stood head and shoulders above most folks. Add those broad shoulders and the trim waist, that devil-may-care smile, those looks just rugged enough to save him from being pretty...

Oh, yeah. He was pretty well perfect.

At least Sarah thought so. And she wasn't alone. She saw the way women watched him when he walked by. Just last week he'd stopped in to say hi at the high school office where she worked part-time. When she walked out to the parking lot with him, Sarah spotted female students and teachers alike watching her husband. And there was no missing the feminine appreciation in their features.

Sarah didn't mind, though, because Dan was all hers and had been almost from the day they met.

The sound of an arrow striking home drew Sarah's attention—Dan's arrow struck just above and to the left of hers. She patted his arm, waggling her brows at him. "You'll win the next one, Danny Boy."

He nudged her away, his deep laughter as sweet as the summer breeze blowing on their faces. You couldn't buy days like this. Not for a million dollars.

Sarah knew it and appreciated it. Deeply.

August and September were too often brutally hot. But July days, like today, had just enough breeze to cool the sun's heat, which made it perfect for hiking.

As Dan reached down for his day pack and lifted it back onto his shoulder, Sarah started walking. "I think I'll scout ahead and see if there's a good spot to settle down for lunch."

"Okay, meet up in fifteen at the most?"

She looked back at him over her shoulder, drinking in the sight of him, basking in the love shining in his face. "You got it, handsome."

Nope. You couldn't buy days like this for all the money in the world.

The woods around them were dense enough that Sarah was out of sight within minutes, but Dan didn't mind. He preferred a more leisurely pace to Sarah's bounding energy. Nor did he worry. Sarah could handle herself out here. She might be small—the top of her head barely reached his shoulder—but she was fit and strong. That was one of the things that first drew him to her. She wasn't one of those fragile women who had to be sheltered and protected. No way. His wife was a tiny package of energy and spunk, and he loved that.

As was the agreement—loser retrieves arrows from the target—Dan went to pull their arrows free. Slipping them into his quiver, he followed Sarah's trail with a practiced eye. No path out here. Just wilderness. Pure and majestic.

He paused, lifting his face to the sun's warmth. He enjoyed hiking almost as much as Sarah did. The rich, earthy fragrance of the Oregon forest filled his senses. He soaked in the towering evergreens all around, sunlight filtering down through dense needles.

"Okay, buddy. No snoozing on the trail."

He chuckled and opened his eyes. His wife was just ahead of him, crouched atop a huge fallen tree. With her quiver of arrows on her belt, her bow slung across her slim shoulder, and her floppy hat set at an angle on her long chestnut hair, she looked like a modern-day Robinette Hood perched there. She sent him a mock glare from on high; he painted his features with equally mock penitence. "Sorry, boss. Not even catnaps, eh?"

"Not even *kitten* naps. You can't afford to slack off. I'm ahead of you five to three on scoring targets."

"Slave driver."

"Count on it."

Her severity lasted another second before laughter overtook it. She plopped down on the log, adjusting her quiver so it was out of the way, then swung those shapely legs back and forth as she pulled her water bottle free. She tipped her head back, taking a long drink; Dan drank in the sight before him.

His wife's beauty was all natural. As natural as the woods around them. The summer sun had kissed her golden skin, making it glow in ways no makeup could. At thirty-four, her smooth features were free of wrinkles, save one or two that danced around her eyes, peeking out from the corners when she laughed. Dan loved those wrinkles. They were testimony to the fact that his wife was happy.

Especially today. Sarah loved being out here, in the forest, hiking and talking even as they tested each other's mettle with a bow.

Which made sense. She belonged here. One look at her showed how at home she was in the woods. She was almost as much a part of the wilderness as the ancient trees reaching over them, creating a lush canopy; as the rich loam of dirt and pine needles beneath their feet.

Which was why Dan made sure they got away like this as often as possible.

The good news was that their town, Central Point, gave them plenty of places to get away from civilization. A small community on the outskirts of Medford, Central Point afforded Dan and his family the warmth of a small town combined with the convenience of a larger city nearby. And, with his sister Annie living right in Medford, he and Sarah seldom had to worry about finding someone to watch the kids for them. Annie adored the kids and loved spending time with them whenever she could.

The bad news was that with all their commitments—their jobs, the kids, the volunteer work Dan did with troubled kids in the area—finding a day to get away was far from easy. Then there was the fact that it got harder every year to get time off. With every county budget cut, the number of deputies shrank, which meant fewer men to handle an ever-growing area. And that meant longer, more frequent shifts.

When Sarah reminded him a few weeks ago of how long it had been since they'd had a day out together, he knew what he had to do. Just as he knew it was going to be a battle.

But it had been worth it.

"So, you ready for me to beat you again?"

Dan arched a brow at his wife's teasing challenge, taking in her teasing smile, her glowing eyes.

Oh, yeah. *Definitely* worth it.

"That sure of yourself, are you?" He stood in front of her. Her smile deepened, and she rested her hands on his shoulders as he lifted her from the log, careful not to catch her quiver or bow on the bark, and set her on her feet in front of him. He buried his face in her hair, breathing in the heady mix of fragrances—summer and forest and all woman.

"Are you trying to distract me?"

He pressed a small kiss to her neck as he scanned the area around them. It was his turn to choose a target. "Mmm. Depends. Is it working?"

Sarah chuckled. "Maybe…"

There! Just down the path. A perfect target.

Sarah wrapped her arms around his waist then lifted her face to his. He leaned close, watching her eyes drift shut. His lips hovered over hers for a heartbeat, then he jumped away, sliding his bow off his shoulder and getting ready to move. "Okay, loser, next target is *mine*! Old tree stump, fifty feet ahead, dead center or no points."

"You are *such* a sneak!" Sarah's laughing response brought a grin to his face. She slid her bow free. "You're gonna pay for that one, bud."

Even as she spoke, she surveyed the area around them, spotting the target within seconds. With a whoop, they raced down the path, Sarah dodging in front of Dan.

Dan yelped and stumbled, barely avoiding a tumble to the ground. He came up with a playful growl, which faded to dismay when he saw his fleet-footed wife already in the firing stance, nocking an arrow.

He drew a few feet closer as she lifted the bow, and he opened his mouth to holler, hoping to distract her, knowing even as he did so it was useless. Nothing distracted that woman when she was focused. He looked at the decaying stump—and frowned.

What was that? He peered more closely, and alarm shot through him.

Bees. Buzzing around the top of the stump. "Sarah, wait!"

Too late. She pulled the string back with practiced ease and let the arrow fly.

"Sarah! Run!"

His warning split the air just as two things happened: Sarah's arrow struck, straight and true, dead center on the target; and she turned to toss him a gloating, "Hah!"

Which meant her back was turned to the stump.

Which meant she didn't see the cloud of angry yellow insects roil up out of their assaulted shelter.

Yellow. Yellow bees. No, not bees…yellow jackets!

Dan's alarm changed to near panic. "Sarah!"

The tone in his voice made her turn and look behind her. In the seconds it took understanding to dawn, the wasps had locked on their own target: Sarah.

Dropping her bow, she sprinted toward Dan, the insects in hot pursuit. When Sarah reached him, he grabbed his wife's hand, and they tore through the woods.

Dan heard Sarah cry out, felt the wasps hitting him and stinging, heard them buzzing at his face, but he didn't stop. He just brushed madly at his attackers with his free hand as he ran.

"Pull your shirt over your face!"

He didn't look to see if Sarah complied. He couldn't. He had to stay focused on the woods in front of them, on getting them as far away from the hive as fast as possible.

How far or how long they ran, Dan couldn't say. All he knew was that the number of wasps swarming around him lessened, until finally there weren't any.

Gasping for air, his lungs burning, he drew Sarah to a halt, pulling her into his arms. "Oh, man! Un…believable!"

Sarah didn't respond. When Dan saw she'd pulled her shirt up over her face, relief swept him. Though he could see welts forming on her hands and arms, if she got the shirt over her face, maybe that was the worst of it.

"Sarah? How bad are you stung, honey?"

Again, no response. She just stood there, fingers clutching his shirt as she dragged in air.

Listening to the wheezing sound of her breathing, dread

clawed through Dan's chest. "Sarah?" He pulled his wife's shirt away from her face and his heart seized.

Her face was pasty white, except for six or seven bright red welts on her forehead and cheeks. Her eyes were wide, and Dan saw something in them he'd never seen before.

Panic.

"Can't…" She gasped, as though sucking air through mud. "Can't breathe…"

Before he could reply, she sagged against him, her hands going limp.

"Sarah!"

Dan lowered his wheezing wife to the ground, kneeling beside her. "Oh, Jesus, *please!*"

His training kicked in, and his critical mind registered the facts: His wife had been stung at least fifteen or twenty times. But most adults could survive as many as two hundred stings unless…

Unless she was allergic.

A memory flashed through Dan's mind. Two summers ago, eight-year-old Shannon had been stung by a wasp. It hurt the poor kid something fierce, and she cried and cried until Sarah finally got her calmed down. As Dan and Sarah settled at the kitchen table, rejuvenating cups of coffee before them, Dan sighed.

"Man, nothing hurts quite like a bee sting."

Sara sipped her coffee. "So I've heard."

"Heard? You mean you've never been stung?"

"Not even once; a fact for which I'm grateful."

Dan had laughed then, telling her she was "blessed among sting-free women." Now…

If she'd been stung before, they would have known she was allergic. And they'd have known to bring along the needed first-aid supplies. Instead, he had the terrifying sense that his wife's first bee sting could be her last.

"D-Dan…"

He grabbed her hand—there were red bumps and splotches all down her arm. He held her limp fingers to his cheek, then used his free hand to jerk his cell phone from his belt clip. "Don't try to talk, Sarah. I'm calling for help."

She said something more, but it was barely a whisper. Her fingers tugged on his, and he could see how hard she was trying to speak. He leaned close to her lips. "Easy, honey. Just whisper."

"Tell…kids…love them."

Please, Jesus! Please, help her!

"You can tell them yourself as soon as we get home." He flipped the cell phone open, but Sarah shook her head, the feeble motion sending panic zinging through him. "Sarah, please…"

"*Tell* them."

Dan clenched his teeth, set the phone down, and took both her hands in his. "I will." The hoarse promise almost shredded his heart. "You know I will—if it comes to that."

She coughed, her eyes drifting shut. A smile trembled on her lips. "You're—you're such a good man, Dan."

"Sarah, please honey, don't try to talk."

She wasn't listening. A tear pushed past her closed eyelid and trickled down the side of her face. "I always saw…God…in your…eyes." She gripped his hand and opened her eyes, though he could tell what an effort it was for her. "Help…kids see…who God is. Help them…really live. Really love." She dragged air in. "And you. Please…Dan…live…love."

She was saying good-bye!

"Sarah!"

"Love you." The words whispered out on a faint breath. Her eyes closed, and she went limp.

"Oh no you don't!" He grabbed the phone, shaking her with his free hand. "You *stay* with me, Sarah! You hear?"

He punched 911 into the phone, then, keeping one hand on Sarah's chest so he could tell if she stopped breathing, he listened to the ring once…twice…

Don't let this happen, Jesus. Please, don't let this—

"Nine-one-one. What's your emergency?"

Dan spoke quickly, identifying himself as a sheriff's deputy and giving information—their names, the situation, their GPS coordinates—as clearly and concisely as possible. But even as he did so, he knew what the 911 operator would say.

"We've notified emergency services, Mr. Justice, but it's going to take them twenty minutes or more to reach your location."

Hopelessness landed on his chest like a leaden weight, and he looked down at Sarah—then froze.

There was no motion under his hand.

"She's stopped breathing!"

Dropping the phone on the ground, Dan leaned over Sarah, his ear next to her mouth as he felt for a pulse in her neck.

No breath. No heartbeat.

As though this were a stranger and not the center of his universe, he tilted Sarah's head back and started the rhythm of CPR. Two breaths. Fifteen chest compressions. *And-one-and-two-and-three…*

All the while, behind the steady count to fifteen in the forefront of his mind chaos reined. Images of Sarah and the kids, memories of laughter and loving, ran rampant…Sarah's voice drifted through, singing the kids to sleep, uttering that deep contented sigh she breathed so often against his chest as they drifted off to sleep, the sound a sweet benediction on the day…and his own desperate prayers, agonized pleas for God's mercy and divine intervention.

…and fifteen.

He pinched her nose shut, placed his mouth over hers, and watched her chest as he gave her two more breaths.

What…?

There was no chest movement. No sign the air was getting in.

He tried again. *Puff. Puff.*

Nothing.

Her chest should be moving. Why wasn't it?

Awareness slammed into Dan. Anaphylactic shock. Severe allergies could cause anaphylaxis, which meant her airway was swollen shut.

Jesus...Jesus! His mind screamed the name, a desperate plea for mercy. *The air can't get through.*

"No..." Dan pressed trembling fingers to his wife's neck, checking for a pulse. "Come on, Sarah. Come on..."

Nothing.

He sat back with a thud, pulling his knees to his chest, lowering his face to his hands.

There was nothing he could do.

The sudden sound of rotors pounding the air brought him to his feet. He waved his arms, hope roaring through him as he watched the chopper lower to the ground. Rushing back to Sarah's side, he pressed his fingers to her neck once again.

Please...please...

A gentle hand settled on his shoulder. "We'll take over now, Deputy."

He looked up, ready to argue, to tell them *he* had to do this, had to save her, but the words died on his lips. The face beside him was familiar.

His gaze fell to the name tag. *Wally*. Of course. Wally Johnson. Dan had worked with him at other accident scenes this summer. He'd been impressed at the way Wally treated people. With respect. And a depth of kindness.

"Deputy?"

Dan let himself be urged from Sarah's side. "She—" He could hardly speak above a whisper. He tried again. "She hasn't been breathing since I made the call to 911. It's anaphylaxis. Bee stings."

Wally and his partner went to work with solemn speed and efficiency. Dan stumbled away, leaning against a nearby tree, watching as they injected Sarah's still form, performed CPR.

Watching. Hoping. Praying.

But even as he did so, he knew. Had known almost from the moment she sagged against him and crumpled to the ground.

It was over.

His sweet Sarah was gone.

FOUR

*"The leaves of memory seemed to make
a mournful rustling in the dark."*
HENRY WADSWORTH LONGFELLOW

*"My heart is breaking as I remember
how it used to be."*
PSALM 42:4

IT SHOULD BE RAINING.

That would have made more sense. Cold, drizzling rain.
Then he'd know the very heavens understood something terrible had happened.

But as Dan stood looking out the window, there wasn't a
drop in the sky. Rather, the sun shone from behind wisps of
cotton clouds. Birds sang glorious rhapsodies as they filled the
trees just outside the window. A teasing breeze lifted the cur-
tains, sending them dancing like giddy schoolgirls when spring
comes to play.

Like Sarah, on the last day of her life.

Dan longed to choke the life from the dark anguish gnawing at him.

How could this be? How could the world go on with such
joyous abandon when his life was so broken?

Widower. That was the kind of thing you said about white-haired men, those who'd shared long, loving lives with the women they adored. Men who talked about their fiftieth and sixtieth anniversaries, about the good old days.

But Dan was only thirty-seven! There wasn't a hint of white in his brown hair. Not unless this past week had put it there.

Raspy fingers of emotion curled around his throat. He shoved his hands deep in his jeans pockets—then allowed himself a small, humorless, smile. His sister Kyla had told him to be sure and wear a suit, but Sarah would understand. She knew suits just weren't his thing. She'd bought the black jeans he now wore for that very reason—so he'd have something at least a little dressy to wear on somber occasions.

Yeah, well…it didn't get more somber than this.

He spread his hand out against the cool windowpane, closing his eyes. *Mom…Dad…I wish you were here.* He missed his parents since their deaths. They'd had him and his sisters late in life, starting with Dan when Mom was forty-three and Dad was forty-seven.

His mom, who had struggled with her health for a number of years, finally lost the battle three years ago, just before she turned seventy-seven. His father faded quickly after that and died a year later. Dan remembered thinking then that losing his parents was the worst pain he'd ever known.

He squeezed his aching eyes tight against new grief. *You always knew the right thing to say. How to help craziness make sense. How to find some semblance of right and justice in even the worst of times.*

Not even his parents could make sense of this.

As though to refute that thought, his mother's tender, peace-filled voice drifted through his mind, speaking words he'd heard from her most of his life…

"God's in control, son. Don't ever doubt it. When things look most out of control, that's when He's at work. His justice will always prevail."

Opening his eyes, he let his hand fall away from the window. How often had she said that to him? God's justice will always prevail. He'd never doubted it. Not for a minute. Not even in the face of this loss.

If only that helped, knowing his mother's words were true. But it didn't. Not at all.

"Danny?"

Warmth flooded him, easing the chill that seemed to have settled deep in his bones.

Danny.

To most people, he was *Dan.* To Kyla, ever the proper one, he was *Avidan.* "Mom gave us specific names for specific reasons," Kyla always said. "I, for one, intend to use them."

But *Danny*? Only one person called him that.

A gentle touch on his arm drew his attention, and he gazed down into the misty hazel eyes of his youngest sister. Eyes that saw so much more than others did.

"So—" he laid his hand over hers—"Ky freaking out?"

Annie's weary smile spoke volumes. The funeral had been hard on all of them, but Annie and Sarah had been good friends. Losing her like this…well, it cost Annie.

Still, Dan could see his sister was doing her best to put on, if not a happy face, at least an uplifting one. That was Annie. Always trying to help people get through the hard times with a bit of laughter.

She shrugged. "Hey, it's in Kyla's contract as the oldest sister."

"She's not *that* much older. And you're not all that young. You're what? Thirty-eight?"

Annie's arched brows warned he was treading on thin ice. "Thirty-three, you beast. You never have been good at keeping track of our ages."

A pang sliced through him. Sarah was the one who tracked ages and birthdays and special family events. Now that duty would fall to him.

"And three years older is plenty, especially when you were *born* old." She flicked dog hair from her pants. "She was less than pleased that I brought my dog with me."

For all his sister's bluster, Annie didn't really mind Kyla's ways. She just loved to heckle her for them. "Kodi's no trouble."

"Yeah, well, tell Sister-Mommy that. She's convinced Kodi's going to do something terrible. Like drool. Or shed." She lifted another dog hair, held it up, and let it go.

Dan watched the hair float down onto the rug. "So where is the fur ball?"

Annie pulled herself to her full height of 5'5", trying to be an imposing presence. At 5'9", Kyla could assume that pose almost without trying. Though she was slim, she gave the impression of strength. An immovable force. But Annie? She weighed all of 135 pounds soaking wet. Needless to say, she wasn't having much luck. Dan was proud of himself, though— he didn't laugh. His sister might be small, but she came by those red glints in her cropped auburn hair honestly. She could be fierce when she was riled.

"That *fur ball,* my good man, is a purebred German shepherd from the finest stock."

Dan swatted at her. It felt good to tease. To pretend they were just getting together for the heck of it—instead of because his world had come to an end. "Yeah. Like she came from the shelter with papers and everything."

She giggled, and the sound did his ragged nerves good. "Okay, but you have to admit she *looks* purebred."

No doubt about that. From the tip of her black, pointed ears to the end of her wagging black tail, Kodi was every inch and pound—ninety-five, at last weighing—German shepherd.

"Anyway, she's tucked away in my room, curled up in her crate."

"So what's the problem?"

Annie planted her hands on her hips. "Oh, let's see. First there's my dog. Then, here we are, at your wife's funeral luncheon, and you're nowhere to be found. Honestly, I think Kyla was about to have me haul Kodi out to find you."

Just what he needed. A certified search-and-rescue dog tracking him down in his own house.

Annie must have read his dismay on his features, because she patted him on the shoulder. "Fear not, dear brother. I saved you."

"Oh?"

"Yeah. Sister-Mommy was about to do far worse than call out Kodi."

His eyes narrowed. "How so?"

Annie's tired eyes regained some of their usual twinkle. "She was all set to send Mrs. Briggs after you."

Dan groaned. Mrs. Briggs was one of the busiest busybodies in existence. If she'd found him, he wouldn't have had a moment's peace until he went back out to mingle with the crowd who'd come to pay their respects.

But if he had to listen to one more person mumble how sorry he or she was, he'd go mad.

"So I stepped in and promised Kyla I'd hunt you down. Which I did." She studied the room around them. "I figured you'd be here. Sarah loved this room."

He let his gaze travel the bookshelves lining the walls. It was this room, a combination office and library, that had convinced him and Sarah to buy the house. When they weren't hiking, they were here, reading, talking. And then, after the children were born, they'd spent a couple nights a week— Family Enrichment Time, Sarah called it—sitting together and reading in this room.

Dan blinked back sudden tears. "I can still feel her here. And if I listen hard enough, I can hear her." He swiped at his eyes with his hand. "Anyway, I needed a break, and this seemed the place to come."

Annie squeezed his arm. "It's okay, Danny. I won't try to drag you back out there. I figure you need some alone time in the face of all that...sympathy."

He should have known. Annie understood him better than anyone except—

His breath caught. He closed his eyes.

Except Sarah.

A thin dagger of ugly truth sliced through him. There was no Sarah. Not any longer.

Annie shifted beside him. "Did I tell you I saw a double rainbow on my drive here from Medford?"

Sweet Annie. Doing all she could to distract him. "Twice. But then, you see rainbows wherever you are."

Annie waggled her fingers at him. "You're just jealous *you* don't have synesthesia."

Dan remembered a time when Annie didn't think her condition was something to envy at all. When she had realized, around age ten, that everyone didn't see the world the way she did, she thought she was crazy.

"No one else tastes shapes or sees words in color! I'm just weird!"

It took them a while to find a doctor who understood the condition, but when they did, he explained it as a "perceptual curiosity that occurs in roughly one in twenty-five thousand people."

Basically, Annie's senses blended the real information of one sense with a perception in another. So she saw the same things other people did, but she *perceived* them differently. The letter *D* to Annie was a deep, rich blue. And that color transferred to things—or people—whose names started with *D*.

Which meant when she saw or thought of Dan, she had the sense of a blue aura around him. Not an aura in any kind of spiritual or mystical sense but a physical sense.

To Annie, that blue was as much a part of Dan as his brown hair and his height. After meeting with the doctor, suddenly Annie wasn't crazy at all. But special.

"Ah, well." She pulled him back to the present as she linked her arm with his. "That's what I get for being an artist. I have a great eye for beauty, and a miserable memory for mundane details."

And what an artist she was. Her works in stained glass had gained national attention and acclaim. Dan wasn't surprised. The beauty she created stemmed from the spirit of true beauty within her. And from her synesthesia. Because she saw things in ways others didn't; she brought a depth of perception to her work, and people loved what she did.

Clearly, God created Annie to be an artist.

He lifted a hand to trace the pattern of one of his sister's creations. When Dan and Sarah bought the home, Annie created a stunning forest scene to go in the library window. So they could be in the woods, she'd told them, even when they were in town.

"Sarah loved this window." He splayed his hand against the richly colored glass. "She always said you gave her her very own piece of God's wilderness."

Annie stood in silence for a moment. "Tell you what. I'll go back and report I found you. And that you'll come out soon, say in a half hour at the most?"

He sighed. "An hour."

"Forty-five minutes."

Dan held out his hand, and Annie hooked her pinkie with his. "Done. That should make Sister-Mommy happy."

"Hey, that's always my goal."

Annie pulled a face at him. "Give her a break, bro. With Mom and Dad gone, *someone* has to make sure you and I behave. Who better than Kyla? I mean, bossing people *has* to be her spiritual gift."

"Which is why she's made the business Dad started into the number one construction business in Portland."

Annie leaned back against the desk. "Really, when you think about it, our sister is pretty remarkable."

He smiled. "That she is. A little...*forceful* at times, but nonetheless remarkable."

"Hey, you know what she always says…"

They spoke together: "'I didn't make it as a businesswoman in a man's world by waiting for someone to tell me what to do.'"

Annie's low laughter coaxed a smile from him. "Sometimes I think Mom should have given her a name that means *control freak* instead of *victorious*."

Dan surprised himself by chuckling. He hadn't laughed in days. He'd wondered if he'd ever laugh again, ever smile again. How could he? Life without Sarah meant…emptiness. But he'd forgotten about Annie. She always made him laugh, even—or maybe especially—at times like this.

He nudged her with his elbow. "And *your* name should mean *imp* instead of *light*."

She leaned against his arm. "You love me, and you know it."

"Yes." He slid his arm around her shoulders, hugging her close. "Yes, I do."

She rested her head against him, and they stood there, the silence a comfort as they stared out at the terrible, sunny day.

"It's a Sarah kind of day."

Dan's brow creased as he gazed down at his sister. "What?"

She spread her hands, indicating the scene in front of them. "Can't you feel it? It's a Sarah kind of day, all full of sunlight and laughter and unbridled joy."

Sorrow battled sweet memory as Dan looked out the window again. Sarah loved every day, rain or shine. Her delight in life didn't come from what was happening on the outside, but from inside. From the deep well of joy within her.

"Sarah would love a day like today."

He smiled. "Only if she could be out in it."

"Hiking out there, in the woods…that was Sarah's truest form of worship."

Their gazes met, and Dan saw something deep in his sister's eyes.

"You know that, don't you, Danny? What happened…you couldn't have stopped it. Sarah was outside every chance she got.

Hiking, biking, swimming. With her not knowing she was allergic to bee stings, it was just a matter of time. If it hadn't happened on your hike, it would have happened someplace else. And this way…" She bit her lip. "Well, at least this way, you were with her."

He wanted to argue. To say he *could* have done something more. But he knew in this, too, his sister was right.

Annie started toward the door, only to halt when it flew open. "Daddy!"

Dan turned as his two children ran toward him, and he went down on one knee. They catapulted themselves into his open arms, clutching him.

"Hey, now—" he forced strength into his arms and his voice. "What's up, you two?"

Shannon sobbed against him, pressing close. Dan flinched as her pendant dug into his collarbone. He'd given her the Aslan pendant for her birthday, six days after her mom's death. He'd considered waiting, but hoped it would give her something to hold on to.

It had. She hadn't taken the pendant off since slipping the chain over her head.

"We couldn't *find* you!" Hiccupping sobs accompanied Shannon's words. "We thought you were gone!"

Aaron released his grip on Dan's shirt just long enough to punch his sister's arm. "*You* thought he was gone. I told you he was here. Dummy."

Normally, he would have chastised Aaron for talking to Shannon that way, but Aaron's words didn't stem from his usual older-brother disdain. No, the cause of his harsh comment was clear in the boy's tone: fear.

He looked over his children's heads at Annie, and she came to wrap her arms around all three of them.

"Your dad's right here, you guys. He just—" she pressed her cheek to Aaron's head—"needed a little quiet time."

Shannon wiped her sniffles on Dan's shoulder then peered up at him. "Were you bad, Dad?"

"Bad?" Dan frowned then gave way to a smile. Ah. Of course. When the kids got to be too much, Sarah used to give them quiet time. "No, hon. Not bad. Just sad."

Aaron's fingers played with a button on Dan's shirt. "You miss Mom."

Dan swallowed his reaction to those quiet words. He needed to be steady for his children. "I miss Mom."

"So do I." A tear trickled down Shannon's pale cheek. "Lots."

Dan stood, taking their hands in his. "I know, honey. Me, too."

"Did God take Mom away?"

Before Dan could reply, Aaron went on. "'Cuz if He did, I'm mad at Him."

Out of the mouths of babes. "It makes me mad, too, that your mom is gone. But I don't think God took her away. I think it's just something that happened. Something really, really bad."

"But…God was there, wasn't He? He could have helped her. God can save anyone, right?"

Dan looked into his little girl's eyes, and the bewilderment there tore at his heart.

What could he say? How could he help them understand when he didn't fully understand himself?

Sarah's last words to him suddenly struck home: *"Help our kids see who God is."*

How do I do that, Sarah? When I'm not sure I know Him the way I thought I did? When I can't help but feel this isn't right… He should have helped you, should have shown us somehow that you were allergic…

Even as the questions raced through his mind, Dan knew what Sarah's answer would be. What it had been over and over again through the years: *"Dan, don't try to explain what you can't. Just say what you know."*

He could do that. "Come here, you two." He led the kids to the overstuffed chair where he and Sarah used to sit together, him deep in the cushions, her snuggled on his lap.

Annie went to lean against the desk. Dan glanced at her, and her gentle eyes told him what he needed to know. She was there if he needed her.

He sat in the chair and opened his arms. The kids didn't need any urging; they crawled into his lap, burrowing close. "God was there, with your mom and me. He's always with us, even when it doesn't feel like it. And yes, He could have saved your mom. But He didn't."

Aaron rubbed a fist at his nose. "Why?"

If only he had an answer for that. "I don't know why, son. I wish I did."

"Did He want you to save her? Because you're a policeman and save people?"

The question cut deep, but Dan tried not to show his pain to Shannon. "I don't think so, honey. I tried…I really did. I…"

Go ahead. Say it. You did your best, right? Funny how it's never quite good enough.

Just like that awful day all those years ago…

For a moment Dan thought he was going to lose it. Right then and there, with his children watching him. But Sarah's voice came to him, low and calming: "*Just say what you know.*"

He could do that. He looked from Shannon to Aaron. "I don't know why God didn't save Mom, but I do know it isn't because He didn't love her. Or you. And it wasn't because He's mean or made a mistake." God didn't make mistakes. Right? Dan just wished he felt a stronger conviction in the knowledge. "I know for a fact that God loves you both, very much. Even more than your mom and I do."

"That's a lot."

Dan smiled at Shannon's words, muffled as they were against his chest. "Yes, it is. A whole lot."

Annie kneeled beside them, reaching out to stroke Aaron's hair. "Do you remember what your mom always used to say about God?"

Aaron leaned against his aunt. "He's in control. Even when it doesn't seem like it."

"Like now?"

"Just like now, Shannon. I know it's hard." Harder than anything he'd ever known. "I know it seems like life is really bad and things won't ever be right again…" He swallowed but couldn't dislodge the lump in his throat. One pleading look at Annie was all it took.

"But God knows everything we're feeling. And He understands and loves us." She touched Shannon's cheek. "Even when we're mad at Him. It's just like when we're mad at each other. As long as we keep talking, we can work through it."

Aaron pursed his lips, thinking. It never ceased to amaze Dan what a deep thinker the boy was. When Dan was twelve, he'd been focused on dogs and football and riding bikes. But Aaron's twelve-year-old mind seemed to gravitate to the big questions in life. Sarah always said it was because God had great plans for their boy.

Dan was sure she was right.

Finally, Aaron gave a slow nod. "Okay."

Dan cocked his head. "Okay?"

Aaron nodded again and slid from Dan's lap. "Okay. I'll keep talking to God."

"Me, too." Determination shone on Shannon's little-girl face as she added her nod to her brother's.

Dan hugged her, then set her on the floor. "And me, too." He mussed her hair, and she caught his hand.

"Love you, Daddy."

This time he managed to speak past the lump in his throat. "Love you, too, Shannon." He looked at Aaron. "And you."

"Well, you two—" Annie reached down to take the kids' hands—"what say we go see how panicked your Auntie Kyla is by now, seeing as we've all deserted her?"

Dan sighed. "Do I have to?"

She hesitated. "Maybe not. At least, not right away." She

looked down at Aaron and Shannon. "Think you two can go find your auntie and give her a big hug? Then ask her for a cookie?"

"Sure." Shannon took Aaron's hand and tugged him toward the door. "We like Aunt Kyla. She's funny."

"Yeah." Annie made a face. "Funny. I've always said what a hoot that Kyla is."

Dan managed a smile through weary lips as Annie followed her niece and nephew toward the door. Just as she reached it, she cast a look over her shoulder. "I don't suppose you have any elephant tranquilizers in the bathroom cabinet, do you?"

At his rueful look, she giggled. "No, I didn't think so. But that's okay. They probably wouldn't be enough to calm her down anyway. So here's the deal. I'll go talk to her, call her *Kylie*—"

"The childhood nickname." Dan almost chuckled. "The one you used to use when you came into her room at night after a nightmare."

"The one that turns her all soft and maternal? Yup, that's the one. Anyway, I'll convince her you need a little more time alone. But listen up. Those forty-five minutes we agreed to earlier, big brother? They're ticking down, starting now."

"I'll be there. I promise."

She slipped out, and as the door clicked shut behind her, Dan leaned his head back. He hadn't realized how tired he was. But suddenly he felt as though a lead blanket lay over him, making it hard to move, to breathe, to think. His eyes drifted shut. "Sarah…"

As though in response to his whispered plea, images swam through his mind, pictures of their life together…Sarah floating down the aisle, the most beautiful bride he'd ever seen…Sarah holding their newborn babies, tears in her eyes…the way her lips tipped when she teased him… On and on they came, one after another, each one ripping an ever larger hole in his heart.

Dan let them come. For here, immersed in memories, he could, for a brief moment in time, be where he most wanted to be.

Where he would never in this life be again.

With Sarah.

A knock at the door sent a stab of shock through Dan. He bolted out of his chair. "Sarah?"

Another knock, this one a little louder and followed by a worried voice. "Avidan? Are you all right?"

Not Sarah. Kyla.

He closed his eyes. Sarah was gone.

Sucking in a ragged breath, he looked down at his watch. Two hours since Annie and the kids left the room. So much for promises.

Dan went to pull the door open. "Kyla, I'm so sorry—"

She stopped him with a gentle hand on his face. Her green eyes softened, and there was a catch in her voice when she spoke. "Oh, Avidan. You've been crying."

He brushed his cheek. She was right. His skin was more than damp. "I was…dreaming, or something. I was in the woods again. With Sarah."

Kyla wrapped her arms around him, patting his back, the action as gentle and soothing as her voice. "I wish I could make it better."

Oh, that a sister's wishes could be granted. "So do I." But nothing was going to make this better. Not for a very, very long time.

FIVE

"The only cure for grief is action."
GEORGE HENRY LEWES

"The LORD will work out his plans for my life."
PSALM 138:8

"I CAN DO THIS."

Dan stood in the doorway, steeling himself. "Come on, Justice. You're an adult. A cop, for cryin' out loud. Nothin' scares you, right?"

Right. Except, of course, the empty room before him. And the thought of sleeping in that empty bed by himself.

He sagged against the doorjamb. Six months. How could that much time have passed already? Six months since the funeral. Six months of living in a house and town where everything reminded him of Sarah. Of all they'd lost.

All they'd never have again.

Six months of putting the kids to bed, then heading for his room with grim determination. Of standing here, in the doorway of his bedroom, telling himself to stop being a fool and get some sleep. Of staring at the quilt Sarah had pulled in place as she made their bed the morning they headed for their hike. Of walking to the bed, lifting the pillow that had cushioned his wife's head, and pressing his face into it, drawing every last bit of her fragrance from it.

Six months of carrying that pillow to the living room. Amazing how accustomed one could become to sleeping in a recliner.

As Dan headed for the recliner one more time, he sighed. At least he seemed to be the only one struggling with the memories at night. The kids had their moments during the day. Like yesterday.

Oh, yeah. That was a doozy.

On Saturdays Sarah always got up early and fixed them all a special breakfast. Pancakes. Waffles. Crepes. Apple-dumpling oatmeal. They never knew what they'd find waiting for them at the breakfast table. But it was always delicious.

Yesterday Dan came to the kitchen for breakfast and found the room in a shambles and Shannon in tears. She'd gotten up early, determined to make a special Saturday breakfast. But nothing went right.

Dan comforted her, saying they could do it together. Aaron had been less than thrilled, but he joined in. Until Shannon turned too quick and knocked a dozen eggs from the counter, sending them crashing to the floor.

The eggs exploded into goo.

Aaron exploded into a rage. "This is *stupid*!"

"It is not!" Shannon's tears erupted again.

Before Dan could say a word, Aaron spat out his fury. "Give it up! Who do you think you are? Mom?"

Oh, yeah. That was a lovely way to start the weekend. By afternoon they had the kitchen cleaned up, and Aaron and Shannon reached a kind of uneasy peace. As for Dan, he went through the rest of the day forcing his lips to smile and his words to be encouraging.

Not an easy task when all he wanted to do was hit something.

Now he sat in his recliner, got the pillow arranged just right, and pushed back. He closed his eyes, slowing his breathing, trying to convince himself he was sleepy. This wasn't so bad, really. Probably better for his back in the long ru—

"Dad?"

He cracked one eye open. Two forms stood beside him.

"We want to sleep in here. With you."

"What…" He pushed up on one elbow. "What's wrong with your beds?" It only took a look from one child to the other to know. His kids had been acting, too. They weren't dealing with the nights any better than he was.

He opened his arms, and both kids climbed up onto his lap, each snuggling down in the crook of an arm. Good thing he had an oversized recliner.

He'd just about drifted back to sleep.

"Daddy?"

He forced his eyes open. Shannon lay with one hand clutching his shirt, the other wrapped around the lion's head pendant. "What is it, Shannon?"

"Can we sing the song?"

He stared at the ceiling, felt Aaron shift and lift his head to look at him.

"Yeah, sing the song, Dad."

A flash of anger left his voice stuck someplace in his throat. He and Sarah used to sing the song to the kids together. From the time they were infants. Just as Dan's mother sang it to him.

Singing it now…without her…

He glared at the darkness. He couldn't *do* this! How was he supposed to raise these two without Sarah? How was he supposed to face one more day knowing she wasn't here? Wouldn't ever be here again?

Suddenly a small, sweet voice filled the quiet room.

"Be not dismayed whate'er betide, God will take care of you.
Beneath His wings of love abide, God will take care of you.
God will take care of you, through every day, o'er all the way;
He will take care of you, God will take care of you."

Shannon's voice was so like her mother's. Dan's eyes closed, his arms tightening around his children. Aaron laid his head on Dan's shoulder and lifted his voice to join his sister's.

"Through days of toil when heart doth fail,
God will take care of you;
When dangers fierce your path assail, God will take care of you.
God will take care of you, through every day, o'er all the way;
He will take care of you, God will take care of you."

As he listened, it was as though he could hear other voices joining in. His mother's. Sarah's. Each letting him know they weren't gone. Not really. They were there, in his children. In his heart.

Finally, with a shuddering breath, Dan opened his mouth and sang.

"All you may need He will provide, God will take care of you;
Nothing you ask will be denied, God will take care of you.
No matter what may be the test, God will take care of you;
Lean, weary one, upon His breast, God will take care of you."

As the sound of their voices drifted into silence, Dan placed a kiss on Aaron's, then Shannon's foreheads. Yes, Sarah was gone. But part of her lived on in the two he held in his arms.

For that, he would always be grateful.

∾

The next day, when the kids were off to school, Dan called his sisters, asking them to pray for him. "We need a change. I'm just not sure what kind."

Kyla and Annie each agreed to spend time every day for the next week reading the Bible and praying, asking God to give them a special verse for guidance. At the end of the week, Kyla and Annie would drive to his house to talk.

Dan sat down for his morning devotions, and words from his reading jumped out at him: "Leave the boat, all of you."

He blinked, read the words again, and broke into a grin. He supposed there was a message in that somewhere. He read the whole chapter, but nothing stood out except those six words.

Yeah, well, that's what he got for thinking he could just open the Bible and get a word from God.

During the week, he read the entire book of Genesis, and still that same verse kept coming back to him, over and over, like maddening song lyrics that wouldn't go away.

It wasn't until he met with his sisters that it made sense. Annie arrived that afternoon, so they came to Dan's for dinner. After putting the kids to bed, the three of them gathered in the library.

Annie had barely shut the door when Kyla jumped in. "Okay, Avidan, what's your verse?"

He fidgeted, scooting to the edge of the couch cushion. "I'd rather one of you went first. Mine is a bit…odd."

"Odd or not—" Kyla sank into the cushion next to him— "let's hear it."

Dan started to argue with her, then sighed, watching Annie take her usual spot, perching on the arm of the couch. "Okay. You asked for it. My verse is Genesis 8:16. It says, 'Leave the boat, all of you.'"

Their reactions weren't even close to what he'd expected.

He thought they'd laugh, maybe tease him. Instead, they just stared, first at him, then at each other.

Kyla swallowed. "Well. That settles it."

Dan frowned. "Settles what?"

Annie looked at her sister. "Yours, too, huh?"

Resignation glimmered in Kyla's green eyes. "I kept hoping I got it wrong."

"Me, too. I mean, mine didn't quite fit with what I thought God was saying, but now—" Annie folded her hands in her lap—"it makes sense."

Dan crossed his arms and stared at his sisters. "You two care to let me in on the secret?"

Annie folded her knees to her chest. "Go ahead, Kyla."

She turned to Dan, and he wondered at the hint of sadness in her eyes. "My verse is Acts 7:3. 'God told him, "Leave your native land and your relatives, and come to the land that I will show you."'"

Dan's mouth fell open.

"Annot?"

Annie followed her sister's lead. "My verse is John 14:16. 'And I will ask the Father, and he will give you another Counselor, who will never leave you.'"

It didn't take a genius to put it all together: The change they needed was a move.

As hard as it was to even consider the idea—to imagine leaving the home he and Sarah had made or the sisters who meant so much to him—Dan had to admit he felt a certainty, deep inside, that it was the right thing to do.

The first confirmation came in the form of a job opening posted on the wall at work. Dan seldom looked at the job postings, but today he was drawn to them. And one sheet in particular caught his eyes. It was a job description for a sheriff's deputy in a rural mountain community about an hour north. Dan read the sheet three times. Each time his heart beat a little faster.

Finally he stuck his head in his boss's office, dangling the job description in front of him. "What's this?"

John Grayson, Jackson County's sheriff, looked up, one bushy brow lifting. "What? You forget how to read?"

Dan stepped inside the office. "No, I mean…we don't have deputies in those mountain communities."

"Yeah, well, we do now. Or we will, when they fill the position."

Dan frowned. "How? I thought the county couldn't afford—"

"They couldn't. But some rich guy decided he wanted to donate money for a new program to get deputies to those remote areas, and this is where the county decided to start. So, the money's there. All they need is a deputy."

Dan looked down at the paper. "I want to apply." He didn't know who was more surprised: Grayson or Dan himself.

The sheriff leaned his arms on the desk in front of him. "Figured you would."

Okay. Dan was more surprised. "You did?"

The sheriff shrugged. "Just seemed a good fit. From what I hear, it's a nice little town. Great place to raise kids. And it's in the middle of the mountains."

He picked up his pen and waved it in the air. "You're always spouting off about how the valley's getting too full of people." He turned back to the report he'd been reading. "Can't hurt to check it out."

Nope. Couldn't hurt at all.

The second confirmation came that evening, when Dan got home and sat the kids down to tell them what he was considering. When he'd given them all the information, he waited, not sure what to expect. Questions? Maybe. Resistance? Possibly. Anxiety? He wouldn't be surprised—

"What's the name of the town?"

Dan searched his daughter's face for signs of apprehension, resistance. He saw only curiosity. And a glimmer of something else…something he couldn't quite pinpoint. "Sanctuary."

"Ohh—" that indefinable emotion deepened, bringing a warm glow to her chocolate eyes—"I like that."

Understanding dawned. Hope. That's what Dan saw in her eyes. Hope.

"Me, too."

Aaron agreeing with his sister? "You do?"

The boy stuck his feet straight out in front of him, wiggling them. "Yeah. Sanctuary." He repeated the town name, as though seeing how it fit not only on his lips, but in his heart. "It sounds like, I don't know…"

"Like home."

Aaron glanced at his sister, apparently letting her words roll around in his head, then nodded, a smile tiptoeing across his mouth. "Yeah." He looked at Dan. "It does. It sounds like home."

Dan leaned back in his chair. Okaaay…God *had* to be at work here. His children never agreed on anything.

Not ever.

Clearly, he was witness to a miracle.

Dan called personnel the next day, and a Realtor the day after that. The job was his in three weeks. His house sold in four.

Before he knew it—less than two months after asking his sisters to pray—Dan stood on the front lawn of the home he and Sarah had shared, surveying the loaded moving truck.

Kyla stood next to him, patting her brow with a monogrammed handkerchief. She'd taken over the second Dan arrived with the moving van, orchestrating them all with precision and authority.

The woman was born to commandeer.

Normally Dan would have given her a run for her money—he was bigger and taller than she; he was sure he could take her—but today he was grateful that someone else took control. He had all he could handle dealing with the grief that kept popping up, seizing his heart and superseding his ability to make logical decisions.

"Well—" Kyla folded her handkerchief into a precise square and slid it into her pocket—"I think that's everything."

"It'd better be. I don't think there's an inch more of room in that truck."

His sister's one raised brow warned him a reprimand was coming. "Well, I *did* tell you to get the larger truck." She gave a little sniff. "I do similar kinds of things for a living, Avidan. One day I hope you'll actually listen to me."

"Only if he's totally lost his mind."

They both turned, Dan to grin at Annie and Kyla to glare at her offending sister. Annie responded to the reprimand by sticking her tongue out.

Kyla drew back. "How lovely, Annot. *There's* a picture to capture in stained glass."

Annie was the picture of wide-eyed innocence. "Ya think? Hmm, it just might work." She struck a pose, her tongue sticking out. "Take a picture of me?"

Dan stepped around the two women, shaking his head. "I'd like to say I'm going to miss these little exchanges between you two…"

Annie's goofy face evaporated. "Aw, that's so sweet."

He reached the front door of the now empty house. "I'd *like* to, but I can't." He winked at them. "'Cuz I won't."

Dan stepped inside, closing the door against Annie's protest and Kyla's indignation. He made one last round through the barren house. It felt so sad…a skeleton of a life that used to be. Pausing in each room, he let the memories drift over him. Good memories. Memories that he'd keep with him always. Memories that gave him the strength to do what he knew he needed to do.

Until, that is, he came to the bedroom he and Sarah had shared. There, the memories were overwhelming, bringing back his loss with renewed sting. He leaned against the wall, taking in the bare room.

Early this morning, the moving truck pulled into Dan's driveway. His sisters arrived mere minutes later, and the day raced by as he supervised the hauling and loading of his and Sarah's life together.

The kids had recovered from their stint in miracle land and were back to normal—aggravating each other at every opportunity. But they managed to keep their exchanges on a mostly friendly, bantering level, which Dan appreciated.

Now, standing in his bedroom, Dan felt the weariness bore into him. He rubbed at his throbbing temples. How could he say good-bye to this place?

To this life?

How could he—

"Daddy?"

He turned, schooling his features into some semblance of peace before he met his daughter's eyes. "Hey, kiddo. I thought you were outside with your aunts."

"I was. But Aunt Annie said she thought it was hard for you to leave. So I came to help." She looked around, wrinkles forming a question mark on her brow as her hand went to the pendant at her neck. "There's nothing here, Daddy."

He followed his daughter's gaze. "You're right. And you know why?" He knelt beside her. "'Cuz everything that matters is going with me."

"Can we go see our new home now?"

He touched his nose to hers, then stood and held out his hand. "You bet we can." With her hand nestled in his, he led her from the room, his steps sure and solid.

If only his heart felt that way as well.

SIX

"Sometimes when you think you are done,
it is just the edge of beginning."
NATALIE GOLDBERG

"The LORD longs to be gracious to you."
ISAIAH 30:18 (NIV)

"YOU FEEL THAT?"

Dan turned to his son. "Feel what?"

Aaron sat as far forward on the seat as his seat belt would allow. "I'm not sure. I just got a kind of…charge, I guess. Excitement. Like we're goin' on a real adventure."

"An adventure." Dan mulled that over. "Yes, I guess you could say that. Starting a new life is definitely an adventure."

"Look, Dad! That's where we turn, right?"

It was, indeed. Dan turned the moving truck off the Crater Lake Highway, just opposite the Sanctuary Ranger Station. His sisters and Shannon followed him in Dan's car. Just after turning off the highway, he came to a large, rustic sign at the side of the road.

The wooden sign hung from a frame of logs, and large letters were burned with artistic precision into the weatherworn marker. Aaron read out loud: "Welcome to Sanctuary, A Little Bit of Heaven on Earth."

Dan looked at his son. "Sounds pretty good."

Aaron glanced at the tall evergreens all around. "It's sure not like Central Point or Medford."

A pang of worry plucked at Dan's innards. He drove on. "Does that bother you?"

"Nah." Aaron grinned. "I was never that crazy about living in town anyway. Besides, I bet we get snow for Christmas up here!"

Relief brought a smile to Dan's face. "I think you can count on that." From what he'd heard, December usually brought as much as a foot of snow up here. All the years they'd lived in the Rogue Valley, Aaron and Shannon had prayed for snow at Christmas. Unfortunately, the white stuff rarely fell on the valley floor, so Christmas after Christmas they were disappointed. A few years there was actually a dusting on Christmas Eve, and both kids ran outside to scrape up what they could into snowballs. But a real snowfall? It just hadn't happened.

There should be snow aplenty in Sanctuary. In fact, though it was late March and warm enough to be comfortable outside, there was still some on the ground now. So that would be a real treat for the kids. Dan planned to let them play outside as much as they wanted.

Anything to distract them from the pain of setting up a new home without their mom.

Aaron spotted another sign just on the outskirts of town. His chin dropped. "Is that right, Dad?"

"Hmm? Is what right?"

Aaron read the sign: "Sanctuary, population 659½." Dan and Aaron stared at each other then broke into laughter.

"A *half*? Does that mean, like, half a person?"

Dan shook his head. "I suppose we'll find out, son. Should be interesting."

Within minutes, they reached downtown Sanctuary—such as it was. Rather than sidewalks, Sanctuary had old-fashioned wooden walkways. Dan wasn't sure if that was for atmosphere or because they'd just never replaced the original sidewalks.

All along the walkways, in front of the few select businesses keeping the downtown alive, were rows of rocking chairs, most of which were in use by locals of all ages.

Dan drove through town slow enough to study the buildings lining the street. Continuing his role as tour guide, Aaron read off the business names as they passed them. "The Sanctuary Trophy Room…"

Dan smiled. The Trophy Room, so called because of the multitude of hunting trophies mounted on the walls, was the town's one somewhat formal restaurant. He and the kids had eaten there once. Aaron thought it was cool; Shannon, on the other hand, couldn't eat a bite. When Dan asked her why, she looked up, her lip trembling.

"I can't eat in front of *them*!" She jerked her chin toward the animal heads looking down on them. "I mean, what if this hamburger is their…their *cousin* or something?"

Needless to say, it would take a little time to convince tenderhearted Shannon to go back there.

"The Sanctuary Beauty and Video Salon…"

Beauty and videos. A different kind of combination, but one that made infinite sense, or so Mabel Jones, the owner of the place, had told Dan on his first visit to town. "Who chooses the videos families watch? The mother. So she can kill two birds with one stone."

"The Sanctuary Fire Station, Post Office, First Evangelical Church of the Savior's Brethren, the Sanctuary Public Library…"

And on the list went. Dan looked forward to getting to know each establishment—and the owners—well. That was one of the great things about living in a small town. Everyone knew you—

"Um…Dad?"

He glanced at Aaron. "You run out of buildings, son?"

Aaron frowned. "Well, no. I mean, yes, pretty much. But that's not why I stopped." He pointed out the truck window. "Look."

Dan directed his attention out the window and had to fight back a laugh. Behold, one of the drawbacks of moving to a small town. While Dan and Aaron had been studying Sanctuary, the good people of the town had been studying them. Anyone seated in a rocking chair leaned forward to watch Dan's truck as it rolled by.

He nudged Aaron. "What say we stop and say hello?"

Aaron peered out the window. "You sure they're safe?"

"Safer than most, I'd guess." He parked the moving van alongside the walkway. A quick look in his side mirror showed him his sisters had followed his lead and parked behind him.

Dan grabbed the door handle, then nudged Aaron. "Ready to check out your new hometown?"

"Let's go!" Aaron hopped out of the van.

Annie was already on the sidewalk, waiting for them. "What's up, brother? I thought we were going to the house first."

He held his arm out for Shannon, who came to stand next to him. "Aaron and I just thought it would be nice to meet our new neighbors."

Annie looked over her shoulder at the rocking chair crowd, several of whom were still leaning forward to watch—and listen—better. "Why bother?" she whispered. "I'm betting they already know everything about you there is to know."

"Either that," Kyla said, joining them, "or they'll make it up."

"What'd that nice-looking young man say?"

Dan and the others turned at the loud, querulous question. Two white-haired women sat side by side in their rockers. A tiny dog decked out in a sparkly collar perched on one woman's lap.

The taller of the two women swatted at the other's arm.

"Lower your voice, Agatha. You want those folks to think we're gossips?"

"Parsnips?" Agatha peered over her glasses at Dan. "What's he got to do with parsnips?"

"For heaven's sake, Aggie!" The taller woman rocked her chair at a furious pace. "Turn up your hearing aid."

Agatha sat back in her rocker, setting it in equally rapid motion, the dog in her lap scrambling to stay balanced. "Fiddle-faddle, Doris. Don't need it. I hear just fine."

"Ha! You can't hear worth spit."

Agatha peered at her friend. "What's that?"

Doris's expression was that of utter innocence. "I *said*, looks like rain's going to hit."

"Rain?" Agatha stared up at the bright sun. "There's not a cloud in the sky, you nit!"

Dan and the kids drew closer, and Aaron nudged him. "Is that a rat on her lap, Dad?"

He coughed to cover a laugh. "No, it's a dog."

Disbelief painted his son's features. "No way."

"It's a Chihuahua." This from Shannon, ever the animal expert. "I think he's adorable!"

Dan slipped an arm around his children's shoulders and inclined his head to the two women. "Morning, ladies. I'm Dan Justice."

"Doris Kleffer." The woman nodded to Dan, a dimple peeking out from the soft wrinkles on her cheek. "And the deaf one here is Agatha Hunter."

"Well!" Agatha let a breath out on a huff. "If you're not going to introduce me, I'll do it myself." She cut the other woman's indignant response off by sticking her hand out to Dan. "Agatha Hunter. This is my friend, Doris. And this hand-some fellow—" she lifted the Chihuahua, whose spindly little legs went rigid—"is Half Pint."

"He's so cute!"

Before Dan could stop her, Shannon stepped forward to

scratch the dangling dog's big ears. Dan's fear that the dog might snap at her faded when a tiny pink tongue shot out, licking Shannon's hands as though they were his salvation.

"He likes you, dear." Agatha's wrinkles folded into a beaming smile. "He can always tell who the nicest people are."

"Miss Hunter, Miss Kleffer, these are my children, Shannon and Aaron."

Agatha frowned. "What's that about a harem?"

"Oh, for the love of *Pete*, Aggie!" Doris leaned over and poked her finger in the other woman's ear, giving a quick turn. A shrill whine sounded, and Agatha tucked Half Pint close and batted her friend's hand away.

"That's *too* high!"

Shannon giggled, and Aaron stepped up beside her, stroking Half Pint's tiny snout with a finger. "Is he a puppy?"

"Oh, no, dear." Agatha was all smiles again. "He's full grown."

"So this is as big as he'll get?" Aaron's amazement amused the two ladies. "Wow. He's gotta be the smallest dog I've ever seen."

"That's why we just count him as a half."

Shannon and Aaron exchanged a look then grinned at Dan. "The population sign, Dad. Half Pint is the *and one half*!"

Dan was about to tell the kids that not even Sanctuary was so small it would list a dog on its official population when Agatha spoke up, pride ringing in her words. "Indeed, he is. Like his father before him, and his mother before that."

Okay. So he was wrong.

Agatha leaned toward Shannon. "You are just the prettiest little thing. Like a little angel come right down from heaven."

Dan nudged Aaron when he groaned. Fortunately, Agatha didn't seem to hear his brotherly disgust.

"What's your name?"

"Shannon Michelle Justice, ma'am."

"Justice?" Agatha looked up at Dan. "Now isn't that fine? You're the new sheriff come to live in town!"

Before Dan could respond, Doris chimed in, holding her hands out to Kyla and Annie. "And these must be your dear sisters." She took Annie's hand, patting it and making a *tsk*ing sound as she looked at Dan. "So sorry to hear about your wife, Sheriff Justice."

Dan didn't know what alarmed him most: being called a sheriff or the fact that his life was so well known by people he'd never met. "I'm not a sherri—"

"Oh, won't it be wonderful, Agatha, to have our very own sheriff living right in Sanctuary?"

Dan tried to reply, but he didn't get the chance. Agatha popped up out of her rocker—Dan would never have imagined those old bones could be so spry—and hobbled over to call down the sidewalk toward the other rocking chairs.

"Come on over, folks! Come meet our new sheriff!"

"Uh, no...hang on. I'm just a deput—"

No one was listening. Suddenly Dan and his family found themselves surrounded by people smiling and talking and patting them on the backs, welcoming them to "our little piece of heaven on earth."

As Dan smiled and did his best to connect names with faces, a shiver crawled across his shoulders. He had the distinct feeling he was being watched. Glancing up over the heads of those around him, he scanned the sidewalk.

And locked gazes with a pair of eyes so cold they were arctic. The kid staring at him was a hulk. Had to be almost as tall as Dan, but he guessed the kid outweighed him by a good fifty pounds. Not that he was fat. He was just big. Defensive-lineman big. No-neck big.

But the kid's size didn't make Dan take note of him. It was the look in those dark eyes. Though Dan couldn't tell the color from here, he had no trouble recognizing the expression carved into the kid's features. He'd seen it way too often in his work with troubled kids. Especially with the boys.

Anger. Arrogance. And just a touch of fear. A bad combination. One that had a nasty tendency to turn troubled kids downright dangerous.

"Come on, Sheriff." Dan looked down at Doris, whose thin hand was resting on his arm. "LouBelle has invited us all to her diner for coffee and fresh baked cake."

He put his hand over hers. "Sounds great. But Doris—" he glanced back to the kid down the sidewalk. He still stood there, leaning against the building like he owned it. "Tell me, who is that boy?"

Doris peered past him then pulled back, lips thinning. "Oh, he's a bad one, Sheriff. Marlin Murphy." Her tongue clucked. "Sixteen and nothing but trouble. That young man is going to come to no good, just like his father."

Before Dan could ask any more, Agatha and several others tugged at him. "Let's go, Sheriff Justice. Cake doesn't stay fresh all day!"

Dan followed Agatha, his family in tow. Several hours later, their arms laden with gifts of pies and cookies and homemade bread, Dan and the others finally made their way back to their vehicles.

"Wow." Aaron shook his head as he climbed into the moving truck. "Those people can *talk*!"

"They can, indeed." Kyla held the car door open for Dan as he unloaded his goods to the backseat. "Something tells me, dear brother, you've not only said farewell to the city, but to the luxury of privacy."

"It'll be fine. I'd rather have folks be friendly and supportive than remote and uninterested." He got into the truck, rolled the window down, then pulled the door shut.

"Well, then, you should be ecstatic," Kyla retorted. "Because they *certainly* are interested."

"Interested…and interest*ing*." Annie's gaze was fixed across the street. When she turned back to Dan, warning bells went off at the gleam in his sister's eyes.

"Okay, infant, what are you up to?"

Her wide-eyed innocence would have done Doris proud. "Me? Not a thing." She leaned against the truck door. "So, to the house?"

Dan frowned. What had Annie been looking at? Nothing was across the street but the tiny house that served as Sanctuary's public library. The tidy structure was adorned on the outside with an abundance of rose bushes, all laden with large, colorful blooms.

A woman stood there, her face hidden behind a wide-brimmed hat. Garden clippers in one hand, a basketful of daffodils in the other, she was the picture of a contented gardener. As a breeze tickled Dan's face, he could just hear the soft sound of the woman's singing.

She had a lovely voice.

The sound of a car starting pulled his awareness back to matters at hand. He glanced toward the car and caught Annie's expression. She looked as though she'd just discovered something...intriguing. He looked from her to the woman at the library.

Oh no.

He knew Annie meant well. She was a romantic through and through. And she always saw possibilities, which made her a gifted artist and, at times, and gigantic pain in the neck as a sister. Though she recognized it was far too early to talk about it, Dan knew, in her heart of hearts, she wanted him to fall in love again, to have someone to share his life with, to help raise the kids. But just because he noticed a shapely woman with an angelic voice who was close to his age didn't mean he was ready, could *ever* be ready, to let another woman into his life.

Grabbing the gearshift, he jammed the truck into gear.

Yes, he and the kids needed a change. And they'd gotten one. A big one. Huge. But Dan loved Sarah—past, present, and future. She was the one and only great love of his life. And though she was gone, his love for her wasn't.

And that was something that wasn't going to change.

Not ever.

Marlin Murphy slumped down in the rocking chair, planted his feet on the railing, and watched the moving truck drive away. "So—" he spoke around the toothpick clamped between his teeth—"law and order's come to Sanctuary?"

Snorts met his proclamation. "Law and order! Yeah, right."

"I'll show that cop law and order. Jerk thinks he can just take over *our* town."

Marlin leveled a glare at the two idiots leaning against the railing. Dicky and Jay Larsen, the brainless brothers. Good thing they got second helpings on brawn, 'cuz they were sure hiding behind the door when brains were handed out. "Why don't you two just shut up?"

Their mouths clamped shut, and Marlin rolled his eyes. Fools. He was surrounded by fools.

Well…not *all* fools. There was always Jayce. Kid was as smart as they came. A little hard to control at times, but that's where the two muscle morons came in.

"Marlin?"

He frowned at Dicky, not even bothering to hide his impatience. "I thought I told you to shut up?"

"Yeah, I know. But are you…? I mean…"

Marlin jerked his feet off the railing and slammed them onto the boardwalk. "*What?*"

Dicky bobbed his head. "Well, that cop. You gonna just let him come to town like that?"

Marlin shot a look at Dicky that shut him up quick.

Slow as ever, Jay piped up. "Yeah."

Oh, joy. Another pea brain country heard from. "Don't be stupid." He snorted. "Oh, sorry. Forgot who I was talking to."

The brothers frowned, and Marlin could tell they were trying to figure out if they'd just been insulted. He stood, rolling his shoulders. "Don't worry about the cop."

Jay's grin was half sneer. "You gonna take care of him, aren't you?"

Marlin pushed Dicky out of the way, striding down the street. The two brothers fell in step beside him, as he'd known they would.

"You gonna do it, huh, Marlin? Take care of the cop?"

A small smile touched his lips. "That's my job, boys. Taking care of things."

"And you're good at it, too."

"Yeah," Jay chimed in. "Really good."

Marlin's smile grew. They had no idea. But they would. Soon enough, everyone—especially the good deputy—would know just how good he was.

SEVEN

"She smiled, and the shadows departed;
She shone, and the snows were rain;
And he who was frozen-hearted bloomed up into love again."
JOHN ADDINGTON SYMONDS

"You have allowed me to suffer much hardship,
but you will restore me to life again and lift
me up from the depths of the earth."
PSALM 71:20

"I CAN'T BELIEVE THEY BLEW UP AN OUTHOUSE."

Jasmine took a serious chomp on her gum, studying the two young boys sitting in Dan's office. "Hey, it's the thing to do for kids out here."

Dan grimaced. "But...an outhouse?" He'd heard that was the most common offense among teens and preteens in Sanctuary, and supposed he should be grateful his first experience with the favored pastime of tiny minds had waited two months to hit him.

"Yeah, well, with so many of the fathers from the area gone, kids find all kindsa ways of getting into trouble."

His receptionist-slash-dispatcher sure seemed to know the area. But it would be a lot easier to take her seriously if she looked a bit less...what was the term Aaron liked to use?

Oh yes. *Bizarro.*

First time Dan met Jasmine, he couldn't believe she was the town council's choice for working with him in the office. The fact that she was barely in her twenties was concern enough. Could a girl that young take this kind of job seriously? Especially when her résumé showed her only experience was several years of babysitting for neighbors and being a part-time cashier at the local market-cum-gas station?

Then there was the way she looked. Jasmine Carlson was…an individual. When he first met her, her hair was short, spiked—and green. And she dressed in black. All black. And in the four months he'd been in Sanctuary, the girl's hair had changed at least a dozen times. Sometimes every week. He never knew what color it would be. So far she'd shown up with blue, purple, bright pink, and the same color red as the old Chevy truck his grandfather used to drive.

Lately, though, she'd taken to wearing it straight and pure black, with purple right around her face. A little too Morticia Addams for his taste, but hey. It beat green.

Then there was that tongue stud. It only took a week of hearing her clack that thing against her teeth for Dan to ask her to leave it out while she was working.

Fortunately, she complied.

Unfortunately, she replaced it with an eyebrow ring.

Ah, well, at least that one didn't make noise.

During those first few days, Dan considered replacing her, but something told him to wait. And watch. And what he saw amazed him.

Jasmine stayed cool under pressure like few people Dan had ever met. Most days the phone didn't ring all that often. Then there were the crazy-making days. Days when the phone never shut up and people came through the door in a steady stream. The first day like that, Dan nearly climbed the walls.

Jasmine, on the other hand, took it all in stride. She managed the phone like a pro and the people coming in like a drill sergeant.

And then there was her work ethic. The girl was as responsible as they came—and she knew how to keep things to
herself. Not once had Dan ever heard of her talking about
things she shouldn't.

Getting accustomed to Jasmine's peculiarities may have
taken a while, but accepting her as a true blessing came fast
and easy.

He stood at the front of her desk, eyeing the two young
boys sitting in his office. "So, blasting outhouses to the sky is
some kind of Sanctuary rite of passage?"

"Could be worse."

It could indeed. Dan had seen that firsthand with the kids
he worked with in Medford, where gang rites of passage ranged
from petty theft to drug dealing to murder. Yeah. He'd take
exploding outhouses any day.

"Well, guess I'd better go read 'em the riot act."

"Go get 'em, Chief."

"*Jasmine…*"

She held up her hands. "Right, right. I'm sorry. You're not a
chief."

"I'm a deputy. Or you could just call me Dan."

She waved him toward his office. "So go, Deputy. Scare the
little monsters onto the straight and narrow." Her lips lifted a
fraction. "If anyone can do it, you can."

He pushed away from her desk. "Gee, thanks. I think."

Straightening to his full height, he stomped toward the
office. The boys threw near-panicked looks over their shoulders
when they heard him coming, and Dan fought not to laugh.

Hardened criminals, these two.

He went into his office, slamming the door behind him and
going to sit at his desk. Pinning the now-trembling boys with a
glare, he launched into his speech about respecting others'
property and the dangers of explosives. He was just gaining
steam, and the boys were turning yet another shade of petrified, when a firm knock sounded at his door.

He looked up, ready to scold Jasmine for interrupting him, and found himself face-to-face with a pretty, fresh-faced young woman. At first glance, with her shoulder-length dark brown hair tucked behind her ears, wide blue eyes, and casual turtle-neck sweater and jeans, she didn't look that much older than the boys slumped in chairs in front of Dan's desk. High school, maybe.

He looked closer.

No, more like a freshman in college.

Strange…he had the feeling he knew her. But he'd remember if he met this girl before. He leaned forward to frown past the intruder, looking for Jasmine. She was sitting there, jaw working on her gum, filing her nails. His frown deepened, and he aimed it at the girl leaning against his doorway. "Excuse me. I'm busy—"

"Yes, I can see that."

Her mature, confident tone was his first surprise. The second was when she walked into his office and put one hand on each boy's shoulder.

Dan firmed up his expression. "I'm sorry, Miss…"

"Wilson," she supplied, confidence still firmly in place. "Shelby Wilson. I head up Master's Touch."

Dan leaned back in his chair. Master's Touch? "I've heard of your group. But how did you come to know about these two?" He indicated the boys.

"Sanctuary is a small town, Deputy." She surveyed the room then went out to the outer office and grabbed a chair, glancing up at Jasmine. "Do you mind?"

Jasmine waved her fingernail file in the air. "Help yourself."

Dan pushed back from the desk and went to take the chair from the woman, then carried it back into his office. She thanked him and took a seat.

"So are you saying Master's Touch is based around here?"

She waited until he was seated to answer. "Not just around here, but here. Right in little ol' Sanctuary."

"You're kidding."

He wasn't sure if she was amused or offended by his astonishment. "Not a bit. I founded the organization, and Sanctuary is my home, so there you have it."

Amazing. A group as effective as Master's Touch, with a network of professionals who worked with problem kids from all over southern Oregon, based in Sanctuary.

"I worked with one of your branch outreach programs when I lived in Central Point."

Her smile was knowing. "I can imagine who they paired you with."

"The worst offenders."

"Makes sense."

He lifted a brow. "It does?"

"That's who I'd pair you with. Kids hell-bent on destroying themselves and anything—or any*one*—who got in their way."

"Yeah, I guess I do look like I'd fit with those kids."

"What you look like is someone who can handle those kinds of kids."

He'd done pretty well. He hadn't been able to get through to all the boys, of course, but he did reach some. Sarah said it was because he opened himself up to them, let them see who he really was.

"Are you still involved in the program?"

Dan hesitated, picking up a pen and scribbling on the paper in front of him. "No. No, I'm not."

Maybe Sarah's assessment was right. Either way, after she died, he couldn't do it anymore. Not for a while, anyway. He didn't have the energy or ability to let anyone inside. "I needed a break, so I pulled out."

"Well, Deputy, let me know if you're ever ready to get back in." Her look was direct, open. "I'd love to have you join us here."

"You have a lot of tough kids, do you?" He smiled, but Shelby didn't return it.

"You'd be surprised."

Not so much. Dan had been a cop too long to doubt kids got into trouble no matter where they were. Fortunately, Master's Touch had an admirable track record for turning serious troublemakers into model students. If he remembered right, Shelby had taught a workshop in the Central Point branch.

That was probably where he'd seen her before.

Get off it, Justice. Doesn't matter if you've seen her before or not.

Right. Forget trying to figure that out. Focus on matters at hand. Or, more accurate, on the woman at hand.

But that was easier said than done. Shelby leaned back in her chair, a smile spreading across her features.

That was the biggest surprise of all. That smile.

As it lifted her lips, warmth filled her features, transforming them from young and sweet to captivating. Her dancing sapphire eyes held a luminous light, and in their depths Dan saw the kind of understanding he usually only saw in other cops. There was a difference, though. In his brethren, the understanding was ragged, a worn-down edge at the backs of their eyes when they met your gaze head-on. But in Shelby…

It glowed.

The effect was like a candle flame flickering to life in a window on a dark, stormy night. A beacon of comfort and safety, an assurance of acceptance and truth.

Deep inside him, something stirred. Recognition sparked. Dan's mouth fell open a fraction. "You work at the library, too?"

She was taken aback for a moment, then laughed. "I take care of the flowers outside the library, if that's what you mean. I'm their volunteer gardener."

"I saw you."

At her raised brows, he backpedaled. "On my first day in town. We were talking with a group of folks, and you were working on the daffodils. And singing."

"Excuse me?"

He leaned back in his chair. "You were singing." He smiled. "Nice voice."

Her responding smile was just slightly tongue-in-cheek. "Thanks."

She turned to the two boys, who'd sat in frozen silence since she came in. Dan couldn't blame them. They were probably trying to figure out if she was their savior or executioner. She had a real air about her, one that had Dan discarding his initial impression.

Shelby Wilson knew what she was up against and wasn't in the least discouraged. As unbelievable as it might seem, she was like Dan. A warrior.

And he'd just been taken captive.

Sitting there, caught between surprise and a bolt of something he hadn't felt since Sarah—pure, visceral awareness—Dan found himself speechless.

Oh, he had plenty to say. He just couldn't seem to find the oxygen or voice with which to say it.

She turned back to him. "I've been looking forward to meeting you, Deputy. I meant to introduce myself sooner, but the last few months have been crazy." Her words gave him a moment to regroup, to suck in air and get his heart started again. "Thanks to characters like these two." She shot a sideways glance at the boys, but not before he saw the twinkle of mischief in her eyes.

"No problem." His own gaze nailed the two troublemakers to their chairs. "I figure we'll just lock 'em up, throw away the key."

The din of alarmed protest the boys raised almost made Dan laugh. Almost. But he managed to keep a straight face as Shelby silenced the two miscreants with a raised hand.

"Bobby, Justin, I should just let the deputy put you in a cell." Their mouths dropped, and Dan could just imagine her satisfaction as she crossed her arms, leaning against his desk. "It's not like this is your first time in trouble, now is it, Justin?"

"No, Miss Wilson."

The younger boy's subdued tone was music to Dan's ears.

"May I assume, Bobby, if I can talk the good deputy into letting you go, that it will be your *last* time?"

The other boy looked up. "It's not *my* fault—"

Her hand shot up again, backing the boy's words into his throat. "We're not talking fault here—" her tone hardened a fraction—"although you are older than your brother. And if I remember correctly, your daddy entrusted you with keeping him out of trouble?"

Bobby stared down at his shoes. This time when he spoke he was equally subdued. "Yes, Miss Wilson."

"Doesn't seem as if you've done a very good job, now does it?"

"No, Miss Wilson."

"I'd like to think I can count on you to do better from now on."

At the softening in her tone, Bobby looked up.

"Because I think Justin is scared. About your mom being sick. And since your dad is so busy taking care of her, he needs you to help him do what's right. To make your folks proud of you both. That's what you want, isn't it?"

Dan watched the play of emotion on the boy's features, wishing he could see Shelby's face. But whatever her expression, it must have hit home. Because young Bobby straightened in his chair, and an air of determination settled over him. "Yes, Miss Wilson. That's what I want."

She took the boy's hand and squeezed it. "I know it is." She peeked over her shoulder at Dan. "Well, Deputy, what do you think?"

He let the boys stew while he seemed to roll the idea around in his head. "Still have to call their parents."

She ignored the boy's groans. "Of course."

"And give them community service, probably about a hundred hours."

"A hundred hours!"

At the older boy's outburst, Shelby turned with a quick frown. "You think that's too much, do you?"

Bobby squirmed in his chair. "Well, gosh…I mean…"

She didn't say anything, just waited. The boy swallowed with difficulty, stubbing his toe into the floor. "Um…no."

"Well then?"

He stared at the floor then dragged his gaze back to Shelby. "Okay."

"Good." Shelby turned back to Dan. "Would you like to call their parents, or shall I?"

He pushed the phone toward her. "You're the boss."

Her smile was just this side of wicked. "And don't you forget it."

EIGHT

*"No straight lines make up my life,
and all my roads have bends."*
HARRY CHAPIN

*"Teach us to make the most of our time,
so that we may grow in wisdom."*
PSALM 90:12

ONE YEAR LATER

"I WANT A UNICORN."

Dan looked up from stirring a bowl of pancake batter. His youngest child stood in the kitchen doorway, the early morning sun lighting her face as she rubbed a small fist into her sleep-filled eyes.

Finally. He'd been calling for her and her brother to get up for almost an hour. Amazing how a child's ability to hear seemed to drop in direct correlation to his or her desire to do what was being requested.

Either that, or sleep made kids deaf. Dan hadn't decided which was accurate.

He'd finally given in to the ultimate weapon: start breakfast and let the smells do what his authority alone couldn't—get them out of bed.

"A what?"

Shannon padded over to lean her elbows on the kitchen island, bending forward just enough to lift her feet off the floor. Dan watched her, marveling. How could one year bring such change?

Last summer, Shannon had been all little girl, playing with dolls and talking to her stuffed animals in the full belief they heard and understood her. And heaven knew there had to be at least a dozen stuffed animals on her bed before she could go to sleep at night. Then just two weeks ago, on the first day of August, Shannon turned twelve.

Suddenly, something changed. It was as though some inner cognition roused from slumber and roared to life, triggering a startling metamorphosis. The stuffed animals and dolls made way for funky pillows on her bed. Her walls were plastered with posters of teenaged actors and singers. And she spent countless hours on the phone with other men's little girls, talking about hair, clothes, and—heaven help him—boys.

Just last week she asked if she could start wearing makeup.

Dan studied Shannon as she stood there, contemplating the delight of her favorite breakfast: shape pancakes. With her drowsy eyes blinking, hair tangled from sleep and tumbling down into her face, cheeks pink and glowing, she looked every inch his baby girl. And yet…

There, just at the edges of her little girlness, Dan could see it. A young woman, ready to burst free. And every time he caught a glimpse of that young woman, he suffered the same soul-deep pang. These last two years without Sarah had been hard, but it was times like this, looking at their beautiful daughter, who every day was becoming more and more a miniature of her mother, that Dan missed his wife the most.

How was he going to handle his little girl becoming a woman without Sarah?

Shannon yawned. "I want a unicorn. You know, a horse with a horn and wings?"

"Unicorns don't have wings, dummy."

Ah, the perfectly honed sarcasm brothers reserved for sisters.

Shannon spun and glared at her big brother, but Dan jumped in, preempting his daughter's answering volley. "Don't call your sister a dummy."

Aaron grabbed a piece of bacon off the plate, munching it as he glanced up at his father. When the kid turned fourteen last year, he took on the mantle of *teenager* with a vengeance. Still, for all his teenager ways, Aaron knew how to turn on the innocence and sincerity. "But Dad, what if she *is* one?"

"Aaron."

"You're always telling us to say the truth. So if she *is* a dummy, then—"

"I am *not* a dummy!" Shannon's foot stomped the floor, accentuating her denial.

So much for stopping the battle before it began. Fortunately, Dan held the big guns. As his offspring squared off, lobbing verbal volleys, Dan turned without a word and unplugged the griddle. Then, his motions slow and methodical, he picked up the bowl of batter he'd been stirring and set it in one side of the double sink. Then he picked up the batter-dipped fork and held it suspended above the dishwater in the second sink.

The bickering voices faltered, then fell silent.

"Hey…"

Brows arched, Dan glanced over his shoulder at his son. "Yes?"

Aaron bit his lip. "Um, what are you doing, Dad?"

"Yeah—" Shannon leaned over her brother's shoulder— "why'd you unplug the griddle?"

Dan let his eyes go wide. Aaron wasn't the only one who could muster innocence when it suited. "The griddle?"

"And what's the bowl of batter doing in the sink?" Aaron's

forehead creased. "I thought we were getting pancakes for breakfast?"

Shannon crossed her arms, accusation shooting from her brown eyes. Eyes so like her mother's that Dan still found his breath catching when his little girl looked at him. "Yeah. Shape pancakes. You promised!"

Dan's gaze drifted from his children to the dripping fork. "Oh…you mean you still want pancakes? You guys didn't exactly jump out of bed when I called you this morning, so I figured you weren't all that excited about it."

They opened their mouths to reply, but he cut them off with a pointed look. "Besides, you seemed way too busy chewing on each other for pancakes."

Those opened mouths snapped shut. Shannon and Aaron looked at each other, then at the floor.

"Aw, Dad—"

Shannon gave her brother a silencing shot with her elbow. Before he could protest, she slid her arm around his waist. "We're sorry, Daddy."

Dan's lips twitched, but he didn't give in. Not yet.

Aaron tried to pull away from his sister, but she tightened her grip on his waist and popped him with her hip.

"Hey!"

"*Aren't* we sorry, Aaron?"

He frowned, took in her exasperated glare, then looked from his father to Shannon. Understanding dawned on his features like sunrise over the mountains.

"Ohhhh…" Aaron nodded, slipping his arm around his sister's shoulders. "Oh, yeah, Dad, we're sorry." Another nod. "Really."

"And truly."

Shannon's added emphasis almost undid him. Dan cleared his throat, stopping the snort of laughter from escaping, and lowered the fork. "So, the war's over then?"

A pair of nods. A shared hug. Shannon rested her cheek on her brother's arm. "All done."

"Well, then—" Dan lifted the bowl from the sink—"what are you waiting for? Someone plug in the griddle. Time's a-wastin', and I have to get to work."

Shannon complied, then climbed up on a stool, resting her elbows on the kitchen island. "I don't like it when you work on the weekends."

Dan held back the sigh. "Honey, we've talked about this. I have to work my shift, and sometimes that means I work on Saturdays. Trouble—"

"—doesn't take the weekends off, so people need you." She plopped her chin in her hands. "Yeah, I know. But we need you, too."

He stopped, a deep ache tearing at him. Such simple words, but oh, what a punch they packed.

Sarah, this is so hard without you... "I know, baby. And I need you guys, too. A lot."

She nodded. "But you gotta work."

"I gotta work."

Shannon peered at the griddle. "I still want a unicorn."

Did all kids change moods in the blink of an eye? "Yeah, I seem to remember you saying that."

"Can you make one, Daddy?"

Aaron leaned on the counter beside his sister. "'Course he can. He can make anything you want." Aaron's nod was pure confidence. "He even made me an armadillo once, when I was little."

"Really? Cool!"

"That I did. Even gave it a real Texas cowboy hat." Of course, it had looked more like a squashed turtle than an armadillo. But hey, it made Aaron happy. Dan dipped up some batter and drizzled it onto the griddle, forming the unicorn's horn with care.

And even if this unicorn came out looking like some kind

of mutant horse from Mars, Shannon wouldn't mind. She'd love it because he made it special, just for her.

He finished the unicorn's body and legs then used a large tablespoon to swoop a tail. Shannon watched, enrapt.

"See?" Aaron poked his sister with an elbow. "What'd I tell you? It looks real!"

Dan studied the unicorn, then smiled. Aaron was right. He'd done an especially good job on this one. It didn't look the least bit like a turtle.

Shannon clapped her hands then hopped down from the stool to hug Dan tight. "Thank you, Daddy."

He returned his daughter's hug, then lifted the perfectly cooked unicorn pancake onto a plate and handed it to Shannon. She stared down at it then back up at Dan. Dismay tugged at him when he saw her lip trembling.

"What is it, honey?"

Big tears slid from her eyes. "I can't eat him!"

"Oh, brother."

Dan shot Aaron a warning glance, then turned the heat down on the griddle and crouched to talk with Shannon. If he'd learned anything in the past few months, it was that Shannon's emotions were all over the map. And some days twelve was a whole lot younger than others. "It's just a pancake."

"No, it's not! You made him so real, Dad. *Look* at him!"

She stuck the plate under his nose, and he obliged her by looking, then eased the plate from her hands. "Tell you what. How about if I take care of him—"

"*Eat* him, you mean."

Dan could have swatted Aaron, especially when alarm widened Shannon's eyes. "Daddy!"

"No, honey. I won't eat him. I'll...I'll..." What on earth would he do with a pancake that wouldn't dismay his daughter? "Tell you what. I'll drive to a nice field somewhere and leave him there—"

"A field with lots of flowers," she said on a sniff. "Unicorns like flowers."

"Right." He stood, set the plate on the counter, and turned the griddle back up. "A field with flowers." He smoothed Shannon's sleep-tumbled hair. "He can live there."

Shannon's chocolate eyes fixed on him. "Don't be silly, Daddy. He's a pancake. He won't *live* there. But it's nice to think he'll be food for deer and squirrels and other animals."

"Right." Could you get whiplash from another person's mood swings? "So, think you could eat a pancake that looks like a flower?"

Her smile was pure sunshine. "A daisy?"

"You got it."

She leaned against his side as he poured the batter into the griddle. Dan glanced down at her and smiled.

For all the posters and boy-talk, there was still plenty of tenderhearted little girl in Shannon. Maybe, just maybe, he had more time than he'd thought to prepare for the changes coming.

Thank heaven.

The cheery sound of chimes from the clock in the living room pierced him. He looked down at his watch to verify the time.

Okay, he wasn't late.

He was *really* late.

Turning back to the griddle, he fought off the sense of defeat. It was so much easier when Sarah was alive. She'd made all the difference, not just in making things go more smoothly, but in helping him deal with the stress of being all things to all people: deputy, employer, father...and now mother.

Can it, Justice. It's not like you're the only single parent in the world.

Duly self-chastised, he flipped the daisy pancake one last time, slid it onto a plate, and delivered it to his daughter's waiting hands. Then he turned to Aaron.

"Okay, son, what's your pleasure?"

Aaron's grin was utter mischief. "An armadillo."

Dan groaned. "You can't be serious."

His son nodded. "With a real Texas cowboy hat."

"Sure you wouldn't rather have a turtle?" Aaron's expression answered him far better than any words could have. Dan sighed, lifted the bowl of batter, and dipped a spoonful. "Okay. One armadillo, Texas-style, coming up."

Almost there.

And there was even a parking place left for Dan in front of his office. Imagine that.

The blare of a horn jerked Dan from his thoughts, and he whipped the car to the left, barely avoiding a white Blazer as it screamed past him.

The guy had to be doing seventy in a thirty-five zone.

Dan flicked on the siren and shoved the accelerator to the floor, praying no one got in the Blazer's way. Or his, for that matter.

The Blazer raced through town, screeched around the curve in the road, and didn't even pause at the intersection with Highway 62. It just fishtailed its way around the corner, then hauled north. He didn't have much time to catch the vehicle before it hit Union Creek—and the curvy roads beyond.

One hand firmly on the steering wheel, Dan grabbed the radio, telling the dispatcher to radio for any other deputies or state troopers in the area. "We're just south of Union Creek."

"I'll put out the call," Jasmine said. "Just be careful."

Gunning his engine, Dan watched the speedometer climb. Eighty. Eighty-five. Ninety.

Lord, keep the road clear!

Finally he gained on the Blazer until he was close enough to see two people were in it. Kids, from the size of them. He was just about to try passing the speeding Blazer when he caught the glimmer of flashing lights up ahead.

Two state trooper cars sat on the highway, forming a road-block.

"Let's hear it for the good guys! Thank you, Jasmine!"

He slowed, watching the Blazer, alert to any signs that the vehicle was going to stop. Suddenly, as though the driver just woke up and realized what was happening, the Blazer's tires froze up, laying rubber and sending smoke curling into the air. It screeched to a halt, just feet from the patrol cars. Dan hit the brakes, spinning his steering wheel so that his cruiser ended up sideways, blocking the highway to the south.

Jumping out of the car, his gun drawn, Dan advanced on the Blazer, watching the state troopers do the same from the other side. No one stepped out of the vehicle. They didn't even roll the windows down.

When Dan was beside the driver's window, he looked inside. A young kid—no more than seventeen or eighteen—sat there, staring at the steering wheel, picking at the leather wrap around the wheel. He was muttering to himself, talking about as fast as he'd been driving.

The passenger, who looked to be a little younger, sagged back against the seat. Asleep. Either that, or unconscious.

Dan looked at the trooper standing near the hood. The man shook his head. "Meth. I'd bet my pension on it."

Dan tapped the window. "Open up, son."

The boy jerked away from the window but turned his head, and though the kid was blinking over and over, Dan could see his pupils were dilated. Not a good sign.

"Open the door. Now."

The kid kept muttering but fiddled with the window button, as though that would open the door. He leaned against the door, jabbing his fingers at the button.

Dan grabbed the door handle and opened the door.

"Hey!" The kid's yelp warned Dan, and he got his hands down just in time to catch the kid before he took a header onto the asphalt. Dan pulled the still-chattering boy from the vehicle, steadying him as he tried to stand.

"I told him you couldn't catch us. Told him we were too fast. Too fast for you. For everyone." The kid jabbered on, looking from Dan to the troopers. "You guys after a criminal? A bank robber or something?"

Dan fought the urge to shake the boy. "No, no bank robber. Just an idiot."

"This one's unconscious." A trooper stood with his fingers pressed to the passenger's throat, seeking a pulse. Better call an ambulance."

Dan turned the driver around, pulling his hands behind his back and slipping the cuffs in place. Then he turned the kid back to face him. "What did you take, son? Same thing as your buddy?"

The boy didn't answer. Just kept looking all around them, ducking his head as though trying to hide.

"Forget it, Deputy."

Dan looked over his shoulder at the trooper.

"He's gone. It's gonna be a while until he can even hear you, let alone answer you." He fastened his gun back in his holster. "You'd think kids in an area like this would have better things to do than meth, wouldn't you?"

"Nah." This from a second trooper. "It's everywhere. City, rural, doesn't make a difference. You can't get away from it."

Maybe not, Dan thought as he led the boy to his cruiser, but he was going to do what he could to keep it out of Sanctuary.

He only hoped it wasn't already too late.

The sun was just about overhead by the time Dan made it into the office.

"Mornin', Chief. Or afternoon, I guess."

He glanced over his shoulder as he hung his hat on the wall peg and fell into his almost daily mantra. "Jasmine, I'm not a chief."

She leaned her elbows on her desk, snapped her gum, and nodded. "Oh yeah. Right. I forgot."

Dan sighed.. That should be Jasmine's middle name: *I forgot*.

She eyed him, brow crinkling. "So how come you carry that hat with you when you never wear it?"

"It's part of the uniform."

"But you never wear it."

"But I always have it with me."

"But—"

"Jasmine!"

Her ceaseless gum chomping actually ceased as she clamped her mouth shut for a moment, then shrugged. "Whatever."

Dan sighed and went into his office. He was glad Jasmine was here. He never could have handled this job alone. Besides, the two of them made a good team, for the most part. She'd actually become his right-hand man. Er…woman.

Whatever.

He was even getting to the point of accepting her constant gum chewing and snapping. And that her memory was worse than his mother's used to be.

"Anyways, Chief—"

Make that his grandmother's. But that was a small obstacle to overcome to have an employee who was responsible, eager to learn, and as reliable as a prize coon dog.

He stood in the doorway of his office. "Not *chief*, Jasmine. Not *sheriff*, or *boss*, or *grand high poobah of law and order*. Just *deputy*. Or *Dan*. But not *chief*, okay?"

Pop! Snap! "Sure. Anyways, I'm glad you're here."

"Oh? Why is that?"

She twisted a strand of purple hair around her finger. "We just got two calls in a row."

Dan's brow lifted. "Two, huh?" Figured. The one day he

was late, trouble put in extra time.

"The first was another break-in." She handed him a slip of paper with the details. "One of those nice homes just up offa Highway 62. The lady who called in said they got a bunch of stuff: laptop computers, CD players, TVs—"

"All things you can grab in a hurry. And sell almost as fast."

"Right." This affirmation was accompanied by a loud pop of her gum.

Dan eyed her. How did she do that? Talk and pop at the same time?

"Second call came right after. It was a crazy kind of call from ol' man Brumby. Sheesh. That guy's a total grump. Did you know Ruby said her sister told her that—?"

"The call?"

"Hmm?"

Dan closed his eyes. One of these days, he was going to get her to focus. "The call. From *Mister* Brumby." Stress on the *Mister*. A subtle hint she should be a bit more respectful.

"Oh, yeah. Right. Well, once he got done bein' mad that you weren't here to answer the phone, and then telling me how I was too young to work in the sheriff's office and how I dressed like some kind of freak—"

"Jasmine."

"Oh. Right. Sorry, Chief."

He didn't even correct her. No point putting another distraction in her path.

"Okay, so anyway, ol' man Brumby—"

Dan sighed and leaned against the doorjamb. So much for respectful.

"—says someone blew up his outhouse this morning. Blew it to 'heckamy and back,' he said." The pop of her gum echoed off the walls like a gunshot. "He talks funny, you know? Real colorful."

"Yes, I know." Dan straightened. "Okay, I'll check out the break-in."

"And the outhouse, right? Ol' man—"

He gave her an exasperated stare.

"Okay, okay, *Mister* Brumby wants you to stop by and investigate, see if you can catch the—get this—*hoodlums* who did it."

Dan held out his hands. "Hey, I live to serve." He headed for the door, grabbing his hat on the way. "Break-in first, then I'll take a run out there. Let me know if you get any other calls, okay?"

"Will do, Chief."

Dan paused then pulled open the door.

So he was wrong. Even his grandmother's memory wasn't *that* bad.

Shelby Wilson hadn't planned to end up in Deputy Justice's arms. She especially hadn't planned for it to happen in broad daylight, in the middle of town. It was simply a twist of fate— and some pretty phenomenal timing.

She'd been walking down the sidewalk, reading through a pile of reports, not watching where she was going, when a door suddenly flew open in front of her. She dodged, missing the door—her reflexes had always been good.

Everything would have been fine if not for the darned rocking chair on the sidewalk. She was so busy dodging the door, she didn't see the chair. Her foot caught, and she pitched forward, her papers flying up and raining down on her. But instead of kissing the boardwalk as she expected, she found herself caught in a very capable pair of strong hands.

"Whoa! Careful, there."

She grabbed on to the arms supporting her, letting her forehead rest for a second against her rescuer, then tipped her head back and saw Dan Justice smiling down at her. He righted her, keeping his hands on her arms.

"You okay, Miss Wilson?"

She stood there, staring at him, her tongue suddenly glued

to the bottom of her mouth. Her head was spinning, and she'd give anything if it had been because of the near fall. But it wasn't.

It was, and this embarrassed her to no end to admit, because of the feel of his strong hands on her arms. Of his strength beneath her fingers.

And because those blue, blue eyes were closer than she'd ever expected them to be.

"Miss Wilson?" Dan peered at her.

"Shelby," she corrected automatically, then could have bitten her tongue.

He lifted one brow. "Shelby, then. Are you okay?"

"Fine." She realized she was still gripping those muscular arms and jerked her hands away, wiping the warmth off on her jacket. "I'm fine. Really."

He bent to gather her papers, and she knelt next to him, waving him off. "Oh, no. Really, don't bother."

His face right next to hers, he angled a look her way, and a smile eased across his lips. "It's no bother, Shelby."

She'd always liked her name. Thought it was unique, pretty. But she'd never liked it as much as when Dan Justice said it, with just a hint of teasing.

Shelby couldn't stop herself. She smiled back. "Thanks, Deputy."

"Dan."

Quick heat in her cheeks sent her gaze scurrying to the papers on the boardwalk. "Dan. Thanks."

He gathered the last of her papers, stood, and held a hand out to her. She slid her hand into his, let him pull her to her feet, then accepted the papers he held out to her.

"It was my pleasure."

As he walked on down the boardwalk, Shelby had the most ridiculous desire to fan herself with the papers.

Oh no, Dan. No it wasn't. She turned and headed on her way. *The pleasure was definitely mine.*

NINE

*"There are always uncertainties ahead,
but there is always one certainty—God's will is good."*
VERNON PATERSON

*How can we understand the road we travel?
It is the LORD who directs our steps.*
PROVERBS 20:24

THIS DAY WAS GOING FROM BAD TO WORSE.

First, he'd spent twice as much time as he'd anticipated with the woman whose home had been burgled. Situated several miles outside of Sanctuary, the clearly custom-built home sat down a long, paved drive, in the middle of ten acres tucked way in the national forest. As Dan followed the immaculately dressed woman from one elegant room to another, writing down all that had been stolen, he got an earful.

"We moved out here to get away from crime," she sputtered. "I thought this was supposed to be a safe, quiet area! Honestly, what is law enforcement for if it can't protect our homes?"

It was useless to point out that no area was safe from some kind of crime or that an expensive home this remote was a prime target for thieves. One look at the place was all it took to know it would be full of treasures just too tempting—and easy to sell—to resist.

Nor did he point out that most everyone in the area knew that two kinds of people gravitated to the remote regions of Oregon: Most were folks who loved simple living, smaller communities, wildlife, wilderness, and nature. But others were far less desirable. People who came out to the boonies to do drugs and other illegal activities without worrying about the law.

Which was why it was such a good thing that they were finally able to have a deputy in Sanctuary again. They'd done their best before that, patrolling this area along with the rest of Jackson County, but it was so much better to live here.

Day to day, he saw who came and went; he got acquainted with the pillars of the community—and with the pits. In the process, he'd run into pretty much every kind of folk, from real live mountain men, complete with scruffy beards, knee-high moccasins, and clothes fashioned from animal pelts; to artsy folks who looked like transplants from the sixties; to those wealthy enough to buy acreage and build million-dollar log homes.

The woman he saw this morning fit in the latter category. And she was far from pleased that her "rustic retreat" had been invaded. When Dan asked what kind of alarm system they had in the house, her manicured hand went to her throat, and she peered down her nose at him like he was three-day-old shrimp. "Alarm system? Good heavens, Deputy, I never *imagined* needing such a thing out here."

Dan took down all the information, then gave her his card and the card of a reliable alarm system supplier.

After an encounter like that, Dan was not looking forward to dealing with James Brumby.

The old codger had lived just outside of Sanctuary for as long as anyone could remember. No one knew for certain how old he was, but Dan figured he was eighty if he was a day.

Brumby, who'd never been married, believed in keeping to himself and letting everyone else do the same. He just worked his place, cut enough wood to last the winter, and even hunted anything that could grace his table—in and out of season, though Dan had never been able to catch him breaking the law. Brumby only called into town when there was trouble.

Like today.

He was one of a kind, Brumby was. A fact for which Dan was immeasurably thankful.

Of course, a man like Brumby lived as far up the mountain as he could get. And the road to get there was as inhospitable as the man. The rutted dirt logging road was worse every time Dan drove it. With all the recent rain, it was slick as well as bumpy. After one particularly jarring bounce that sent the cruiser sliding from one side of the road to the other, Dan put on the brakes and looked in his rearview mirror.

Nope. He was wrong. No matter what it felt like, he hadn't left his kidneys back there in the road.

Thank heaven he was almost to Brumby's place. Of course, that wouldn't be any more fun than the drive. Because once there, Dan would have to deal with Brumby's security system: four very large, very vocal, very unfriendly dogs.

Dan parked the cruiser next to the fence surrounding Brumby's property and opened the car door. He'd no sooner stepped out of the vehicle than the dogs were at it, barking and snarling and doing their best to shred the thick wood fence between them and Dan.

"Nice doggies…" he muttered, watching the beasts try to reach him. "Nice big, ugly doggies."

Since he'd been to Brumby's a few times before, he knew to call and let the man know what time he'd be arriving. Even so, the old fella took a considerable amount of time to get from the house to the fence.

Brumby aimed ineffectual swats at the dogs as he shuffled up to the gate. "Hush up now, boys! It's Deputy Dan. He's a friend."

He started to open the gate, the yapping monsters at his side, their eyes gleaming as though already anticipating how Dan's leg would taste. Dan grabbed the gate and jerked it shut again. "James, would you please put the dogs inside?"

The man's rheumy eyes peered at him. "Why, the boys won't hurt you none, Deputy. Not with me standing here."

Dan eyed the growling guardians and shook his head. "You're probably right, but I'd hate to take a chance." He met Brumby's gaze. "I mean, if one of the boys bites me, he might get sick." Dan had heard early on how particular James Brumby was about what he fed his dogs. "These big boys usually have pretty sensitive digestive tracts, you know."

Brumby looked down at them. "Well, they *are* used to only the best beef for chow…"

"Exactly. Besides, if I got bit, well, I'd have to write up a report, have the dog taken to animal control."

That did it. Brumby shuffled back toward the house, calling the yapping "boys" as he went. Three of the four bounded after the man. The last dog—an animal that looked like a cross between Cujo and a really ugly grizzly—didn't budge. It glared at Dan, a guttural growl emanating from its massive chest.

"Duke!"

Dan jumped. Brumby's growl was as bad as the dog's.

"You get in here. Now!"

With a final snarl in Dan's direction, the hulking beast turned and ambled into the house. Dan pushed the gate open and stepped in. He slid on his latex gloves and pulled the evidence bags from his pocket as Brumby led him around back, showing him what was left of his outhouse.

There wasn't much.

"You cleaned everything up?"

The old man shrugged his bony shoulders. "Well, sure. The boys were all over the place, grabbing wood and chewin' on it. One of 'em even had a nail he was chompin' on. And some wire. And the area stunk to high heaven. 'Course I cleaned it up."

So much for preserving the integrity of the crime scene.

Dan moved closer, hoping to find some bit of evidence. Tape, batteries, twisted iron wire, fragments of metal, maybe even a footprint…anything. But Brumby was nothing if not thorough, especially when it came to the boys' safety. And he and the boys had effectively obliterated whatever footprints might have been there.

No way he was going to find evidence now. But he pulled his camera out of his pocket and took pictures of the scene. Knowing even as he did so that it really didn't matter much. This kind of mischief usually was the handiwork of the same group of kids.

Sanctuary was a warm and welcoming place, but it had challenges. With the Oregon lumber industry falling off so badly, many of the men had to go as far away as Alaska to find work. Which meant they were gone for months at a time. The women had to work as well to make ends meet, which left the kids unsupervised. So, as kids will do, they ran loose.

When kids out here ran loose, they often got bored. Then they got creative.

They'd started with blowing up outhouses. Then, just in the last year, they'd exchanged outhouses for mailboxes in town. Gave "Air Mail" a whole new meaning. The post office finally got tired of replacing their outside mailboxes and just took them out. So now, apparently, the kids had gone back to outhouses.

The whole time Dan was at Brumby's, the old man went on and on about how bad kids were nowadays, how they didn't have respect for anyone or anything. He followed Dan back to the front gate, expounding on his solution for what ailed America: "Round up all these wild kids and put 'em to work."

Dan smiled at Brumby. "Doing what?"

"Diggin' new outhouse holes, for one thing!"

Chuckling, Dan let himself out the gate, then closed and latched it.

"They're getting meaner, too. You know some kids tried to do my boys in?"

Dan paused. "How's that?"

"Set out meat with glass in it. Woulda cut the boys to shreds. But they's as stupid as they are mean."

"The boys?" Dan frowned.

"No. Ain't you listenin'? The kids! The meat they stuck that glass in was spoiled. Smelled like a dozen week-old skunks. Good thing, though. I smelled it 'fore I put the boys out and went to take a gander. Found the meat all over the ground." He spit. "I'm tellin' you, Deputy. I see any of those kids on my property again, I'm gonna get my gun."

Dan stopped cold at that. "Now, James."

"I'm too old to keep rebuilding outhouses and digging new holes. Gonna give me a heart attack. So I figure it's either me or them."

"It better not be, James."

"But—"

"I mean it, now." He gave the old man a stern look. "If you see kids hanging around, you call me. Write down their descriptions. Take a picture of them, if you want. But you shoot someone, and I'll have to come up here and haul *you* back to town."

"But I—"

"Then who will look after the boys?"

Brumby glanced over his shoulder to where the dogs watched them through a window, barking with all their might. "Now, Deputy, you know ain't no one but me can watch out for my boys."

"Exactly. So don't go doing anything that'll land you in jail."

"Jail?" He gaped at Dan. "You'd put me in jail for shootin' trespassers?"

Dan's eyes narrowed. "For shooting kids? In a heartbeat."

Brumby clamped his mouth shut.

"So no guns, right?"

Brumby's mouth settled into a hard line.

"You see anyone, you call me. Right?"

The old man gave a grudging nod.

"Good. I'll hold you to that."

With a snort, Brumby turned and went back inside—but not before he held the door open and let the dogs scramble out after Dan again. Thankfully, he was back in his cruiser before they slammed into the fence.

He stared after the old man, then turned the key in the ignition. As the engine jumped to life and he put the cruiser into gear, Dan cast one last look over his shoulder at Brumby's place.

He'd been right. This little visit to Brumbyland was no fun at all.

"So? Anything fun to report?"

"Fun?" Shelby took a bite of her burger, studying her friend.

Jasmine's long-suffering sigh was pitiful. She waved her black-nailed hands at Shelby. "Fun! *You* know." She bobbed her head, dropping her voice so no one would overhear. "Between yooou…and the chief."

The bit of burger slammed to a halt in Shelby's throat. After a couple of seconds of coughing and slurping water, she planted her hands on the table and gave the woman opposite her a hard look. "Jasmine, you are one of my all-time favorite people, and when everyone else says how crazy you are, I just tell them you're creative, but *have you lost your mind*?"

Jasmine took the gum out of her mouth and stuck it to the side of her plate, then lifted her gyro. "Fine. Don't tell me. It's not like everyone in town doesn't know you two are interested in each other. After that display in broad daylight earlier today." She batted her eyes, her voice going all syrupy. "Oh, Dan. Thank you for saving me from that nasty fall."

It took a few seconds for Shelby to realize she was sitting here with her mouth hanging open. Actually, it took Jasmine muttering around a bit of gyro, "Close your mouth before the flies get in." But Shelby couldn't help it.

She was stunned. Mortified. And panicked.

If Jasmine was saying things like this to her, what was to keep her from saying them to...to...

No!

Shelby grabbed Jasmine's wrist, jerking her gyro to a halt, making her take a bite out of thin air.

"*Tell* me you haven't said anything like this to Deputy Justice."

Jasmine's purple lips compressed, and she pulled her wrist free. "Don't be a dope. Of course I haven't."

Sweet relief made Shelby's knees weak, so it was a good thing she was sitting down.

"'Course, that doesn't mean anyone else hasn't. Like I said, everyone in town knows about it."

Shelby's head dropped to the table.

Jasmine tapped the back of Shelby's head. "You do realize your cheek is in your plate, don't you?"

"I don't care."

"You should."

She peered up at Jasmine. "Oh? Why?"

"Because the chief just came in."

"*Wha—?*"

"Hey there, ladies."

She closed her eyes then forced herself to open them and look up. Sure enough, there he was. Deputy Dan Justice. Tall, handsome, and looking at her like she had gone round the bend.

Way round.

"Shelby, you feeling okay?"

Actually, she wasn't. She felt decidedly ill. But she plastered a smile on her face. "Just fine."

He bit his top lip and gave a slow nod. "Oh. Okay. Good."

She frowned at him. What was that look for?

Fighting a grin, he reached out and plucked a piece of parsley from her cheek, holding it out to her between his fingers. She looked from it to him then back at it.

"I…uh…" She grabbed her purse. "Excuse me." She hopped up, slipping past him. "I have to go."

It was a coward's exit. Shelby knew that. And she didn't care one jot. Or so she told herself as she scurried back to her office.

Pity she'd never been a good liar.

"I'm outta here, Chief."

Dan glanced up from his desk. "Jasmine."

She rolled her head back and looked to the ceiling. "So-rry! *Deputy*. I'm outta here, *Deputy*."

He looked at his watch. "Three o'clock? Kinda early to be knocking off, isn't it?"

"Going to the valley to get my hair cut, remember?"

Oh yes. She had told him about that. "Right. Sorry, I forgot." He tipped his head. "So how come you don't just go to the Beauty and Video Salon like everyone else in town?"

She snorted. "Yeah, right! Like I'd let Mabel Jones *touch* my hair. She'd probably chop off an ear or somethin'. I mean, hey, you know what they call her?"

"Jasmine."

But there was no stopping the girl when she was onto a juicy tidbit about one of the townspeople. She popped her gum, savoring it as much as her next words. "The *Slasher*."

Dan leaned his arms on his desk. "You know very well that's because she was an English teacher way back when and used to mark kids' papers up with a red pencil. It has nothing to do with cutting things."

"Sure." Another juicy pop. "That's what you say now. But I'm the one who'd have to go under the knife."

"Scissors."

"Whatever! Suppose I wasn't paying attention and used bad grammar? I mean, she might shave me bald for using a dangling particicle."

"Participle."

"See?" She shivered. "I'd be in trouble for sure." She turned and grabbed the doorknob.

"Hey."

She looked over her shoulder. "Yes?"

"You know James Brumby? I mean, not do you know who he is, but do you really know him?"

With a sigh, she walked back to him. "Sure. Why?"

Dan filled her in on Brumby's threat, and she leaned against his desk as she listened, a spark of concern lighting her brown eyes. When he finished, she shook her head.

"Not good."

He'd been afraid of that. "Why? He's just blowing off steam, right? He wouldn't really shoot at anyone."

Her look was answer enough. "Not only would he shoot, but he'd hit whatever he aimed at."

Oh, great. Dan rubbed his temples. More good news. "So he can shoot?"

"Hey, Old Man Brumby may be a crotchety ol' coot, but he can outshoot most anyone in Sanctuary. And that's saying something." She pushed away from the desk. "Now, I *gotta* go."

"So go. Who's stopping you?"

Dan fought off a smirk when she fixed him with a glare then marched to the door and jerked it open. Her muttered "*Men!*" drifted back to him, tweaking the corners of his mouth. But his smile vanished when Jasmine's final words hit him.

"I don't know what Shelby sees in you!"

He stared at her. "Shelby sees something in me?"

Jasmine popped her gum. "Not if she's as smart as I think she is." With that, she was gone.

Dan leaned back in his chair. He'd known Shelby for a

while now, had always thought she was great. Good at her job. Wonderful with the kids. But today when she flew into his arms, when he held her, when she looked up at him with those big blue eyes…

Well, things shifted. He hadn't asked them to. Hadn't even wanted them to. But they'd shifted all the same.

Oh, boy. Had they ever.

He'd sat in his car after that little encounter, heart aching. All he could think of was Sarah. What would she think of him? Of the way he'd reacted to Shelby? Of the emotions he let himself feel? Not for long, of course. But they'd been there. No denying it.

Emotions he hadn't felt since losing Sarah. Emotions he hadn't even realized he'd missed. But there was something so exciting, so full of promise in them.

His heart had leapt to embrace them.

Remembering, he bowed his head. "Sarah…I'm sorry."

He missed her so much. Not having her with him left a huge, gaping hole in his gut. Like a part of him had been torn away, left to fester, never healing. And yet. When he'd looked down at Shelby today, there was a fraction of a moment when he didn't hurt. When the ache was replaced with anticipation.

Maybe…He closed his eyes, not sure he could even consider the thought. But he let it come.

Maybe it was time. Maybe he was ready to care again.

Of course, he'd figured that the feelings, the unsettling surge of attraction, were just on his side. But if Jasmine was right…

Get over yourself, Justice. Quit mooning about Shelby Wilson and focus on your job. And James Brumby.

Ah yes. James Brumby. He was sure Jasmine was right about that. If there was one thing the menfolk of Sanctuary prided themselves on, it was their shooting skills. Dan discovered that fact a few weeks after moving to town.

Late one night someone had called in a report of a carload

SHATTERED JUSTICE   *115*

of young men driving through town and shooting at street signs. Dan was at the scene in a matter of minutes—as was most of Sanctuary. As he checked out the street signs, Dan was relieved to find them undamaged.

"Well, wasn't anyone from town."

He'd turned at the slow drawl and found Amos Abbot, the editor of the *Sanctuary Sentinel,* standing there, a coat thrown over his pajamas, his feet clad in slippers. "Oh? Why do you say that?"

Amos indicated the still-intact sign. "They missed. Had to be someone passin' through, Deputy. Folks 'round here, they don't miss."

Dan hadn't been sure if that bit of news was comforting or unnerving. Now, thinking of James Brumby, he had no doubt.

Unnerving. Definitely unnerving.

TEN

*"Look up and not down. Look forward and not back.
Look out and not in, and lend a hand."*
EDWARD EVERETT HALE

*"Dear children, let us stop just saying we love each other;
let us really show it by our actions."*
1 JOHN 3:18

NOON. THE MAGIC HOUR.

Dan pulled his cruiser into his usual parking place, slid from the car, adjusted his utility belt, and walked toward the promised land.

Lou's Diner and Deli.

To the untrained eye, it looked like a little hole in the wall, a greasy spoon best avoided for the sake of one's gastrointestinal tract. But to those who live in Sanctuary, Lou's was the doorway to delight.

Forget the sad exterior with faded, peeling paint. Forget the sign that looked as though it came off the underside of a wagon dragged across the states with the town's founding fathers. Forget the gaudy neon signs in the windows, the dusty county fair posters from 1967, and the front door that squeaked loud enough to bring the mice in town running.

No sir, none of that mattered. Not when LouBelle Watson got to cooking. No one created culinary masterpieces like Lou did. Her fare was plain, to be sure: eggs, bacon, ham, hash browns, biscuits, hot cereals for breakfast. Soups, sandwiches, burgers, fries for lunch. Meat loaf, roast beef, fried chicken, fish, and spaghetti for dinner. Which made Lou's genius that much more amazing. By adding just the right touch of this or pinch of that, she transformed what might otherwise be a simple grilled cheese sandwich into a matchless melt-in-your-mouth morsel.

And then there was her dessert menu. Just the thought of that menu—and the delicacies it promised—set Dan's taste buds into overdrive.

He pushed the front door open, inhaling as he stepped inside. Luscious aromas filled his senses, and he let out a soft sigh. No matter what happened during the day, no matter how crazy things got, he could always count on lunch at Lou's. No one knew how to fill an empty stomach—or lift a sagging spirit—like the petite diner owner.

"Well, don't just stand there, boy. Take your seat."

Dan dodged the diminutive gray-haired woman zipping past him, her arms laden with plates of food. There was as much spring in her step as any of the rabbits Dan was forever chasing out of his garden.

"Yes, ma'am." He moved to slide into his booth.

Most of regulars who ate at Lou's had their own booths. No names on them or anything, but folks knew which booth or table belonged to whom, and they respected each other's right of ownership.

Most of the regulars had been coming to Lou's since they were kids. Of course, Lou treated all of them—even those pounding down the door of senior citizen status—as if they were still barely in grade school. When Dan made lunch at Lou's a more-or-less daily excursion, he accepted that Lou would treat him that way, too. Which she did with glee, even going so far as to insist he drink milk instead of coffee.

Truth be told, though, Dan didn't mind Lou's coddling. In fact, he kind of liked it. Almost as much as he liked watching the other customers as he ate. Dining at Lou's wasn't just about the food, delicious though it was. It was about the company, too. And as Dan settled into his booth and glanced around, he saw that the regulars, or the Lou Crew, as he'd dubbed them, were there in force.

Amos Abbot perched on his stool at the counter. He saluted Dan with his cup of coffee. "Afternoon, Deputy."

Dan nodded to Amos and to the man sitting next to him. Gordon Gossier, the town crier. At least, that's what Doris and Agatha called him. From the day Dan had hit town, those two had made it their personal duty to fill him in on the "good folks of Sanctuary." They pointed Gordon out to him during his first week in town.

Dan had spotted the two women sitting in their rockers in front of the Beauty and Video shop. He stopped to chat and was listening to a litany of Doris's latest physical ailments when she suddenly stopped rocking and leaned forward, staring across the street.

"Well, look there, Agatha. It's the town crier."

Agatha peered at her friend. "Brown dryer? Don't be silly. The dryers in the Laundromat are white. Besides, what *that* has to do with your lumbago is beyon—"

"*Crier,* you nit! Town *crier.*" Doris swatted Agatha's arm. "Turn up your hearing aid."

"I will not burn it up! There's times I need the silly thing." She sniffed. "Though not as often as some people like to think."

"Town crier?"

Doris looked up at Dan's question, clearly delighted to have an audience that could hear. "Gordon Gossier." She pointed a knitting needle at the stout man across the street. "You can be sure of this, Sheriff Dan, no one beats Gordon at spreading news—"

"Or rumors—" Agatha's white-capped head was bobbing her agreement. "The man's a veritable *fount* of tittle-tattle."

Dan frowned. "Tittle-tattle?"

Agatha's veined hand waved at him. "Oh, you know, who is doing what with whom, when and where and why. He seems to know everything about everyone—"

"And has no qualms sharing his wealth of information." Doris sat back in her rocker. "Fast and efficient. That's our Gordon. Why, we hardly need phones with him around."

"Indeed." Agatha's head was bobbing again. "You're so right, Doris. So right."

Dan smiled at the memory. He'd discovered Agatha and Doris were right on the money about Gordon. Which was likely why he always sat next to Amos. Where better to get the latest scoop than from a newspaperman?

Wilson and Edwina Casey, who'd been married just over sixty years, sat in the booth across the way from Dan. Almost every day, their weathered hands were entwined. Today was no different, and even from across the room Dad could see the way their eyes shone as they looked at each other. It always got to Dan, watching them…

He and Sarah would have been like that.

Dan waited for emotion to clog his throat, but it didn't come. Instead, he just smiled. That had been happening more and more. Especially since that day on the walkway with Shelby. When he thought about Sarah there was more gratitude than pain.

A quick look around the diner showed the other regulars of the Lou Crew were at their posts: Jessie Matthews, the local librarian, was seated across a table from Camilla Wright, the clerk at the town's gas-station-cum-grocery-store. Mabel Jones, Jasmine's slasher beautician, sat at her usual booth, studying the hairstyle magazines spread out on the table in front of her.

There were one or two folks Dan didn't know. Tourists, no doubt. Visitors who stopped in at Lou's generally fit into one of three categories. They'd heard about the place so weren't put off by the exterior. Or they were brave-hearted souls, whose pioneer spirits wouldn't let them turn away when things got ugly. Or they were flat-out starving and painfully aware there weren't a whole lot of choices for places to eat between Sanctuary and Shady Cove, almost an hour down the highway.

Too bad he hadn't been here when the new folks arrived. First-timers were always surprised when they first met Lou. For some reason, most folks expected to see a big burly lumberjack of a guy. Lou wasn't even close. Barely five feet tall, weighing probably a hundred pounds soaking wet, she looked more like a misplaced munchkin than a lumberjack. But for all of her sweet smiles and grandmotherly hair and dress, Lou was no one to mess with.

She could be a terror, when needed. A tiny terror, but a terror nonetheless.

Dan cast a final look around the diner. Yep. Everyone was here.

Well…almost everyone.

"She'll be here, Deputy."

Dan turned and caught the twinkle in Edwina Casey's eyes. "Who will?"

"Good try, Deputy." This bit of laughing sarcasm from Gordon at the counter. "But it's a waste of energy. Everyone here knows who you're lookin' for."

A tiny wave of heat inched up Dan's neck, into his face. After that day a few weeks ago, when Shelby tripped, it took a couple of days for her to be comfortable around him. Neither of them said anything, but he was pretty sure they both were aware of the shift in their friendship. Thankfully, they managed to get it back on track. And though a suggestion of something more existed, neither of them was in any hurry to push it.

Pity the folks in town weren't as patient. They'd been making little comments. Dan did his best to just let them slide on by, like he hadn't heard them. But this time, there was no denying it.

"Now, you all leave the deputy alone," Lou said from behind the counter.

Dan sent a grateful smile her way. She nodded to him. "The usual, Dan?"

"Absolutely." At least *someone* knew how to mind her own business.

Lou slid one of her golden-brown grilled cheese creations onto a plate, making his mouth water. She added a spoonful of coleslaw and a slice of orange to the plate, then made her way around the counter, bestowing that broad grin of hers as she set the plate in front of him.

Along with a tall glass of milk.

Dan eyed the glass. "Lou…"

She waved her hand in the air. "Growing boys need milk."

"Lou, I'm six foot four. If I grow any more I won't fit in my cruiser."

"Then the county will just have to buy you a new car."

"I don't *want* milk—"

She patted him on the cheek. "'Course you do. Everyone likes milk."

"Lou—"

"Give it up, Dan. You *know* you'll never win."

He looked past Lou's elfin form to find Shelby standing there, amusement dancing in her blue eyes.

"I just love hearing the voice of reason." Lou leaned close and pseudo-whispered into Dan's ear. "Brains *and* beauty. Makes a pretty attractive package, don't you think, Deputy?"

The diner went silent. A quick look confirmed Dan's fear—everyone had stopped eating and was staring at him.

So much for Lou knowing how to mind her own business.

It had been a long time since Dan blushed, and here he'd done it twice in the space of five minutes. What was he supposed to say? That he agreed? Well, of *course* he did. Dan had thought Shelby was a very attractive package, inside and out, since coming to Sanctuary almost a year and a half ago. Was even more convinced of it after she'd landed in his arms.

So much so that he made a decision. He'd been feeling it was time to get back into volunteer work with kids, so why not kill two birds with one stone, so to speak? If he volunteered with Master's Touch, he'd have a good reason to spend more time with Shelby. That'd be a safe way to explore things a bit.

A whole lot safer—he thought, sitting here, staring up at Lou as she waited for a reply—than commenting on his opinion of Shelby in the middle of the day with an all-too-interested audience.

Fortunately, Shelby's light laughter saved him from having to respond. "LouBelle Watson, you are a troublemaker."

The older woman's smile was saucy. "You only say that because it's true." She made her way back toward the grill. "Hamburger, Shelby?"

"With fries." She slid onto the empty seat across from Dan and focused her attention on him. "Got a few minutes to talk?"

He finally found his voice. "Sure. What's up?"

"I need you."

Dan's heart did a quick jump. "Oh?"

She nodded, snatching the pickle off his plate and taking a bite of it. "I've got a boy who just entered our program, and I think you'd be perfect to work with him."

"Oh." Was that disappointment curling through his gut? *Grow up, Justice. You're worse than a junior higher with a crush.* "How old is this kid?"

"Thirteen going on forty." She reached into her purse and pulled out some papers, tracing a finger down to the information she wanted. "Born July 17, 1991, and he's had a truly rotten life. Both parents are gone—his dad is in prison; his mom just vanished when Jayce was a few months old. His paternal grandmother has done her best with him, but he's a smart kid." She set the papers on the table. "Really smart."

"Ah." Dan took a bite of his sandwich. "Let me guess. Bored in school, so he ditches? Bored in life, so he invents his own activities? Activities that are less than constructive."

"Or legal, unfortunately." She stretched her hands out across the table, drumming her fingers softly. "But I'll tell you something, when I look in this kid's eyes…"

She fell silent, and Dan studied her. "What?"

"He's on the edge, Dan. He's been in the system off and on for years. You'd think he'd be hard and cold, but there's something in his eyes that gets you—" she pressed a fist to her chest—"right here. A longing. Like he wants to come home but doesn't know where home is."

The sadness in her tone set him on edge. He wanted to reach out, draw her close, and protect her.

Shelby straightened, leaning back against the seat. "I'm afraid if we don't reach him soon…"

"You'll lose him."

She nodded, and he saw how that grieved her.

"Well, then—" he plucked what was left of his pickle from her fingers, downing it in one decisive bite—"we'll just have to make sure that doesn't happen."

ELEVEN

"If you haven't any charity in your heart,
you have the worst kind of heart trouble."
BOB HOPE

"Share each other's troubles and problems,
and in this way obey the law of Christ."
GALATIANS 6:2

"NOW THAT'S WHAT I CALL A GOURMET MEAL."

Dan couldn't restrain a guffaw. "A hamburger and fries qualifies as gourmet?"

Shelby folded her hands in front of her. "Not just any burger and fries, of course, but Lou's burger and fries?" She dipped the last fry on her plate in a concoction she'd made by mixing mayo and catsup together, then popped it in her mouth, closing her eyes as she chewed. "Mmm. Definitely gourmet." She opened her eyes and licked her lips. "You'll have to bring Jayce here one of these days."

"Yeah. Jayce." Dan picked up his unused knife and drew circles on the tablecloth. "So tell me about this kid. Thirteen going on forty, you said?"

"Right." She reached into her oversize purse and pulled out a manila folder. Opening it on the table in front of her, she slid a picture across to Dan. "Deputy Justice, meet Jayce Dalton."

He studied the photo, taking in the firm jaw, the short-cropped golden hair, the gleam of defiance in those unsmiling blue eyes. "This kid *looks* forty."

"I know, but then, he hasn't ever really been a child. His father worked in lumber before Jayce was born. After that industry collapsed and he lost his job, the father just drifted from one dead-end job to another. Couldn't seem to hold anything for more than a month or two. He finally gave up. Made ends meet by breaking into homes of very wealthy people."

Dan paused, a French fry halfway to his mouth. "Brilliant."

"Well, kind of, actually. Mr. Dalton had an uncanny knack for choosing homes containing small but especially valuable property. Apparently he made a pretty decent living."

"Goody for him."

A rueful smile played at the corners of her mouth. "Yes, well, never fear. While the man had excellent taste in choosing his targets, he was a sadly inept burglar. He managed to pull off three fairly substantial jobs, but on the fourth he found himself surrounded by police, guns drawn and aimed right at him."

"Chalk one up for the good guys."

Shelby chuckled, tucking Jayce's picture back into the folder and closing it. "Indeed. To his credit, Mr. Dalton offered no resistance as they cuffed him—"

"Perps usually don't when you've got your gun on 'em."

She ignored that. "He just asked that he be allowed to call his mother so she could watch out for his boy. When the gavel fell at Mr. Dalton's trial, he'd been sentenced to nearly twenty-five years in the Oregon state penitentiary."

"And Jayce?"

"He moved in with his grandmother, who, despite a heart condition, did her best to raise him. Unfortunately, his early years gave him a bit of a bad taste for rules and regulations."

"A rebel is born, eh?"

She slid the folder from the table and put it back in her

bag. "An unusually bright rebel, who found all kinds of creative ways to get into trouble. By the time he was in grade school, he was known as 'that Dalton kid,' an inveterate troublemaker. A reputation that's still in force today."

She reached for her check, but with one deft movement, Dan snagged it before her fingers made contact. Her brow furrowed. "Dan."

He slid from the booth, pulling out his wallet. "Know what *my* daddy taught me? Never let a pretty woman pay."

He held his hand out, pleased when she laid her hand in his and let him help her from the booth.

"Sounds like your daddy was a nice man."

He liked the feel of her hand tucked in his. "The very best."

"Explains where you get it from."

Whether it was her words, her warm smile, or the gentle squeeze on his hand, Dan wasn't certain. But he suddenly had the sense of being on unfamiliar—and unstable—territory. Dropping her hand, he turned and headed for the register.

By the time he paid their bills, he had regained a bit of composure. "So anything else you want me to know about Jayce?" He held the door open for her as they exited the restaurant and walked toward her car.

"Jayce was picked up for various minor offenses."

"Such as?"

"Oh, you know, truancy, loitering—nothing big." She paused beside her car, turning to face him. "But in the last few years, Jayce has gotten into increasing trouble, culminating in being picked up a few months ago for theft."

Dan's brows rose.

"That's when his grandmother called Master's Touch. It was clear she was pretty much at her wit's end. She's convinced Jayce is a good boy at heart; he's just fallen in with the wrong crowd."

Dan's expression must have given him away, because Shelby poked him in the ribs. "Didn't anyone ever tell you skepticism isn't attractive in a man?"

He rubbed the spot she'd poked. "Ouch."

Her lips twitched. "Baby."

"Bony fingers."

"Brat."

Dan laughed. "No denying that." He leaned against her car. "About Jayce, you have to admit that's what they all say. 'Junior's a saint; it's the other kids who lead him wrong.'"

She conceded his point, though the uptilt of her lips told him she wasn't in complete agreement. "You're right, of course. But in this case…"

He slid his hands into his pockets. "You think Granny's right."

"I do. Have you encountered a boy yet named Marlin Murphy?"

"Yeah, I've met the kid. A bruiser who heads up a gang of bullies. I've gotten calls about them for vandalism and shoplifting, and most everyone figures these are the thugs blowing up mailboxes and outhouses."

Shelby leaned her elbow on the top of her car and rested her chin in her hand. "And yet these bastions of society continue to roam the fair streets of Sanctuary."

"I can't exactly haul them in without hard evidence."

"More's the pity."

"Don't tell me that's the group this Jayce kid is involved with."

"One and the same." She straightened, searching in her purse for her car keys. "Mrs. Dalton says Jayce seems to admire and want to please Marlin, which, of course, convinces her the boy's in the fast lane to following in his daddy's footsteps. So she's determined to break his ties with our man Marlin and his—" she snickered—"'gang of scallywags,' as she called them."

"That must have gone over big."

"Like showing *Bambi* at an NRA meeting."

His burst of laughter made her smile as well. "Anyway, after Mrs. Dalton and I talked, she asked if I'd go with her to tell

Jayce he was going to take part in our program."

"Needed backup, did she?"

"Hardly. More like she wanted me to be there to haul him away if he didn't agree. You should have seen her, Dan. She's this little white-haired lady, but when Jayce started to give her grief, she just squared off with him, poked a bony finger in his chest, and told him, 'It's either that, boy, or I turn you over to this lady to take you to Family Services. Take your pick.'"

"Whoa." Had to admire that kind of grit. "So what do you think? Is our boy a victim of bad environment and worse friends? Is there something worth salvaging in this kid?"

Shelby pursed her lips. "I've only been around Jayce a few weeks now, but I think something is really good about this boy. It's just buried under a lot of garbage." She unlocked her car door. "Which is where you come in."

He straightened and bent one arm, flexing his muscle. "You want I should take out the trash?"

She swatted him. "I want you should help this kid see he's got options." Opening her car door, she slid in, turned the key in the ignition, and pressed the button to lower the window. She leaned on the still-open car door, looking up at him. "And maybe let Jayce get a glimpse of something really wonderful."

"You mean me?"

She pulled the car door shut. "I mean God."

All teasing was gone from Shelby's expression. In its place was warmth. Trust. And something else.

Something that both soothed and unnerved him.

She put her hand over his where it rested on the car door. "First time I met you I knew I saw Him in your eyes, Dan. Jayce will see Him, too."

As Shelby's car pulled away, an echo whispered through Dan: "*I always saw God in your eyes...*"

But as Dan walked to his car, he couldn't tell whose voice was speaking—Sarah's...

Or Shelby's.

TWELVE

"This is the way of peace: Overcome evil with good,
falsehood with truth, and hatred with love."
PEACE PILGRIM

"Oh, the joys of those who do not follow the advice of the wicked,
or stand around with sinners, or join in with scoffers."
PSALM 1:1

FUNNY. THIS SEEMED LIKE SUCH A GOOD IDEA YESterday, as Dan looked into Shelby's imploring eyes. Now?

Now it was a truly rotten idea.

Probably because the eyes he was looking into now were about as far from Shelby's as it got.

Sure, they were blue. But where Shelby's eyes glowed with warmth, these baby blues were pure ice. Crater Lake in January.

And hard? They made obsidian seem soft and cuddly.

Dan could hardly believe those eyes belonged to a kid. But then, like Shelby said, Jayce hadn't had much of a chance to be a kid.

When Shelby had introduced them, Jayce didn't say a word. He just stood there, hands stuffed in his pockets, those icy eyes fixed on Dan, watching. When Shelby walked away, saying she'd give them some time to get acquainted, Dan tried to read the boy's reaction. He looked like a rabbit about to bolt.

Either that, or a predator about to strike.

Dan was sure of this much: Jayce Dalton had a chip on his shoulder the size of Mount St. Helens. But who could blame him? How many adults in his short life had tried to gain his trust, to explain away the pain of his thirteen years, only to let him down?

How many more—his own mother included—had just gone straight to the letting down?

Not exactly solid ground for building friendship, trust. Much of anything.

"So—" Dan motioned toward the door with his head— "you wanna go shoot some hoops or something?" Master's Touch had an outdoor recreation area. It wasn't fancy, but the kids enjoyed it.

Jayce shrugged, looking away.

Now *there* was an action Dan recognized all too well. He'd seen it from Aaron many times, and the message was textbook teen: *You can make me be here, but you can't make me enjoy it.*

Oddly enough, he found that encouraging. For all that Jayce had been through, he was still just a kid. Maybe the key wasn't so much making up for his past as just treating him the way Dan tried to treat Aaron. With a firm hand balanced with respect and love.

Dan sat, stretched his legs out in front of him, and crossed them at the ankle. "Yeah, I hear you."

The crease between Jayce's eyes told Dan he'd achieved his first objective: confusion. Keep the kid off balance. "You don't want to talk. Don't want to be buddies. You're here because you have to be. Well, same here."

A cynical twist touched the boy's mouth.

"Don't believe me, huh?"

Jayce faced Dan, the beginnings of curiosity peeking out of his eyes. Of course, Dan had to look pretty hard to see it under the layers of scorn.

"Fine. Up to you. But I'm just telling you, your grand-mother made you come; my mom made me."

Jayce snorted. Well, not a snort so much as a huff. Or a hiss. Whatever. At least it was some kind of sound. That was a step up from stony silence.

"What? You think I'm too old to do what my mom says?"

He watched the battle on the boy's face. He didn't want to give in, to say anything. But Jayce just couldn't hold back. "No."

Ooo. A word. Progress. "No?"

Definitely a snort this time. The kid dropped into a chair opposite Dan, draping a leg over one arm. He didn't so much sit on the furniture as subdue it. "Don't be stupid, man. Moms are moms. You're never too old to do what your mom says."

Not the reply Dan expected, though he didn't let that show on his face. "Got that right. Or your grandmother."

From Jayce's reaction, Dan guessed the kid was trying to decide if Dan was making fun of him. Finally Jayce gave a little lift of his chin. "So, why'd your mom tell you to come here?"

Dan opened his mouth to answer, but Jayce cut him off. "No, wait, let me guess." The sneer was back, torquing his lips into a less-than-attractive shape. "So you could save the rotten kids no one else wants?"

The sarcasm was thick, but Dan wasn't fooled. Something else was there, too. Something he was sure Jayce Dalton would do everything he could to hide, if he even knew it was there.

Fear

Dan *felt* it emanating from the boy—like some trapped ani-mal digging its way through the kid's protective shell.

"No, my mom knew saving people wasn't my job." Jayce's brows lifted at that, but Dan didn't give him the chance to com-ment. "She just thought it was a good thing to do. Helping others. Wherever I could, however I could."

Another snort. Dan was starting to miss the silence. "And you're just now starting? That's sad, man."

Dan went still. The kid's tone…the little twitch of his lips…

If he didn't know better, he'd think Jayce was teasing him. "Actually, I've been doing it since I was about your age."

His gaze flipped to the ceiling. "Oh, man. Give me a break. Am I supposed to go all warm and tingly?" He wiggled his fingers in the air. "Bonding moment. How touching."

Okay, then. Welcome back, sarcasm. Dan kept his reaction casual. "It's the truth. Not believing it doesn't change anything. It's still the truth."

Jayce chewed the side of his lip then nodded. "Truth is truth. Whether you believe it or not. Okay, so score one for the lawman. You're not as dumb as you look."

"Gee," Dan tried not to sound as underwhelmed as he felt, "thanks."

"So how come you're not already all connected with some other kid?"

Dan shifted in his chair. Did this kid ever ask easy questions? "I…took a break."

Jayce smirked. "Oh, I see. Got tired of givin'? What'd your mom say about that?"

Dan wanted to throw something at the boy, but the chair was too big and there weren't any rocks at hand. So he settled for the truth. "She didn't say anything. She's dead. Died almost five years ago. And I took a break because my wife died two years ago."

Jayce held Dan's gaze then a small exhalation escaped him. "Man. That stinks."

Funny. People said all kinds of things when they heard about Sarah. Too often their comments sounded almost practiced for effect and eloquence. Mini sermons to help him accept the burdens God had given him. He'd wanted to clamp a hand over those yapping mouths, just to stop their careless words from slicing and dicing his already shredded heart.

And yet here was this belligerent kid, someone Dan barely knew, and with those three words he gave Dan what all the mini sermons never could. Understanding. And comfort.

"Yes, it does."

A crease drew Jayce's brows together, and his hawklike gaze fixed on Dan. "So…your mom, she didn't really tell you to come *here*, then."

Sharp kid. Shelby had warned Dan. "Nope. Miss Wilson told me that."

Dan almost fell out of his chair when Jayce grinned. "Give it up, then. I mean, you might try to argue with your mom, but Miss Wilson?"

Dan grinned in return. "I hear you. *She's* scary."

"Dude. That's one woman you do *not* mess with." Jayce pushed out of his chair and ambled toward the outside door. He paused, hand on the doorknob, glancing back over his shoulder at Dan. "So we gonna shoot some hoops, or you just gonna sit there?"

Dan hopped up and went to join Jayce. He put a hand on the kid's shoulder, then pulled it back when Jayce jerked away like he'd been burned. His hand in the air, Dan took in the red seeping into Jayce's lean cheeks. "Sorry."

The boy rolled his shoulders. "I just don't like being touched, okay?"

"No sweat. And no touching. I got it. So, hoops?"

"Hoops."

Dan followed Jayce outside. "Just be prepared to go down in flames."

"In your dreams, old man."

"Old? Look, you infant, nobody calls Dan Justice *old*. Not nobody, not no how."

Jayce just emitted yet another snort and jogged toward the basketballs. That was okay; Dan didn't mind. Not even a little. Because when Jayce called him *old*, he'd done so with humor—and a touch of something else. Something Dan was pretty sure this kid didn't give away very often.

Respect.

∾

Anger.

Hot rage tipped with fury.

Cold hatred wrapped in wrath.

It consumed Marlin Murphy, making him shake, as he sat there watching Jayce Dalton and that cop.

Shooting baskets. Laughing. Talking. Jayce smiling at that cop like he was something special.

Pain from his gritted teeth radiated up Marlin's jaws. Into his temples. But the clenching didn't ease. Not one bit during the hour and a half he sat there, across the street from the basketball court.

Watching.

Just when Marlin thought he would erupt, the crud cop tossed the ball to Jayce, then went back inside. Marlin wanted to surge across the street. Grab the punk kid by the front of his sweaty shirt. Bury his fist in the smile Jayce still wore.

Ask him just what the heck he thought he was doing.

Instead, he forced himself to stillness. Trembling from the rage flowing through him. Then finally, he saw what he'd been waiting for. Mr. Law and Order walking out of the center, getting in his big, fancy SUV, and driving away.

In seconds, Marlin was up. On his feet. Across the street.

Jayce was just leaning over to pick up a basketball when Marlin slammed into him from behind. Sent him flying, face-first, into the brick wall of the building.

"Hey—!" But Jayce's yelp was cut off.

The sound of flesh and bone meeting with concrete was music to Marlin's ears. He buried his fingers in Jayce's shirt and jerked him to his feet. Marlin noted the blood running from the punk's damaged nose with a slow twist of his mouth.

"Hey, Jayce, ol' pal." His anger snarled free. "Have a nice time with the man?"

Jayce's hands planted against Marlin's chest. "Are you *nuts*?"

Marlin shoved his face close to Jayce's. "*I'm* not the one making nice with a cop, dirtbag."

Jayce pushed against Marlin's chest, twisting and jerking free. Marlin let him go, knowing he wouldn't get far. The kid might not be as big as Marlin, but he was strong and wiry. Aspects that made him a definite asset to Marlin.

No way some badge from the city was going to waltz in here and take those assets away. Not now. Not when he was so close to achieving everything he'd been working toward.

Jayce wiped his sleeve across his bleeding nose. "I just shot hoops with him, man!"

"For an hour and a half."

Something flickered in Jayce's eyes, and though Marlin maintained his scowl, he smiled inside. *Yeah, punk. That's right. I know what you're doing. All the time.* With that message delivered and received, Marlin relaxed a fraction, pulled the pack of cigarettes from his pocket.

"And you didn't just shoot hoops. You were talking." He tapped a cigarette free. Slipped it between his lips. "What were you talking about, Jayce?" He lit the end, drew in the heat, then flicked the match away. Arching a brow, he pinned the silent boy in front of him with a lazy glare. "Or should I say *who*?"

Jayce crossed his arms over his chest. "Get over yourself, man. You think every conversation with a cop is about you?"

Marlin almost smiled at that. "You know, Jayce, you got guts. Fighting back when you're cornered, man. I like that." He inclined his head. "Right place and time, that'll work for you."

One massive hand shot out, grabbing Jayce by the front of his damp, bloodied shirt, and slammed him back against the wall.

"Wrong place and time?" He drew in on the cigarette, took it from his lips with his free hand, then held it next to Jayce's face. "Best-case scenario, it'll get you hurt. Worst case…" He let the heated tip just touch Jayce's face. "It'll get you *dead*." He bellowed the last word in the kid's face.

"Go ahead!"

Marlin had to hand it to the kid. He didn't even flinch when the cigarette connected.

Defiance glowed in Jayce's eyes. Hatred oozed from his voice. "Go on. *Do* it."

Marlin considered it. Considered cracking the kid's head against the wall, smashing it like last year's Halloween pumpkins.

Then he let go and stepped back.

Jayce's low, sneering chuckle was like shards of glass across his skin. "You need me, Marlin. You know it, and I know it. You can talk all you want, but you won't kill me."

"No." Marlin spit the word out, tossing his cigarette to the ground and smashing it with his booted toe. He turned, slow and easy. "But there are people I *don't* need."

Good. Alarm. That was more like it. Let's fan the flame a bit… "Your sweet little grandmother, for one." A step forward.

Jayce didn't budge, but his jaw tensed. "You wouldn't."

Marlin's laughter escaped. "You know better." His gaze drifted to the building behind Jayce, traveled up to the window above them. The one belonging to an office.

Her office.

The lovely, oh-so-caring Shelby Wilson.

"And your do-gooder friend, for another." His smile turned cold. Suggestive. "Of course, killing the delicious Miss Wilson isn't the best option…"

Jayce's hands drew into fists, and this time he took a step forward. "Shut *up*!"

Heat surged through Marlin. That did it. Got to the kid. Broke that eternal calm he wore like some kind of medal. Anticipation uncoiled, rose like smoke from a fire. *Come on….come on…* "Oh no, I wouldn't dream of killing her. Not for a while—"

"You won't *touch* her!"

Oh, yeah. It was comin'. Marlin's pulse raced. His breathing sped up. Man, not even crank had a high like this. Laughter rasped up his throat then out into the charged air. "Oh, I'd do more than *touch*."

Jayce launched at Marlin like a rabid cougar. Marlin opened his hands, ready to receive it. Revel in it. The one drug that never let him down.

Pure, sweet violence.

It wasn't the yelling that made Shelby run.

She'd heard plenty of yelling in her career. Heated exchanges when emotions ran high and intellect took a backseat. More times than she could count she'd had to go toe-to-toe with some kid who towered over her, not flinching, not giving an inch. Not caring when he screamed right in her face.

No, yelling didn't bother her. But the *tone* that came flying in through the open window… That bothered her. A lot.

A glacial fury. A low hiss, like slender streams of gas escaping a broken gas pipe, filling a room with unseen but undeniable danger.

This was a sound she'd only heard a few times, but unless stemmed, it would end in disaster. Little wonder, then, that she bolted out of her chair and raced down the hallway.

She didn't even pause when heads turned her way as she cut through the rec room, shoving open the door to the basketball court outside. She rounded the corner then jerked to a halt.

Oh, Lord…help me!

Jayce Dalton was unloading on Marlin Murphy. The screams Jayce emitted sent shivers across Shelby's shoulders. Screams of someone who had vanished into rage.

Marlin was taller, heavier, and—Shelby had always thought—the clear winner in a battle between the two. But what she saw in front of her changed her mind.

Jayce was on top of Marlin, his fists working fast and furious. In the heartbeat she stopped and stared, she thought Jayce was going to take the kid. Then Marlin found an opening and landed a punishing blow to Jayce's jaw. He grunted and collapsed like a marionette whose strings had been cut.

A string of obscenities slashed the air as Marlin grasped Jayce's unconscious form, tossing him to the side, surging to his feet with a roar. His breath came in gulps, blood trickled from his bruised face, and when he turned, staring down at Jayce, Shelby knew.

If she didn't act, Jayce would never get up.

Without giving herself time to reconsider, she grabbed a baseball bat from the equipment rack, then raced toward Marlin. "Stop!"

The bruiser looked up, fist poised, and froze. His blazing eyes narrowed as Shelby came to Jayce's side, bat at the ready.

Marlin lowered his fist, his bloodied lips twisting into a sneer. "Hey there, beautiful. Welcome to the party."

His tone skittered over her like spiders in the darkness. She firmed her grip on the bat. "Back off, Marlin."

He spread his hands in front of him. "You got it all wrong, baby. Your boy here started it. All I did was finish it."

"So it's finished." She didn't blink. Didn't flinch. Just kept her gaze pinned to his, ignoring the instincts screaming at her to run—as fast as her feet would carry her. "So take off. You've made your point, whatever it was."

Marlin's gaze roamed from the bat to Shelby herself. His sneer shifted, morphed into something uglier. More threatening.

More frightening.

"I haven't even *started* to make my point."

"Well, that's too bad. Because you're done."

Both Shelby and Marlin jumped, turning to look at the source of the firm command. Dan Justice stood there, hand resting on his sidearm, glare firmly fixed on Marlin. He looked all business. Totally serious.

And utterly, knee-weakeningly wonderful.

"Dan..." She breathed his name out on a sigh that held equal parts relief and joy.

He smiled, but his gaze stayed glued to Marlin as he approached. "I believe the lady told you to leave, Murphy. So unless you want to be charged with trespassing—"

"Hey, no problem." Marlin nudged the unmoving Jayce with his foot. "I'm done here anyway." Those cold eyes came back to Shelby. "For now."

With that he walked toward Dan. Shelby bit her lip when she realized the bully's intention—to make Dan step aside. But if he thought the deputy would give way, he was sadly mistaken.

Marlin paused in front of Dan, their gazes locked in a silent wrestling match of wills, until, with a muttered curse, Marlin sidestepped the granite that was Dan Justice and stalked off the basketball court, through the fence, and across the street.

Shelby knelt at Jayce's side, then looked up when she felt a tug. Dan had hold of the bat and was pulling it with gentle pressure.

"Don't think you need this now."

She managed a smile—though she couldn't keep it from trembling. "Thank God." She put her hand over his where it rested on the end of the bat, squeezed it, then let go. "I've never been so glad to see someone in my life, Dan. How'd you know?"

He knelt on the other side of Jayce. "One of your kids called me. Said something was going on out here, and it wasn't good." He looked down at Jayce. "I'd say that was an understateme—"

"Aahh!"

The scream sent Shelby and Dan pulling back as Jayce exploded to life. He jerked into a sitting position, fists ready, shaking his head, as if to clear it from the remnants of the fog that had held him unconscious all this time.

"It's okay, Jayce."

At Dan's voice—a voice so calm and confident that she felt herself relax—Jayce relaxed, too, let his hands lower.

"Mar—" He grimaced. "Mar…lin?" The word came out slow. No wonder. From the looks of the bruises already forming on his jaw, talking was not going to be Jayce's favorite pastime for a while.

She laid a hand on his shoulder. "Marlin's gone."

Jayce sagged back to the ground. "Good." He closed his eyes, forced his wounded lips into a slight smile. "Didn't…want to haf…t' teach him…'noth'r less'n."

Dan's gaze met Shelby's, and they smiled. He slid a supporting arm under Jayce. "C'mon, Rocky, let's get you inside."

Jayce snorted, then groaned as if the action cost him. "Rocky's…a wuss."

But for all his bravado, he didn't argue when Dan lifted him to his feet and supported him as they walked back toward the center.

Shelby followed, tears and laughter playing an internal tug-of-war with her heart. But one emotion stood out as clear as any she'd ever felt.

Gratitude. That God had been watching. And that He'd sent a protecting angel.

In the form of Deputy Dan Justice.

THIRTEEN

> *"We can do no great things,*
> *only small things with great love."*
> MOTHER TERESA

> *"Ears to hear and eyes to see—*
> *both are gifts from the LORD."*
> PROVERBS 20:12

JAYCE DALTON WAS A TROUBLEMAKER.

Oh, not on purpose. In fact, Dan figured the boy didn't even know the trouble he was causing Dan at home. And if he was really honest, it wasn't Jayce causing him trouble.

It was Dan himself.

When he'd first told Shannon and Aaron he was going to start doing volunteer work with Master's Touch, they asked him why. He sat them down and told them the story they'd heard over and over, but one he knew they loved. About his mom and how she'd chosen his name with such care and prayer.

"Avidan, right, Daddy? That means *justice*."

"That's right, Shannon. Your grandmother and grandfather raised me and your aunts to live up to our names, to let God show Himself through our words and actions. And one way they did that was by encouraging us to get out and help others."

"That's why you and mom used to work with underprivileged kids when we lived in the valley."

Dan nodded to Aaron. "Right."

"But you quit when Mom died."

He leaned forward, taking Shannon's hand. "I did. When your mom died, I needed some time just to be with you two. And by myself."

"You needed to let your heart heal, huh, Daddy?"

Before he could answer his daughter's insightful question, Aaron perched on the arm of the couch. "Is your heart healed now, Dad?"

The husky tone in the boy's voice almost undid Dan's composure. "Not entirely, son."

Aaron looked away. "Mine either."

Shannon slid onto Dan's knee, snuggling against him. "Mine still hurts when I think of her. I miss her, Daddy. Lots."

He held his daughter close. "I know, guys. It's hard. And I don't think the hurt will ever completely go away. But I also think one way we help it to heal more is to listen when God calls us to help others who are hurting, too. Maybe even more than we are."

Shannon considered that. "Like who?"

"Well—" Dan leaned back in his chair—"there's a boy at Miss Wilson's organization, Master's Touch. His mom abandoned him when he was just a baby, and his dad's in prison for stealing things. He lives with his grandmother, but he's been having a hard time. And Miss Wilson thinks I can help him."

Of course, Shannon's tender heart was won right away. So much so that when Dan came to her room for prayers and tuck-in time every evening, Jayce was on her prayer list.

Aaron was less enthusiastic.

When Dan came into his room that first night after telling them about Jayce, Aaron lay in bed, hands folded on his quilt—a queen-size quilt Sarah made for him when he started school—staring at the ceiling.

Dan sat on the edge of the bed. "Something bothering you?"

Aaron didn't answer right away. Dan waited, giving the boy time. Finally, Aaron pushed himself to a sitting position, but he still didn't look at Dan. Just stared down at the quilt, fingering the tiny stitches.

"This must have taken her a long time."

Dan looked down at the patches, each one stitched with a Scripture reference, verses Sarah chose just for Aaron. He knew almost all of them by heart. "Yes." Dan traced *Proverbs 5:1*.

"'My son, pay attention to my wisdom, listen well to my words of insight.'"

His son's words were so full of sorrow, of longing, that Dan almost couldn't stand it. He forced down a swallow, touching another square: *Psalm 28:7.*

Aaron didn't hesitate. "'The LORD is my strength and my shield.'"

Dan's finger touched the square closest to his son's hands. The one Sarah had placed at the top, where Aaron would hold on to the quilt as he pulled it over him. *Proverbs 10:1.*

"'A wise son—'" Aaron halted, then after a moment he went on. "'A wise son brings joy to his father.'"

"And to his mother. You were, you know. A real joy to her."

Aaron nodded. If he'd been a little younger, Dan was sure he would have let his sorrow flow. But Aaron was at that awkward place. Too old to act like a child; too young to take on the role of an adult.

"I miss her." Though the admission was soft, it held volumes of pain.

"Me, too. I miss her every day."

"I wish…I wish she was here. I wish she didn't have to die."

Dan wanted to be strong for Aaron. To be the kind of man he knew Aaron was becoming. A man who took the good and bad of life, standing tall on the sure knowledge of God's presence. His truth.

Instead, he felt weak. And lost.

"I'm sorry, Aaron. I'm so sorry." *I'm sorry I couldn't save her.*

Dan wasn't sure how long they sat there, engulfed in the heavy silence of shared pain. But after a while Aaron slid back down under the quilt.

"You think you'll be able to sleep?"

Aaron pulled a hand out from the quilt and held it out to his dad. "After we pray."

Dan took his son's hand in his, and they bowed their heads. "God, this is really hard. Harder than anything we've ever done. So we just ask You to be with us. To help us. Amen."

"Amen." Aaron let go of his hand and lay back against the pillows.

Dan squeezed Aaron's shoulder, then kissed his son's forehead. "Good night, son."

"Dad?"

Dan paused.

"Do you have to do the thing with that kid?"

For a moment, Dan didn't follow. "You mean Jayce?"

Aaron rolled onto his side. "Yeah. Jayce."

"No, I don't have to. Why?"

"I dunno." Aaron yawned. "I just...I like it better when you spend time with us than with someone else."

Dan didn't argue with Aaron. Didn't point out that Aaron had a father and Jayce didn't. That Aaron got to see him every day, and Jayce would only see him once a week at the most.

No, he learned a long time ago to let the boy work through things for himself.

"Well, I've already told him I'll see him for a little while this weekend. I don't think it would be fair to back out, do you?"

"I s'pose not."

"Tell you what, how about if you think about it? Pray about it? And we can talk it over when you're ready. Okay?"

Aaron's eyes drifted shut. "Okay, Daddy..."

Daddy. Usually, Aaron was too busy being a teenager to call him that. Dan smiled, touching his now-sleeping son's cheek.

Nice to know the little boy was still there, inside the teen.

The next day, Shannon came up with the answer to Aaron's objection without even knowing it. She asked Dan for a picture of Jayce.

So a few days later, when he met with the boy, Dan asked Jayce if he could take some shots of him for his daughter.

"What, she doesn't have enough posters of movie stars for her walls?"

Dan snorted. "Nah, she's just fond of stray animals, that's all."

"Ha ha."

"Seriously, she wanted a picture of you because…" He wasn't quite sure what Jayce would think of this next part.

"Because?"

Well, here goes nothing. "Because she prays for you every night."

Jayce stared at him, disbelief etched in his young features. "She what?"

"Prays for you. Every night."

Confusion creased the edges of his eyes. "She doesn't even know me."

"Doesn't matter. She's heard me talk about you, and she's decided she likes you. So she's praying for you."

Dan had seen Jayce silent before but never speechless. The boy opened his mouth, closed it, opened it again, then just shook his head. Dan held the camera up, eyebrows raised, and Jayce shrugged.

"Go for it."

So Dan did. When he printed out the pictures, he left them on the kitchen table with a note for Shannon to take a look and pick one out. He came into the kitchen a little later and found not Shannon but Aaron sitting there, the pictures spread out in front of him.

"This is Jayce?"

"This is Jayce." He looked over his son's shoulder at the shots. Jayce was photogenic, no denying that. If he could just get the kid to smile.

Aaron picked up one of the pictures, studying it, then laid it back down. He pushed his chair back and looked up at his dad. "I thought he was my age."

"He's close. You'll be fifteen in a week or so. Jayce will be fourteen next July. So you're about nine months older than he is."

Lines puckered Aaron's forehead, as though his thoughts were especially weighty. "He looks…old. Sad."

Dan's heart warmed at the concern on his son's face. "He is, Aaron. His spirit is old and worn out because of all he's been through. And his heart is sad. He tries not to let it show, of course—"

"But you can see it. In his face. His eyes."

Dan looked at the pictures. "Yes, you can."

Aaron stood and started out of the kitchen then hesitated. He turned back to Dan. "I'm glad you're spending time with him."

His heart swelled with pride in his son. "You sure?"

"Yeah. I mean, I've been thinking about it. If it's hard not having you around once in a while, it's gotta be the pits not having a dad around at all." He went to pull the fridge open, and his voice came to Dan from behind the door. "So I think you should do it." He shut the door, as though to add emphasis to his words, and popped open the soda he'd found. "Okay?"

"More than okay. Thanks, Aaron."

He lifted the can. "You bet, Dad."

That night, Aaron joined Shannon in her prayers for Jayce. And from that time on, they lifted the boy to heaven every night, asking God to love him and take care of him. During the past eight months, they asked more questions about Jayce.

One question in particular, though, kept showing up as Dan worked with Jayce. It was this question that led Dan to the conclusion that, even when he didn't know it, young Mr. Dalton caused trouble.

"When do we get to meet Jayce?"

Dan wasn't sure why he was so hesitant to bring Jayce and his kids together—it made sense; they'd all get along—but something held him back. Some desire to keep his personal life separate from everything else. To protect it.

Protect them.

If Jayce didn't know Shannon and Aaron, then Marlin Murphy didn't know them, either. But if Jayce started spending time with Dan's kids…

Just the thought of that jerk even looking at his children made Dan's jaw tense.

He figured the intensity of his feelings had something to do with losing Sarah, but he didn't really understand it. And until he did, he couldn't give in to the kids' request.

A few days ago, Shannon had been looking at the calendar in the kitchen where Dan wrote down all their activities. The calendar had come with a bunch of stickers to mark special occasions, and she loved to go through and look at the stickers. She frowned when she spotted a birthday cake sticker on an upcoming Saturday.

"Dad? Whose birthday is this?"

He looked where she was pointing. July 17. "Oh, that's Jayce's birthday."

"It is?" She clapped her hands, eyes sparkling. "That's so great!"

Dan mussed her hair. "I'm glad you're so excited for him. Too bad we won't be here." He went back to finish pulling the dishes from the dishwasher. "That's the week we're going camping up by Diamond Lake."

"I know! It's perfect!"

Aaron just entered the kitchen. "What's perfect?"

Shannon poked her finger on the calendar. "*This* is! It's Jayce's birthday. And *this* is the perfect birthday present for him."

Dan knew where this was going and tried to stop it, but he wasn't fast enough. Aaron caught his sister's vision.

"You mean take him camping with us? Cool!"

From that moment the two of them were at Dan, pleading. And he resisted. This was *family* time, just the three of them. Yes, he liked Jayce. A lot. But take him with them? Dan didn't even know if Jayce's grandmother would agree.

Of course, he didn't know she wouldn't, either.

Then just this morning, Shannon went into turbo-plead. She knew they only had a few days before they left, so she followed Dan around the house, eyes and tone equally imploring. "*Please*, Daddy."

It wasn't easy to resist those big brown eyes looking up at him with just the faintest shimmer of tears. But he forced himself to be strong.

"Daaaaddy…"

"Shannon, that's enough. I said no, and I meant it." For a moment he thought she'd given up, but he should have known better. Shannon was like her mother: tenacious.

"He doesn't have anybody else."

"He has his grandmother."

"To take him camping?"

Score one for the imp.

"Come on, Daddy. You keep saying how you like spending time with Jayce."

"Yes, but—"

"And how he needs to learn what a loving family is like."

"I know, but—"

"So won't he get both if he goes camping with us?"

Dan eyed his youngest child. "Shannon, this is *family* time."

Her smile bloomed. "And if Jayce comes with us and learns about Jesus, *he'll* be family, too, right? Don't you want that?"

His daughter's question rolled around in his mind, a pinball of guilt bouncing from one objection to another. *Did* he want Jayce to be a part of their spiritual family?

The answer surprised him. No, he didn't.

Okay, why not?

That answer wasn't so surprising. It clawed at him every day, crawling through his gut, reaching bony fingers up into his chest and squeezing.

Fear.

Okay again. Of what?

Of letting someone else in, because…because…

He closed his eyes. Because caring meant taking the chance that one terrible day, you just might lose the person. And he'd had his fill of loss. More than his fill.

More than twenty people's fill.

Do not be afraid.

How could he avoid it?

I will protect you.

Dan longed to believe that, to rest in it. But it was so hard, especially when he kept seeing Sarah's white face, feeling her still chest beneath his fingers…

I am with you.

Dan swallowed. *I know, Lord. I know. But what if—?*

I am with you.

Dan drew in a slow breath. It was true. More than that, it was enough. And it was time to start acting as though he really believed it.

"Daddy?"

He opened his eyes and saw the concern on Shannon's sweet face. He gathered her in his arms. "It's okay, honey."

Her arms slid around his waist. "I didn't mean to upset you."

"You didn't. You just helped me understand something that's been bothering me."

"I did?"

"You did. What was that question you've been asking me all day?"

"Daaaddy!"

"What was it?"

She looked to the ceiling, then with a heavy sigh repeated, "Can Jayce please go camping with us?"

"Okay."

Shannon pulled back as though to see him more clearly, to make sure she'd heard what she thought she had. "Okay?"

Dan stroked her soft cheek. "Okay, Jayce can go camping with us."

With a squeal that would do Flipper proud, Shannon threw her arms around Dan's neck. "Thank you, Daddy! You won't be sorry!"

If only he could be as certain of that as she was.

FOURTEEN

> *"Take the first step in faith.*
> *You don't have to see the whole staircase,*
> *just take the first step."*
> DR. MARTIN LUTHER KING JR.

> *"You will show me the way of life,*
> *granting me the joy of your presence"*
> PSALM 16:11

TENT PEGS WERE NO HELP AT ALL WHEN ONE WANTED to take a picture.

Dan stood in the woods, pegs in one hand, digital camera in the other. Oh, sure, he could take the shot with one hand. But his one-handed shots were getting more and more blurry lately.

He slid the offending pegs into his back jeans pocket, then snapped pictures of Aaron and Jayce laughing together as they helped Shannon set up her tent. Why had he been so worried?

The two boys hit it off the minute they met. Though their life experiences couldn't have been more different, they were teenagers. They spoke the same language: fluent sarcasm.

Shannon, now, that was a different story. One look at her and Jayce stared at his feet, red seeping into his features. Of course, that made perfect sense to Dan. Sure, most girls his

daughter's age were pretty. But Shannon? Well, she had an indefinable sort of beauty. Dan thought it was her smile.

Sarah said it was her spirit.

Either way, people always said she looked like an angel.

What amazed Dan, though, was that she acted like one so
often. Sure, she had her moments. What kid didn't? But when
it really mattered—as it did in that awkward moment with
Jayce—Shannon simply shone. Before Dan had a chance to
think of a way to ease Jayce's discomfort, Shannon walked up
and threw her arms around him, hugging the stuffing out of
him.

Dan waited for Jayce to jerk free. He still remembered
Jayce's reaction when he touched the kid's shoulder at the center. But the boy stood there, enduring the hug for a full beat
before he eased free, his face beet red.

His face split with a broad grin.

The kids' nonstop chatter punctuated the drive up the
mountain. Shannon rode in the front seat with Dan, the two
boys in the back. But Dan hardly saw his daughter's face the
entire hour's drive. She turned as far around as her seat belt
would allow, joining her brother in firing question after question at Jayce about his likes and dislikes, his life. They weren't
intrusive, just eager to get to know him. And much to Dan's
amazement, Jayce was equally eager to share.

By the time they reached their lakeshore campsite at
Broken Arrow, the kids seemed fast friends.

Their first task had been putting the canoe in the lake and
securing it with a chain and padlock so no one could mistake it
for a rental. Then it was back to the campsite to set everything
up. Dan told the kids they could take the canoe out as soon as
camp was ready, then he sat back and watched his two fly into
action, snagging Jayce in their current. Aaron and Shannon
never stopped talking.

"Remember the time we…?"

"Oh, yeah! And how about that time Mom…"

"That was so great!"

On and on they went. Dan listened, laughter mixing with tears as they regaled Jayce with family history. It was so good—and so hard—to hear them talk about their mother this way.

"Is it hard to do?" Jayce looked at Aaron from where he was pounding tent stakes into the ground. "You know, drive a canoe?"

Dan was proud of the fact that Aaron didn't laugh at Jayce's question. "Nah. You'll be steering like a pro in no time."

"We can even take the fishing gear with us." Shannon was so excited she was talking almost double time. "Right, Dad?"

"Don't see why not. As long as you're careful."

Dan finished setting up his tent, then went to where he'd laid out the fishing gear. He double-checked the kids' tackle box then picked up the new rod he'd bought just the day before. It was a beauty—a Penn trolling rod combo. Dan fingered the slick graphite frame. So it was a bit pricey. It was for a good cause.

He turned and carried the rod toward the kids, who were just finishing up with their tents. "All set?"

"You bet!" Aaron's gaze rested on the rod, and excitement sparkled in his blue eyes. He and Shannon had gone with Dan to the sporting goods store, but it was Aaron who lifted the rod and handed it to Dan. "This one."

Eyeing the price tag, Dan drew a breath. "You sure?"

"Absolutely. It's the one I'd want."

"Ohh!" Shannon practically danced beside them. "I can't wait! He's gonna love it!"

Dan had no doubt she was right. He caught his children's attention, and they looked from the rod to him then exchanged smiles.

Dan held the rod out to Jayce. "Happy birthday, Jayce."

The boy went still. His gaze traveled from the rod, to Aaron's and Shannon's smiling faces, then up to Dan. "This…this is for me?" He frowned. "Why?"

Dan had expected the shock he heard in Jayce's voice. But he was stunned at the emotions battling in the boy's features: suspicion, resistance, pride…and a stark longing that ripped at Dan's heart.

It just wasn't right for a kid to be so beat down he couldn't even believe someone would give him a birthday gift.

Lord, help me get through—

He glanced at Aaron and Shannon, standing just behind Jayce, and saw the mixture of excitement and apprehension on their faces. They were as invested in this as Dan.

No, Lord, help us *get through to Jayce.*

Without thinking, he put his hand on the boy's shoulder. Jayce tensed beneath his touch but didn't pull back. Dan was grateful for the change. "Because it's your birthday, Jayce, and because we wanted to."

Shannon slipped her arm around her dad's waist. "We picked it out, just for you. It's a great pole."

"*Rod,* dummy." Aaron was at Jayce's side, nudging him with an elbow. "She tries, but she's a girl, you know?"

Shannon stuck her tongue out at her brother, and Dan thought he saw the hint of a smile tug at Jayce's mouth.

Aaron took the rod from Dan and held it out for Jayce to inspect. "This thing is übersweet, man. And check out the reel. It's got a heavy-duty line clicker."

Jayce eyed Aaron. "Clicker?"

He threw an arm around Jayce's shoulders, shaking his head. "Man…we got a lot to teach you." Aaron handed the rod to Jayce. "So we'd better get started, huh?"

Jayce hesitated, then his hands closed over the rod and he gave a slow nod. "Yeah." His sigh was part surrender, part delight. "Yeah, let's get started."

Within a half hour they were down at the lakefront. Dan ran through the dos and don'ts of canoeing, then watched the three of them settle into the canoe—Aaron in the stern, Jayce in the bow, and Shannon in the middle.

Dan relaxed into the lawn chair he'd set up on the shore, propped his feet up on the cooler, and flipped open the novel he'd brought along—a supernatural thriller about a submarine that went missing in WWII and suddenly showed up fifty years later. "You guys make sure you stay in my sight, okay? And life jackets go on the bodies, not under the seats."

Aaron gave him a thumbs-up as they paddled away. Dan kept looking up from time to time, but it seemed everything was going great. The kids were tossing their lines into the water, and their laughter drifted to him, a beautiful sound on the warm summer breeze.

Only one thing would have made it all perfect. But that one thing was gone. Forever.

Suddenly the words on the page in front of him blurred. Dan closed the book, leaning back and turning his face to the sky. *God, will the hurting ever stop? The piercing loss when I hear the kids laugh—but not Sarah?* He rubbed a hand over his eyes. *Sarah, I miss you so much…*

A yelp jerked his eyes open, and he looked at the canoe just in time to see Jayce jerking on his pole.

"I got one! I *got* one!"

Dan jumped up, almost as excited as Jayce sounded. "Keep tension on the line, son!"

Aaron waved at Dan to show they'd heard, and Dan could hear him guiding Jayce as the fish went first one way then the other.

"Watch it!" Aaron leaned forward. "He's heading under the canoe."

Shannon joined in. "Don't let your line go slack. You'll lose him!"

"Whoa! I think I got a whale here!" Jayce jumped up from his seat, and though Dan couldn't see his kids' faces, he heard the alarm in their voices.

"No!"

"Sit down!"

Too late. Jayce threw his weight to the side, trying to keep tension on the line. The canoe tipped one way, then the other—and over it went.

A chorus of cries split the air as the kids flew into the lake. Dan ran out into the water, ready to plunge in to save whomever needed saving, but the oddest sound stopped him.

Laughter. Hilarious, sputtering laughter.

All three of the kids popped up next to the capsized canoe. Aaron and Shannon splashed at each other. Dan surveyed the situation, making sure everyone was okay—and his eyes widened.

Jayce's flotation vest kept him afloat, which was a good thing. Because he held both his hands high. In one, he clutched his rod.

In the other he held a squirming fish.

"Oh, *man*!" Aaron swam over to Jayce. "How'd you *do* that?"

"I have no idea!" At Jayce's stunned words, all three exploded into laughter.

"Aaron!"

He turned at his dad's voice, looking back at the shore.

"Can you and Shannon right the canoe?"

"Sure!"

Dan hoped his son's confidence was deserved. Happily, it was. "Well, hon," Dan spoke to the silence around him, "looks like the training we gave them actually paid off." Dan couldn't be sure, but he thought he felt a gentle touch on his cheek. It was just the breeze, of course, but it made him smile all the same.

Within minutes the canoe was upright, drained as best it could be, and Aaron and Shannon were back in. They took Jayce's rod and the fish, then helped him back in the canoe, balancing carefully as he came over the side.

When they reached shore, a beaming Jayce stepped out, dripping wet, and held up his still-wriggling trout for Dan's inspection.

"It's a beauty, all right." He slid his arm around Jayce's shoulders. "Now follow me, and I'll show you the best part of all."

Jayce's eyes lit up. "What's that?"

Dan grinned. "Cleaning your catch."

That night they feasted on freshly caught fish—courtesy of both Jayce and Aaron, who'd proven themselves master anglers—cooked over a campfire. Shannon took a bite of the fish Jayce caught and sighed. "Your fish tastes best of all, Jayce."

Pleasure lit the boy's face with a warmth Dan had never seen before. Any doubts he still held about bringing Jayce on this trip vanished like the smoke rising into the sky from their fire.

By the time they'd taken care of cleanup, the sun was kissing the tips of the mountains around them. As the shadows lengthened, Dan went to his tent and pulled a worn cloth-bound book from his duffel. He held the book in his hands, eyes skimming the title. *The Lion, The Witch and the Wardrobe.*

So much of their lives had been turned upside down, but he and the kids managed to hold on to their nightly story time. As they sat together, the kids snuggled up in the crook of his arms, reading those familiar stories seemed to soothe the kids' grieving spirits.

And Dan's, too.

As he read, Dan could swear he felt Sarah beside him, could hear her voice reading along with him, could even see her shed a tear when Aslan lay down on the great table, ready to die.

And in those dark, pain-filled days just after Sarah's funeral, when Dan read the part about Aslan rising again, about him running and leaping in the utter ecstacy of new life, Dan felt the promise deep within. Sarah's story wasn't over. It was only interrupted.

Eternity was waiting. They would be together again.

Dan and the kids had just started *Prince Caspian,* the fourth Chronicles of Narnia book, the weekend before this trip. No matter how many times they went through the series, they never tired of them. How could they? These books—and the characters held within—were the dearest of old friends.

Even so, Dan had decided against taking the books on the camping trip. Sure, they loved the story, but Jayce? What would a kid from Jayce's background think of these fantastical stories? About a magical wardrobe and a lion that spoke?

Dan shook his head. He could just imagine Jayce's reaction, and the last thing he wanted was for the boy to hurt Shannon's, and even Aaron's, feelings. No, this trip had enough potential emotional land mines already. No point in taking chances that weren't necessary.

Of course, just because *his* mind had been made up didn't mean the issue was settled. Which he found out as he packed his duffel bag for the camping trip. Aaron, who was sitting on his bed watching Dan, put a hand on his arm as he was about to zip the bag shut.

"Hang on, Dad."

"What?"

"You forgot something." He hopped off the bed and ran from the room. When he returned, Shannon was with him. She held a book out to Dan. *The Lion, the Witch and the Wardrobe.*

Trepidation tripped up his chest, drawing it tight. "We read this one already."

Aaron didn't hesitate. "I know, but this is the one we need to read on the trip."

"I thought we'd leave the book home. I don't want it to get damage—"

"Dad, you *have* to take it!"

Okay. He'd expected Shannon to object. But this vehement comment from Aaron stunned him. "Why?"

Shannon looked at Aaron, and he nodded. "Go ahead. Tell him."

"Well, Aaron and I talked about it, and we both have a feeling."

"A feeling?"

"A really, really, *really* strong feeling."

"Really strong," Aaron echoed, and Dan fought back a chuckle.

"Okay, a feeling about what?"

"That we need to read on the trip. And it needs to be this book. For Jayce."

"For…" Dan took the novel from Shannon, holding it in his hands, letting his fingers trail over the embossed title. *Just ask the question.* "But guys, what makes you think Jayce will like these stories? What if he thinks they're stupid?" He looked from one of his children to the other. "How will you react if he makes fun of them?"

Shannon's response was the last thing Dan expected. She reached up and patted his hand, like a mother patting away a somewhat slow child's objections. "You're so silly, Daddy. Jayce will love them. God told me so. Besides—" she took the book from him and gave it to Aaron, who placed it in Dan's duffel bag—"he needs to know."

"To know what?"

Aaron answered him. "About Aslan."

Dan had just stood there, mute. When did these two grow from childish thinking to spiritual maturity—and how on earth did he miss it?

"Move, frog breath!"

"You move! I was here *first!*"

Thus jolted from his reminiscence, Dan turned to find his "spiritually mature" offspring wrestling for the best position around the campfire.

So maybe they weren't quite finished with childish thinking, after all.

He was ready to tell the two of them to knock it off, when Jayce stepped between them and sat on the contested log.

Aaron and Shannon both turned to gawk at him. He crossed his arms and stretched his legs out in front of him. "See what happens when you waste your time fighting? You both lose."

Dan restrained a smile as red bloomed on Aaron's cheeks. For a moment he thought the two boys were about to have their first fight, then Aaron exhaled and a rueful smile slid across his features. "So what you're saying is, a log's a log. Shut up and sit down?"

Jayce nodded. "See there? You're a lot smarter than you look." He reached out to smack Aaron's arm. "Have a seat, dude." He glanced at Shannon and patted the log on his other side. "You, too, squirt."

Dan's brows arched at the tinge of red coloring Shannon's cheeks. Concern slithered through his chest as he made his way back to the fire. Jayce was a good enough kid in the right setting, but he still had a lot of problems. Dan would rather not have his little girl forming a crush on a kid with so much to overcome.

He joined the kids near the fire and lowered himself onto one of the logs. "You guys ready to read?"

"Absolutely!"

"Read what?" Jayce's response wasn't anywhere near as positive as Aaron's.

Aaron didn't hesitate. "The best story you've ever heard, that's what."

Shannon, who'd been hovering, finally settled on the ground between the two boys, leaning against her brother's leg. "You'll like it, Jayce."

Thus reassured, Jayce looked up at Dan and shrugged. "Go for it."

Dan opened the book. *Here goes, Lord.*

Dan started reading. "Once there were four children…" At first Dan glanced up every few words, trying to gauge Jayce's reaction. But soon the story wove around him, and he was too engrossed to remember to worry. As they followed the children's journey through the wardrobe, Dan was only vaguely aware of the dying daylight around them. It didn't matter, though. The kids kept feeding fuel to the crackling fire, so it gave off plenty of light for reading.

Not until Dan's voice began to crack did he stop reading. And the moment he did so, all three of his listeners erupted.

"Hey!"

"Daddy!"

"Aw, c'mon, Mr. Justice. You *can't* stop there!"

Dan held up his hands, laughing. "Have mercy, you guys. My voice is about shot."

"Man!"

There was no missing the disappointment in Jayce's tone. Dan closed the book with gentle firmness. He should have known Shannon would be right. She usually was when it came to reading people. When he looked up from the book, he found her smiling at him, a little gleam in her twinkling eyes. She didn't need to speak a word for him to get the message.

See? Told you so.

"Okay, you three, let's put the fire out and get some sack time. Tomorrow's another day, and—"

"We need a good night's sleep to do it justice," his offspring chorused.

Jayce looked from them to Dan then back again. He stood and grabbed the pail of water to douse the fire. "And people think *I'm* crazy."

"Nah—" Aaron stirred the soggy ashes with a stick—"they think you're trouble." His grin was just visible in the moonlight. "Goes to show how much they know, huh?"

Jayce's relaxed chuckle was music to Dan's ears. He watched the kids amble off to their respective tents, soaking in the sound of their happy chatter.

He never would have imaged things would go so well. Aaron's words echoed in his head: *"Goes to show how much they know, huh?"*

Dan stood, tucked the book under his arm, and looked up at the star-studded night. "And I guess it goes to show how much I know, too." Good thing he had the kids. And good thing they'd inherited their mother's inner eyes, that looked deep into the heart and saw people the way God did.

With faith.

With truth.

And, most important, with love.

Dan unzipped his tent and cast a final glance up at the sky. "Help me see with eyes like that, God. With eyes like Yours."

As he stepped into the tent, his whispered prayer eased into the night, caught the dancing breeze, and rode it to the heavens.

Shannon pulled her sleeping bag higher over her shoulder, burrowing down inside its warmth. She'd opened one of the tent's window flaps so she could see the night sky.

It was beautiful.

Mom always used to talk about what an artist God was. And she was right. No one but an artist could have created a sky like that, with so many stars twinkling that it looked like God had spilled silver glitter across the heavens.

She turned her head toward the boys' tent, listening, but all she heard was the sounds of the night. Was Jayce looking up at the sky, too? Had he ever seen a sky like this before?

Shannon doubted it. From what he'd said on the drive up, he spent most of his time in town. And most of that he was inside. "Easier to stay out of trouble when you stay in your room all the time." The sound in his voice when he told her that made her heart really, really sad.

But then, lots of things about Jayce made her sad. The way his mom left him. That his dad was in prison and Jayce never got to see him. And then there was that side of Jayce—that quiet, almost scary side. She'd only seen it for a second, when

Aaron asked him about his friends. Then Jayce changed the subject. Fast. Aaron didn't even seem to notice.

But she did.

She saw a lot of things others didn't see. Especially with Jayce. It was funny, but from the minute she met him, Shannon kind of felt like he…belonged to her. Like she was responsible for him. She didn't know why, exactly, but that was okay. Jayce needed someone to feel this way about him. Someone to care about him, to pray for him.

To love him like a mother would. Like his mother should have.

Lying there, with God's stars shining down on her, Shannon knew she was right. Deep down inside, she just knew. God brought Jayce to her. And she would do her best to help him see how really special he was.

But how?

Her fingers went to the pendant hanging around her neck, and she fingered the fine detail of the lion's head. As she did so, an idea came to her.

She hesitated, then flipped the sleeping bag back and went to kneel beside the window flap. She spread her palm across the screen, looking up at the night sky.

"Mom?" Shannon gripped the pendant with her other hand, unable to stop the tears from rolling down her face. "Mommy?"

The night breeze stirred the trees, filling the darkness with a soft rush of sound.

Shannon drew her knees to her chest, never taking her eyes from the stars. "I wish you were here, Mommy." She rubbed away the tears stinging her face. "You'd like Jayce so much. You'd make him feel special." She paused, then lifted the pendant from around her neck and held it in her hand. "Like you always made me feel special."

The golden lion's face caught glimmers of moonlight, and Shannon could almost believe it was crying, too. She closed her hand around the pendant and nodded.

"I know what you'd do, Mommy. How you'd show Jayce you loved him, that God loved him." She turned her face to the sky. "So since you can't do it, I will. Is that okay?"

She waited, holding her breath, and though no sound came, she felt the answer deep inside.

Warmth. Peace.

And a firm, loving *yes*.

Shannon crawled back into her sleeping bag. She slipped the pendant under her pillow and lay down.

A yawn took hold of her, and she patted the pillow, smiling. "Night, Mommy. I love you."

FIFTEEN

"A loving heart is the beginning of all knowledge."
THOMAS CARLYLE

"My heart has heard you say, 'Come and talk with me.'
And my heart responds, 'LORD, I am coming.'"
PSALM 27:8

IT WAS SO QUIET HERE.

Jayce liked that. The quiet. The way you could just sit here, lean back against a tree, close your eyes—and feel like you were all alone. No one to hassle you. No one to tell you what you could and couldn't do.

No one to threaten. To show how easy it was to get to an old woman alone. To hurt her.

No one to make you do things you didn't want to do.

He opened his eyes, looking up at the blue, blue sky through the thick branches of the tree. Man, it would be nice to just stay here. Live here.

Free.

Don't kid yourself. One hour out here alone, and you'd be scrambling to get back to town.

No. He wouldn't.

Yeah? And when it rains? Snows? What then? You just sit out here and freeze?

He'd find shelter. He wasn't stupid.

Says who? How smart is giving in? Doing things you say you hate?

Jayce gritted his teeth. *I don't just say I hate them. I do hate them.*

But you're so good at them. Why do you think Marlin keeps coming to you?

Because he wants the rep, but he doesn't want to risk getting caught. He's like those jungle dogs…those jackals. He waits for someone else to make the kill, then he moves in and claims the prize. Jayce pushed back against the tree, felt the rough bark digging into his skin. *He's nuthin' but a coward who won't do his own dirty work.*

A coward? If you're so brave, let's see you say that to his face.

Jayce longed to tell Marlin what he thought of him and his crew. What they could do with their threats against his grandmother. And Shelby. But one thing you didn't do with a scared jackal was back it into a corner.

Not unless you wanted to get torn to shreds.

I know why Marlin comes to you. Because you're born to the work he gives you. A regular chip off the ol' block. You know what they say, like father, like so—

Jayce stood, pushing away from the tree. "I'm not like him!"

Coulda fooled me.

He started walking. The dark voice chuckled, a deep rumble in the pit of Jayce's gut. He clamped his hands over his ears, but it didn't help. The voice was always there. Taunting.

Hateful.

You only hate me because I speak the truth.

"Shut *up*!"

"Jayce?"

He spun around—then stopped cold.

Shannon stood there, eyes wide and hesitant as she watched him.

See? Even she knows who you really are. Look at her. The look on her face. Like prey that's just realized it's too late to run.

Jayce willed the spiteful voice into silence, forced the churning emotions away.

A gentle touch startled him. He looked down at Shannon's hand, resting on his sleeve.

"Are you okay?"

Shock ran through him. The voice was wrong. She wasn't afraid. Not at all. The only thing Jayce saw in her expression was concern.

Caring.

The last of his anger melted in an overwhelming warmth. Looking into this girl's eyes, the resentment that dogged him couldn't hold up.

Instead, what he felt was something it took him a while to recognize.

Peace.

"Yeah, I'm fine." He gave her hand an awkward pat, and her quick smile made him glad he'd done so. Then he looked around. They were in the middle of nowhere. "Hey, what are you doing way out here anyway? Where's Aaron? And your dad?"

"They're back at the camp. I wanted to talk with you."

"How'd you know where I was?"

She bit her lip. "Well, I saw you leave after you got your chores done, and…um…I followed you. I lost you for a little while, then I heard your voice. And that's when I found you again."

He eyed the woods. "Do you know how to get back to camp?"

"Sure!" She turned and started walking. "It's this way."

Relief lightened his step as he fell in beside her. "You like it out here, don't you?"

"I like it a lot. I mean, living in town was okay. There was always lots to do and stuff. But out here…" She stopped, reaching out to break off the tip of a tree branch. She crushed the needles in her fingers then cupped her hands and inhaled. "Smell that." She held her cupped hands out to him.

He let the strong fragrance seep into his lungs.

She started walking again. "It just feels and smells so good out here. You know, fresh and new. Like every day is another chance."

"Another chance for what?"

"Oh, everything!" She lifted her hands, as though to embrace the world. "Life. You know, all of it." She shrugged, and he watched a hint of pink slip into her cheeks. "I don't know. Just for being, I guess."

Did all girls her age think like this? He wasn't sure, but he had the feeling Shannon was different.

Something tugged at him, a kind of longing that dug deep, making him ache until realization hit with the force of a fist.

He wanted to be like that.

Special. Happy. In love with the world and everything around him.

But being that way…that was for kids like Shannon. Kids whose parents loved her like they should. Kids whose parents spent time with her, talked with her, laughed with her.

Kids whose parents didn't land in jail.

He brushed the depressing thought away. "So what'd you want to talk with me about?"

"I have something for you."

"Yeah?" As before, his mood couldn't help but lift when he looked at her. "Did you catch a fish and want me to clean it for you or somethin'?"

She giggled. "No, you goof. Look—" she pointed just beyond them—"there's the camp."

He followed the direction of her finger. Aaron was visible just beyond the trees, sitting near the campfire toasting something.

"Here."

Jayce turned his head, looking down at Shannon's now-outstretched hand. A pendant lay there. He peered close.

"Oh, man…"

A golden lion's head, with amber eyes catching the sunlight and sparkling as though they were real. It was so lifelike Jayce almost expected it to open its mouth and roar.

"It's a pendant. You know, a kind of necklace." She held it up, and he saw that the lion's head was strung on a leather cord. "I got it for my birthday a couple years ago. It's Aslan."

He stretched a finger out to touch it. "Man, that is so cool." He met Shannon's eyes. "It looks just like I pictured him."

Shannon turned it over. "There's something written on the back."

Jayce read the engraving: *Shannon, See life with God's eyes. Love, Mom.*

"It's for you."

He stepped back. Had he heard her right? "I can't take this. Your mom gave it to you."

"And I'm giving it to you. I even took it off the chain and put it on a leather cord, 'cuz I thought that was better for a guy."

"But…why?"

The light in her smile was almost more than he could bear.

"Because you remind me of him."

Now he was *sure* he hadn't heard right. "Of Aslan? I remind you of Aslan?"

Shannon reached out and slid the cord over Jayce's head. "You're just like him." She stepped back, surveying her handiwork. "You're big and strong and wild. And you growl loud and show your teeth. Everyone knows you're not a tame lion. But you're good." Her open hand rested on his chest, just over his heart, and that gentle touch warmed him to the core. "Down inside."

Jayce had to try twice to speak. "You think I'm good?"

"Nope."

What an idiot! He'd almost believed her. He should have known she was just setting him up for someth—

"I don't think so. I *know* it."

It was weird. Jayce had the sense that he was outside himself, watching himself stand there like a dope, staring at Shannon, mouth hanging open. But he couldn't help it. There had to be something, some hint that she was teasing.

Nothing.

Shannon meant every word.

He reached up and closed his fingers around the lion's head, feeling the carving with his thumb.

When Mr. Justice handed him that rod and reel the first day they got here, Jayce thought it was the best gift he'd ever received. He was wrong.

Nothing would ever compare to this.

"Do you like it?"

Jayce let go of the lion's head, but he felt it resting against his chest. "Yeah. I like it a lot." He gave her a gentle nudge with his elbow. "Thanks, squirt."

He let her hug him and didn't even have to work hard at not pulling back.

She skipped away, heading through the trees back to their campsite.

She thought he was good. Like Aslan.

No one had ever said anything like that about him before. But the weird thing was, he believed it. Not just that she meant it, but that she just might be right.

You're kidding yourself. There's nothing good about you, and you know it.

For once, the voice inside didn't bother him all that much. Because he'd made up his mind. If he wasn't good, the way Shannon thought he was, then he'd just do whatever he needed to do to change that.

If Shannon thought he was good, then good he'd be.

Because there was no way in this world he was going to let her down.

Dan moved as silently as possible, slipping behind a large tree so Jayce wouldn't see him.

He hadn't meant to eavesdrop on Shannon's conversation with the boy. He'd just been going out to look for the two of them. He was almost on top of them when he heard them talking. Not wanting to intrude, he stopped—and heard the whole exchange.

Now, Dan watched Jayce walk toward his tent, a battle raging inside him. On the one hand, he was proud of Shannon. More proud than he could say. She'd seen a hurting boy and reached out to show him real, honest love. Maybe even the first love of its kind Jayce had ever experienced.

Oh, Dan believed the boy's grandmother loved him, but she was worn down by the hassles and failures. Shannon didn't have any of those things to weaken her faith in Jayce.

On the other hand, the concerns Dan felt last night at the campfire came storming back to twist his innards. Shannon was at such a crucial age, where feelings got out of control way too fast. He'd seen too many little girls who should be playing with dolls getting involved and in trouble.

That would not happen to his daughter. No way. No how.

Dan tromped back toward the campsite.

Time for a little father-daughter talk.

The opportunity Dan needed came just a few hours later.

They'd all gone down to the river after lunch to get in some swimming and canoeing. After an hour or so of hard play, Aaron and Jayce decided to hike to Silent Creek. An old codger at the South Store had told them there was no place like Silent Creek for catching fish, so they figured they'd land dinner.

That left Dan and Shannon to walk back to the campsite.

She chattered away, all excitement at the fun they'd just had. And then she gave him the perfect opening. With a sigh the size of Texas, she looked up at Dan and said, "Jayce is really a wonderful boy, isn't he, Daddy?"

Dan chose his words like a man whose answer would win or lose him a million dollars. "Yes, honey. Jayce is a great kid. Out here, with us. He's relaxed and having fun, and I'm glad to see that."

Shannon's chestnut head bobbed. "Me, too. Jayce needs to have fun."

"Right. Just like we all do. But—"

The rest of his planned speech jerked to a halt when her soft little hand slid into his. "No, Daddy."

He looked down at those suddenly somber eyes. "No?"

"Not like us. We have fun all the time, you and me and Aaron." Her lips twitched. "Well, you and me. Aaron's just a nit."

This time it was Dan who tugged at her hand.

"I'm kidding, Daddy. But not about Jayce. He needs to have fun in a different way."

"Different how?"

"Because his eyes didn't know how to smile. Or his heart. Because he was sad all the way down, and nothing was making it better. Because part of Jayce is broken."

She looked up at him. "If Mommy were here, she'd help Jayce, too. She'd hug him and help him laugh. And she'd help him see how much God loves him."

Dan cupped his daughter's precious face in his hand. "Yes, she would do all that."

She leaned her cheek into his hand. "But you know what, Daddy?"

"What's that, love?"

"I don't think Jayce knows God." She sounded so grieved for him. "And Mommy's not here to help him. So *I'm* gonna do it."

They started walking again. "Do what, hon?"

She swung their joined hands. "Let him see God in me. You know, like Mommy did. I'm gonna talk to him and like him and love him the way Mommy would."

Dan stared down at his little girl. Did she even realize what a wonder she was? *Sarah, she's so like you...*

A sweet light dawned on her features as she smiled. "I'm letting God show me how to be Jayce's friend and his pray-er."

"His pray-er?"

Shannon skipped beside him. "Sure. The one who prays for him. His pray-er."

"Oh." Dan squeezed her fingers. "I see."

"Anyway, I'm praying for him every day, asking God to touch and love him. 'Cuz he doesn't have anyone else to do it. And 'cuz God gave Jayce to me."

Dan's steps faltered a bit at that. "He what?"

The look she bestowed on him was pure Sarah: impish wisdom.

"Daddy. You don't think Jayce is with us by accident?"

"Well, no, but—"

"God knew he needed someone to love him kind of like a mommy would, right? Like his mommy didn't."

How on earth did she know that? Dan only mentioned the situation with Jayce's mom once, but apparently that was enough. That hard fact of Jayce's life had planted itself in his little girl's tender heart, blooming in compassion and kindness when she finally met the boy.

He stopped, kneeling and pulling Shannon close. "Honey, I'm proud of you for wanting to help Jayce—" his voice roughened, but he kept on—"the way your mommy would have." He leaned back so she could see his face clearly. "But it's not all up to you, you know. You can't make up for what his mom did or didn't do."

She placed her hands on either side of his face and touched her forehead to his. "'Course not! But God can. I'm just letting

Him use me when He wants to." She pulled back, her head tipping to the side. "That's okay, isn't it, Daddy?"

All those nagging concerns faded away and Dan knew Someone else walked the path with them, placing His hand on Dan's shoulder, reassuring him that all was well.

"Yes, it's okay. I wasn't sure at first, but now—" he stood— "it's more than okay. It's right."

Aaron couldn't believe his eyes.

He blinked. Then looked again. He saw what he thought he saw.

Shannon's lion. So how come Jayce was wearing it?

Sudden anger slithered through him. He liked Jayce. A lot. But if he'd stolen that from Shannon...

"Hey, you think it's break time or somethin'? I'm not packin' this tent up by myself—" Jayce's laughing challenge screeched to a halt when he saw Aaron's face. "What's wrong?"

Aaron's gaze dropped to the pendant. "That's my sister's."

Jayce lifted his hand to the lion's head. "Yeah, I know."

Scorching heat coursed through Aaron as his anger turned up a notch. "Did you know our mom gave it to her?"

Jayce started to answer, but Aaron cut him off.

"Just before she died."

The way Jayce's eyes widened, Aaron knew that was a surprise.

Jayce looked down at the lion. "Oh, man..."

Yeah. Aaron gritted his teeth. *Now you know, huh? What a crud you ar—*

"Then I can't take it."

Darn right you can't.

"I don't care what Shannon says, I gotta tell her I can't take it."

What? Aaron's eyes narrowed. "What do you mean, what she says?"

Jayce took the leather cord from around his neck. "She said

she wanted me to have it. Said I reminded her of Aslan." He shook his head. "Can you believe that? I mean, your sister is really somethin' else."

Like a dog that knows it's done wrong, Aaron's anger tucked its tail between its legs and ran yipping for cover. "Yeah. She is."

If the sincerity on Jayce's face hadn't been convincing enough, his words sealed the deal. Aaron knew his sister well. She thought Jayce was just this side of wonderful. And if anyone would give away something she loved to someone she loved, it was Shannon.

"She's somethin' else. And I'm an idiot."

Jayce cocked his head. "You're what?"

"Man, I'm sorry, Jayce. I saw the lion, and I just thought…"

Understanding turned Jayce's eyes hard. "You thought I stole it."

Aaron swallowed, feeling more miserable by the second. Why did he do that? Why did he just jump to conclusions like that? Mom always told him he needed to stop and really think before he decided he knew what was going on.

"You're such a smart boy, Aaron," she had said over and over. "But being smart doesn't always help you understand people. You have to listen with your heart as much as your head."

Too bad he hadn't remembered that a few minutes earlier.

Jayce was turning, ready to walk away, and Aaron grabbed his arm. "Wait."

When Jayce spun back to him, his hand fisted over the lion. Aaron jerked back, then straightened his shoulders and faced his friend.

"Look, I'm a jerk. I should have known you wouldn't do that to Shannon."

Jayce didn't answer, but the tight look on his face said it clearly: *Yeah. You should have.*

"I just…I get a little stupid, sometimes, about things my mom gave us."

Jayce paused. "What do you mean?"

He really didn't want to talk about this, but Aaron figured it was the only way to help Jayce understand. "Like, if mom gave us something, we have to make sure we don't lose it. Or…" He looked away. "I dunno. It's stupid."

"Or you'll feel like you lost part of her?"

Aaron stared at Jayce. "Yeah." Relief flooded that one word, even as understanding flooded his heart. *Okay, Mom. I get it. This is how it feels when someone listens to you with his heart instead of his head.* "So when I saw you wearing the lion, well, I got mad. Like you were trying to take away part of Mom." He kicked at the ground. "Pretty lame, huh?"

The hand that came down on his shoulder was gentle. "Nah. It's not lame. It makes sense. I mean, I never knew my mom, but there's this little blanket, you know, that she bought for me when I was a baby. Just before she left."

Aaron nodded.

"I still have it. I stick it inside my pillowcase, so it's right by me when I sleep." He stared at the ground. "It's kind of like…I don't know…"

"Like she's holding you."

Jayce gave a slow nod. "Yeah. Like that." He let go of Aaron's shoulder. "Anyway, no sweat, man. I understand. I guess it makes sense you'd think I stole it."

"No." Aaron shoved his hands in his pockets. "It didn't make sense at all. You're my friend." Something flickered in Jayce's eyes, but Aaron didn't stop. He wanted Jayce to know. "And I shoulda trusted you."

Jayce didn't say anything for a second, then he gave a small smile. "So, I guess we both jumped to conclusions."

"Cool."

Jayce frowned. "Cool?"

"Yeah." Aaron grinned then knelt to fold the tent. "That means it's over with, and we don't have to do it again."

Jayce stared at him for a heartbeat, then shook his head. "You're as strange as your sister."

"Hey! No need to be insulting."

Jayce laughed.

"And Jayce?"

"Yeah?"

Aaron pointed to the hand still holding the lion's head. "Don't try giving that back to Shannon. If she gave it to you, she really wants you to have it. You'll just hurt her feelings if you give it back."

Jayce looked from Aaron to the pendant.

"I'm not kiddin', man. You don't want to hurt her, do ya?"

The uncertainty faded from Jayce's features. "No." That was it. One word. But as he said it, he slipped the cord back around his neck, then bent to help with the tent.

Strange, though… Aaron couldn't get rid of the weirdest feeling. That Jayce's response wasn't just agreement.

It was a vow.

Dan grabbed the last sleeping bag and tossed it into the back of his SUV.

"We have it all?"

Jayce turned to survey the empty campsite. "Unless you want to take the trees with us."

"Smart aleck."

His only response was a particularly mischievous grin. Then his expression changed. "Hey, I just wanted…you know. To say thanks." He looked around them. "This was good."

Dan smiled. "Yeah, it was."

"And I wanted to let you know, so there aren't any misunderstandings—" he pulled the lion's head pendant out of his shirt—"Shannon gave me this. If you don't want me to have it—"

"Why wouldn't I want you to have it?"

Dan watched the play of emotions on the boy's face.

"I dunno. 'Cuz her mom gave it to her?"

Dan leaned against the vehicle. "And now Shannon gave it to you."

"Yeah."

Dan pushed away and shut the tailgate. "Then she must think very highly of you." Dan angled a look at the boy. "That's a good thing."

"Yeah." Jayce slid the pendant back inside his shirt. "Yeah, it is." He took a deep breath. "I like the way it smells out here. Like trees. It's how my dad's clothes used to smell, back when he worked the trees."

Dan had been about to call for Aaron and Shannon, who'd gone down to the lake for one last look, but he hesitated. This was the first time Jayce had talked about his father. "He was a logger?"

"A choke setter."

Dan lifted a brow. Choke setters fastened steel cables or chains around piled-up felled logs so they could be moved to the landing area. They faced dangers of all kinds, from rolling logs to rough terrain. A family friend, like many in Dan's father's generation, had been a logger. A choke setter. When a machine operator had made a mistake, the cables the friend just set around the logs snapped, and the logs rolled right over him, killing him. "Hazardous job."

"Yeah, but they said Dad was good at it. And the way he talked about it, I could tell. He loved logging, trees."

Jayce's eyes had a faraway look in them. "He lost his job before I was born. But when I was little, he used to take me to the lumberyard with him sometimes, just to show me the different kinds of lumber. Tell me what trees they were from. Like he was teaching me how to be a logger someday. Like he believed the industry would bounce back."

The boy's lips lifted in a small smile. "I was pretty young, but I felt…I don't know, good. Like when we were there in the yard, my dad and I were close. Connected."

He blinked. "'Course, the lumber industry took another

dive, and they finally closed the yard down." An indefinable emotion darkened his features as he looked down at the ground. "I keep hoping someday it'll be used again. Not like now."

Dan reached out to squeeze the boy's drooping shoulder. "Must be depressing to see the place deserted."

Jayce looked up, and Dan saw the sorrow there.

"I'm sorry, Jayce."

He shrugged. "You didn't close it down."

"No, I mean I'm sorry...about your dad. That you don't get to see him."

Another shrug, this one more curt. "That's the way life is, you know?"

"But it shouldn't be." Dan held the boy's gaze. "You deserve better."

The snort told Dan Jayce didn't buy that for a minute. "Yeah, like a kid with a dad in prison deserves anything—"

"Your value lies in who *you* are, Jayce. Not in who your dad is."

Dan could see, in the haunted look in the boy's eyes, that his words struck a chord.

"Haven't you heard, Mr. Justice? Everyone says I'm my father's son." He looked away. "Even Gram."

"No."

Jayce turned back, his brow wrinkled.

"You're your own person, Jayce. You make your own decisions about how you live your life. You can take the same path your father did, or you can choose another way. A better way."

Suspicion glinted in those blue eyes. "You talkin' about God?"

Dan laughed. "I'm talking about doing what's right. And yes, God makes that a lot easier. He wrote the Book on right and wrong, you know."

Humor wrestled with doubt on Jayce's features, until a smile finally emerged. "Yeah, I think I did hear that somewhere before."

"So are we going home, or what?"

Dan and Jayce turned to see Aaron and Shannon coming through the now-empty campsite. Dan smiled. "We are going home. Okay, you monsters—" he let the teasing affection in his tone encompass all three of them—"pile in."

"Shotgun!" Aaron ran to pull open the front passenger door. Dan wasn't the least surprised when Shannon didn't protest. As much as she loved riding shotgun, she was content this trip to sit in the back. With Jayce.

The kids got in the car, shoving and nudging each other, filling the air with their teasing laughter. Dan lagged behind, soaking in the sight and sound of their happiness.

How could a week just disappear in a heartbeat? It seemed they'd only arrived yesterday, and yet they'd been here five days. Five days of fishing and swimming and canoeing and telling stories and watching the kids grow ever closer. Aaron and Jayce were as comfortable—and as competitive—as any two brothers Dan had ever seen. And Shannon alternately bossed and hugged on them both with impunity.

Surprisingly, Jayce didn't even protest. He took Shannon's bossing with a rueful grin. A grin that reminded Dan of how *he* used to look when Sarah bossed or mothered him.

Ah, Sarah, I miss that. Miss feeling the way you made me feel when we were together, laughing. He felt the void inside as he opened the car door and slid behind the wheel. But as he inserted the key into the ignition, he felt something else.

Something new.

He paused, focusing, trying to understand. And when he did, his mouth dropped open a fraction.

He missed Sarah. With all his heart. But he also missed being part of something bigger than himself. Part of a team.

No. Be honest. Not part of a team.

Okay. Fine. Part of a couple. He missed being part of a couple.

"What's wrong, Dad? You forget how to drive? Want me to drive home?"

Dan started, then waved his son off. "Yeah, in your dreams, kid." He turned the key in the ignition, letting the realization settle in.

Maybe…just maybe…he was ready to explore feeling that way again. Maybe it was time to open another door.

And let a certain someone with crystalline eyes and brown hair come in.

SIXTEEN

*"We can cure physical diseases with medicine,
but the only cure for loneliness,
despair, and hopelessness is love. "*
MOTHER TERESA

"Against all hope, [he] in hope believed."
ROMANS 4:18, (NIV)

IT STARTED SMALL, LIKE A SPLINTER JUST LARGE enough to feel but not large enough to see and remove. It nagged at the edges of his awareness, entering his dreams, turning them dark and foreboding. The sound continued as images loomed, threatened, increased as shadowy figures reached for him…

Jayce awoke with a heart-pounding jerk and bolted to his feet, standing in the middle of his bed. Sweat-drenched and trembling, he crouched, peering into the darkness around him. What…? What woke him?

He dragged in ragged breaths, struggling free from the disturbing images and emotions that invaded his dreams. As his eyes adjusted to the nighttime, so, too, his hearing sharpened, tuned in—

He turned his head.

The sound came from his window.

Stealth, as natural to him as breathing, filled his every movement from the bed to the floor, across the room to the window. Gaze sweeping, scanning, alert to any hint of movement—

There. A shadowed form. Just outside the window.

As he drew near, moonlight illuminated the form—and the edge of fear that had settled over Jayce slipped away as suddenly as it came. In its place was a dull, throbbing irritation.

Frustration hissed through his teeth as he snatched the window lock open then thrust the window up with a low, muttered obscenity. Grabbing his jacket from the desk chair, he slipped through the window, dropping to the ground outside. He stalked away from the house, then, when he was far enough away that his grandmother wouldn't hear them talking, he spun to glare at the hulking boy at his side. "What do you want?"

Marlin Murphy smiled, but clear warning burned in those dark eyes. "Hey, can't a guy stop by to see a friend?"

Jayce crossed his arms. "I asked you what you want."

The other boy's smile faded, leaving his lips thin and twisted. "Where you been, Dalton? You were supposed to meet us last week, remember? We had business."

Marlin looked down at his hands, flexing his fingers, then angled a look back up at Jayce. "I warned you about making nice with the law, man. And what do you do? Take a trip to the mountains with the jerk."

He sneered at Jayce's surprise. "You didn't think I knew where you were? Oh yeah, I knew. I heard all about the big plans. Campin' in the mountains with good ol' Deputy Dan and his kids. Just like one of the family. Make you feel good, Jayce? The way that little girl looks at you like you're worth somethin'? Shannon, right? That her name?" His mouth twisted. "Cute kid. I bet she's cute, even when she's crying."

Jayce was no stranger to anger. But hearing Marlin talk about Shannon did something to him. Grabbed him by the back of the neck and shook him, like a Doberman ripping into a poodle.

"Shut…up." His words slid out on a growl with lethal force that brought Marlin's head snapping up and narrowed his eyes.

"You think you can take me?" A cruel mockery of laughter escaped him. "Pretty stupid after our last dance. Even more stupid than bein' a no-show when we're supposed to meet."

Even if the moon hadn't been bright enough to see the hatred glinting in Marlin's eyes, Jayce had no trouble hearing the threat in the crud's voice.

Marlin didn't like much. Money. Power. That was pretty much it. He'd dropped out of school a couple years ago, when he was fifteen, because he said it was a waste of time. That it wouldn't do a thing to help him get either one of those things. And they were what drove him.

Money, power, and one other thing. His favorite thing of all. Hurting people.

Marlin could do more than hurt Jayce, though.

Marlin could kill him.

Sure, Jayce would get his shots in like last time. He knew how to fight. But he didn't kid himself. In the end, Marlin's size and bulk would win, and Jayce would be finished.

For good.

So what? You have so much to live for?

Jayce flinched then relaxed. For a second he'd thought—

"Did you *hear* me, you little jerkwad?"

Understanding stiffened Jayce's spine. Oh, man. He'd thought it was Marlin asking him what he had to live for. Marlin sounded just like the voice. Why hadn't he ever realized that befo—?

Go for it. Let the crud take you out. You'd be better off. Your grandmother would be better off.

"Aw, you scared, little Jayce? Want me to go get your grammy?"

Go on.

It wouldn't be hard. A few well-chosen words, a shove, and Marlin would be out of control.

Do it!

Not with his jacket on. It was too heavy. It'd get in his way as he fought. Jayce grabbed the zipper, jerked it down—and it snagged. Caught. Muttering an oath, he looked down and found himself staring into a pair of amber eyes.

His pendant. Aslan.

And suddenly the voice inside wasn't dark or menacing. It was soft and gentle, full of a sweetness Jayce had never heard before.

"You're just like him…you're not a tame lion. But you're good…down inside."

Jayce eased the zipper free from the leather cord, then closed his hand over the pendant. He'd almost forgotten what he promised himself. What he promised Shannon, though she didn't know it.

But he knew. And that's what mattered.

He squeezed the pendant hard, then let it go. But he could feel its imprint in his palm as he faced Marlin. "I didn't show because we're done."

Something flashed on Marlin's face. Shock? Alarm? Before Jayce could decide, it was replaced by a cold, hard stare that promised pain.

"Done?" Marlin took a step forward. "I got news for you, you worthless piece of trash. We're not done until *I* say so."

"I've done everything you told me to. I've delivered your packages without asking questions. I've stood guard and let you know when the cops were around. I stole and lied and done things that would kill my gramma if she knew. I'm *sick* of it. Sick of you. Sick of *me* when I'm around you."

Jayce stood his ground, not flinching, not looking away. He held Marlin's merciless gaze, but from the corner of his eye he caught the other boy flexing his big hands. Stretch, clench.

Stretch, clench. Like he was crushing his own bones.

Or getting ready to crush Jayce's.

Yeah, well, Marlin was probably going to beat him to a pulp. So be it. He'd been hammered on by bigger and badder than Marlin, and he was still standing. If that's what it took to make the guy leave him alone, to be free, it was worth it.

He waited for the first blow. But it didn't come.

Instead, Marlin's cruel mouth twisted into what Jayce supposed was a smile, and Marlin shifted his eyes, looking just past Jayce. At the house. His grandmother's house.

Alarm rammed through Jayce, and he spun, scanning the shadows.

"You kill me, you know that? All worried about little Shannon." Marlin's voice turned to granite. "When there's so much to worry about right in your own home."

It only took a moment to see them. Marlin's crew. All standing next to Grams's house.

Holding gas cans.

"Funny thing, fire. One little spark, and it's gone. Outta control." He moved to stand beside Jayce, slipping his arm around Jayce's shoulders, digging his fingers into Jayce's arm. "I heard they think fire's alive. You know, 'cuz it doesn't just burn things. It eats 'em. *Consumes* 'em. Fast. Like it's starvin'. Someone old, not real steady on her feet. Why, she wouldn't have much of a chance."

He pulled his arm away, leaving Jayce's arm throbbing, a sure sign Marlin's meaty fingers would leave bruises to remind him of this little lesson.

"Yeah." Marlin started toward the house. "Dyin' like that. That'd be a bad way to go."

Anger wasn't the only companion Jayce had carried through his life. Another even more familiar emotion hung on him, taunting him. And it came now, despised, compressing his chest until taking a breath was like being cut in half.

Hopelessness. And as it curled itself through and around

him, Jayce knew. It didn't matter. Nothing that he did, nothing that anyone else thought—not even someone as special as Shannon—mattered one bit.

This was his life. There was no escape. Period.

"All right."

Marlin stopped. "Excuse me?" Victory all but screamed in his smug tone. "Did you say something?"

"All right. You win."

Cruel laughter lifted on the night breeze. "I win." Marlin turned, his malicious gaze raking Jayce. "Well whaddya know? It's true."

Jayce could tell Marlin wasn't going to let it go, so he ground out the expected response. "*What's* true?"

Marlin pointed to the sky. "God is in His heaven, dude, and all's right with the world."

"*God?*" The word spat out before Jayce could stop it, as did the near hysterical laughter ripping from his throat. "You think *God's* on your side? Are you *crazy?*"

In three quick steps Marlin was in his face, grabbing a fistful of Jayce's jacket—then he stopped. "Ow! What—?" He shook his hand then reached out and snatched Jayce's pendant.

"No!"

His protest didn't matter. Marlin jerked on the pendant, clearly bent on ripping it from the cord. But the leather wouldn't give. His movements sharp and swift, Marlin cinched the cord above the pendant in his fist, making it into a noose, snapping Jayce's neck back and drawing him up on his toes.

Jayce grabbed at the cord with both hands, struggling to keep it from cutting off his air entirely.

"So who'd you steal this from?" Marlin eyed the pendant.

Jayce sucked just enough air to spit out a reply. "I didn't steal it."

A greedy light glittered in Marlin's eyes, and Jayce wanted to scream. He knew what that look meant.

"Looks like real gold." Marlin turned the pendant, running

this thumb over the back— then frowned. Reaching into his pocket, he pulled out a small flashlight, turned it on, and read the inscription.

When Marlin's eyes came back to Jayce, the greed he'd seen there moments before was gone.

Something far worse had taken its place.

"So your little girlfriend gave this to you, did she?"

Jayce sucked in air. "She's not my girlfriend."

"Too good for the likes of you, huh? Wouldn't wipe her feet on trash like you?"

Jayce yanked at the cord. "You sick jerk! She's just a kid!"

Marlin tugged the cord higher. "Got you thinking about God, huh? You thinking about God, Jayce?" He stuck his face close to Jayce's. "I *am* god, you little puke. I'm *your* god. You live, you die—"

Another tug on the cord. Jayce felt his vision going black.

"—it's not God's call. It's *mine*."

Suddenly Jayce was free. As he sucked in oxygen, Marlin took hold of his jacket and threw him backward. Jayce went flying, landing on the ground so hard it knocked whatever air he'd managed to drag in from his burning lungs.

Marlin towered over him, a hulking shadow blocking the sky…

"*My* call."

…the moon, the stars…

"Don't you ever forget it."

Hope.

Everything was gone.

SEVENTEEN

"Enemy-occupied territory is what the world is."

C. S. LEWIS

"The enemy said, 'I will chase them,
catch up with them, and destroy them.
I will divide the plunder, avenging myself against them.
I will unsheath my sword; my power will destroy them.'"

EXODUS 15:9

"TALK TO ME ABOUT MARLIN MURPHY."

Jayce's head jerked up, the look in his eyes far from accommodating.

He and Dan were on their way home from catching a movie down in the valley, and Dan decided to put the drive to good use.

"Why?"

"Because I know he's a friend of yours. And that worries me."

"Marlin's not my friend."

The harsh edge to Jayce's words drew a glance from Dan. Jayce released a huff. "You saw what he did to me at the center. Why would you think he's my friend?"

Fair question. Deserved an honest answer. "Because you hang with him."

"Yeah, well…" Jayce turned to stare out his window. "Not by choice."

He muttered the words so low Dan wondered if Jayce meant for him to hear them. "Meaning?"

"What?"

"What did you mean, not by choice?"

Nope. If the red that seeped into Jayce's cheeks was any sign, he hadn't intended for Dan to hear that.

"I dunno. Look, Marlin doesn't have friends. He has…"

"Accomplices?"

His jaw tensed. "Do we have to talk about this?"

Okaay. Dan gave the boy a sideways glance. "What would you rather talk about?"

"Anything." He pulled a pair of sunglasses from his coat pocket and slipped them on, leaning his head back against the headrest. Sunglasses at night. Clearly he wanted to hide. "Anything but Marlin the Miserable."

Dan let the silence grow for a beat then launched in. "So tell me what you think of God."

He peered at Dan over the sunglasses. "You gotta be kiddin' me."

Dan negotiated the turn just before the Lost Lake bridge. He glanced at the lake, loving how the water shimmered in the moonlight. "Marlin or God. Take your pick."

With a weighted sigh, Jayce plucked the sunglasses from his face. "Right. Okay. God. He's there. But that's pretty much it."

"Think so, huh?"

"Hey, I know you think He's all around us and inside us. And that He's all involved in our lives and stuff. But—" his shrug was eloquent—"I don't see it. Or I guess I don't see Him."

"Not at all?"

Jayce opened his mouth to reply then closed it. Thought for a moment. Then glanced out the passenger window again. "Maybe a little."

"Hey, a little is good. I'll take a little."

Jayce shook his head. "You have got to be one of the strangest ducks I've ever met. You and your family."

Dan grinned. "Just wait'll you meet my sisters."

"Stranger than you?"

"Way stranger."

With a chuckle, Jayce slid his sunglasses back in place. "Now *that'd* prove God was real."

Dan laughed. "How's that?"

The grin that lifted Jayce's lips was pure mischief. "'Cause someone being stranger than you? That'd *have* to be a miracle."

The battle was about to begin.

Dan leaned against his cruiser, which was parked in front of his office, arms crossed, watching Marlin as he sauntered down the sidewalk toward him. The kid walked like he owned the world. Sadly, too many treated him that way as well. Younger kids looked up to him as some kind of rebel hero. Older kids tried to emulate him, as if he were the epitome of cool. Adults? Well, a few ignored him. Others hurried to get out of his way when he walked by. And then there were folks like Aggie and Doris.

Just yesterday Dan had glanced out his office window to see the two old women perched in their rockers. They'd been talking, rocking away, when suddenly their chairs came to an abrupt halt. Dan stood, concerned there was a problem. He walked to the window and frowned when he spotted Marlin, his gang in tow, ambling toward the two ladies.

Grabbing his jacket, Dan was out the door, ready to protect them from Marlin and whatever verbal abuse he might choose to unleash. But he needn't have bothered. Aggie and Doris stiffened in their rockers, backs ramrod straight, chins lifted a fraction, fixing Marlin with eagle-sharp glares.

He caught their stares, and for a heartbeat Dan thought the kid was going to say something smart. But Doris's already stern features turned downright formidable. Marlin stopped, took a step back, and scooted past them with only a glower tossed over his shoulder.

Watching Sanctuary's resident bad boy taken down a peg by those two did Dan's heart some serious good. He joined the ladies on the boardwalk.

"You know, I pray for that boy every day."

Dan tried not to let his surprise show at Doris's comment. "You do?"

She nodded. "I figure anyone that angry has a whole lot of hurt inside."

"Not only that, he's got to have a lot of hurt."

Dan and Doris looked at Aggie. Her eyes went wide. "What?"

"Yes, I pray for that boy. Almost—" Doris offered to Dan in a low aside—"as often as I pray for Agatha's hearing."

He laughed.

"What?" Aggie scooted her chair closer. "Speak up, Doris! I can't hear the punch line to your jokes!"

"Agatha Hunter, you *are* the punch line."

"Oh…phoo." Aggie's chair set to rocking. "Anyway, that Murphy boy, he needs our prayers. Lots of them." She pinned Dan with a firm look. "You pray for him, don't you, Sheriff?"

He'd long ago given up correcting these two when they called him that. "Well…"

"'Course he does, Aggie. Sheriff Dan's a solid Christian. He knows the best thing to do is pray for your enemies."

Dan chuckled. "I'll tell you something, ladies; you put me to shame."

"Oh?" Doris's nose took on more wrinkles. "Why is that?"

"I've done a lot of things about Marlin Murphy. Checked into his background—"

"Ooh. That was terrible. The way his father treated him."

"And killing himself that way. With a gun." Aggie clucked her tongue. "Such a waste."

"—but I confess, I've never prayed for the kid."

Both women's rockers halted at that. Then Aggie started her chair into a slow, easy motion. "Well, now...that is a bit of a surprise."

"Your being a believer, and all."

Dan smiled. He couldn't help it. He hoped when he reached these ladies' age, he would be as firm in his faith—and as willing to speak truth—as they were. "You know what I think?"

Aggie's forgiveness for his lack was clear in the warm smile on her features. "What's that, Sheriff?"

"I think God sent you two as my own personal angels. To remind me what I need to be doing. And I promise to pray for Marlin from now on."

They giggled like a couple of schoolgirls. "Angels! Doris and me? Well, I mean, I can see why you'd think *I* was an angel..."

"Oh, plah, plah, plah, Aggie. Like *real* angels need hearing aids."

And on they went, until Dan had to head back to his office before he burst out laughing. But as he walked across the street, he knew things had changed. He'd meant what he said. He would pray for Marlin.

But it was time to do something else as well. Something he'd been thinking about for a while.

It was time to talk with Marlin Murphy. Face-to-face.

So today he watched what had become the bane of his professional existence draw closer. Though only eighteen, Marlin was almost as tall as Dan. Combined with his considerable bulk, that made him an imposing figure. Marlin might be a hulk, but Dan knew the kinds of moves to bring hulks tumbling down.

He'd dealt with more than his fair share of kids like Marlin. The old adage *Never let 'em see you sweat* held true with them. You had to be as bold and in-your-face as they were. Not belligerent, just not a doormat.

As Marlin and his crew drew parallel with the cruiser, Dan pushed away from his leaning position and straightened to his full height. Times like this, he was grateful for his father's genes. His dad had been six feet two. Dan topped him by a good two inches.

Dan knew the moment he came into Marlin's line of sight. Alarm flashed across the kid's features, then disappeared as the cool facade slipped into place. Marlin stopped—his gang stopping with him—arms crossed, and tilted his head to eye Dan.

"'Sup, Sheriff Taylor? Barney Fife get lost and you want us to find him for you?" The four boys with Marlin snickered.

Dan just smiled. "Aw, Marlin, I wouldn't ask you to do that. I know you've got far more important things to do."

Surprise flickered in Marlin's eyes, and his responding smile was smug. "Yeah? Well, good. I like it when people recognize I'm important." He cast a look of triumph at his gang, as though to say, "See? Even the deputy stays outta my way."

Dan assumed a relaxed pose. "Sure. It's hard work to find flunkies stupid enough to do your dirty work while you just sit around and reap all the benefits."

The sudden hard set to Marlin's features almost made Dan laugh. "Especially now that you've lost one of your main go-to guys."

"Zat so?" Marlin's voice had lost that lazy, confident drawl. Instead there was a definite edge to his words. "Care to elaborate?"

"Wow, Marlin. *Elaborate*. Big word for such a small man." He didn't give any indication he'd noted the way Marlin drew himself rigid at the insult. "But I think you know who I mean. Jayce Dalton. He has been somewhat absent from your following of late."

Dan's eyes drifted from one of Marlin's crew to the next, noting how each of them dropped his gaze, staring at the ground. Like puppies pretending to be brave until an alpha male looked at them—then they piddled all over the floor and themselves showing how submissive they were.

"Ah, my man Jayce." Marlin's tone was as unpleasant as his smile. "He's been on a bit of a hiatus." He paused. "Oh, sorry, Andy, didn't mean to use big words again. 'Specially not when they're clearly over your head."

The kid was good. He really looked like he felt bad. "Your concern is touching, Marlin. But no worries. I've known *hiatus* since I was in grade school. But hey, I'm glad you've finally learned what it means. Nice to see you bettering yourself."

Marlin's gaze narrowed. "Yeah, well, then you'll be thrilled to know *my* man Jayce is right back on the job. Not—" he smirked at his cronies—"that there's any kind of real job going on. I just mean he's as much a part of our little group as ever."

Dan studied the boy's face, and his heart sank. He could usually tell when someone was bluffing, and Marlin had the smug expression of someone who knew what he was saying was not only true, but that it was bad news for the listener.

And it was. Bad news.

Shannon would be brokenhearted if she knew Jayce was hanging with Marlin again. Dan had been so sure Jayce was out of Marlin's gang. That he'd changed...

Let it go, Justice. Focus on the issue at hand.

He focused on Marlin and gritted his teeth. The malicious glitter in the kid's eyes said he knew he'd struck home. That his words had nailed Dan, throwing him off.

Dan forced a nonchalant expression to his features, let a tiny smile tip his lips. "Marlin, Marlin." He shook his head, not hiding the condescending tone in his voice. "Haven't you learned by now? Things are seldom what they seem." He shrugged. "Any good leader knows that."

Two spots of red surged into Marlin's cheeks. Score one for the good guys. "But hey, don't let me burst your bubble, man." Dan stepped aside. "And don't let me hold you up. A big man like you must have lots of *business* to attend to."

Glowering, Marlin started to pass Dan, but his hand shot out, catching the boy's arm. He felt the muscles tense, but he didn't let his gaze waver as Marlin spun toward him. Dan met the boy's angry stare without flinching.

"Just one more word to the not-so-wise, Marlin. I know what you're up to. And I'm watching you. You mess up—you're mine."

A muscle jumped in Marlin's jaw, but he didn't reply. He just stared at Dan a moment longer. Then he jerked his arm free, spun on his heel, and went on his way, his gang in his furious wake.

Dan watched them go, hands in his pockets. So, the lines were drawn. But it wouldn't end here. In fact, if what he'd just seen in Marlin's dark eyes was any indication, it was just starting.

Well, so be it. Dan wasn't about to let Marlin ruin Sanctuary. Any more than he would let him run Jayce's life. Jayce was just starting to see how good life could be, how full when someone really cared about him.

Speaking of which…

His first planned encounter for the day was done. Now, on to the second. Dan smiled.

With any luck, this one would be far more enjoyable.

EIGHTEEN

"Suddenly, I saw you there..."
GEORGE GERSHWIN

"You alone [O God] know the human heart."
1 KINGS 8:39

SHELBY WILSON, DIRECTOR.

Shelby sat at her desk, staring down at the desk sign she held in her hands. She'd worked so hard to earn that title. Director. Woman in charge. She Who Must Be Obeyed.

And yet...

Looking at the title now, she felt nothing. Empty.

She set the sign back on her desk with a sharp bang. "Snap out of it, Shelby! You do important work here. Work that matters."

So how come lately, no matter how many kids seemed to improve or find homes where they could be nurtured and grow, she didn't feel anything?

Maybe because you've forgotten someone?

She had not! She'd given each case at Master's Touch her

personal attention. Why, she'd even found the right family for the most impossible kid of all.

She jerked open a desk drawer, pulling out a folder of photos, then plopped down in her chair and spread the pictures out on her desk. Shelby studied them, one by one—Shannon and Jayce holding up a huge fish, laughing so hard they looked about to drop the creature on the ground; Aaron and Jayce flexing their muscles over a pile of wood they'd chopped for the campfire; all three of the kids setting up tents, faces intent on the task at hand.

When Jayce Dalton showed up at Master's Touch, he qualified as poster boy for the consequences of too little, too late. No one could get through to him. Not even Shelby. But a few months with the Justice clan and that belligerent, bleak bad boy was all but gone. In his place was a boy whose ready smile won people over before he spoke a word.

Shelby picked up a picture of the three kids standing near a canoe, arms draped across each other's shoulders. Clearly, Jayce and the Justice family were devoted to each other.

Her eyes fell on another picture, and picking it up she sat back in her chair with a heavy sigh. Dan Justice smiled out at her, eyes crinkled at the edge of mirth, and she could almost hear his deep voice cutting loose with that rich laughter that seemed to come from his very core. She loved hearing him laugh.

You love hearing him, period.

She didn't deny it. There was no reason for it. Heaven knew, the man hadn't given her any encouragement. And yet, Dan had somehow worked his way into Shelby's heart. Just the sight of him sent a surge of warmth through her. And when his eyes met hers…it was like coming home to a place she'd never known.

So comfortable, so peaceful—she never wanted to leave.

So maybe you've found the perfect family for the one you forgot, too.

Shelby gripped the picture, muttering under her breath, "Name one person I forgot! Go ahead. I dare you."

Shelby Wilson.

"Oh!" The word sucked in on a startled breath. Shelby looked down at Dan's picture and suddenly felt like weeping.

Yes, okay. She'd forgotten one person. Herself. All these years she'd been so focused on helping the kids, she figured she'd have time later for all the dreams she used to have. Silly things.

Like love, a husband, children?

Yes. Silly things like that.

But before she knew it, years had passed, and she was still alone. Sanctuary wasn't exactly a wellspring of eligible men, either. Not men under sixty, anyway. And then, Dan Justice came to town.

Shelby fought the attraction she felt for him. After all, there were bound to be an abundance of women vying for his attention. And she refused to enter some ridiculous female competition to catch his eye.

So here she sat, mooning over his picture, while the man hardly seemed to know she was alive. Aside from when he dropped in to give her regular reports on how things were going with Jayce, she seldom saw him.

Oh, they smiled at each other every Sunday at church, but so what? That put her on par with the sweet white-haired ladies in the back pews. Dan smiled at *them* every Sunday, too.

She glared down at his picture. "How can such great eyes be so blind?"

She tossed the picture back on her desk, and it skittered across the surface, sliding off and fluttering to the floor.

Just in time to be stepped on by a size-thirteen shoe, as the object of her frustration materialized and entered her office.

Shelby jumped to her feet, a bundle of shock and alarm. "Dan!"

"Shelby!" Dan responded with playful force. "Okay, now we both know who we are."

Glancing down, he lifted his foot. "Oops!" He bent over and plucked the photo from beneath his foot.

Don't look at it. Please, don't look at it...

Clearly, the man didn't have an ounce of ESP in him. He looked at the photo, and his brows lifted. But he made no comment as he handed the picture back to Shelby. She considered that a definite mercy.

"I was just reviewing Jayce's file—" she jabbered, gathering up the photos and stuffing them back into their folder—"you know, just as part of my job. I mean, that is my job. To keep track of the kids we work with. Keep the files updated."

He just leaned in her doorway, watching her, lips tipped in a slight smile.

"Anyway, I'm updated now. Or, I mean, the file is. Updated. So." She sank into her chair. *Where* had the dratted man come from anyway? And why on earth couldn't he give a girl a little warning?

"So."

Dan's rich voice pulled her from her miserable thoughts. "So—" she drew a breath—"what brings you to my humble abode, Deputy?"

"Deputy?" Dan's smile grew a fraction. "Now, Shelby, I thought we were past the formal stage."

She was ready to reply, but the look on his face...well, she'd never seen him look at her like that before. His blue eyes were warm and soft as a caress. His smile held a gentle tenderness—and something more.

It was that something more that rendered her mute.

As though sensing her inability to form a coherent sentence, Dan continued. "Anyway, what brings me by is food. I wondered if you'd like to join me for some."

Shelby's lungs—and her rising hopes—deflated.

How silly of her to think this was anything more than her being a lunch buddy. "Sure." She did her best to sound casual. "Lunch at Lou's. Works for me."

"Not for me."

She paused in the act of pulling her purse from a bottom desk drawer. "You don't want to eat at Lou's?"

The warmth of his chuckle sent shivers down her spine. "I don't want to eat lunch. I was thinking more of dinner. Bel Di's in Shady Cove."

She straightened. Bel Di's was a wonderful restaurant well known for its luscious cuisine—and its romantic atmosphere. "Dinner. At Bel Di's."

"You and me."

She blinked. "Together."

"Unless you'd rather run alongside the car, of course."

Her laughter joined his, easing the shocked tension that held her in its grip. "I'm sorry, Dan." She shook her head, certain, if the heat scorching her checks was any indication, that she must be as red as the light on top of his cruiser. "You just took me by surprise."

His gaze met hers and held. "Well, then, I'd say we're even." He pushed away from the door frame. "So Friday night work for you? Say around five? I'll make reservations for six, so we can just take our time and enjoy the drive. Sound good?"

She nodded. "Sounds great."

With a tip of his head, he was gone. Leaving Shelby to sit there, staring after him. She lifted a trembling hand to her still-warm cheek.

So this was what it felt like to have a dream come true. Stunning. Unsettling. Exciting.

And utterly, completely wonderful.

"Aggie, I swear! If you don't control that rat of yours, I will!"

"Half Pint is *not* a bat!" Agatha Hunter wrapped her veined hands around the yapping, stiff-legged little dog on her lap.

"Rat. I said *rat!*"

"—and well you know it, Doris Kleffer. He's a registered

Chihuahua with a lineage, I daresay, far more distinguished than yours!" The woman's white hair all but trembled with her indignation.

Shannon bit her lips to keep from laughing out loud. She'd walked down to the store with Aaron, who had a list of groceries from Dad. When Shannon saw Miss Hunter and Miss Kleffer sitting in their chairs just outside the store, she told Aaron she'd wait for him out here. She wouldn't miss sitting and listening to these two women. They were funnier than Saturday cartoons!

Besides, Miss Hunter's little dog, Half Pint, was adorable. Shannon remembered the look on her dad's face when he first saw the dog—and when he discovered Half Pint was the famous ½ on the population sign for the town.

"Only in Sanctuary," he'd sighed.

It was true. No place else was like Sanctuary. And no people were like the people who lived here.

"Piffle!" Doris shot back at her friend's assertion of Half Pint's stature. "If that minuscule mutt is a real dog, I'll eat my shoe."

"Moo shoo?" Aggie sniffed. "What do *I* care if you eat Chinese food?"

Doris planted her hands on the arms of her rocker and shouted. "My *shoe*! I-will-eat-my-*shoe*!"

"Shannon!"

She jumped and went to stand beside Miss Hunter's rocker. "Yes, ma'am?"

"Please go get Miss Kleffer a shaker of salt." She aimed a syrupy smile at the woman rocking next to her. "She'll need it to season that shoe and make it palatable."

"Oh!"

Ignoring Doris, Aggie lifted Half Pint and pressed a kiss to his little snout. "Pity we can't make her tongue more palatable as well."

"Plah, plah, plah."

"Doris Kleffer, you just stop it right now. You always say that ridiculous thing when you know I'm right—"

"Then I'm surprised you ever hear it. Since I can't remember the last time you were right."

"—but no one knows what it means. *Plah, plah, plah?* I'll bet *you* don't even know what it means."

Shannon couldn't help it. She was lost in giggles.

"Now, Aggie, don't change the subject. You know this all got started because your puny little pup was raising a fuss over nothing."

Agatha patted Half Pint's trembling head and leaned closer. "Shows what you know. It wasn't over nothing. It was over them."

Shannon and Miss Kleffer followed the other woman's nod. When Shannon saw Jayce standing there, she smiled. "Oh, Miss Hunter, Jayce is a nice boy."

The woman's long fingers waved in the air. "Not *him*, child. That other one."

Shannon didn't recognize the large boy talking to Jayce. But apparently she was the only one.

"Oh." Doris sat back in her rocker. "Of course. Well, my apologies to Half Pint, Aggie. I don't blame him for barking." She aimed a glare across the street. "That boy is no good. No good at all."

"I don't care how tall he is. He's no good." Aggie's rocking punctuated her words. "Why, just last week he tried to kick Half Pint. *Imagine.* A boy that big trying to kick my little baby."

Shannon frowned. What kind of creep tried to kick a little dog like Half Pint? And why was Jayce with someone like that?

Aggie patted Shannon's hand and smiled up at her. "We need more children like you, dear. Sweet and kind. Like an angel on earth."

Shannon smiled and thanked the woman then went to sit down again. She pushed the rocker, setting it in motion, trying to focus on what the two women were saying. But her attention kept straying back across the street.

She watched Jayce and the other boy talking, taking in the stiff set of Jayce's shoulders. He didn't look happy. In fact, he looked kind of mad.

Just then the larger boy reached out, punching his finger into Jayce's chest. Shannon jumped up. "Hey! Stop that!"

Both boys turned, and Shannon felt the impact of their full attention. Though they were across the street, she could see Jayce's eyes drop into a frown. Was he mad at her for speaking up for him? Boys could be silly about things like that.

Jayce turned back to the other boy, grabbing his arm, trying to pull him away. The boy didn't budge. He just kept his gaze glued to her. Shannon crossed her arms and stared back.

You don't scare me, she told him with her eyes.

He smiled. But it wasn't a nice smile. Not even a little. Then he took a step forward, toward Shannon.

Her heart jumped. Okay, maybe he did scare her. A little.

Jayce grabbed the boy's sleeve, and his voice raised enough for Shannon to hear it. "Forget it, Marlin. She's not worth it." Jayce's gaze raked over her, and though his voice dropped and she couldn't hear the rest of his words, Shannon had to bite her lip to keep from crying.

Jayce looked at her like she was a stranger.

No…worse. A nuisance.

She stared at the boardwalk, and when she looked up again, Jayce and the boy were gone.

"Are you all right, dear?"

Shannon turned back to the two women and realized they both were watching her. She shrugged. "I'm okay."

Miss Kleffer *tsk*ed, then looked across to where Jayce had stood. "You steer clear of that boy, child." Her old eyes, when they returned to Shannon, were more serious than Shannon had ever seen. "He's dangerous."

"Who is?"

Shannon turned and saw Aaron standing there, a sack of

groceries in each arm. "Nobody," she mumbled, going to take one of the sacks.

"That hulking Murphy boy."

"Did that creep give you some kind of trouble?"

Shannon had seen her brother get steamed before. Plenty of times. And usually at her. But she'd never seen him look like this. Serious. Protective. She had the sense that if she said the wrong thing, he'd go hunt Marlin Murphy down and take his head off.

Well…try, anyway. Marlin was almost twice Aaron's size.

"No. Don't worry about it." She bid the ladies good-bye and started down the boardwalk toward home.

Aaron fell in step beside her. "Shannon?"

She sighed. "He didn't do anything to me. He was just on the other side of the street." She hated to tell him this part, but it wouldn't be right to hide it. "Talking with Jayce."

He stopped then fell into step with her again. "Jayce?"

She nodded, feeling more and more miserable.

"That doesn't make sense." Aaron's brow was all wrinkled, telling her he was bugged. "He's smarter than that."

"Jayce is really smart."

"So what would make him hang with a guy like that?"

Shannon didn't know. But one thing was certain.

It couldn't be good.

NINETEEN

*"If it is your time, love will track you
down like a cruise missile."*
LYNDA BARRY

*"For when you grant a blessing to your servant,
O Sovereign LORD, it is an eternal blessing!"*
2 SAMUEL 7:29

CINDERELLA WAS A LIAR.

So, for that matter, were Sleeping Beauty and Snow White. Shelby had seen enough of life to realize *happily-ever-after* were just words to end a fairy tale.

So why on earth was she sitting here, under a star-studded sky, looking out on a peaceful meadow and feeling for all the world like the Grimm brothers got it right? *All* of it.

"You cold?"

Oh. Of course. *That's* why.

She studied the man beside her. Relished the way those cobalt blue eyes gazed down at her. Savored the glimmer of tenderness in their depths as they roamed her face. His arm around her shoulders tightened, and she gave up.

The Grimm brothers won. Fairy tales *were* real.

Her capitulation started out with a simple dinner in Shady

Cove, where she and Dan talked about everything, from her childhood and growing up in Sanctuary, to how he and Sarah met, what their life was like, and how he and the children were doing without her. It meant a great deal to Shelby that Dan could talk with her about Sarah—though she had to admit it was a bit imposing to hear how much they'd loved each other.

But as the evening progressed, that was less of a concern. When they got back to Sanctuary, Dan turned to her. "You ready to go home, or are you up for a little walk?"

Gladness rippled through her that he didn't want the evening to end yet. "A walk sounds great."

They strolled along the boardwalk. And though the stores were all closed, it was a warm August night, so Shelby wasn't surprised to find folks sitting in the rockers, chatting. They'd met a number of people, stopping to talk, and the whole time Dan held her hand captive in his.

At first that made Shelby nervous. But when she tried to pull away, mindful of not starting any rumors, Dan just smiled, folding his fingers around her.

"Let 'em talk." He tugged her hand into the crook of his arm.

Tingles ran along her skin, and she was more than happy to comply.

"Evening, ladies," he said to Doris and Agatha when they approached the two seated in their rockers.

"Hello, Sheriff." Agatha peered at them then glanced at Doris.

"Hello, Shelby." Doris inclined her head. "Nice night for a walk."

"It is, indeed." Dan looked up at the night sky. "God's quite the artist, isn't He?"

"I should say so." Aggie looked like the cat that got away with eating a ton of canaries. "And I swear, it's almost as bright as daytime with that full moon up there."

"A perfect night for romance, don't you think?"

Shelby almost swallowed her teeth at Doris's comment, but Dan just smiled. "Know what, Doris?"

She leaned forward in her chair. "What?"

"I was thinking the same thing." He glanced at Shelby then back at the old woman. "You wanna take a walk with me, beautiful?"

"Oh, you!" Doris swatted at him, but a pretty pink painted her thin cheeks. "Get on with you youngsters."

Laughing, Dan drew Shelby along. From there they walked to his SUV. He opened the door for her, helping her inside. Then before closing the door, he leaned against the doorway. "How about a drive?"

Shelby felt like she was in a dream. And she hoped she didn't wake up for a long, long time. "I'd love it."

He drove out of town, up Highway 62 to the north. Shelby relaxed back against the seat, smiling when his fingers closed over hers again. He pulled onto a side road, driving until they came upon a large meadow. Killing the engine and the headlights, he tugged on her hand.

Shelby didn't resist. She slid close, and when his arm draped around her, she knew she was right where she wanted to be. Not just now.

But forever.

"Well…" Dan's deep voice was filled with regret. "I suppose we'd better head back."

She leaned her head against him. "Let's just stay here."

"All night?" Laughter laced his tone.

"No." She let out a small sigh. "Forever."

His chuckle washed over her, the sound sweet and tender. She held on to that sound, hearing it over and over, letting it warm her as they drove back to town. When they reached her house, Dan opened her car door, then took hold of her by the waist and lifted her from the vehicle. For a moment he stood there, his hands at her waist, looking down at her. Then slowly, so slowly, he lowered his head and pressed a kiss…

To her forehead.

But far from being disappointed, Shelby was touched. More deeply than she'd been in a very long time.

"I'll see you tomorrow."

She nodded, then walked to her front door and pulled it open. Slipping inside, she eased the door shut, leaning back against it as she listened to his SUV start up. She moved to the window, watching as Dan drove away.

Knowing without an iota of doubt that her heart went with him.

Dan stood outside his house, staring up at the stars. It had gone so well tonight. Better than he'd imagined. He felt so comfortable with Shelby. They talked and laughed and seemed to finish each other's sentences. Just like he and Sarah used to do.

Sarah.

Dan waited for the stab of pain to come. But instead, what filled him was a quiet peace. Almost a benediction of sorts. As if something within him was finally letting go…saying good-bye.

At least for now.

Inhaling the crisp night air, he turned, going inside the house. He'd barely closed the door when the question came.

"So? How was it?"

Dan should have known his sister wouldn't let him get past her without an inquisition. He came to join Annie in the kitchen. "The kids in bed?"

"All tucked in and ready for you to come say good-night." She held up an empty coffee cup, brows lifted, and he nodded.

"Yeah, I'll take some. Thanks."

She poured the rich, dark liquid and handed him the mug. "Okay, answer my question."

"Annie…"

She held up a hand. "Listen, I came all the way up here

from Medford to be with the kids so you could stay out nice and late—"

"And I appreciate that."

"—and all I ask by way of payment for my valuable time are a few juicy details." With that she planted her elbows on the counter and leaned toward him. "So spill!"

Holding back a grin, he held the coffee mug over her head. She eyed it, then him. "Do it, and I'll set my dog on you."

The shepherd was curled up on the couch, snoring to beat the band. "What's she gonna do? Drool me to death?"

Annie slapped at his arm. "Avidan Timothy! If you don't tell me how your date was…"

He let the threat hang in the air for a second as he sipped his coffee. Then he turned toward the living room. "Great."

She scampered from behind the counter, on his heels. "Really?"

Dan glanced over his shoulder. "You're squealing."

"I can't help it!" She plopped down on the couch. Kodi shot awake, then, seeing it was her beloved mistress, stretched out so she was lying across Annie's lap. Annie didn't seem to mind a bit. She grabbed the dog and hugged her. "Uncle Danny's got a girlfriend! Isn't that exciting?"

"She's not a girlfriend, Annie." He sat in his chair, breathing in the scent of his coffee. "Not yet."

"Ooo, I can't wait to call Kyla."

"Sure you wouldn't rather just wait for the evening news?"

"Ha ha. Listen, I told you when you moved to Sanctuary that Shelby was something special. And Kyla had said the same thing whenever she came to visit you. So you can't blame me for being pleased that you finally admit we were right."

"Those words never escaped my lips." And they never would. Admit his sisters were right? Ha! He'd never hear the end of it.

Annie gave Kodi a gentle shove off of her, then stood. "Well, time for this pumpkin to head back to the patch, bro. Go tell your kidniks good night, and I'll see you later."

He set his coffee down, engulfed his sister in a hug, and went to do as he was told. He tapped his knuckles on Aaron's door.

"Come in."

Dan opened the door and went in to sit on his son's bed. "Hey, buddy. You look wide awake."

Aaron fingered his quilt. "I couldn't sleep." He kept his gaze on the quilt. "Didja have fun?"

Was that apprehension in Aaron's voice? "I did."

Aaron was silent for several seconds, then his eyes met Dan's. "Are you in love with Miss Wilson?"

He should have known that was coming, should have read it a mile away. But the question took Dan by total surprise. "I…well, I mean…uh…" He clamped his mouth shut. He sounded like an idiot.

"Yeah." Aaron's word was weighted with weary understanding. "I know what you mean. There's a girl at school who makes me feel that way, too."

They sat in silence for a moment. "Aaron?"

"Yeah, Dad?"

"Would it bother you if I was? In love with Miss Wilson?"

He looked down at the quilt again, plucking at the fabric. "It did at first. I mean…" Heavy sadness filled the look he lifted to his father. "She's not Mom."

"No." Dan shook his head. "She's not."

"But then, no one is Mom but Mom. And you won't find anyone just like her, because there isn't anyone out there like that, you know?"

He did, indeed.

"So I've been thinking about it. You and Miss Wilson seem like good friends. And I like Miss Wilson, so it's a good thing if you and she get to be friends. Like you and Mom were friends. Not the same but kinda."

Dan stared at his son. When had Aaron grown so wise?

"I love you, son."

Aaron smiled up at him. "I love you, too, Dad."

"You ready to get some sleep?"

Aaron's grin peeked out. "Can I have some hot chocolate first?"

Dan chuckled. "Only if you share."

"Okay, but I get the little marshmallows." Aaron pushed the quilt back and slid out of bed.

Dan caught him and pulled him into a hug. "I'm glad you're my son."

The boy hugged him tight. "Me, too, Dad." He pulled back with a grin. "I always said you deserve the best."

Soft laughter followed them as they made their way to the kitchen, ready for the perfect end to a perfect day.

"Perfect. Just *perfect.*"

Jasmine looked up at Dan's sarcasm, her plucked brows and the eyebrow ring disappearing into the fringe of the Lucille-Ball-red hair on her forehead. "Oooo, sounds to me like you'd better do lunch on your own, Shelby."

The other woman, who just came in the door, looked from Dan to Jasmine, then back again. "What? Oh, Dan. Don't tell me you're going to work later? It's Saturday. You promised to take the afternoon off." She planted her hands on her hips. "One of the last nice weekends in September, and you're going to work."

Dan shoved away from his desk. "No, I'm not." He grabbed the papers he'd been reading and tossed them into the trash.

"Hey!" Jasmine jumped up and pulled them out of the garbage. "I thought you needed these reports to figure out what Monstrous Murphy's up to."

"Yeah." Dan shoved his hands into his pockets. "So did I. But they're worthless."

"What are they?"

When Dan didn't answer, Jasmine turned to Shelby. "Police reports about Marlin."

Dan shook his head. "That's what they were supposed to be. But that kid covers his tracks better than anyone I've ever met. Every time the police came anywhere close to nailing him, someone else stepped up to take the fall. So those things—" he waved at the police reports—"are about as helpful as a squirt gun at a forest fire."

He paced in front of his desk. "People have reported seeing Marlin's idiots at different times with large amounts of drain cleaner, rubbing alcohol, brake cleaner, lithium batteries, cold tablets…"

"Stuff you'd use in a meth lab."

Dan nodded at Jasmine. "And they're always careful not to have any of that stuff when I'm around. So I've never seen anything suspicious that I can use to pull them in for questioning. Man! I'd give anything to know if that kid is just playing with meth, or if he's a serious cooker. And to know how Jayce is mixed up in it all."

Jasmine dropped the papers back into the trash can and perched on the edge of her desk. "I take it you've asked Jayce about it?"

"And *that's* about as helpful as *spitting* on a forest fire." He was letting his temper get the best of him, but blast it! Something big was either about to happen or was actually happening, and he couldn't figure out what. And he'd bet his pension Jayce knew what it was. But for all that he and Jayce had grown closer, Dan couldn't break through the shell he kept around his relationship with Marlin Murphy.

Why did Jayce protect that creep?

Shelby touched his arm. "How about we go get some lunch? You might think better on a full stomach."

He found a smile. "You just want to steal my pickle."

"Oh, please!"

Dan arched a look at Jasmine, but she wasn't the least

affected. She made a gagging motion, then shooed them away. "You two are so sweet together it's making me ill. Please, go. Eat. Get away from me."

"Whatever you say, boss." Dan pulled the office door open, then jumped back when two small bodies tumbled in almost on top of him. He recognized the yelps right away.

"What are you two doing here?" He eyed his offspring. Had they been listening at the office door? Why on earth would they do that?

"We…uh…we were coming to see if…if…" Aaron looked at his sister, and she jumped in to help.

"If you wanted to buy us lunch."

Clearly, those two were up to something, but he didn't have time to figure out what.

"Sorry, guys. You're on your own today." He stepped aside so Shelby could exit. "I'll be home for dinner, okay?"

Shannon's response was oddly meek. "Okay, Daddy. We'll see you later."

She sounded so nice and obedient. So why, Dan wondered as he followed Shelby from the office, did it make him so uneasy?

TWENTY

"The tragedies that now blacken and darken the very air of heaven for us, will sink into their places in a scheme so august, so magnificent, so joyful, that we shall laugh for wonder and delight."
ARTHUR CHRISTOPHER BACON

"Should we accept only good things from the hand of God and never anything bad?"
JOB 2:10

AARON WAS SITTING ON THE COUCH, ENGROSSED IN his book, when Shannon dropped down beside him.

"Do you mind?"

She didn't answer. Instead, she reached out and plucked the book from his hands.

"Hey!"

She closed the book and put it on the coffee table. "We need to talk."

"I don't need to do anything except finish my book. Now give it back before I—"

"Aaron, come on! You heard what Dad said about Marlin when we overheard him talking at his office. And about Jayce." She sounded so serious, Aaron bit back what he'd been about to say—which basically was to tell her to go jump.

"Yeah, I heard him."

"Well? Didn't that worry you?"

He pulled one leg under him. "Sure, but what can we do about it?"

"I have a plan."

When he just stared at her, she leaned closer. "A *real* plan. And I think it just might work."

Aaron groaned. "Great. If you think I'm going to join you in some lame plan—"

"Just listen. We want to know what Marlin's up to, right?"

"Yeah, so?"

"And we want to know how much Jayce is involved, right?"

He bobbed his head from side to side. "*And*?"

"I've been following Jayce."

Alarm jolted through Aaron, and he sat up straight. "You what?"

"It's okay. I've been careful. He doesn't know I'm doing it."

He faced her. "How do you think Jayce would feel about you following him?"

Her features clouded. "He wouldn't like it. But sometimes you have to do things people don't like to protect them." She tugged at Aaron's arm. "Jayce is our friend, Aaron. He needs us."

He narrowed his eyes. "*Us*? What *us*?"

"You and me, *us*. We're going to follow Jayce again. Tomorrow. I think something's happening. I don't know for sure, but—"

"Forget it." He grabbed his book from the table and headed for the deck off the kitchen. She followed right behind him.

"Come *on*, Aaron! Dad's working tomorrow, so we don't have to worry about him. And it's Sunday, so we'll have all day to track Jayce, which means we'll have a good chance of seeing what's going on."

"Shannon…"

"Look, do you want to help Daddy? And Jayce?"

He sighed. "Of course."

"Then this is the way to do it. We'll head out early tomorrow morning, and we'll be back before dinner when Dad comes home; we can tell him what we found out."

"Assuming we find out anything that matters."

She didn't reply, but he could tell from the look on her face that she thought they would. Aaron stood there, one hand on the sliding glass door, the other clutching his book. Finally he stepped away from the door. "Okay."

Shannon squealed. "Really?"

He cuffed her with the book. "Well, *some*one's got to go to keep you out of trouble."

She threw her arms around him. "Thank you, Aaron. This is going to work. I just know it. Now come back into the living room, and I'll fill you in on what I've seen so far."

He followed her, tapping his book against his leg as he walked. "All I can say is, we'd better do some serious praying tonight."

"For safety?"

"That," he said with a sigh, "and for Dad not to kill us when he finds out what we've done."

"Oh." Shannon's nod was slow and thoughtful. "That's going to take a *lot* of prayer."

"Amen, sister." He threw his arm around Shannon's shoulders. "Amen."

TWENTY-ONE

"The great snake lies ever half awake,
at the bottom of the pit of the world,
until he awakens in hunger."

T. S. ELIOT

"A bruised reed he will not break, and a smoldering
wick he will not snuff out, till he leads justice to victory."

MATTHEW 12:20 (NIV)

IT WAS A BEAUTIFUL DAY.

Of course, most folks would disagree. Foggy days weren't generally considered "beautiful," especially in Sanctuary where the dense mist could actually keep people housebound for days on end. And especially this early in the season.

Sure, fog was expected from December on, and lots of it. But in early October? No way. And yet, here it was, cloaking the world all around them with a misty beauty.

Dan loved this kind of weather. Maybe it was the cool, moist air. Or the way the fog hung there, seemingly inert, but if you just concentrated hard enough you could see how it was in constant motion, drifting past.

With fog—especially thick fog, like today's, where you almost couldn't see the front of your car—the day seemed clean. Quiet. Peaceful.

Yeah. It was a beautiful day.

Dan leaned back against the car seat, poured coffee from the thermos into his cup, and sipped it.

Come to think of it, most of the days lately had been beautiful. And the nights. His first date with Shelby had been...amazing. They'd been so comfortable together. He never dreamed he could feel that comfortable with anyone again. The drive down to Shady Cove seemed to take five minutes instead of forty, and their time together over dinner had only brought them closer together.

They'd gone out several times a week since then, sometimes to dinner, other times just for a walk or a drive. Some nights they spent at his house with the kids who seemed as fond of Shelby as he was. The more time he spent with her, the more certain he grew that he'd been given something he thought was impossible.

A second chance at the love of a lifetime.

He looked out the windshield, drinking in the way the haze hung in the tall evergreens around him. Too bad he had to work today. Shannon and Aaron loved the fog as much as he did. They begged him this morning to let them go hiking while he was at work, but he'd been firm.

"I don't want you kids out alone in this. If I was with you, it'd be different. But I can't be today. So stick close to home."

They hadn't been happy with him, but those were the breaks. Parenting didn't mean always making the kids happy but making them safe.

Still, he had to admit he felt a little guilty. Here he was, sitting on one of the many deserted roads just off the old highway, enjoying the fog-drenched world, and the kids were stuck at home.

Ah well. There had to be some benefit to being an adult.

Squawk! Screech! "Chief?"

Dan cringed. They really had to get that radio fixed. He grabbed the mic and keyed it. "Dan here."

"Hey, I just got a call from ol' man Brumby."

Dan waited for her to talk about what a grump the man was, but she didn't. "And?"

"Well, it's strange. He said there's some kind of trouble up at his place. He was talking real fast and sounded like he was all out of breath, and those crazy dogs of his were yelping in the background, so I couldn't really understand him."

The pop of her gum sounded like an explosion over the radio. Dan gritted his teeth. "Does he want me to come out there?"

"I think so. I don't know. He sounded really weird. Kept talking real fast, rambling on and on about how he was calling like you told him to, that what happened wasn't his fault, that no one could see in this fog." She fell silent for a moment. "Chief? He didn't sound like himself. He sounded…"

Dan frowned. "What, Jasmine?"

"Scared." Oddly enough, so did she. Few things rattled Jasmine, but this call had clearly done so. Which meant something was wrong. Very, very wrong.

"Did he say anything else?"

"Well, I'm not sure."

"What is it?"

"Chief, he was babbling something fierce, but I think I caught something about people up there. About them being hurt."

Dan waited. He could tell she wasn't done, but she was having a hard time getting it out.

"I'm almost sure he said they were lying on the road in front of his place. Bleeding. Dying."

Dan examined the gray soup around him, then pulled out onto Highway 62 and headed south. "You notified the EMTs?"

"Gonna call 'em soon as we hang up, Chief."

"Let me know their ETA, Jasmine."

"Will do. Over 'n' out."

"Jasmine, you don't have to—" Dan sighed. He'd have a

better chance of changing the color of grass than getting her to drop her radio lingo. "Never mind. Justice out."

Normally, he'd have been at the accident site within ten to fifteen minutes at the most. Today, it took him twice that. Twenty-five minutes. An eternity if someone was hurt. Bleeding...

He crept along, fingers tight on the steering wheel, praying all the way, hoping against hope the victims were only injured, that they'd hold on until he and the EMTs got there.

The logging road cut off the highway, turned from paved to gravel, then snaked its way up the mountain.

Screak! "Come in, Chief."

He grabbed the mic. "I'm here. You reach the EMTs?"

"They're on their way, but it's gonna be a while. Fog's gettin' worse."

Great. "Thanks, Jasmine."

"Sorry the news isn't better, Chief."

So was he. He'd handled accidents before. Bad ones. And he'd dealt with his share of fatalities.

But it was never easy.

He peered out the window at the engulfing shroud. Knowing how the road climbed up the mountain, Dan figured he'd break through the fog, but the weather wasn't giving an inch today. What had seemed so peaceful and beautiful a half hour ago suddenly seemed menacing.

He crawled around the last corner before Brumby's place and pulled the cruiser to the side of the road.

He stepped out of the car and listened. Silence. Where were the dogs? For that matter, where was Brumby? Well, before he went to find the man, he'd better set out some flares so the EMTs knew this was the scene of the accident.

It only took him minutes to set up the flares and road flashers, then he grabbed the first-aid kit from the trunk and walked to the fence. "James! James Brumby!"

He listened. Fog seemed to amplify sound. Even if Brumby

had the dogs closed up in the house, Dan should be able to hear the boys' fierce barking.

But it was silent as a tomb.

Brushing off a sudden chill, Dan hollered Brumby's name again. Why didn't he respond? The man was a lot of things, but deaf was not one of them. He tried once more then waited.

No sign of the man anywhere.

Well, he couldn't wait any longer. Best to see if he could find whoever was hurt. The fog captured the glow of the flares, blending the red light with the bright white of the strobing flashers and turning the world around Dan eerie, haunting.

A shiver spidered up his spine as his gaze swept the ground.

He almost stepped on the first body. One second there was nothing but fog; the next he hit a leg with his foot.

"Whoa! Sorry about that." Dan knelt, setting his equipment on the ground and kneeling beside the still form. "It's okay; I'm the deputy sheriff. I'm here to help you."

No response. No sound. No movement.

Dan could see the still form now, lying facedown in front of him. His heart seized. Either it was a short adult or…

A kid. No more than a teen, from the size of him. *Oh, Jesus*—his prayer was equal measures supplication and sorrow—*a child? Why a child?*

He reached out to feel for injuries, then when he saw the victim's back, his hands froze in midmotion. There was a fist-sized hole in the kid's coat, right between the shoulder blades.

Dan took in the dark stains soaking the jacket around the hole.

Blood.

This kid had been shot.

Dan stared down at the wound, utter disbelief wrestling with fury, as James Brumby's voice drifted through his mind: *"I'm tellin' you, Deputy. I see any of those kids on my property again, I'm gonna get my gun."*

"Brumby, you old fool." Dan felt for a pulse in the neck, and for a moment he was back with Sarah, pressing his fingers to her neck. He pushed the memory away—along with the emotions it sent flooding through him. He couldn't afford those emotions right now. He had to focus.

No pulse. The victim's skin was like ice, and Dan knew that had nothing to do with the weather.

His fingers slid away.

Nothing he could do for this one. Best to move on, see who else was hurt. Pray someone was still alive.

He only walked a few more feet before finding a second victim lying sprawled on her back. This one was even younger than the first. A little girl, from the long brown hair spread across her face. Dan ground his teeth, dread a weight in his heart and mind. *Are they all children, God? All of them?*

Dan knelt beside the still form. She had to be Shannon's age, even had long chestnut hair like Shannon's. *Jesus, Jesus…help this little one's family…*

He pressed his fingers to the death-cooled neck. Praying. Waiting…

Nothing.

Bitter defeat squeezed his eyes shut. *God, it's not right! She's so small.* He opened his eyes, saw the gunshot wound in her chest, reached gentle fingers to brush away the hair covering her still face. *So youn—*

Air wedged in his throat. His mind saw. Grasped. But didn't understand. Refused to understand.

It couldn't be.

Fingers trembling, he touched her cheek, the fluorescent orange Band-Aid he'd put there just this morning.

No.

"I told you to stay home. I told you not to go out in this." He took hold of the slim shoulders, shoulders that fit in his hands the way her mother's always had. "God, please…not Shannon. Not my Shannon!"

But it was. His little girl, lying in the dirt, skin so white. So cold.

Understanding had fled at the first sight of her face; now it came surging back, raking every nerve. "*God!*"

He pulled her to him, willing the life to flow from his own heart into hers. "Shannon, please baby, please…"

But it was too late. He knew it, even as he cradled Shannon, her blood sticky on his hands.

How could this have happened? Agony sliced through his veins, turning his blood hot, boiling. Where was Aaron? He was supposed to watch his sister. They were supposed to stay together.

Dan went still.

They were supposed to stay together.

Oh, Jesus…no. You couldn't. You couldn't let that happen.

Easing Shannon back to the ground, he made his clutching fingers release her, made his trembling, stiff legs stand and walk back to the first body. It still lay there, facedown.

No…no…no…

But as he studied the form in front of him, he saw. Saw the jacket Aaron had begged for week after week. The jacket his son had been so sure he couldn't live without. The jacket Dan finally broke down and bought him as an early birthday present.

Aaron's jacket, ravaged by the bullet that pierced and destroyed.

Aaron's favorite shoes and the jeans Shannon patched for him using hot pink thread because she knew it would make him crazy—both splattered with blood.

A soundless scream clawed up his throat, pried his mouth open, and exploded into the suffocating mist.

Suddenly he was on his knees, doubled over, fingers digging into the hard, unyielding gravel, as his life slowly but oh-so-surely unraveled.

∽

"Dan?"

He heard the voice but didn't move. Couldn't.

A strong hand gripped his shoulder. "Dan? C'mon, man. It's Tony. I'm here with the squad."

Dan's eyes opened but only a slit. The ghostly glare of the flares and strobes he'd put out had been joined by brighter colors. The EMTs. The ambulance. They were here.

But it was too late. *Too late.*

The pressure on his shoulder increased. "C'mon, buddy. I know it's bad, but we need you with us here. How many vics are there?"

How many? Dan shook his head. His whole world. "I don't know."

"You don't—"

Dan surged to his feet and spun to face the man beside him. "I. Don't. Know."

Tony backpedaled. "Whoa, okay, man. Don't freak on me."

A shocked cry split the air, and Dan and Tony turned. Jack, another EMT, was kneeling beside Aaron's body. Jack's day job was as a coach. A football coach.

Aaron's football coach.

His stricken gaze went from Aaron to Dan. "I'm sorry. Oh, man. I'm so sorry."

"*What* is going on?" Tony took a step toward Jack, then jerked to a halt. Stared. Dan watched the tumble of emotions paint his friend's features: astonishment, dawning understanding, horror.

Tony turned back to Dan, his gaze sliding past Dan to Shannon's still form. When he met Dan's eyes, Dan just stared.

"Who did this?"

Dan felt his hands clench. "Brumby. James Brumby."

Tony looked around them. "Is he here somewhere?"

"I don't know." His tone hardened. "But I'm going to find out."

A hand closed on Dan's arm. "No, you're not."

He stared at the man holding him, rage burning in his throat as he growled out a warning. "Let me go, Jack. Now."

The EMT squared off with Dan. "I'm sorry, but you're in no shape to go after Brumby."

Dan jerked his arm free. "You think I'm going to just let him go? After he did *this*?"

"He's not going to get away. We'll call Sheriff Grayson. Get him and some other deputies up here to go after Brumby. But you're not going by yourself."

"You think I can't get past you, Jack?"

"I think you can't get past us both."

Dan looked at Tony, who now stood beside his partner.

"This is bad, Dan. But Jack's right. You can't be the one to take Brumby."

He considered rushing them, knocking them both out of his way, forcing his way into Brumby's house, wrapping his fingers around the man's scrawny neck...

He closed his eyes. Nodded. "Call the sheriff."

Dan turned and walked back toward the place where his children lay. The place where their lives had ended.

And his along with them.

TWENTY-TWO

"There is eloquence in screaming."

*"O God, you have ground me down
and devastated my family."*

JOB 16:7

SHELBY WAS JUST LEAVING CHURCH WHEN SHE HEARD her name being called.

She turned to find Jasmine standing there. "Hey, girlfriend. What are you—?" Her teasing smile faded when she saw the look on Jasmine's face.

Something was very, very wrong.

Jasmine took her hand. "Shelby…" Jasmine's voice broke.

"What is it? What's wrong?"

"It's Dan…"

Terror seized Shelby, and she thought her knees might give way. "Oh, Father, no! Is he?"

"No. No, I'm sorry. He's fine."

Shelby swatted Jasmine's arm. "Don't ever do that again! You scared the *life* out of me."

Jasmine rubbed an unsteady hand over her eyes. "*He's* fine,

227

Shelby. But Aaron. And Shannon. They're dead. Shot. James Brumby killed them."

The words struck her but didn't connect. Hit but didn't make sense. Shelby frowned, and the meaning of what Jasmine was saying squeezed past her denial.

Aaron and Shannon, the lights of Dan's life, were dead.

Dear God in heaven… She put her hand against the side of the church, steadying herself. *Wasn't it enough for him to lose Sarah? But the children? Lord, the* children?

How is he going to survive this?

Dan's blood surged through his veins with such force it made his head ache.

Hurry up…

He stood next to the cruiser, watching the sheriff and his men move in on Brumby's place. They called out. Announced their intent. When no response came, they broke down the door.

Dan watched the officers flow into Brumby's house, every ounce of control focused on keeping him where he was—where the sheriff told him to stay or he'd get fired.

He wanted to be there. To hear for himself what had happened.

To look his children's killer in the face.

Within minutes, several officers came out of the house. One signaled to Dan, and he broke into a run. But the deputy stopped Dan before he entered. "It's empty."

Dan's gut twisted. "Empty?"

"No one's in there. No humans. No dogs. Nothing. The guy rabbited. But don't worry, Dan. He's on the run with a bunch of dogs. We'll catch him."

Dan went inside, saw for himself that what his friend told him was true.

Brumby was gone.

There would be no arrest. No answers.

And no justice. Not for you. Not for your kids.

The bitter words cut through Dan, and he turned, going back to his car. But before he reached it, Sheriff John Grayson was at his side.

"I'm gonna have Pete drive you home."

Dan squared off with his boss. "I'm fine."

"No, you're not. And I'm not letting you behind the wheel of a cruiser." John nodded to a deputy standing nearby, then met Dan's glare. "This isn't a suggestion, Deputy. It's an order."

Dan spun, but John's hand caught his arm. "We've notified your sisters, Dan. Annie's at your house now. A friend of Kyla's is flying her down from Portland. I just wanted you to know."

He stared down at the ground, afraid if he looked at John, he'd lose it. "Thank you."

John's hand squeezed his arm then let go. Dan walked to the cruiser, slid in on the passenger side, and stared out the windshield. His gaze focused outside, and as realization assaulted him, he leaned forward, gripping the dashboard.

The fog was lifting.

He'd been so preoccupied he hadn't noticed there was no longer anything blocking his sight. Blocking anyone's sight.

God? You let it lift now? His fingers dug into the dashboard. *Why didn't You do that sooner? Why didn't You let Brumby see who was out there?*

"Dan?"

He spun and found himself facing Pete, one of the newer deputies, seated behind the steering wheel. Dan didn't speak. Just sat there.

"Dan, you okay?" Pete glanced away. "Look, forget I said that. Stupid question." He turned the key and the engine jumped to life.

Jumped to life…

Dan's lip curled. Humorless laughter coursed through him. Everything was alive.

Everything but his wife. His children.

Pete's discomfort was evident in his jerky actions, the glances he kept throwing at Dan. "Let's get you home, buddy."

Home. Dan sagged back against the seat.

What home?

No. Don't. Don't give in. Think. Focus:

On his sister. At least one, by now, if not both, were waiting for him.

On Pete and his driving. Clean. Crisp. Economy of movement.

On the sound of the tires on the road. Gravel crunching. Slight squeal as they turned onto the highway.

Focus. On anything and everything but the silent screaming filling his mind.

She couldn't stop shaking.

Annie Justice sat at her brother's kitchen table, sipping the cup of tea she just brewed. She stared at her hands, commanding them to be still. To stop trembling.

They wouldn't listen.

Neither would the rest of her.

Because this can't be real. Please, God…this just can't be real.

With an impatient huff of air, she pushed the mug away and stood. Quick steps took her through the spacious kitchen and out into the great room. Annie recalled the first time she'd seen this house. Dan had asked her and Kyla to take a look at it with him, to see if she thought the kids would like it.

The moment Annie saw the house, she knew it was perfect. Large and warm, just the right home for a new start. Even the ever-practical Kyla had fallen in love with the place.

"Oh, Dan," she'd said. "It's a sanctuary within Sanctuary. It's perfect for you and the kids."

Dan and the kids.

Annie blinked back tears, walking through the living room,

touching books, knickknacks, throw pillows…anything the kids might have touched.

For years she'd thought of her brother in terms of Dan and Sarah, like it was one word: *DanandSarah*. It only made sense, because they were so much a part of each other. It took Annie almost a year to finally start thinking of her brother as *Danandthekids*. Again, one word. All connected.

Now?

She jerked to a halt in the hallway and rested her forehead against the wall. Now what? How would Danny come back from this? He'd survived losing Sarah because of the kids. They pulled him out of grief's abyss, back into life. They became his reason for going on. Reminded him there was still living to do.

She turned her head, and her forehead bumped against something. Opening her eyes, she pulled back, focused. And a small cry escaped her.

Dan, Sarah, Shannon, and Aaron. They all smiled at her from a family portrait, taken over three years ago. Annie laid her hand on the picture.

Jesus, how is he going to survive this?

"Annot?"

She spun on a gasp.

"Easy, little sister, it's just me."

Kyla. The sight of her brought the wash of tears Annie had managed to hold back, and she fell into her sister's arms, weeping.

"Here, drink this."

Kyla handed a warmed-up cup of tea to Annie, noting her younger sister's drawn features. Annot was so sensitive. Such was the price of an artist's temperament, she supposed. Thank heaven she didn't suffer from the same quirks.

But there was no defense against this kind of news. Sarah's death…that had been terrible. But she'd been an adult. Somehow, losing children…

It was crazy. Senseless.

Kyla didn't do senseless. That was more Annot's world. Ever since they were children, her little sister spent her time living in her imagination, seeing colors where there were none, singing songs she heard in her head.

Then there was Annot's room. Chaos. That was the only way to describe it. Kyla's room, by contrast, was clean and well ordered. A place for everything and everything in its place.

Until Annot came in, that was. Then Kyla spent all her time putting things back after her sister pulled them out and left them in the middle of the floor.

It drove Kyla nuts.

And yet, she loved Annot. Treasured her, probably for the very reasons she drove her nuts. For her free spirit and open heart. Both of which were breaking at this moment.

Kyla stepped over Kodi—the huge, black beast sprawled out on the floor in front of the couch—and sat next to her sister. Kyla tried twice to speak, but her voice wouldn't work.

Annot nodded, patting her hand, and the understanding in that gesture was almost Kyla's undoing.

Father, this isn't right! You know how much those children loved You. How much Avidan loves you! How could this happen to them? How could You let those children die? And like this? She caught her breath. *Oh, Father, not like this!*

Annot took her hands, and Kyla forced herself to speak. "Do you know when Avidan will be here?"

"Soon. I got a call about fifteen minutes ago saying they were on their way."

Kyla stared down into her coffee. "Are they sure? Both of the children…?" She couldn't finish. She didn't need to.

Annie looked down at their linked hands. When she could speak, the words came out ragged. "They're both dead, Kylie." She tightened her grip. "We have to pray. Now."

"Of course—"

"No!" Annot pulled at their hands, the action as desperate

as her cry. "You don't understand! We have to beg God to help us. To give us the words. For Dan." She clenched her teeth, fighting against a flood of emotion. "Because I'll tell you something, Kylie, I don't have *any* idea what to say to him. All I feel…all I know right now…is *anger.*"

Annot was gripping her hands so hard they hurt. Kyla eased her hands free and took hold of her sister's shoulders. "I know this is crazy, but none of it—" she gave Annot a gentle shake—"*none* of it changes who God is."

"How could He let this happen?"

Her sister's wail broke her heart, and Kyla pulled Annot close, embracing her, letting her weep against her. The storm raged, then slowly, surely, subsided.

"I'm so glad you're here."

The whispered words brought a flood of memories, of times Annot would come to Kyla's room after a nightmare, seeking safety…when her younger sister came to her with a broken heart after some boy hurt her…. All their lives, Kyla knew, no matter how her little sister shone, she needed Kyla. For comfort. For security.

Hearing that long-ago little girl voice of Annie's now…Kyla's lip trembled. She choked on a sob. And tears streamed down her face.

At the first hint of her pain, Kodi was there, laying her snout on Kyla's leg. Annot almost smiled.

Though it was beyond Kyla's comprehension, Kodi absolutely adored her. Kyla sniffed back her tears, looking down her nose at the walking fur machine. "What's this about?"

Annot allowed a smile. "You know what they say, 'all creatures great and small.'" She shrugged. "Maybe Kodi wants to pray with us."

Kyla dropped a hand on Kodi's broad head—and she wasn't sure who was most surprised at the action, Annot or herself. "'Where two or three gather…'" She took Annot's hand again. "Well, it can't hurt."

"Exactly."

Bowing their heads, the two went before God, crying out their pain.

"Father God—" Kyla gripped Annot's hands tighter, needing her sister's strength to get the words out—"we're so lost. We want to help our brother, but don't know how to do that in the face of this...insanity."

"Lord," Annot came in, "Dan has been through so much. Please, Father, please, put your hand on him. Even now as we're praying, touch him with Your peace. Your presence."

"Don't let the enemy win in this, God. Don't let him tear apart our brother, your son. Your warrior. Dan has fought for You, for others, all his life. Please, somehow help him endure this terrible loss. This..." Kyla struggled, seeking the right words. Suddenly they came to her. "This horrible injustice."

Annot's fingers gripped her hands even tighter. "Kylie's right, Lord. This just isn't right!" Her words broke, but she pushed on. "I don't understand why this had to happen, but I know You, God. I know Your love. And somehow...somehow You'll make things right. For Danny. For all of us. Because Your justice doesn't fail."

As the prayer went on, Kyla felt it. A cloak of calm, settling over them. As though it soaked up their tears, bound their broken hearts, and imparted God's peace.

When their words ran out, and the amens were said, Kyla settled back. The tension pinching her temples eased. She even stroked Kodi's ears. "It's going to be all right." As she spoke the words, she felt such...confidence. An almost reverent relief. As if the deep, unanswerable questions had been answered, though no words had come to them.

The sound of the front door opening brought both sisters to their feet. Annot told the dog to stay, then she took Kyla's hand and they went to meet their brother.

At the door, they jerked to a stop.

Avidan stood there. Hands limp at his sides. Face ravaged

by shock. Sorrow. Though he looked at them, his eyes were blank. As though he didn't recognize them.

Or didn't see them.

"Danny?"

Dan flinched, his head jerking. He blinked, and Kyla could almost see his eyes, his mind, come into focus. With a hoarse cry, he came toward them. They rushed forward, opening their arms. Kyla felt shaken to the core when, in the wake of this shattering sorrow, their big brother became a terrified, weeping child.

Kyla and Annot did what they could for him. They offered arms to cradle. Whispers of shared sorrow and comfort. Hearts filled with prayer.

And the unmovable anchor of truth. Truth they knew and believed but couldn't speak. Not yet.

God was with them.

TWENTY-THREE

"Who ever said that misery loved company?
[His] misery did not love company.
[His] misery loved to be alone.
[His] misery threatened to bludgeon company."

FRANCINE PASCAL

"Therefore I will not keep silent; I will speak out in the anguish
of my spirit, I will complain in the bitterness of my soul."

JOB 7:11 (NIV)

TWO ELEGANT CASKETS. SIDE BY SIDE. ADORNED WITH blankets of flowers, stuffed animals, and cards.

It was the most horrific sight Dan had ever seen.

He practically cowered at the back of the church narthex, hands buried in his pockets, counting the seconds as they dragged by. Waiting to be free.

Annie and Kyla stood at the front of the church, reading notes and remembrances about Shannon and Aaron. He listened as story after story was shared, some drawing sobs, some stirring laughter.

It would be his turn soon. But he wasn't ready. He didn't know what to do with his hands. Putting them in his pockets seemed too casual. Keeping them at his sides was stiff. Uncomfortable. Folding them in front of him looked stupid.

Are you nuts? Who cares where you put your hands? Just get up there. Say something. Anything.

He peered through the doorway at pew after pew of mourners. Adults. Children. Teens. So many had come to say good-bye. They were sitting there, listening—and waiting for him. He was supposed to walk up the aisle, stand before those two cases holding his children prisoner, and face a church full of grieving friends and family. To say…say…

What?

What was there to say? No words, spoken or otherwise, mattered. Nothing would help this make sense! Nothing!

Bitterness dug its claws deep as it clawed across his heart, his spirit.

How could this have happened? How could he possibly be here again?

Lost.

Desperate.

An aching emptiness where his heart used to be as he stared at a casket—no, *two* caskets, this time. Caskets for his children.

And his heart.

"Mr. Justice?"

Dan turned at the broken voice. Jayce stood there, eyes red, swollen.

"Mr. Justice. I'm so sorry."

He wanted to speak words of comfort, of shared love for these two now lost to them. To embrace the stricken boy standing there, hands clenched together so tightly they were white.

But he couldn't.

Couldn't speak. Couldn't move.

He was no longer made of flesh and blood. Instead, he'd turned to stone. Cold. Unmovable. A statue staring down at the living, unable to care or feel.

"Mr. Justice?"

The confusion in Jayce's voice tugged at him. Almost drew him out of the pit closing in on him. A plea rose from within him.

Don't close the boy out. Please, don't do that to him. He doesn't deserve it.

Deserve it? *Deserve* it?

Did Aaron and Shannon *deserve* to die? Did Sarah? Did he *deserve* to suffer this kind of pain? Loss?

What did *deserving* have to do with *anything*?

He stared at Jayce, watched shock then pain twist the boy's features. The color drained from his young face, and he spun—

Only to run square into Shelby Wilson as she slipped into the narthex. She caught Jayce, took one look at his face, and turned to Dan. "What's going on?"

His stare transferred to her. This woman he'd been dating, who touched his heart in ways he never expected. Who brought to life emotions he never thought to feel again.

And as he looked at her, he felt…nothing. Not for her. Not for Jayce.

My children are dead. My life is over.

"Dan?" Shelby hugged Jayce with one arm, reaching out her free hand toward him. "Dan, please. Let me help."

He lowered his gaze to her outstretched hand. That small, warm hand. Hands so like Sarah's. And Shannon's. But his wife and daughter's hands weren't warm. Not any longer.

Sickened to the core, he turned, forced his marbleized limbs to move. Walk away. From the funeral.

From death.

From everything.

And everyone.

"Jayce, it will be okay."

He wanted to laugh. To show Miss Wilson he didn't believe. No, even more, that he didn't *care*.

"Dan's just…he's hurting right now. So much that he can't

think straight. He's saying things he doesn't mean. Can't mean."
Her hand trembled on his shoulder. Was that supposed to be a
comforting touch?

Think again.

"He cares about you. Please don't think he doesn't—"

Jayce ran.

Her voice called after him, but he didn't stop. Just kept his
feet moving, pounding the ground beneath him.

All Miss Wilson's talk, all her reassurances were just words.
Stupid, empty words.

Jayce knew the truth. Saw it in Dan's eyes.

Yeah, he'd let himself start calling Mr. Justice *Dan*. Never
out loud. Just in his head. Like they were friends. Close.

Like *Deputy* Justice cared about him.

He should have known it was all just a cop keeping a kid
out of trouble. Nothing but talk.

Was Shannon just talk?

Pain knifed through him, and he staggered, stumbling to a
stop. Legs aching, lungs screaming for air, he doubled over, one
hand fisted around the Aslan pendant.

No. Shannon wasn't just talk. Neither was Aaron. They
only said what was true. What they meant. Their eyes showed
that as clear as their words. And their actions.

But Deputy Justice?

Jayce gulped in air, pushed himself straight, and started
walking.

What Jayce saw in his eyes today was a question. One simple
question. A question Jayce had asked himself every day since the
terrible news about Shannon shattered his world.

A question he couldn't answer.

Why wasn't it you?

Dan just reached his car when he heard someone call him.

"Deputy Justice, a moment, please."

He hesitated, hand on the car door. The last thing he wanted right now was to talk with Agatha Hunter. Or Doris Kleffer, who was bound to be at her side.

Just go. Pretend you didn't hear her. Pull the car door open, get inside, and go!

He tensed, fingers gripping the door handle, ready to bolt—and stopped.

He hesitated one second too long. A tremulous hand dropped onto his arm. Dan lowered his head to look into those ancient, ageless eyes. An odd question rambled through his fogged mind.

How old was Agatha?

He had no idea. Had never thought to ask her or anyone who knew her. But he could see a life well lived in the eyes trained on him.

Dan laid his hand over hers where it rested on his sleeve. For all that he'd considered running from her, he was glad she caught him. If anyone could speak comfort in the face of this insanity, it would be Agatha.

"Deputy Justice, I only have one thing to say."

He waited, ready for the balm on his raw, aching wounds.

"I'm disappointed in you."

His mouth fell open. His eyes creased into a stupid stare. "I…wh-what?"

She delivered a sharp pat to his arm. "You heard me, young man. Disappointed."

Dan took a step back, but she gripped his sleeve, not letting go.

"That boy needed you, Deputy. A word, a touch, anything to tell him he still mattered. And you let him down."

"Boy?" He looked around them. "What—Jayce? You mean Jayce?"

Her head bobbed. "I do, indeed. Young Jayce Dalton, who was doing so well. I heard it all, Deputy. All the boy said." She eyed him. "All you *didn't* say."

"Maybe you didn't hear what you thought."

It was a low blow, and Agatha didn't let him get away with it. "Do you think for a minute I would take a chance on not hearing what's being said about that precious little girl and boy, Dan?"

He couldn't hold her steady gaze. He looked down at the ground. "I'm sorry. Of course you wouldn't."

"As much I detest this hearing aid, it does its job when I let it. Although today, I almost wish it hadn't. I almost wish I'd missed what you did to that boy."

Dan had had about as much as he could take. "Look, Agatha—"

"No, Dan Justice, *you* look. Look deep inside yourself. More than once I've listened to you talk about God. About His goodness and mercy. About His place in your life."

Dan gritted his teeth. "I just lost my children!"

"I *know* that, boy." The raw pain in her words hit him like a stinging slap.

"Don't you see, Dan? We *all* lost them. Those children of yours…we loved them. They were part of this town, part of each of us who lived here. Shannon…"

She drew in a ragged breath. "That little girl brought more joy to my days than I could ever express. And that sweet boy. Those children were a gift." Her fingers gripped his arm. "A gift right from heaven. For all of us."

Pain wrapped its spiny fingers around his neck. Squeezing. Squeezing…

"But Dan, your little girl—she was God's gift for *that young boy*. Don't think we didn't see, didn't know how she loved him. Why, she talked about him near as much as she talked about you."

"I can't—I can't talk about this now. Don't you under-stand?"

"Don't *you* understand? That's the question." She let go of his sleeve but didn't back away. "I know you're in pain. Of course I know that! Nothing makes sense, nothing is right. Will ever be right again."

She did understand. Then why was she being so—?

"But feeling pain is no good reason for causing pain, and well you know it."

Dan wanted to run. From the woman. From her relentless words. *God, please, make her stop…*

"Your little girl saw that boy the way God saw him. He knew it, even if he didn't understand it. And it changed him, opened him up."

"How do you know all this?"

She folded her hands in front of her. "Just because I'm old, boy, and have trouble hearing at times, don't think I'm blind. I saw the way his face changed. The way his *life* changed. Your daughter did that because she loved with a pure, godly love."

Images flooded Dan's mind. Shannon smiling, reaching up to hug him. Shannon laughing, singing. Shannon holding the Aslan necklace out to Jayce. "That's all Sarah and I ever wanted…for Shannon and Aaron to know God. To know His love."

"And show it. And so they did. You taught them well. Until now."

The last two words brought his head snapping back to face her. "What does that mean?"

Those eyes studied him, so full of sadness that he almost couldn't bear it. "You know what it means, Dan Justice. God brought Shannon into Jayce Dalton's life. But He brought others as well. Aaron…and you."

"I don't have anything left to give him!"

"You didn't have anything to give him in the first place." She said it quietly, gently. "Not of your own. All you've ever had to offer that boy—or anyone—is what God gives you. What He does and says through you." She tugged her shawl closer around her lean frame. "Same as any of us."

He rubbed trembling fingers over his eyes. "What do you want from me, Agatha?"

"Nothing."

His hand dropped, and he stared at her.

She sniffed, her chin raised another fraction. "Don't look at me like that, boy. It's the truth. *I'm* not the one who wants something from you."

Dan bit his lip, holding back the angry tirade burning his tongue. "Fine. What does Jayce want from me?"

Her steady gaze bored into him.

"Well?"

Her lips thinned. "If I didn't know better, I'd call you a fool. That or plain stupid. But you're neither, and well I know it." She lowered her head, shaking it. "Go on, then. Run. For all the good it will do you."

She sighed, so much sorrow in that low sound. Then her back stiffened, her shoulders came back, and she lifted her gaze to his. "I can't stay out here any longer. I have to say good-bye to two precious angels." She turned, making her way back toward the church.

Dan followed her painstaking progress, then realized two people stood on the outside steps, waiting for her. As he expected, one was Doris. The other—

Dan's heart lurched.

Shelby. Even at this distance, he could see her face. See the hurt in her pinched features.

Hurt he had put there.

He jerked the car door open and slid onto the seat. Gunning the engine, he pushed the accelerator to the floor, but not fast enough to escape the echo of Agatha's words.

"Go on, then. Run."

"For all the good it will do you."

TWENTY-FOUR

"Mankind fears an evil man but heaven does not."
MENCIUS

*"The wicked say to themselves,
'God isn't watching! He will never notice!'"*
PSALM 10:11

EXHAUSTION. UTTER. COMPLETE EXHAUSTION.

That's what sat on Shelby's shoulders as she pulled the doors of the center shut at the end of an especially long, tiring day.

She walked to her car, pressed the button on her keychain to open the door. *God bless whoever invented remote access.* It was a woman's best friend, especially late at night like this. What was it about darkness that made things seem so much more sinister?

Sliding inside, she pulled the door closed, hitting the lock. She leaned her head back against the seat for a moment, resting. Why did everything seem so much harder these days? Why couldn't she seem to rejuvenate?

The answer floated through her mind in an image. A face. A man's face, with a strong chin and killer blue eyes.

"Go away, Dan." She brushed at her eyes. It was just fatigue. Those weren't tears. "Please, just for one night, leave me alone."

Slipping the key in the ignition, she turned it.

Nothing.

Shelby frowned and turned the key again.

Zilch. Zippo. No joy in engineville.

Great. Just great. Now what was she supposed to—

A knock on her car window just about sent her through the car roof. She turned and in the darkness made out a young man's face. Of course, she couldn't lower the window at all. Not without power. So she yelled through the glass. "Yes?"

"Do you need help?"

The words were muffled, but Shelby heard them. Weary relief flooded her. *Thanks, Lord. I appreciate the angel.*

She unlocked the door and pushed it open—then realized, too late, what a mistake she'd made.

The young man reached inside and hauled her out of the car. She screamed, trying to pull away from him, but he was far stronger than she. And suddenly, he wasn't alone. Two forms came toward them out of the dark. One Shelby didn't recognize. The other…

O God…help me.

The other was Marlin Murphy.

"What's this? The fair Miss Wilson has car trouble?" Marlin's lips twisted in what she supposed he considered a smile. "Now that's a pity, isn't it, boys?"

As his goons echoed their "sympathy," Shelby backed up against her car, fighting the panic creeping through her. *Jesus, help me. Please, help me.* She felt her keys in her hand and eased them so that the keys slid between her fingers in a kind of pseudo brass knuckles. It wasn't much of a defense, but it was something. They'd do some damage if she could just hold on to them.

Murphy's goons stood on either side of her, not touching her, but close enough that she felt their breath fanning her cheeks. Murphy stood in front of her. Again, he didn't touch her. But he didn't need to to make her skin crawl.

"So what do you say, pretty lady?" He crossed his arms. "How 'bout we give you a ride home?"

"Sure," goon number one said with a chortle. "We could do that."

"We'd only take one or two detours." This from goon number two, who apparently was feeling left out.

"Oh—" Murphy's voice dropped, the throaty sound pure threat—"they wouldn't be detours, boys. They'd be the main attraction." He reached out then, let his fingers just brush her cheek. "Or, to be more accurate, *you'd* be the main attraction."

The feel of his touch was almost her undoing. She willed strength to her trembling limbs. He might overcome her, but not before she made him pay.

"Whatsa matter, babe? Struck dumb with gratitude?" He fingered her necklace, a cross the kids had given her for her birthday a few months ago, where it lay against her skin. "Hmm, pretty." He held her gaze as he slid his fingers behind the delicate chain, then yanked. The chain broke, and he held the necklace in front of her. "Think I'll keep this to remember you by."

Shelby glared at him but held her silence. She wouldn't play his game. Wouldn't give him the satisfaction of hearing the tremor in her voice.

"Aww—" he leaned closer, and she closed her eyes, fighting back a whimper—"don't be like that—"

"*Back off.*"

Murphy and his pals spun, eyes narrowed, hands fisted— and froze when they found themselves facing Deputy Dan Justice, his shotgun at his side.

If Shelby's knees weren't shaking so bad, she would have flung herself into Dan's arms. But she could only sag back against her car, swept by a relief so forceful it brought tears to her eyes.

As for Murphy, well, Shelby had to give it to the kid. He recovered quickly. He straightened, then held out his hands. "Hey, Deputy, relax. We're all friends here."

"I said, back off from the lady."

Even Murphy seemed to realize Dan's tone brooked no resistance. He took several steps away from Shelby, his goons at his side. With one smooth movement, Dan jerked the shotgun, cocking it as he lifted it.

"Whoa! What are you *doing*?"

Dan ignored Murphy. Instead, he eyed his two pals. "Beat it." They stared at him, gape-mouthed.

"*Now!*"

Their legs scrambled, and they disappeared into the night. Keeping the shotgun trained on Murphy, Dan walked toward him. The kid stood his ground, though Shelby could see beads of sweat on his brow.

She felt a stab of alarm herself when Dan walked until he was right in front of Murphy, the end of his shotgun pressed into the boy's chest.

"Dan."

One look from him was all it took for her voice to dry up and blow away. The man was stone-cold furious.

He turned back to Murphy. "I should haul you to jail and throw away the key."

Marlin just smirked. "On what charge, Deputy? All we were doing was talking."

Dan's jaw tensed. "Score one for the punk. You're not as stupid as you look." Marlin's eyes narrowed at that, but Dan didn't give him a chance to speak. "I want you to know something, son."

"What's that, Dad?"

For all his bravado, Shelby heard the uncertainty in Murphy's growl.

"I'm a man of my word."

Murphy frowned. "Okay. So?"

Dan leaned forward, so his face was right in Marlin's. "So if you *ever* touch Miss Wilson again, if you even look her way, I will personally see to it that you don't bother anyone. Ever. Again." He ground the words out, emphasizing the last few by poking the shotgun into Murphy's chest. "We clear?"

"As crystal," Murphy hissed the words through clenched teeth.

"Now get lost."

Unlike his buddies, Marlin didn't run. He took a step back, turned, and walked away, vanishing into the darkness, like a wraith in the mist.

"D-Dan…"

At her broken plea, he was at her side, his arms around her, holding her tight against his chest. She gripped his uniform, trembling from head to toe. "I…was so…s-scared!"

"I know. It's okay now. You're safe."

The words, his touch, were like finding a fresh spring in the middle of a desert. It had been so long since he talked to her, and now here he was. Saving her. Holding her.

She wasn't sure if she wanted to laugh or cry.

So she did a little of both.

Dan guided her to her car and eased her onto the seat. He knelt beside her, watching her face as she regained her composure.

"How…" She looked over at him. "How did you know?"

For a minute she thought he wasn't going to answer. Then he lifted his shoulder. "If I see your office light on when I patrol at night, I stick around until you get in your car and head home. Tonight, I had a call, so I had to leave before you did. But I figured I'd come back by and make sure you got home okay." His gaze hardened. "Good thing I did."

Before she could agree, he reached under the dash and pulled the hood release. He went to the front of her car, then, after a few seconds, called out, "Give it a try."

She turned the key, and the engine sprang to life.

He closed the hood then came to shut her car door. She pressed the button to lower the window. "They messed with a couple of wires. Easy enough to do, and easy enough to fix."

"Dan, I—"

"You shouldn't work this late by yourself, Shelby."

Her words of thanks stuck in her throat at the clipped, remote words. She looked up at him, and her heart sank when she saw the distant expression on his features.

So that was it? He let himself show he cared and then *poof*! It was back to Mr. I-don't-even-know-you-exist?

"Dan, please."

He stepped away from her car. "You'd better get going. I'll follow you home to make sure there's no—"

She shoved the car into gear. "Don't bother, Deputy. You've done your duty."

Stepping on the gas, she steered her car onto the road and sped away. But almost against her will, she glanced back in the rearview mirror, and what she saw haunted her.

One solitary form, standing in the darkness, head bowed in defeat.

Dan wanted to pray.

He wanted it more than he could remember wanting anything for a very long time. But here he sat, in his cruiser, staring after Shelby's car…and nothing came.

No words. No sense of God.

Nothing.

He gripped the steering wheel, his fingers aching. Longing for the days when he could turn to God for counsel, for peace in the face of turmoil. For wisdom when he was at a loss. But somehow, over the last few months, every time he tried to pray all he found within himself was silence.

Cold, empty silence.

"Come on, Justice," he muttered, hitting the steering wheel with the palm of his hand. "Just *do* it. Just say the words. You know God's there."

He tried. Gritted his teeth and tried to force the words out. "God…Jesus…"

But speaking their names felt so…vacant. Like nothing within him connected to them any longer.

Maybe that's because there's nothing to be connected to?

He stared out at the night from the darkness of his car. No. No matter what happened, Dan knew God was there. That He was real. That Jesus was who He said He was.

Dan just didn't trust anymore that that made much of a difference.

Defeat pressing in on him, he started the car and headed home. Back to solitude.

To silence.

To the nothing his life had become.

Marlin didn't do well with defeat.

That night, after his little encounter with the deputy, he hunted down his guys and taught them a lesson about bailing before he said they could. Then, with that worked off, he contacted Jayce. Just one quick phone call.

"We gotta talk."

"What? Why?"

Marlin spat the words at him. "Just *meet* me."

It took a couple of days, but here they were. On the outskirts of town, in a nice secluded spot. Marlin and the boob brothers. And as they watched Jayce approach, Marlin couldn't wait to share his news.

"What's up?"

Marlin raised a brow at Jayce's curt question. "My, my, testy today, aren't we?"

"What do you want, Marlin?"

He stiffened then forced himself to relax. *Take your time. Work the punk.* He looked at the brothers. "He wants to know what I want."

They took the cue and snorted.

Marlin turned back to Jayce. "I just wanted to give you something."

Jayce's brow creased. "Give me something?"

"Yeah, a little present." He reached into his pocket.

"You're gonna like this, you little crud."

Marlin shut Dicky up with one well-aimed glare. This was *his* show. He didn't need backup. He pulled out Shelby Wilson's necklace and held it out to Jayce, who studied it, eyes growing wide.

"That's—"

His gaze came back to Marlin's, and the alarm in his eyes almost made Marlin laugh. "Yeah. It is."

Jayce took it from him. "How did you get it?"

"I took it. Right off her pretty little neck." He moved to put his face right in Jayce's. "And I could have taken a whole lot more, boy. You know I could have."

Jayce fisted his hand around the necklace. "What do you want, Marlin?"

"I want you to remember. You do what I say, when I say it. Because if you don't…" He shrugged, stepping back. "Well, I can get to the people you care about." He poked a finger into Jayce's chest.

Slipping the necklace into his pocket, Jayce turned away.

"Don't forget, boy."

Jayce hesitated, then his words, heavy with resignation, drifted back over his shoulder. "I won't forget."

"See there?" Marlin crossed his arms and grinned. "I told you boys Jayce would be reasonable. All he needed was the right motivation."

TWENTY-FIVE

> *"The tragedy of life is what dies inside a man while he lives."*
> ALBERT SCHWEITZER

> *"People ruin their lives by their own foolishness and then are angry at the LORD."*
> PROVERBS 19:3

"DADDY."

Dan turned. *"Shannon!"* He knelt, opening his arms, and his little girl ran to him. He hugged her close, tears flowing.

It had been a dream. All a terrible, terrible dream.

"What was?"

At the sound of that voice, Dan surged to his feet. Sarah. She stood there, Aaron at her side, his hand in hers.

"What was a dream, hon?"

Dan walked toward her, reaching out to touch her face. So afraid she'd vanish…

"Don't be silly." She smiled, pressing her hand over his where it lay against her soft cheek. *"I'm not going to vanish. I'm always here. Always with you."*

"But you were gone."

She took his hand in hers. *"I love you, Dan."*

He pulled her and the children into his arms. "I love you, too. All of you."

Shannon hugged him tight, and the feel of those small arms around him was heaven.

"Daddy, you're so silly." She grinned up at him. "This isn't even close to heaven. Heaven's lots better."

He tousled her hair. "You know that for a fact, do you?"

She didn't answer, just looked at Sarah.

"Dan, we need you to help us."

He frowned. Suddenly they weren't in his arms but standing in front of him. "What?" He shook his head. "Help you? How?"

"You have to find us, Dad."

Aaron's soft words pierced him. "Find you? But you're right here."

"No, Daddy." Shannon's gaze was so full of love. "Inside. You have to find us inside. But there's too much stuff in the way."

He tried to draw closer to them but couldn't. Something held him fast, just out of their reach. "What is? What's in the way?"

Sarah's sweet smile both touched and tortured him. "You know, Dan. You've known all along. If you don't clean out the barriers—" sadness filled her eyes—"you'll lose us."

"No!" He couldn't stand that. Not again. Please, God, not again.

"Don't let us go, Dad." Aaron took his sister's hand. "We love you."

"Wait. No! Don't go!"

But nothing he said mattered. Bit by bit, they faded, pulled away from him until they were wisps in the dark air.

Pain tore through Dan's gut, and he screamed out his agony. But even that sound was caught and carried away. He couldn't hold on to it. Because another sound tugged at him. A constant irritating sound that grated on his nerves, tugging him from the darkness.

Suddenly he understood. His family wasn't being pulled away. He was. Pulled away from them, toward the nagging sound outside. No matter how he cried out against it, he couldn't stop it.

~

He should be happy the storm woke him.

Instead, he was angry. That he'd lost Sarah and the children again. That he couldn't hold on to them.

He dragged out of bed, coming to the kitchen for coffee. Or so he told himself. But he knew he wasn't after coffee.

Dan looked down.

The gun lay there, solid, heavy in his hand.

Dan's fingers convulsed on the weapon. *Justice*. What a laugh. There was no justice. No right. No wrong. No innocent. No guilty.

That's just the pain talking. You don't believe that.

His hoarse laugh sliced through the silence. Believe? What did that matter? Did it stop evil? Save those who deserved it? Make the guilty pay?

Hardly.

Justice was a myth. A nice little fairy tale to make children feel safe so they could sleep—

Sorrow cut as deep as any shard of glass, piercing him. His gaze lowered to the cold steel in his hand.

He let the weapon settle into place. Nestle in his palm.

Escape. It was so close. So easy. Just lift the gun, point it—

No.

Dan spun. He could have sworn the word was spoken right behind him. But no one was there. He leaned against the kitchen counter, one hand clutching the gun, the other planted on the cool tile.

He needed to do this. Needed to get away. Needed...

You need sleep.

Dan closed his eyes. Sleep. The thought of it drew him.

Go to bed, Dan. Rest. Think about this tomorrow.

Dan's lips lifted. What was that Bible verse? Something something trouble...

Oh yeah. "Don't worry about tomorrow, for tomorrow will

bring its own worries. Today's trouble is enough for today."

Today's trouble. Yesterday's trouble. They were more than enough. He could scarcely think straight for their weight on his soul.

Rest...

The word whispered through him, and Dan looked down at the gun.

He could do this. He really could.

He moved his thumb, flipping the safety back on.

He just wasn't going to do it tonight.

Dan opened his eyes.

Another day. So he was still alive.

Pushing himself from bed, he went through the motions of getting ready. Shower. Shave. Take vitamins so he could live a long, healthy life.

Alone.

Always alone.

By the time he made his way to the kitchen, he was dressed and pressed and ready to clock in. He looked good on the outside. That's what mattered. As for the inside...

"Hi there, brother."

Dan stopped. What was his sister doing up this early? Usually Annie slept until he was gone.

"Thought I'd fix you a nice breakfast today. I mean, anything's got to be better than the coffee and gum you usually have."

Her smile was forced. Overly bright. He knew she was worried about him and considered telling her not to bother. He was fine. But the words wouldn't come.

"Oh, by the way, Shelby called again last night. Just wanted to say she's thinking of you." She poured him a steaming cup of coffee and added a couple dollops of milk. "You know, Danny, it wouldn't kill you to talk with her. She cares a great deal about you. And you haven't spent any time with her since the funeral."

His mouth felt like it was full of sand. He shook his head when she held out the coffee cup. "I gotta go."

Annie was out of the kitchen and in his path before he finished turning away. "*Stop* it!"

He stared at her. Such passion. Such heart.

Such a waste of energy.

"Stop what?"

She grabbed his arms. "Dan, what are you *doing*? Stop acting this way. Like you don't feel anything. Don't care. I know that's not you—"

He reached down and gently but firmly pushed her hands away. "You're wrong, Annie. This is me." He walked to the door, pulled it open. "It's all that's left of me."

With that, he walked out the door, steeling himself to face another empty day. Another day of penance for being alive.

A few more feet. Just a few more, and I'm there.

Annie groaned, pushing herself up the driveway to Dan's house. Her legs burned, her breathing came in ragged gasps, and sweat trailed down her face.

Now *this* was more like it. She felt great!

Or she would, if it weren't for Kodi trotting at her side, not even winded. It just wasn't fair. When Kodi wasn't working or training, she spent most of her days just lying around sleeping. And still she stayed in excellent shape. All Annie had to do was miss a few days of working out and running a mile was murder.

Whoever coined the term *it's a dog's life* must not have had a dog. Dogs had it great.

Staggering the last few steps to the front door, she slid the key in and opened the door. She glanced down at Kodi. "Sit. Stay."

True to her training, Kodi's backside dropped into a sit, and she waited, her amber gaze glued to Annie as she entered the house, dropped her keys on the counter, then filled Kodi's water dish with fresh water.

Setting the dish on the floor, Annie waited another beat, then, "Release."

At the magic word, the shepherd leapt to her feet, bounded inside in two huge strides, and planted her monstrous paws on Annie's chest.

With a yelp, Annie went flying. Fortunately, she'd been standing in front of the couch. Oh well, she thought as she sprawled on the cushions, she needed a nap anyway.

Kodi went to lap up her water then sauntered back and plopped her still-dripping snout in Annie's lap.

"Ew, ick!" Annie sat up, brushing the dog away with a laugh. "I swear, dog, you are the sloppiest drinker I've ever seen."

Kodi circled twice, then plopped down with an ecstatic groan, that crazy grin on her doggie face. Annie knelt next to her, rubbing the dog's ears. "How can anyone resist that face?"

As she pushed to her feet, Annie wished she had an answer. Because Dan resisted not only Kodi's face, but every other face around him.

She went into the kitchen, turning on the burner under the teakettle. Opening a cupboard, she pulled out mint tea bags and the container of honey. Nothing soothed like hot tea and honey.

She should know. She'd drunk enough of it while staying with Dan. Things had been so tense. Annie thought it would be like it was after Sarah died. That Dan would struggle with emotion, breaking down at times, talking his pain through at others.

None of that happened.

Instead, in the almost five months since they'd found Shannon and Aaron dead, her brother acted like he was auditioning for a role in some zombie movie. All through the investigation into the shootings, the fruitless search for James

Brumby, and the painful days following the funeral, Dan drew more and more closed.

It was like he'd died right along with Shannon and Aaron.

To say Annie was concerned was the understatement of the century. Which was why she was still here and not back home in Medford. Fortunately, she could work from pretty much anyplace. That was one of the joys of working in stained glass.

She'd driven back to Medford after the funeral and gathered up what she needed to finish the commissioned pieces she'd been working on, loaded everything into her minivan, and drove back to Dan's. He set up a temporary studio for her in the heated garage. Not the same, of course, as her studio at home with its perfect lighting, but it would do. So she spent her days working. And praying.

And her evenings trying to break through the armor her brother had formed around himself.

So far, she'd been a dismal failure.

Annie went back to the living room, sitting on the floor next to Kodi. With a happy pant, Kodi flopped onto her side along Annie's thigh.

Well, at least her dog cared about her.

The only thing Dan seemed to care about anymore was his job, and he kept a professional distance even from that. Every once in a while, just to see what would happen, Annie tried to stir something in him. To make him react, even in anger.

But it just didn't happen. From all she could see, Dan didn't get angry, didn't even question God. He just went…cold.

And he'd never done that before. Even with Annie. She'd always been able to get through to him. But now…

"I'll tell you something, though." Kodi's ears perked up, and she tipped her head as she honed in on Annie's voice. "I'll bet you anything there's a boatload of grief and anger trying to come to the surface. But you know Dan."

Kodi's head tipped the other way, as though to say she did,

indeed. Annie nodded. "Right. My dear brother is as stubborn as they come. If he's decided he's not going to feel, then by heaven, he won't feel. Not a thing."

The shrill whistle of the teakettle broke the air, and Kodi sat up, ears at attention. Annie jumped to her feet, but didn't get to the kettle fast enough.

The dog tipped her head back and cut loose with a long, mournful, "Arrrrooooooooo-ooooo!"

"Okay, okay, I'll shut it off. Stop howling, you nut!" Annie snatched the kettle from the burner, but it took a few seconds for the whistle—and the howling—to die out.

Her mug of tea poured, Annie settled on the soft couch cushions. Kodi came to lie at her feet. Or, more accurately, *on* her feet.

The dog wasn't happy if she wasn't touching someone. That was okay, though. It kept Annie warm. And she needed that, because she was going to be sitting here awhile.

She knew better than to try and talk her brother out of his emotional desert anymore. She was here to listen, to help take care of whatever daily details she could.

And to pray. Most of all to pray.

Because only God could reach Dan now.

Cupping her hands around the mug in her lap, she bowed her head. "Father, I don't understand any of this. Not Sarah's death. Surely not the kids being killed. It's crazy, Lord. Crazy and wrong. But I know You, God. I know You're grieving just as we are. Just as Dan is. Please, Father—" she gripped the mug—"You know how much it hurts to lose a child. You know the hard, cold place where Dan is caught. Please…touch my brother. Bring him back. Somehow, show him You're with him, that You love him."

She wiped at her eyes. "Please, Lord. Open his heart and eyes so he can see—really see—that You haven't abandoned him."

❧

Abandoned.

Dan studied the house, the yard. That's how it all looked. Abandoned. Like Brumby hadn't just run but never intended to come back again.

He shouldn't be here. Sheriff Grayson had made it clear: The investigation of the shootings was out of Dan's hands. He wasn't involved.

Dan's lip curled. Not involved. Get real.

He pulled a penknife from his pocket, slicing the police tape on the front door of Brumby's house. Pushing the old door with his shoulder, he walked inside. But what he saw didn't make any sense.

The dogs' food dishes were there, half full, food scattered around on the floor. His gaze came to the table in the middle of the cluttered room. It was clear now, but he'd read the police reports from that terrible day. The deputies found a plate of partially eaten eggs and toast, a cup half full of tepid coffee.

The conclusion the deputies reached was a reasonable one: Brumby had been sitting there, eating his breakfast, when he heard the kids' voices outside. True to his threat, he'd grabbed his gun. Gone outside. Probably hadn't even yelled a warning before he fired.

Shannon and Aaron didn't even know what hit them.

For just a fraction of a second, the hard shell of ice that had formed around Dan's heart cracked

"No."

He gritted his teeth, forcing the feelings back. Embraced the numbness that kept him together.

Good thing Annie wasn't here. She'd been watching him with those hawk eyes of hers, seeking any sign of emotion from him. She thought he needed to let his emotions out. To *feel*.

She was wrong.

He didn't have time for feelings. He had a job to do: catch

James Brumby. That was all that mattered.

Another quick look around the room told him nothing had changed since he'd been here a week or so ago. He'd come today hoping to see signs of someone rummaging through the garbage, of things being moved.

Something—anything—that hinted Brumby was still around.

Instead, he just found further confirmation that the man was long gone. Probably for good.

Kicking trash out of his way, Dan walked to the back door. He pushed it open, walking out into the junk heap that Brumby called a backyard—a narrow strip of fenced-in grass between Brumby's back door and the woods bordering his property. Gnawed bones from the butcher were scattered around, along with chewed-up plastic water dishes and dried piles of dog refuse. Clearly this area was the boys' domain.

There had to be something he'd missed. Something they'd all missed.

Nothing.

He walked to the back of the yard, his steps careful, and inspected the six-foot fence. The wood was old, weather beaten, in sad need of a new coat of paint. Dan scanned the rough surface—then stopped.

What was that?

Daylight shone through a fine crack from the top of the wood to the bottom. Was a panel of the fence separated from the rest? Placing his hand against the wood, Dan pushed, and sure enough, the panel in front of him fell back onto the ground.

Apparently Brumby had made a gate in his fence. But why?

Dan stepped through, searching the tangle of brush, blackberry bushes, and woods. Blackberries were everywhere out here, so Dan wasn't surprised to see walls of twisted vines behind the fence. The blackberry thicket was almost six feet high and probably five foot or more deep. Dan walked along the fence, senses heightened, alert to anything out of the—

There.

A thick section of what seemed to be dried bushes and brush, piled in front of the blackberry thicket. Dan grabbed branches, pulling the brush free, muttering as vines caught and punished his bare hands. He grabbed a large pile, jerked it free—and stared.

What on earth?

It looked as though someone had been living back here. They'd hacked a little alcove out of the thicket, creating a kind of vine cave. But with vines full of thorns all around? That could *not* be comfortable.

Dan stepped closer, pulling his flashlight free and shining it into the dark indentation. This was no hideout.

It was a lab.

A meth lab. Or the remains of one.

Piles of trash littered the ground. Empty antifreeze containers. Smashed packaging from cold and allergy pills and Epsom salts, propane tanks, bottles with rubber hoses stuffed in them, pillowcases stained red. Patches of stained, dead vegetation bore mute evidence of someone dumping chemicals.

Dan stepped back and keyed his shoulder radio. "Jasmine, come in."

She was on the air in a flash. "Yo, Chief. What's up?"

"You'd better contact the sheriff and tell him to get on up here to James Brumby's place."

"You're at ol' man Brumby's? But I thought the sheriff told you—"

"Jasmine. Let me worry about Sheriff Grayson. Just call him. And DHS. Tell him I need them here, too."

"DHS?" That stopped her. Dan didn't call them out very often, but the Department of Human Services was responsible for cleaning up meth labs.

"Call 'em, Jasmine. Now."

"You got it, Chief. Over and out."

"Justice, out."

He lowered his hand then turned to study the abandoned lab again.

"Brumby, you old fool. What did you get yourself into?"

Annie jerked awake.

"What? What did you say?" But the words that had called to her, pulled her from sleep, were mere wisps of sound, vanishing in the air.

With a moan, she rolled onto her back, staring at the ceiling. At first, she couldn't figure out where she was. Then it came back…she was at her brother's house, lying on his couch. She'd been praying. She must have drifted off into a deep slumber.

Swinging her legs to the floor, she barely missed knocking against Kodi, who sat in front of her. *What's wrong?* her amber eyes seemed to ask.

Annie leaned forward. "I'm fine, Kode. Relax. I'm fine."

Kodi was so tuned in to Annie, it was unsettling at times. But that was one reason they did so well in search and rescue. When they were working, they operated almost as a single unit rather than human and dog.

Kodi scooted closer and laid her snout on Annie's leg. Clearly, she didn't believe Annie's assurances. It figured. Annie was still shaking from…from…

She frowned. From what? A dream? She stood, picked up her now-empty mug, and went to set it in the sink. Kodi followed, leaning her shoulder into Annie as she walked. Annie shoved back with a knee.

"Stop it, you worrywart. I'm fine."

It had taken major effort for Annie to break the shepherd of those herding instincts when they worked. But when they were at home, it was a lost cause. When Kodi was excited or worried, she tended to throw body blocks. Annie had to watch herself, because Kodi didn't realize her own bulk—or strength. She'd sent Annie flying a couple of times.

She smiled. It was a small price to pay for a dog like Kodi.

Another nudge, this time from Kodi's snout, told Annie the dog was still uneasy. Crouching in front of the sink, Annie framed the dog's face with her hands. "You're something else, you know that?"

Kodi sat, staring at her mistress, the question still very evident: *What's wrong?*

Annie didn't deny it this time. She stroked Kodi's long black snout. "I don't know. Something woke me. Somebody was talking to me. Telling me something…important. I think."

She shook off the odd feeling trying to settle over her and stood. "Maybe I just need more sleep."

The ringing of the phone made both Annie and Kodi jump. Annie grabbed the receiver. "Hello?"

"Annie? It's Shelby. Shelby Wilson. I…I'm sorry to call again. I tried Dan's cell phone and work phone, but…well, either he's not getting my calls, or he's just not retur—" She stopped and took a deep breath. "Never mind. Is he there?"

Annie glanced at the clock. One-thirty? It was later than she'd realized. Dan should be home by now for lunch, but Kodi would have awakened her if he'd come in. Why hadn't he called?

"No, Shelby, he's not here. But he should be soon."

She was silent for a moment then let out a long breath. "Listen, Jayce is in trouble. Jayce Dalton, the boy—"

"I know who Jayce is." Shannon had talked of little else those last few months of her life.

"Oh. Anyway, he's in trouble, and Dan is the only one who can help."

As Shelby spoke, Annie felt something stirring inside her. An odd sense of excitement. "Would you mind filling me in?"

As Shelby did so, certainty settled over Annie like a warm woolen cloak. Dan was supposed to save Jayce Dalton.

How, Annie didn't have a clue. Considering that Dan had cut the boy off even more completely than anyone else. But that didn't matter. God had the *how* well in hand. All Annie had to do was her part.

"Shelby, listen, when do you need to know Dan's answer?"

"The sooner, the better."

"Tomorrow?"

"That'd be great." Surprise mixed with relief in Shelby's response.

"Dan will call you tomorrow."

Hanging up, Annie stood there, hand resting on the phone. Time to call in the cavalry. Lifting the receiver, she dialed her sister's number.

Kyla spoke before Annie had the chance even to say hello. "I wondered when I'd hear from you."

"Oh? Why is that? No, wait, first tell me how you knew it was me."

She chuckled. "Caller ID, silly."

Annie smiled. "Yes, but it's *Dan's* number showing."

"And Avidan is working. So knowing you're still there…"

"Fine. Now, why have you been wondering when I'd call?"

"Well, I've been up since about five-thirty this morning, praying. I woke up with this feeling hanging over me that something was going on, and I figured it had to be about Avidan."

Annie explained Shelby's phone call and request. Kyla didn't hesitate. "I've got a friend with a plane. He told me he'd fly me down anytime it was necessary."

"It's necessary."

"I'll be there in a few hours."

"See you soon." Annie set the receiver back in the cradle. "Well, this should be interesting, huh, Kodi-odio? Dan's being called to help Jayce. But I think it's more than that. I think he's going to save Jayce. And you know what?"

Kodi cocked her head, ears perked.

"If Dan does this, if he listens to his heart and does what's right, I have a feeling Jayce may very well turn around and save Dan." Annie smiled. "Wouldn't that be something?" She clapped her hands. "And wouldn't Shannon be tickled?"

Kodi's bark voiced her exuberant agreement.

TWENTY-SIX

*"In some way, it is natural for us to wish that God
had designed for us a less glorious and less arduous destiny;
but then we are wishing not for more love but for less."*
C. S. LEWIS

*"Then one day I went into your sanctuary, O God…
I realized how bitter I had become, how pained I had been
by all I had seen. I was so foolish and ignorant—I must have
seemed like a senseless animal to you. Yet I still belong to you."*
PSALM 73:17, 21–23

DAN KNEW SOMETHING WAS UP THE MINUTE HE GOT home.

For one thing, Kyla was there. Not that she couldn't visit, but coming all the way from Portland without telling him first…well, that didn't bode well. Besides, with the demands of overseeing the family construction business their father started, Kyla didn't usually take time off on the spur of the moment.

Not unless something was wrong.

For another thing, his sisters' expressions. He could tell when they'd been "plotting." He'd seen those looks far too many times in his life.

Like the time Annie decided he should start dating a girl from next door, so she enlisted her older sister's help and arranged a meeting by sending him and the girl notes, supposedly from each other—"MUST talk with you. Urgent! Matter of life and death!" Once he discovered what was going on, the only lives at risk that day were those of his beloved sisters.

Then there was the time Kyla had been a senior in high school and wanted to borrow the car he'd saved a year to buy, then spent the next year restoring. Dan was clear: not in this lifetime. He should have known his sister's capitulation came too readily. Sure enough, she got Annie to talk him into going for a walk with her. When they got home, his car was gone. Of course, Kyla returned it—with a dent in the front bumper.

More times than he could count—or even remember— these two had conspired together to convince, sway, influence, or motivate him as they saw fit.

From the looks on their too-angelic faces, they were at it again. Even the dog, lying next to Annie's feet, looked like she had something up her furry sleeve.

He planted his feet, crossed his arms, and fixed them with a stare. "Okay, what's going on?"

They scooched apart, making room for him on the couch between them. Annie patted the cushion. "Have a seat, big brother."

Dan pressed his lips together. Whatever they were up to, it had to be big. "I'd rather stand, if you don't mind."

Kyla stood, Kodi following at her side, and came to take his arm. "As a matter of fact, Avidan, I do mind. Please, come sit down."

He resisted for a moment, then with a sigh gave in. Might as well hear what they wanted. The faster they told him about it, the faster he could say no. He let Kyla lead him to the couch. No sooner had he settled on the cushion than Kodi came to plop down on top of his feet.

Dan wiggled his feet beneath the beast. So much for a quick escape. "Okay—" he looked from one sister to the other—"let's hear it."

Annie jumped in. "Shelby Wilson called."

Dan stiffened. What was this? Annie knew he didn't want to talk about Shelby.

"Dan? Did you hear me?"

"Yeah. Shelby called. What did she want?"

"To talk with you."

He waited.

"About Jayce Dalton."

At the name, emotions flooded Dan. Shame. Resentment. Frustration. Embarrassment. Regret. But he pushed them all way, keeping his stare bland. Noncommittal.

Empty.

"What about him?"

Kyla joined in. "Jayce is in trouble, Avidan. He's been picked up by the police. A gang of boys broke into the store at the Union Creek Lodge. Jayce was the only one they caught. He won't say who broke in or what they were doing."

"He told the police he was just out walking and heard the glass break in the windows. Went to see what was happening. But the police believe he was standing watch."

A flash of concern burned through Dan, but that, too, was consigned to the edges of his awareness. *Don't look interested. Don't let them think they've caught your attention.*

When he didn't say anything, Annie went on. "Would you like to know what was stolen?"

"Does it matter?"

"I think it does."

Against his better judgment, he inclined his head.

"They cleaned out the shelves of cold medicines. Diet pills." Annie scrutinized his face as she listed each item. "Drain opener. Epsom salts. Rubbing alcohol. Matches. Duct tape…"

Dan's interest was piqued, in spite of himself. "Supplies for a meth lab."

At Annie's nod, rage smoldered deep in Dan's chest. Was Jayce mixed up with Brumby somehow? Had he been involved in the meth lab behind Brumby's home?

Had he been involved...?

Dan stopped breathing. Every sense focused on the question now slamming into his mind, his heart.

Had Jayce been involved in the shootings?

Dan almost came off the couch. Almost roared out a denial that it could be possible. But he didn't move. Didn't give any sign that he was being torn apart inside.

Kyla laid a hand on his arm. "Avidan, Shelby called because Jayce needs your help."

He froze. "My..." His throat closed, choking off the word. When he could speak again, his voice was rough. "Why me?"

"You *know* why, Danny. Because of your relationship with Jayce. Because you know he's not a bad kid."

Enough. Dan shoved at Kodi, sending her scampering off his feet, then stood, walking away. But his sisters didn't let go that easily. Quick footsteps behind him warned they were right on his heels. Through the kitchen. Out the sliding glass doors. Onto the patio.

Annie closed the sliding doors, keeping Kodi inside. The dog sat, staring. Clearly of the opinion she should be out there with the rest of her pack.

Trade you places, Dan thought.

Kyla stepped in front of him. "Avidan, you have to talk with us about this."

"Why? Because Sister-Mommy says so?"

She ignored his sarcasm. "You told us yourself you were called to help Jayce."

"That boy is *not* my problem."

"How can you say that?"

He glared at Annie. "*Leave* it! This doesn't concern you!" Then he aimed his glare at Kyla. "Either one of you. It's none of your business!"

"Yes, it is!" Kyla sounded as heated as he. "It's about *you*. Doing what's right. And that concerns us because we love you!"

He pulled back. "Then leave me alone. If you love me so much, leave me be!"

"Why?" Annie took a step closer. "So you can bury yourself in your anger, your grief? So you can shrivel up inside until there's nothing left?"

"Avidan, please. This boy's own family has let him down all his life. You know how he feels about you. How he looks on you like a fath—"

"*No!*"

The denial exploded from him, fueled by a desperation so intense it hurt. His chest ached, burned—like someone was shoving a molten spear right through him. "I'm not that boy's father. He isn't my child!"

His trembling hands gripped the rail, digging into the wood, his voice raising as he spat out each hateful word. "My children are *dead*! Or had you *forgotten* that?"

Annie didn't turn away. She faced him head on.

When Dan and the girls were kids, they used to fight all the time. Their parents often despaired of their reaching adulthood without doing one another in. But they did so, and discovered siblings made the best of friends. Since that auspicious discovery, they seldom exchanged angry words. In fact, Dan couldn't remember the last time either of his sisters got truly mad at him.

Well, he wouldn't have trouble remembering this.

Annie wasn't just angry. She was furious. Hurt. Devastated. All these emotions played on her features as she stood there, mute, shaking like someone coming out of hypothermia. Tears slipped from her glaring eyes, ran down her usually smiling face, but she didn't seem to notice. Didn't rub them away.

Dan had a flash of the look on Shelby's face at the funeral. Was he going to alienate everyone who cared about him?

Regret pierced him.

"Avidan Timothy Justice, you're being an idiot."

And vanished as quickly as it came.

He squared off with Kyla. "I beg your pardon?"

"I said, you're being an idiot. To say something like that to Annie...to even *dare* suggest we've forgotten about Shannon and Aaron." Now her voice matched Annie's body, trembling so she had to speak through clenched teeth. She clamped her mouth shut, a muscle working in her jaw. Dan flinched as one lone tear escaped Kyla's eye, drifting down her cheek.

Kyla never cried. Not even when they were kids.

"Yes," she finally managed. "I think *idiot* pretty well sums it up."

He couldn't argue with her. After all, he'd just managed to hurt his sisters so profoundly, they'd both cried in the space of two minutes. And all they'd been doing was trying to help.

Oh yeah. *Idiot* worked.

Words swirled through him, a vortex of confusion and anguish. He longed to tell them, to try and explain all that was trapped inside him. To spew out the unbearable tangle of emotions, then beg them to help him sort it all out.

Help it make sense.

But how did he voice things he didn't even begin to understand? Things he felt but couldn't describe?

How did he explain what he knew but couldn't believe?

That he was in hell.

A powerful need to scream, to strike out and hurt as he'd been hurt, took hold of him, making him shake so bad inside that he wondered if he'd break into a million pieces.

Spinning on his heel, he pushed the sliding doors open and strode past Kodi, whose watchful gaze followed his every step. Grabbing his jacket off the coatrack, he pulled the front door open. He had to get out of here.

"Where are you going?"

He paused, hand on the door, unable to look at his sisters. "Out. I need..." What? What did he need? He let his hand fall, forced himself to turn and face the two women he knew loved him deeply. "Look, I'm sorry. I didn't mean to hurt you. Either of you. But this thing with Jayce—"

Emotions crowded his words out, shoving them to the back of his throat. It took a couple of deep breaths before he could continue. "You're both convinced God is calling me to this. To help Jayce. Fine. Whatever. But it's not *your* place to make me believe it." He slipped his coat on, his tone turning hard. "That's God's job. So here's the deal. If He wants me in this, let Him tell me Himself."

He jerked the front door open, then paused. "If He has the nerve, after what He's taken from me."

Dan could tell, from the silence behind him, that the low words had shocked his sisters. So be it. It felt good to finally speak what he hadn't allowed himself even to think over the last several months.

His wife was dead. His children were dead.

God had a lot to answer for.

Silence.

That's what met Dan's exit.

Pure, stunned silence.

Then, as though she couldn't stand it a moment longer, Annot started for the door. But Kyla reached it before she did, barring her sister's way.

"I'm going after him, Kylie."

The desperate edge to her words tugged at Kyla's heart. At the place that wanted to join Annot, to run after Avidan, throw her arms around him, and weep. "No."

"No?" Annot's word rang with astonished frustration. "*No?*"

"No."

"Do you really think you can stop me?"

Kyla started at that. "Probably not. You are, after all, a runner, and you have a runner's muscles and strength."

"Exactly." Determination filled Annot's words and features. "So move, before I move you."

"If you do that, you'll be making a serious mistake."

Her sister's laugh showed she was unamused. "Oh, really? Well, let me tell you something, big sister—"

"Shut *up*!"

Annot's mouth fell open, and she stared at Kyla like she'd suddenly grown fangs. Kyla grabbed her sister's arm and tugged her to the window. Together, they caught a last glimpse of Avidan walking with quick, hard steps into the engulfing night.

Annot sagged beside her, and drawing a calming breath, Kyla encircled her sister's shoulders. "Don't you see? He's got to do this alone. Just him and God. They have to wrestle this through, or it will never be settled."

Annot lifted a hand, laid it against the cold glass, as though she could reach through it, touch Avidan's heart and spirit. "Are you sure?"

At the soft, pleading question, Kyla nodded. "I'm sure. I don't know why, but I'm sure."

Annot gave one, tremulous sigh, then turned to bury her face in her sister's shoulder. Kyla held her as she wept, whispering gentle assurances to her little sister.

And to herself.

TWENTY-SEVEN

*"There will come a time when you believe
everything is finished. That will be the beginning."*
LOUIS L'AMOUR

*"God has made my heart faint;
the Almighty has terrified me.
Darkness is all around me;
thick, impenetrable darkness is everywhere."*
JOB 23:16–17

SHELBY COULDN'T SLEEP.

She tossed and turned, punching the pillows into submission. But nothing worked. Finally, she threw the covers back and got out of bed. Shoving her feet into her slippers, she padded to the kitchen.

Maybe some chamomile tea would help.

She'd just put the pot on the burner when it started. The gnawing sense that something was happening. And without thought, her mind flew to the one person she'd been thinking of almost nonstop for the past five months.

Dan.

Forget it! Haven't you spent enough time thinking about him, praying about him? Haven't you given enough of your time, your heart, to him?

You'd think so, wouldn't you?

Five months. Twenty-one weeks. Roughly 150 days. 3,600 hours. 216,000 minutes…

Well, a lot of time. Time she'd had to accept Dan was out of her life. To move on.

Instead, she spent all those months, weeks, and days, doing pretty much one thing.

Thinking about Dan.

Oh, she was *pathetic*!

Why couldn't she get over him? After the way he hurt her, she should be able to write him off in a heartbeat. But those pesky heartbeats just kept whispering his name. Even though the way he looked at her now—when he looked at her at all— tore her apart. All tenderness, all connection was gone.

She might as well have been a total stranger. In fact, he'd probably treat a stranger with more care.

So why waste your time thinking about him?

Shelby pulled the tea bag out of the box. Why, indeed?

Well, there was Jayce. He'd been so lost, sitting in that jail cell. It had taken all of Shelby's control not to grab him and run for the nearest exit. But then, she'd be little help to him if she was in a cell of her own. When it came down to it, there was only one person right now who could help Jayce.

Mr. Personality. Dan Justice.

She dunked her tea bag. There was, of course, that one other reason to think about Dan.

She was in love with the jerk.

Pulling the tea bag up by the string, she grabbed it, ready to toss it in the disposal. Then she yelped when it burned her hand. Quick tears sprang to her eyes. "Oh, *darn* you, Dan! Now look what you've done!"

Flipping on the faucet, Shelby held her hand under the cold water. As she did so, the urging came back. And this time, it was stronger. And clearer.

Something was happening. With Dan. He needed her.

Not in person, but in prayer.

She rummaged in the drawer and pulled out a washcloth, which she soaked in the cold water. Pulling some ice from the freezer, she wrapped it in the washcloth, then used that as a compress for the burn on her hand.

Thus patched up, she went into the living room and plopped down in her oversized chair, pulling her knees close to her chest.

"Okay, God. I'll pray for him. Because You're asking me to."

But as she bowed her head, she knew that wasn't the only reason. No matter how often she got burned because of Dan Justice, she'd always be drawn to thinking of him, praying for him.

It was like that when you loved someone with all your heart.

Whether you wanted to or not.

The dam broke.

Beneath a black sky, where any light was muffled by low-hanging clouds, Dan's hardened heart melted, and words flowed.

"I spent my *life* serving You! Serving others! And *this* is my reward? My wife dies in my arms. My children are murdered. Their killer gets away scot-free. What kind of reward is *that* for living a life devoted to God? To *almighty God*?"

He spewed the bitter words. "Tell, me, Jehovah Jireh, where's the *justice* in that?"

Curse God.

He wanted to. His lips itched to throw God's failure in His face.

"Suffer the little children, You said. They're precious to You, You said!"

Curse God.

Bile rose in his throat, and he raised his fists to the sky. "*Why*? Why Aaron? Why my boy, when he was so close to being a man? A man after Your heart. That's what You wanted, wasn't it? And God…God! Why Shannon? When she loved life so much? Loved *You* so much?"

He wanted to weep. And to laugh. To punch God in the face. And throw himself on God's mercy. He wanted answers. And sweet, comforting silence.

The conflicting emotions writhed within him, and he stopped walking, pressed his hands to his temples. Was this what it felt like to go crazy?

Curse God! Curse God and die!

He wanted to die. To join his love, his sweet children beneath the ground. To dwell with them in silence. Away from this pain.

Dan opened his mouth, willed the curses to come. But his mouth would not move. And what filled his mind wasn't curses, but his mother's voice.

Singing.

"Be not dismayed whate'er betide, God will take care of you.
Beneath His wings of love abide, God will take care of you."

He couldn't stop himself from reaching out for his mother's voice, for the love and comfort it embodied—even if he had to endure lyrics he no longer believed. Dan listened, but instead of comfort, the words of this once-beloved song took the sharp blade of conviction and plunged it deep.

"No matter what may be the test, God will take care of you;
Lean, weary one, upon His breast, God will take care of you.
God will take care of you, through every day, o'er all the way;
He will take care of you, God will take care of you."

As the echo of his mother's voice faded, Dan longed to believe, to rest in the song his mother sang to him all through his childhood. But how could he?

How can you not? How can you doubt what you know is true?

How can you think for a moment it's true when your wife, your children lie beneath the ground? How could a loving God let that happen?

Dan pressed his hands to his ears, the questions so heavy they drove him to his knees. As he hit the ground, one last plea broke free. He didn't know if he spoke it, thought it, or prayed it. He just felt it push through the cordon of confusion, scattering the last of his defenses like twigs before a surging flood.

Help me!

In that moment, it came—a rushing, sweeping stillness. All sound, all light, all awareness…everything was cloaked, enveloped. And though silence reigned in the night around him, a cacophony of words poured through him. Words he'd read all his life.

Words he now admitted he hadn't even begun to understand.

"I Am."

Trembling overtook Dan. He couldn't bear the intensity of those words, of the voice that seemed to speak them. Terror, wonder, shame, relief—one emotion after another coursed through him.

"The Alpha and the Omega, who is, and who was, and who is to come. I am the First and the Last. I am the Living One; I was dead, and behold I am alive for ever and ever! And I hold the keys of death and Hades."

Death and Hades. The companions Dan had embraced, taken within himself. Nurtured with bitterness. Sheltered with anger.

Companions that settled around his heart and spirit, forming the shell he thought protected him. Now he saw it for what it was.

Deception. Destruction. His death, even as he lived.

Spiritual death.

He could no longer abide these things, and yet he couldn't

release them. He wasn't strong enough to let them go. Not by himself. So he lifted his face to the heavens and stretched his arms out at his sides.

He was ready.

For death.

For life.

Whatever God chose.

Because he had nothing left. Nothing within to anchor him. Nothing around to hold him fast. He was shaken and cast atop ocean swells, carried away from all he'd ever known.

"Take me. Please…set me free."

No sooner had his words whispered into the night than he heard the response.

"It is done. I am the Alpha and the Omega, the Beginning and the End. To him who is thirsty I will give to drink without cost from the spring of the water of life. He who overcomes will inherit all this, and I will be his God and he will be my son."

His son. God's son. Like Jesus, God's only *begotten* son.

God knew what it was to lose a son. To watch Him grow from infant to toddling child, from toddler to teen to tall, strong adult. Knew what it was to see that Son taken, beaten, the very skin torn from His frame.

To watch that beloved Son die an agonizing death. To have a part of His heart torn away by the very ones His Son died to save.

This is real love, my son.

The whisper came from nowhere—and everywhere. And Dan understood. Yes, he'd served God. Yes, he and Sarah and the children had loved God. But so, too, He had loved them.

Even unto death.

And by that death, He'd set them free. Not just for this life. But for eternity.

Dan lowered his head, a weary whisper escaping him. "Jesus…"

There, in silence and shadow, Dan finally met the One he

thought he knew. He looked on the face of truth and understood.

He'd never known God.

He'd known his idea of God, his impression of Him. But God, the One true God?

He hadn't had a clue.

Not until this moment. Not until he reached the end of himself.

And found there, in the eternal abyss, fullness beyond anything he'd ever imagined. Fullness that flowed into him, sealing cracks and crevices, replenishing dry ground, breathing peace in place of turmoil, and filling him with soul-deep certainty.

He lowered his arms and sagged to the ground, lying on his back, not caring that the cold seeped through him. He raised his gaze to the sky—it was alive with twinkling starlight.

The clouds were gone.

Mind and spirit were clear—really clear—for the first time since Sarah died. He didn't understand why things happened as they had. But he could live with the questions now. Because he could rest in this one truth: God was God.

And he accepted another fact he could no longer deny. God *was* calling him. To help Jayce.

Dan pushed himself from the ground, brushed leaves and twigs from his clothes. "Okay. You win. I'll do it." He started walking back toward his house. "Just so you understand I'm not doing it because I want to, or because I care about this kid. I'm only doing it because You're telling me to."

An answer drifted through his heart: *Obedience is enough, my son.*

For now.

TWENTY-EIGHT

*"Only he who believes is obedient and
only he who is obedient believes."*
DIETRICH BONHOEFFER

*"You can make many plans,
but the LORD's purpose will prevail."*
PROVERBS 19:21

WHEN DAN WALKED BACK INTO HIS HOUSE, HE WAS
greeted by silence.

Where on earth were the girls?

He walked through the house, nerves growing ever more
on edge when he found no sign of them. Finally he peered out
the sliding doors to the patio.

They were seated on the bench swing, heads bowed.

The sight of his sisters praying for him did something to his
heart. After the way he'd yelled at them, the hurtful things he'd
thrown at them, they had every right to be angry. Resentful.

And yet, here they were.

He pulled the sliding door open and stepped outside.

Both sisters turned, and when they saw him, they jumped
out of the swing and rushed toward him, Kodi hot on their heels.
Dan just had time to brace himself before his sisters threw their

arms around him, hugging him like they would never let go.

They all spoke at once.

"I'm sorry…I'm so sorry…"

"I'm so glad you're back!"

"Are you okay?"

Laughing, Dan hugged them back. "Let's go inside and talk."

Annie made for the kitchen. "Would you like some coffee? It's cold out there, and you were gone awhile."

"That'd be great." He sank into his large, overstuffed chair, which sat next to the couch. Kodi sat next to him, laying her head on his leg, and Dan scratched her ears.

When they were all settled, he in his chair, coffee in hand, his sisters on the couch, Dan told them what had happened. When he finished, Kyla leaned toward him and took his hand.

"I wish I could take this pain away from you, Avidan."

His smile was weak. "Me, too." He gave her hand a squeeze then turned to Annie. "Anyway, one thing I know now is that you were right. I need to do what I can to help Jayce."

"Oh, Danny! I'm so glad."

He still wasn't sure if he was or not. "Tell me again what happened."

Annie shared the details of the robbery and the police picking Jayce up. "This isn't the first time, either. A month ago or so they caught him trespassing late one night. He'd climbed the fence into the old, abandoned lumberyard. They caught him as he was leaving."

Questions perched on Kyla's brow. "The lumberyard?" She looked at Dan. "What was he doing there?"

"His dad used to take him there. Jayce said it was the one place he and his dad were happy. I'm guessing he wanted to feel that again."

But Annie wasn't done. "A few weeks later, Shelby said there was a break-in down in the valley, on the east side of Medford."

The east side. That meant big, luxurious homes.

"Over ten thousand dollars worth of items were stolen from the home. When the police arrived, the thieves were just getting into their truck to pull away. One kid didn't make it onto the truck. A deputy jumped out and chased the kid while another cruiser went after the truck. The truck got away; the kid—"

Dan already knew. "Jayce Dalton."

Annie nodded. "Jayce Dalton. He got caught, but the police didn't have any solid evidence to hold him on."

"He was at the scene."

Dan looked at Kyla. "Circumstantial. Without hard evidence, fingerprints, finding some of the goods on him, they can't hold him."

"Right." Annie folded her legs beneath her. "So they let him go. But this time…"

"This time?"

"Jayce's grandmother relinquished custody of him."

Dan sat up at that. "What?"

"She just couldn't deal with the boy any longer. He was out of control. She said…"

When she bit her lip, Dan knew he wouldn't like what came next. "She said?"

Annie's eyes held a deep regret. "She'd started to hope when he was spending time with you. That he really seemed to be straightening out. But since you…you…"

"Go ahead. Say it. Since I abandoned him."

Kyla touched his arm. "You had to take time for yourself, Avidan. There was nothing wrong in that."

He didn't respond. Just inclined his head to Annie, who continued.

"Anyway, since then, he's just gotten deeper and deeper involved with a gang of boys headed up by some tough."

One guess who that was. "Marlin Murphy. I should have known he wouldn't leave Jayce alone." Dan had always viewed regret as a waste of emotional energy. Folks did the best they could with what they knew, and that was that. He gave himself the same measure of grace.

Until now.

Deep, wounding regret flowed through him for what he had—and hadn't—done. He'd known he shouldn't have walked away. Not from Jayce. Not from Shelby. Not from his sisters.

Yes, he had reasons. But reasons didn't stop consequences. That those consequences affected him was only right.

But knowing those consequences hurt those he cared about?

That wasn't right. Not by a long shot.

"So where do things stand with Jayce? Has he been arrested?"

"No."

A twinge of relief touched him. That was something.

"He's being held and will appear before a family court judge tomorrow. Apparently it's a judge Shelby knows. He was ready to turn Jayce over to the foster system, until Shelby talked with him."

"And now?"

Annie shifted on the couch. "That's where you come in. Shelby convinced the judge to hold off his decision until you talk with him. She's almost certain, if you agree, that the judge will…um…"

He frowned. Annie vacillating was never good.

Kyla nudged her. "Go ahead. Tell him."

"Yeah," he added his voice to Kyla's, "go ahead. Tell him."

"Shelby was almost sure the judge would release Jayce into your custody."

Dan sat back in his chair. "Into my *what*?"

"Your custody."

"As in to *live* with me?"

Annie nodded, and he stared down at his hands, trying to take this news in. Turning it over in his mind, his heart.

Jayce Dalton. Living in his home. His responsibility.

Unable to sit still any longer, Dan went to look out the window at the star-studded sky.

The clouds were still gone. The night was clear.

As was his heart.

This request wasn't coming from Shelby. Or from the judge. It came from a far higher authority. *God, You're asking too much.*

My son, I ask only what I gave.

Dan looked down at the floor. *Only what You gave. But Father, You gave everything.*

There was no reply, but then, Dan didn't need one.

He moved to stand in front of his sisters, perched on the edge of the couch, watching him. "So we'd better get busy if we're going to have Jayce's room ready by tomorrow."

Both women jumped off the couch and swamped Dan with more hugs. Then Kyla glanced toward the back bedrooms.

The kids' rooms.

Dan's throat caught. They'd already gone through the rooms, packing away clothes and toys and all the odds and ends that had been reflections of his children's tastes and loves. The closets and dressers stood empty, the beds bare. So either room should work fine for Jayce.

Should.

But Dan didn't think he could do it. Didn't think he could even consider surrendering one of those rooms to someone else. Fortunately, Kyla saved him from blubbering all over himself.

"The guest room is the largest of the three bedrooms, so I vote we make that into Jayce's room." She looked at Annie. "That means you have to switch all your things to one of the other rooms."

"Consider it done."

"Good. I'll run out to the store and pick up a few things to make the room more fitting for a boy Jayce's age." Kyla glanced at Dan. "Okay?"

"Okay." He watched Annie head down the hallway, and Kyla grabbed her jacket and purse and made for the front door.

He'd never met two women more ready and willing to take on whatever came their way. And he was more grateful than ever that they were on his side.

Heaven knew he needed all the help he could get.

TWENTY-NINE

"Character cannot be developed in ease and quiet.
Only through experiences of trial and suffering
can the soul be strengthened."
HELEN KELLER

"But he knows the way that I take;
when he has tested me, I will come forth as gold."
JOB 23:10 (NIV)

"I'M AFRAID."

Dan spoke the words out loud, into the silence. "No, that's not right. I'm petrified. Stark raving terrified. So freaked I'm about to lose my mind."

Yup. That pretty well covered it.

When he woke this morning, things had changed. While last night hadn't given him all the answers, it had pierced his armor. No, more like cracked it wide open. Shoved it away from his heart until it shattered in a million pieces.

Then when he went to the kitchen to scrounge some breakfast, he received his first shock of the day. Annie's bags were packed and by the door. He looked from them to her.

"Goin' somewhere?"

"Home."

Dan stared, sure he'd heard wrong. Kyla left last night. He

expected that. She couldn't be gone too long from her work. But Annie leaving? She *couldn't.* Not now! Not when he was getting into this deal with Jayce. He needed her here.

She hugged him. "It's time for me to leave, Danny. God made that clear to me when I woke up."

His arms closed around her. "But—"

"It'll be okay." She stepped back. "*You'll* be okay. You don't need me here. You've got God."

He couldn't exactly argue, so he helped her load up her car, gave Kodi a final scratch behind the ears, then stood there waving until her van was out of sight. Then with a heavy sigh, he made his way back inside.

I sure hope You know what You're doing, Lord.

Just a few hours later, here he was, about to lay himself on the line for Jayce when he wasn't at all sure he wanted to. But something else worried him even more.

Shelby. He was about to see her again. And his defenses were all but obliterated.

It was hard enough to resist her when he was numb. Now?

He snorted. *Just run up the white flag, boy. One look from those baby blues, and you'll crumble like yesterday's Ritz crackers.*

By the time he reached the justice building, he had to force himself to release his death grip on the steering wheel. He rubbed at his aching fingers, then opened the car door.

Time to pay the piper.

Shelby stood, waiting, on the outside steps. He spotted her first and stepped back behind the low-hanging branches of a tall evergreen. Feeling incredibly foolish, like a junior higher spying on a girl he likes, Dan peered through the tree's branches.

He couldn't quite make out her expression, but her stance was tense. Was she nervous? Angry? Dan squared his shoulders. Only one way to find out.

With sure steps he started walking. Shelby saw him within seconds, and she kept her gaze on him as he approached. He climbed the steps until he stood just below her. Words rushed to his lips, but he couldn't get them out. Not with those baby blues looking down at him.

He didn't meet her eyes. Couldn't. Was too afraid of what he'd see there. *Say something!* he begged her, but she stayed silent. Serve him right if she never spoke to him again outside of work obligations. Desperation started to crawl across his nerves, and he gave serious consideration to racing back down the steps. But just as he was about to rabbit, she reached out and put a hand on his arm.

"Thank you for coming, Dan. This means a lot to me. And to Jayce."

Dan met her eyes and felt as though someone had smashed a two-by-four into his temples. He expected anger. Frostiness. Condemnation. But what he found was compassion. Tenderness.

And something more.

Something he wasn't the least bit ready to face. And though his heart screamed at him to apologize, to open himself up to her and share what he'd been feeling, he just inclined his head. "Jayce meant a lot to Shannon."

Shelby's hesitation told him just what she thought of that brilliant comment. But it was the best he could do. Shoot, with the emotional battle taking place inside him, he was lucky he could form words.

"Judge Richards is waiting for us in chambers."

The judge was a lean, serious-featured man in his late fifties. When Dan and Shelby entered his chambers, he indicated two chairs in front of his desk and, when they sat, got right to business.

"So, Deputy, am I to understand you will accept responsibility for this minor? This—" he shuffled through some papers on his desk.

"Jayce Dalton," Shelby supplied.

The judge's nod was abrupt. "Precisely. Jayce Dalton."

Dan gripped the arms of his chair. "Yes, Your Honor."

"You're aware of the trouble the boy has been in?"

"I am."

"Your Honor, as I explained yesterday, Deputy Justice and the minor in question have a relationship through Master's Touch."

The judge's lips thinned. "Apparently not too successful a relationship, considering what the boy's been up to."

Dan grimaced. Wasn't this guy supposed to be a friend of Shelby's? Then why be such a hard case?

Shelby cast a look at Dan, and he got the sense she wanted him to say something. But what was he supposed to say? "Yeah, you're right, the kid's trouble. But my daughter saw something more in him, and God told me I was supposed to do this, so I'm willing to try."

Yeah. That'd help.

With a small frown, Shelby scooched to the edge of her chair. "The minor had been doing better, Your Honor. He was doing well in school, applying himself. You can see from his record that it had been some time since he was in any kind of trouble."

The judge scrutinized the papers in front of him again. "So what happened?"

Shelby started to answer, but the judge held up a hand. His gaze pierced Dan. "I'd like the good deputy to answer this one, Miss Wilson."

A dozen replies flitted through Dan's mind. But he discarded them, opting instead for the truth. "I bailed."

The judge blinked. "Excuse me?"

Dan looked away for a moment, then met the judge's hard gaze again. "Your Honor, you may or may not know about my children. My son and daughter. That they both were murdered several months ago."

The judge considered that. "Yes, I do recall reading about that."

"Well, after the funeral, I wasn't in any shape to help Jayce.

Or anyone, for that matter. So I walked away. From him. From everyone."

The judge sat back in his chair, tenting his fingers so that they met just at the tips. "I see. And this was how long ago?"

"In early October."

"And why, Deputy Justice, should I believe you're in any better shape now, half a year later, to help this minor? Or, as you so eloquently put it, anyone else?"

Dan leaned forward, resting his arms on his knees. "I don't know."

There was that pinched look again. Clearly not the answer he'd been looking for.

"I wish I could say something convincing here, Your Honor, but I can't. This isn't easy for me. I lost my children. That's a pain I don't think will ever go away. But I promise you I'm ready for this. And I'm determined to do whatever it takes to help Jayce."

As Dan spoke, the truth of his words penetrated deep into his own heart. He *was* ready for this. He wanted to do it. He hadn't realized how much until this very moment. Sitting back in his chair, he felt himself relax. This was right. More than that, it was what God was calling him to.

"Jayce Dalton is a good kid, Your Honor, deep inside. My daughter saw that in him, and she helped me see it, too. Yeah, I messed up. I don't deny it. My only excuse is I was in shock. I said and did a lot of things I wish I hadn't."

He could feel Shelby's gaze shift to him at that confession, but he didn't look at her. He had to stay focused. "All I can do is promise you it won't happen again. I've been in this business a long time. I know what it will take to help Jayce. And I'll be there for him. I'll keep an eye on him and work with him as hard as it takes to get him through this. This kid deserves a chance. I'd appreciate your giving him—and me—that chance."

Silence filled the room in the wake of Dan's outburst. The

longer it stretched, the more peaceful Dan grew. Since a situation like this would usually have him all but crawling the walls,
that peace was evidence enough that everything would work
out.

The judge sat there, staring at his desk, seemingly deep in
thought. Shelby shifted in her chair, as though she was going to
rise, and Dan put a hand on her arm, staying her. He shot one
glance her way, telling her to wait. Be patient. She studied him
a moment, then acknowledged with a small nod and settled
back in her chair.

After a few more minutes of silence, the judge picked up
his pen and signed the papers in front of him. His sharp gaze
nailed Dan. "Okay, Deputy, you've got your chance." He held
the papers out to Shelby. "These are my orders to place the
minor, Jayce Dalton, in the custody of Deputy Dan Justice.
However, I've made the stipulation, Miss Wilson, that you will
oversee this custody arrangement."

Shelby hesitated, and Dan's heart plummeted. Was being
around him such a burden now that she'd jeopardize Jayce's
future? "But Your Honor, my work—"

"Your supervision, Miss Wilson, or no dice."

Dan held his breath, until Shelby gave a curt nod.

"Agreed." She took the papers from the judge. "Can we
take the minor with us now?"

"The papers releasing him into your custody forthwith are
with the others I just gave you."

Dan stood and held out his hand. As the judge took it, Dan
held his gaze. "Thank you, sir. You won't be sorry."

Judge Richards studied him, clearly not convinced. "See
that I'm not, Deputy."

Jayce sat on his bed in the detention cell, staring at the wall.

Exactly where you should be. Locked up. Just like your old man.

He turned his face to the wall. He'd given up trying to

silence the voice. Nothing he did worked. All he could do was not let it get to him.

Yeah. Right.

How could you get caught? How stupid can you be? Marlin can't be pleased.

Hang Marlin.

Yeah, big talk when he can't get to you. But your grandmother…he can still get to her, now can't he? And you can't exactly protect her in here, can you? 'Course, that's not your problem anymore, is it? After all, she's the one who gave up on you.

Jayce stood and paced. Maybe if he stomped his feet loud enough he could drown it ou—

"Let's go, kid."

Jayce spun. An officer was sliding the key into the cell door. "Go?"

"You're free. Released into custody."

Jayce scowled. "Custody? Whose?"

The officer pulled the door open. "I guess you'll find out in a few minutes. Now let's go."

As Jayce walked, he tried to keep his mind quiet, calm. Whoever was here for him, it didn't matter. He was free. And that meant he could run. Go somewhere. Anywhere. So long as it was away from this stinkin' town.

Jayce saw Miss Wilson as he came around the corner. For a moment he felt a surge of relief, then he spotted the man standing at her side. He jerked to a halt. Anger rose in him, and he took a step back.

"Come on, kid. They're waiting for you."

"No."

The officer grimaced. "Don't give me problems here, boy. You've been released into the deputy's custody. That's it."

If Jayce had learned anything in his bouts with the law, it was that arguing only made things worse. Usually for him. So he ground his teeth and walked over to Dan Justice. Dan lifted his chin in silent greeting.

Jayce didn't respond. He stood there, stone silent, as Deputy Justice finished whatever he was doing. He jumped when a hand touched his arm. Turning, he met Miss Wilson's blue eyes.

"I'm so glad to see you, Jayce."

And he was glad to see her, too. He'd thought for sure he was on his way to a foster home. He blinked fast and hard to hold back the sudden sting at the back of his eyes.

"Everything's going to be okay." She smiled. "You're going to stay with Dan for a while."

His mouth fell open. "I'm...I'm *what*?"

"Staying with me."

Jayce turned, glaring at the man who now stood before him. "And if I don't want to?"

"I'm afraid it's not up to you."

The deputy's words stirred the embers of anger within him, breathing them into flame.

"Look, let's not fight right here in the entrance of the Juvenile Services Center. Come outside. I've got something to say to you. When I'm done, if you want, you can just take off."

"Dan!"

He ignored Miss Wilson's alarmed yelp. "Deal?"

Jayce narrowed his eyes. "I can go?"

"As fast as your legs will carry you."

"Done." Jayce walked out the front door of the center, out to the parking lot. Then he turned, crossed his arms, and glared at the deputy. "So? Let's hear your big speech. I got places to go."

"I...um, I'll be over there." Miss Wilson started to walk past the deputy but grabbed his arm and went up on tiptoe to whisper in his ear. Jayce heard her all the same: "I hope you know what you're doing!"

Deputy Justice gave her arm a squeeze, and she walked a little distance away. Far enough to be out of the conversation, but not so far that she couldn't hear.

Jayce wouldn't put it past her to try and tackle him if he took off.

Deputy Justice leaned back against his cop car, hands in his pockets. He looked…different. More like he used to look. Before that day.

So what? You going soft? He looks like he used to, so suddenly you trust him? After what he did?

No. Jayce wasn't stupid. No way he'd trust this man again.

"I know."

Jayce jumped then gave the deputy a glare. "You know what?"

"That you don't trust me. I wouldn't, either."

What? Could the guy read his mind?

"I'm sorry, Jayce. I blew it."

He didn't reply. Just continued to glare.

"When you came up to me at the funeral, I just lost it."

Why? Jayce would never voice the question, but he so wanted to know. *Why?*

"Because I was afraid."

Shock pierced Jayce. "Afraid? Of me? Give me a break!"

"Of how you made me feel." His brow creased. "No, that's not right. Not how I felt but *that* I felt. At all. I'd just lost the two people I cared about most in the world. And then there you were, and I wanted to care. Wanted to reach out, to comfort you. And I couldn't."

Jayce stared at the ground. Hard.

"I knew if I let myself talk with you, cry with you, that would be it. I already cared about you. If I spent time with you, I'd just care even more. And I couldn't let myself do that. Because you might…I might…"

Jayce lifted his head and met the man's eyes. "Because something might happen and I'd be gone, too."

"So I pushed you away. And Miss Wilson. And I ran." He shook his head. "Funny thing, though, I didn't get far."

"You got far enough."

At his bitter words, Dan sighed. "Yes, eventually. But right then, when I walked way from you two, I got corralled by someone who read me the riot act for doing that."

Who did that? Jayce tried to remember, then his eyes widened. "You mean that old lady?"

The deputy gave a lopsided smile. "Yeah. Agatha Hunter. She told me how disappointed in me she was. How I was letting you—and Shannon—down."

Shannon. "That musta made you mad."

His smile grew a little. "Didn't make me happy. And unfortunately, it didn't stop me. It took a while—a long while—but I finally realized she was right. Mrs. Hunter, that is. I did let you down. And Shannon."

Jayce could tell how much that hurt him.

Yeah. Sure. He makes you feel sorry for him. Thinks everything can be like it was.

The voice grated on Jayce's nerves. He wanted to tell it to shut up. But instead he stared down at the ground, wrestling with the knowledge that lay like a lead pipe in the pit of his gut.

Things would never be like they were.

"Shannon's gone."

Jayce's head snapped up. Exactly. And without her, how could things ever be right again?

"So is Aaron. It took me a while to accept that."

Jayce recognized the rough sound in the deputy's voice. That's what you sounded like when pain grabbed you by the throat.

"And to accept that I'm still here. And so are you. I think God brought you and me together for a reason. Maybe for you. Maybe for me. I don't know. But I want to find out. Or try."

The deputy pushed away from his cruiser. Took a step toward Jayce. "I know I let you down, and I know saying I'm sorry doesn't change that. But I *am* sorry. And I'm here."

His gaze caught Jayce's and held it. "I'm here, Jayce. For

you. I'm not saying this is a permanent situation. We both need time before we make that kind of decision. But I'm asking you: Give me a chance. That's all. Just a chance."

Forget it! Take off. He said you could. Just listen, then you can leave. Remember? So go!

Jayce might have been more inclined to listen to the voice if it didn't sound quite so panicked. That fact combined with the look on the deputy's features made up his mind.

"Okay."

"Oh, thank heaven!"

Jayce and the deputy both looked at Miss Wilson. She clapped her hands over her mouth then took a step farther back. "I'm just over here. Don't mind me."

The deputy turned back to Jayce. "You sure?"

Say no! Get out of here! Run!

Jayce clenched his hand into a fist. *Shut. Up. Just…shut up. I'm not stupid. I'm sure not saying I trust him. But his house is as good a place as any to stay while I figure out what to do next.*

Besides, there would be pictures at the deputy's house. Pictures of Shannon. Of them camping. He'd never had a chance to see those pictures. And he really wanted to.

"I'm sure."

With that, Deputy Justice turned and unlocked the car. "Then let's go home."

THIRTY

> *"The most precious possession that ever comes
> to a man in this world is a woman's heart."*
>
> JOSIAH G. HOLLAND

> *"When they walk through the Valley of Weeping,
> it will become a place of refreshing springs,
> where pools of blessing collect after the rains!"*
>
> PSALM 84:6

I CAN'T TAKE THIS!

The thought repeated in Shelby's mind, and yet she didn't stop. She just kept walking. Up the driveway. To the front door. Where she rang the bell and waited.

The door opened and Dan stood there, that welcoming smile on his face. "Hey, come on in. We've been waiting."

Not as long as I've been waiting for you.

Shelby pushed the rebellious thought away and pasted an easy smile on her face. What was Judge Richards thinking? Bad enough that she had to see Dan at church every week, but spending time with him like this?

It was harder than she ever imagined.

"Jayce, Miss Wilson is here. You ready to go?"

Shelby didn't have to force a smile that time. The warm tone in Dan's voice as he called to Jayce lifted her lips with ease.

Whatever the judge had been thinking to put her in the position he had, he'd done the right thing putting Jayce with Dan. These last two months together had been good for both of them.

A person would have to be blind to miss how much Dan cared for the boy. Shelby was certain Jayce felt the same about Dan, but those walls of his were still as high and thick as ever. With Dan, anyway. At least he didn't have any walls with her. The phone call from him last week proved that.

"Hey, Miss Wilson. It's Jayce."

"I know." She smiled into the receiver. "I recognized your voice."

"Cool. Listen, we—Deputy Dan and me—we want to take you out. You know, for Mother's Day."

She'd been stunned. "Mother's Day?"

"Sure. I mean, I know you're not really my mom, but you're the closest thing I've ever had. So what do you say? Wanna go?"

Jayce's simple words had touched her deeply, so of course she accepted.

That's why you accepted, eh? Because of Jayce? Didn't have anything to do with going out with Dan?

Shelby gritted her teeth. *Shut u—*

"Yo, Miss W!"

She gave a little yelp as she was engulfed in a hug, spun in a circle two times, then let go so abruptly she almost fell on her face. Only Dan's quick action to catch her prevented a close encounter with the floor.

"Whoa!" Dan's laughter brought her head up, and their eyes met. His arms around her tightened a fraction, then he pulled back, set her on her feet, and stepped away.

"You two ready to go? Don't want to be late."

There it was again. That brusque, dismissive tone he'd taken to using anytime they got too close.

"Hey, chill out, Deputy." Jayce halted in the act of putting his coat on. "No need to go postal on us."

Dan blinked. "Postal? I wasn't being postal."

Jayce shrugged his coat on. "Sounded postal to me." He glanced at Shelby, and she bit her lip.

"Maybe a *little* postal."

Dan's features clouded. "I was *not* postal."

"Ooo, more postality." Jayce pulled the front door open. "*That'll* convince us—"

"Can it, Jayce." At Dan's low mutter, Jayce's eyes went to the ceiling.

Shelby chuckled at the response. Did they know how much like father and son they sounded? "Okay, you two. Let's not start out the night being disagreeable. It's my special day."

Dan's hand at her back directed her out the front door, which Jayce now held open. Dan leaned close to her ear. "I am *not* being disagreeable!"

"Yeah," came Jayce's voice from right behind them as they walked toward Dan's SUV. "And Santa doesn't wear red."

"You're just lucky we're still going to see a movie."

Shelby cocked her head at that. "I am? Was there an alternative?"

Dan unlocked the doors to his vehicle. "This crazy kid wanted me to take you out to the old lumberyard for a candlelight dinner for three."

"For three, huh?" She giggled. "Real romantic."

"Hey, the deputy doesn't exactly excel in the romance department. I figured you'd need me to coach him."

She waved his teasing aside. "But the lumberyard?"

Jayce grinned. "I like it there, okay? I figured we could take a little table, set it up with candles and a tablecloth…but no. Mr. I-Hate-Adventure over here wasn't interested. Too bad. I think he should check the place out. You know, for its romance factor."

"It's May, you nut. We live in the mountains. It's still cold outside at night."

Dan's comment only broadened Jayce's grin. He took hold of the door to the backseat, but Dan stopped him. "Jayce, you take shotgun. That'll give Shelby the whole backseat to stretch out."

Jayce stopped, his hand on the door handle. He looked at Shelby, who'd been about to open the door to the passenger seat. Touches of heat tinged her cheeks, but she did her best to look nonchalant as she traded Jayce places.

Fine. If Dan didn't want her sitting next to him, it was no big deal.

As they started the drive to the movie theater in White City, an awkward silence filled the vehicle. Finally, Shelby tapped Jayce on the shoulder. "So, tell me what's happening with you and school."

Clearly grateful for the neutral topic, Jayce waxed eloquent for the rest of the drive. Shelby hoped it was because he was excited, and not because he sensed the tension between her and Dan. But when they pulled into the movie theater parking lot and Jayce echoed her relieved sigh, she knew her hopes were not to be realized.

They got their tickets, waited while Jayce loaded up on pop and popcorn, then made their way to the theater. Jayce and Dan stepped aside, letting Shelby in first. She sat down, then glanced up at the two guys. They were both just standing there, looking at each other. Jayce was nodding for Dan to take the seat next to Shelby; Dan was doing the same at Jayce. Shelby felt her face flame and glanced around to see if anyone had noticed this little interplay.

Not anyone.

Everyone.

Every eye in the theater seemed riveted on the three of them. Of course, neither Jayce nor Dan seemed to realize that. They were too focused on their little war of wills.

Finally a guy from two rows back, who looked to be in his twenties, leaned forward. "If you guys don't want to sit with her, *I* will. She's too fine to sit there alone." As Dan and Jayce started, then looked around, the guy winked at Shelby, who wished the floor would open up and swallow her. "Whaddya say, beautiful? Come sit with me and I promise to appreciate you." He tossed his head at Dan. "That should be a welcome change."

The effect on Dan was, to say the least, fascinating.

He straightened to his full height, shot the guy a scowl, and moved to take the seat next to Shelby. Sitting down, he slid his arm across the back of her chair, forming an effective barrier between her and her would-be suitor.

As Jayce took the seat next to Dan, Shelby glanced over Dan's arm to the young man behind them. He caught her look and winked again, then settled back in his seat. "Hey, can't blame a guy for trying."

"Don't encourage him."

At Dan's hissed chastisement, she turned to refute his accusation and found herself almost nose to nose with him. Their eyes widened, gazes caught. Eternity settled into a skipping heartbeat as they stared at one another. For the barest moment, Dan's eyes softened, grew tender. "Shelby...I..."

At the ache in his tone, her heart constricted, her breath stalled.

But the moment shattered when Dan suddenly pulled away, turning to stare at the ads flashing on the movie screen.

Shelby turned to stare at the screen, too, but it was hard to see it through the sudden tears smarting her eyes. At least her voice was steady when she muttered, "I *wasn't* encouraging him."

Dan's shoulder jerked. "Fine. But guys like that don't know when to quit."

"Yeah?" This low growl came from Jayce. "Well, at least they know when to start."

Shelby couldn't help it. She *really* wanted to agree. Especially when, the moment the lights went down, Dan removed his arm from the back of her chair and sat there, stiff and distant.

The movie was typical guy fare—lots of action, explosions, and car chases. Though Shelby usually enjoyed those kinds of movies, too, this one couldn't end soon enough.

The walk to the car and the drive back to Sanctuary were both painfully silent. Until, that is, they got back to Dan's house. Shelby planned to hop in her car and drive home, but the minute they parked, Jayce jumped out of the car, slammed the door, and stormed into the house.

Dan and Shelby stared first after him, then at each other.

"What's wrong with him?"

Before Shelby could answer, Dan was out of the car, stalking up the path to the front door. Loathe to leave these two in the moods they were in, she got out and followed. When she came inside, she found the two of them facing off, Jayce's angry voice ringing through the room.

"Man, what is your *problem*?"

"Problem?" Dan scowled. "I don't have a pr—"

"Oh, right! You don't have a problem. Then why are you treating Miss Wilson like dirt?"

Oh, no! Shelby's heart plummeted and her cheeks warmed. She snagged the boy's sleeve. "Jayce, please—"

He pulled away. "No. I mean it, Miss Wilson. I'm sick of the way he treats you. The way he talks to you."

If her cheeks had been warm before, they were nuclear now. "It's really okay."

Jayce's jaw tensed. "Naw, man, it's *not*. It's really not." He turned, his gaze riveted on Dan, who glared at them both. When Jayce spoke again, though, it startled Dan as much as it did Shelby, because in place of the anger was an undercurrent of thick tears. "It's really not, man."

Dan took a step toward the boy and laid a hand on his shoulder. "Jayce—"

He shrugged Dan's hand off. "All she's ever done is try to help us. Both of us. God knows she was there for me when no one else was." His pointed look at Dan was clear. "Anyone who looks at her can see how much she cares. About me." He clenched his fists. "And about *you*, though I sure can't figure why."

"Oh, Jayce, please—"

The wretched look he directed at her stopped her words cold.

"I wish I was older." The words came out low, rough, and he gave a sharp shake of his head. "I just hope someday a woman like you looks at *me* the way you look at him."

He swallowed hard, then glared at Dan. "You shoot off all this talk about being kind and loving and treating women with respect. But you know what? That guy at the movies tonight? He was a total stranger, and he treated Miss Wilson with more respect than you do. He was right, too. She *is* fine and beautiful. She's something special, man. So why don't you open your eyes and see that? She deserves to be appreciated."

Jayce spun and strode down the hallway, and the *click* of his bedroom door as it closed sounded like cannon fire in the suddenly still room.

Shelby stood frozen, emotions churning within her. How was she going to make it out of the house before she burst into tears? She stared at the floor, swallowing hard. When she finally steeled herself enough to look up at Dan, she found him watching her.

Say something! Her eyes implored him. *Please say something...tell me what you feel...if you feel.*

But he didn't say a word. Just kept his gaze fixed on her, some unfathomable emotion deep in their depths.

With a choked sound, she turned.

"Shelby." One word, so raw, so full of desperate entreaty, it had to come from the depths of him. But she didn't stop.

She couldn't.

Jayce's words had struck home. As had Dan's silence.

She pulled the door open and walked through. As she closed it, she leaned her head against the cold wood.

"Happy Mother's Day to me," she whispered to the darkness and let the tears flow.

The firm, final sound of the door closing behind Shelby echoed within Dan even hours later.

He stood on the back porch, staring up at but not really seeing the night sky. Instead, what filled his mind was the look on Shelby's face. That pleading, grieved look.

One word. That's all it would have taken from him. One word. The word screaming through his mind as he'd listened to Jayce, then her. The word raking at him now, though it was too late.

Stay.

Because encased in that one word would be everything else he longed to say to her.

Don't leave me. I'm afraid. I can't make it without you. I need you.

I love you.

But even as he'd tried to form the word, to give it voice, fear stopped him, leaving nothing but pained silence.

Then…she walked away. And that solid, final click as the door closed ate at him. Because he feared it wasn't just the door to his home that had closed.

But the door to Shelby's heart.

THIRTY-ONE

PAPERWORK.

Dan hated paperwork.

One of these days, paperwork was going to do him in. Every time he found his desk buried under a pile of forms and reports, all he could do was stand there and ask himself—

"So when's the big announcement?"

Dan started. "What?"

Jasmine grinned from behind the bright blue glasses she was wearing. She didn't need glasses; she just liked the way they looked. She'd chosen this pair, she told Dan, because they matched her hair so well.

That, too, was bright blue.

"You know—" she waggled her brows, making her eyebrow ring jump up and down—"the announcement. About you and Shelby?"

Now Dan was *totally* confused. He came out of his office to stand by her desk. "Jasmine, what are you talking about?"

She studied him a moment, then tossed off a shrug. "Okay, okay, I can take a hint. You don't want to talk about it."

"Talk about *what*?"

"You know! *You* and *Shelby*." Her head bobbed side to side, adding emphasis to each word.

"Me and Shelby what?"

The girl let her breath out on a sharp huff and sat back in her chair. "You've been spending a lot of time together, right?"

"Well, yes, but—"

"Nights, daytime, even breakfasts together at Lou's."

Dan scowled. Just what he needed after that disastrous night at the theater last month. Shelby still spent time with him and Jayce. But things weren't what they had been. And his regret continued to gnaw at him.

"What is this? Am I under some kind of surveillance?"

Jasmine snickered. "Just the same ol' Sanctuary surveillance we're all under every day. You know. Everyone knows your business…"

"And what they don't know, they make up. Right. Well, I've got news for you and the Sanctuary grapevine: Shelby and I are friends. Period. Nothing more."

Jasmine snorted. "Yeah. Okay. Right."

This was too much. Paperwork *and* gossip? Nobody deserved this much grief.

Dan stalked to the coat rack where his jacket hung, talking through gritted teeth. "I'll say it one more time, so listen up. Shelby Wilson is a friend. The time she's spending is with Jayce, not with me." Truth be told, she'd probably be happy to never see him again. "Because that's what the court ordered."

He pushed his arms into the jacket sleeves, then turned back to Jasmine. Elbows planted on her desk, her chin resting in her hands, she watched him with wide, innocent eyes. "Whatever you say, Chief."

"And stop calling me *Chief*!"

With that semi-tantrum, Dan jerked the office door open and stormed to his cruiser. He'd no sooner grabbed the car door handle than he heard his name. A groan worked its way up from deep inside when he recognized the voice.

Aggie Hunter.

Am I being punished, God? Did I do something this bad today? Whatever it was, I'm sorry. Believe me, I'm sorry.

He turned, looking across the street. Aggie and Doris were in their usual rocking chairs, waving him over.

After that day at the funeral, it took Dan a long time to look Agatha Hunter in the face. Partially because he was so angry. But also because he eventually realized she was right. And that just made him angrier.

He'd avoided her as long as he could. Then, one day when he was leaving the office, deep in thought, he looked up and she was there.

"Deputy."

He couldn't exactly ignore her. "Miss Hunter."

She hesitated, seeming a bit unsure of what to say next. "Dan—" her rheumy eyes were resolute—"I know things aren't right between us."

When he didn't deny it, she smiled. "I've always respected that about you, Deputy. You don't candy-coat the truth." She grew serious. "And you know that makes things hard sometimes. When you have to say things you'd rather not say but you know you have to. Because you're responsible for speaking truth."

He did know how that felt. Had to deal with it far too often. He allowed a slow nod.

Her wrinkled hand came to rest on his arm with a feather-light touch. "I hated hurting you, boy. Especially on that terrible day. But I don't candy-coat, either. Not when there's so much at stake. We'd just lost two beautiful children, and I couldn't stand the thought of losing another." She patted his arm. "Especially not one Shannon loved so dearly."

Dan put his hand over hers. "I understand, Aggie. You did the right thing."

Relief and gratitude shone in her eyes. "Thank you, Deputy. And so did you when you took that boy in."

From there they went on to talk about Jayce. It wasn't a long conversation, but it was enough to let them both know they were back on track.

Now, nearly eight months later, it was as though things had never been strained between them. Aggie and Doris were as talkative as ever. He'd never met two women more determined to know all there was to know about everything.

They asked after Jayce whenever they saw Dan. Jayce said they caught him, too, whenever they saw him.

"Those are two crazy ladies," he'd commented just a few nights ago.

"Crazy like foxes," Dan muttered.

"Foxes?" Jayce stared at him, mouth hanging open. "You think they're *foxes*? You seriously need to go on a date, man!"

Dan started to explain the phrase, then he caught the twinkle in Jayce's eye. The kid was teasing him. That still made Dan smile.

Aggie's rocker was in slow-and-easy mode. "So, how's our good deputy this fine spring day?"

Dan looked at the overcast sky, then back at Agatha and her little Chihuahua. "Aren't you exaggerating a bit, Agatha?"

Her brow furrowed. "What's that about eggs? What eggs?"

"Ignore her, Dan." Doris gave her companion an arched glower. "She does it on purpose. I swear, I'm starting to think this old crony hears better than the rest of us."

"Oak roany steers? What in the name of persnickety are oak roany steers?" Aggie was looking from side to side, perplexity peeking out of the creases on her forehead.

"Never mind about persnickety, Aggie. We've got *serious* concerns to address with our dear deputy."

Dan leaned against the railing. "Oh? And what concerns are those?"

Doris straightened in her chair, her hands resting in her lap. "Has there been any progress in finding James Brumby?"

Just what he needed. A reminder that Brumby was still running around, scot-free. "No."

"I just don't understand how a man and four dogs can disappear like that." Doris leaned forward. "Do you?"

"No." *Don't get irritated, Dan. Just answer their questions.* "I don't. I wish I did."

"Of course you do." Aggie tugged on her friend's sleeve, as though to stall any further discussion of James Brumby. Bless her heart—

"Have you discovered anything further about that terrible drug situation?" Aggie clipped Half Pint onto his leash and set him on the boardwalk to wander. "Why, just the thought of such a thing in our lovely town…it makes me want to weep."

Doris's head bobbed. "Weep. Absolutely."

"Well, I for one am glad you're still investigating it all."

"Even though the good sheriff told you to stay out of it. The investigation, that is. Not the meth lab." Doris's brow furrowed. "Although I suppose you're supposed to stay out of the lab as well."

Dan didn't even wonder how on earth they'd learned what the sheriff told him. Or that he was continuing to investigate the lab and the shooting. These two knew everything. His rueful chuckle wasn't lost on them.

"You are heading for a breakthrough, aren't you?"

"I wish I could say I was, Doris, but every lead I've managed to scrounge up just fizzled out. I've talked to the principal at the school. She said they've been working against the drug situation for years, but she has no proof who is involved. I've had meetings with kids and their parents. No luck. I even went down to the valley and talked with the DARE team. They've got their suspicions, but again, no proof.

If anyone around here knows anything, they're not talking."

Aggie plucked Half Pint from the boardwalk and clutched him to her, both trembling—Aggie from indignation; Half Pint from being squeezed so hard. "Not talking? Why ever not?"

Oh, if only more people had the courage of these two little ladies. "Because they're afraid. And I can't blame them. Now if I'm right about who's behind all of this—"

"That Murphy boy."

The ladies said it in unison and with the utmost conviction. If Dan had worn dentures, he would have dropped his teeth. Aggie waved his amazement away.

"Deputy, please. We've lived in Sanctuary most of our lives. I remember Marlin when he was tiny."

"Even then he was a terror," Doris agreed. "Did you know I used to be a school teacher, Deputy? I taught first grade." Her face glowed with happy memories. "Oh, it was such fun at first. But those last few years—" She grimaced. "Children are so different than they used to be."

Dan didn't disagree. "Marlin was one of your students."

"He was. That was my last year teaching. Oh, I remember how Marlin used to torment the other children."

"Of course, that father of his was no help."

Dan's attention spiked. "Father?"

"Oh, yes." Doris *tsk*ed. "Mike Murphy. Such an unpleasant man. So angry at everything and everyone. Mean spirited and manipulative. Why, everybody just knew he was involved in terrible things." She dropped her voice to a whisper. "Drugs, even!" Her sigh overflowed with sadness. "And oh! The terrible way he treated his son."

Stories like this never ceased to anger Dan. "He beat him."

"No one could say, for certain." Aggie sounded so sad. "But I think he must have. I do know he yelled at the boy. Constantly. Said horrid things." She blinked, as though struggling against tears. "No child should have to endure such things."

Doris reached out to pat Aggie's arm, then looked up at Dan. "I tried to help the boy, to let him know not everyone was like his father. But it was no use. Every time I'd start to break through the walls he had up, his father would lay into him."

Aggie stroked Half Pint's ears. "And Marlin would come to school worse than ever."

Doris's sigh was heavy. "I think, without really knowing it, he wanted everyone else to be as unhappy as he was. It was so sad."

Yes, it was. And it helped Dan understand what drove Murphy. Violence begets violence. "So where's his father now? I don't recall ever seeing him. Or his mother, for that matter."

"Oh, dear." Doris cringed. "The mother, well, none of us ever knew her. When Mike moved to Sanctuary, it was just him and Marlin. And he wasn't exactly talkative. Not about his wife, or much of anything else."

"But he still lives around here?"

Aggie shook her head. "Oh, no, Deputy. He died." She clutched her hands. "Shot himself with his favorite gun. Marlin was fifteen at the time. He was the one who found his father and called the police."

This sobering news hit Dan square in the chest. Abandoned by his mother. Abused by his father. Scarred by the suicide, by seeing his father that way…

There was plenty of fodder to feed the rage inside Murphy.

Still, that didn't excuse criminal acts. And Dan was certain the thefts in the area and the meth lab all led back to Marlin Murphy.

If only he had some kind of proof.

Unfortunately, as he'd learned on those police reports, Marlin covered his tracks well. The kid might be a thug, but he was a crafty thug. He ensured other kids took the fall for what he did.

Kids like Jayce.

"Well, enough of this sad talk." Doris brushed at her lap, as though ridding herself of troublesome crumbs, then aimed a seraphic smile up at Dan. "Now, Deputy, on to what really matters."

"Oh, indeed!" Aggie hugged Half Pint. "Do tell us, Deputy, how goes it between you and Shelby Wilson? Are there wedding bells on the horizon?"

Dan's mouth opened, but no words came out. Just an odd, choked kind of sound.

Eyebrows raised, a little smile teasing her lips, Doris leaned toward Aggie. "Aren't men just the cutest thing when they blush?"

That was it. Dan jumped off the railing, muttered something about having work to do, and made a quick exit, the ladies' soft laughter following him all the way across the street.

Jerking the car door open, he slid behind the wheel and took a quick look at himself in the rearview mirror.

Yup. He was as red as a tomato.

And there was nothing cute about it.

He put the car into gear, rolling down the window as he drove out of town, letting the cold air slap him in the face. As he was about to turn onto Highway 62, the radio squawked to life.

Screech! Skrawwwk! "Come in, Chief."

He grabbed the mic. "Go ahead."

"Hey, you need to run up to Brumby's place."

Dan's gut seized. "Brumby's? What for?"

"We just got a call from some hunters. They were in the woods behind Brumby's house, and they found something."

Dan's pulse skipped. "Another meth lab?"

"Uh, no."

He waited, but all he heard was white noise. Finally he keyed the mic. "Care to share?"

"Huh?"

Dan drew in a heavy sigh. "Jasmine, what did they find?"

"Oh! That."

It was all he could do to keep from smacking his head against the steering wheel.

"You'll never believe it. I mean, I couldn't believe it."

Dan leaned his head back against the head rest. "Try me."

"Well, Chief, it's a body. They think they've found a body."

James Brumby and the boys never left home.

When the large hole behind Brumby's place was finally dug up, there wasn't one body in it, but five bodies. One human. Four canine.

No wonder Dan hadn't been able to track Brumby down.

He took statements from the hunters. Listened as the shaken man whose dog made the discovery related how one of his hounds caught a scent, ran like the wind, then just started digging at the ground like he was crazy.

"One thing about ol' Bo. Once he gets a scent, he don't give up. Well, by the time I reached him and got him pulled off, he'd dug up what was buried. I looked down—" the hunter shuddered—"an' there it was. This arm. Jus' comin' up outta the dirt. I could tell the rest of the body was still buried, so that's when we called you."

The grave was excavated, the contents bagged and tagged and sent to the lab for analysis. When the report from the crime lab finally came in a few days later, Dan sat at his desk, staring at the information in front of him. James Brumby and his dogs were shot. All of them. Several times. But what was most astonishing was the approximate time of death.

According to the report, they'd been dead since early October.

When Shannon and Aaron were killed.

And that sent a shattering realization pulsing through Dan's mind: If James Brumby died when the reports said he did, then it was likely he didn't shoot Shannon and Aaron. But if it wasn't him, then who? And *why*?

Dan went over and over the reports, both from the lab and from the investigation since the shootings. *Think, Justice. Think it through.*

The thefts in the area started up just a year before he came to town, and increased in frequency just a month before he arrived. Reports on the meth lab he found at Brumby's place showed the lab was probably abandoned about a month before Dan found it.

So Brumby was killed around the same time as Shannon and Aaron. Shot, as they were shot. The lab was abandoned around the same time Shannon and Aaron were killed.

It all had to be connected.

He grabbed the phone. He'd have forensics do some ballistic comparisons on the bullets taken from Brumby, his dogs, and—he gripped the receiver—those taken from Aaron and Shannon. If they matched, that'd be the evidence he needed to link it all.

"Yeah, sure. I can check that out. I'll get back to you soon."

"Thanks, Gene. I appreciate it."

Dan hung up the phone, then sat back in his chair. People coming and going behind Brumby's would have gotten his boys all stirred up. Knowing Brumby, one or two incidences of the boys going off, and the old man would get suspicious. Figure something was going on besides kids blowing up outhouses. Maybe he started to snoop, and when he found the lab…

Dan rubbed his hand across his forehead. But why were Shannon and Aaron at Brumby's? Had they gone out there with someone? Someone connected to the meth lab?

His hand stilled. Dropped to the desk. His gaze drifted to the photo he had framed and set on his desk. The picture from the camping trip.

The picture of Shannon, Aaron, and Jayce.

Jayce.

Dan stood. No. He wouldn't believe it. Couldn't. There was no way Jayce would have had anything to do with hurting

Shannon or Aaron. No way. He liked Aaron. And the kid *adored* Shannon. Hurting them would have taken a heart so hard that life meant noth—

Dan froze.

Of course.

Marlin Murphy.

If ever there was someone capable of killing without a second thought, it was that kid. And if Aaron and Shannon somehow found out about the meth lab…

For a fraction of a second, Dan considered tracking Murphy down, hauling him in, and interrogating him until he got some answers. But the tiny voice of reason prevailed. He had no proof.

How did that old saying go? "Never try to teach a pig to sing. It's a waste of your time and annoys the pig."

Talking with Marlin would be the same: a waste of Dan's time. And it would probably set Marlin off, let him know Dan was onto him. Dan didn't want to do that. Not yet.

He headed for the door. Okay, so he couldn't talk to the crud himself. Fine. There was still someone he *could* talk to. Someone who knew Murphy better than he ought to. Someone who might have answers without knowing it.

And someone who, one way or another, would share those answers with Dan.

THIRTY-TWO

*"If I find in myself a desire which no experience
in this world can satisfy, the most probable
explanation is that I was made for another world."*

C. S. LEWIS

"I will be his father, and he will be my son."

2 SAMUEL 7:14

JAYCE SAT IN THE PASSENGER SEAT, STARING OUT THE
car window, not letting on just how nervous he was.

When Deputy Dan showed up at school to pick him up
early, Jayce had asked what was going on. Dan's response was
silence. The same silence that hovered between them on the
drive to the house.

As they pulled into the driveway, Jayce was out of the car
and at the front door in a heartbeat. But Dan was right behind
him, following him inside.

"Sit down, Jayce. We need to talk."

Jayce did as Dan ordered. Because that's what it was. An
order.

"I want to know where to find Marlin Murphy's meth lab."

If he'd picked up a bat and taken a swing at Jayce's head, Dan
couldn't have shocked him more. "What are you talking about?"

Dan stood in front of him, arms crossed. "Look. I know Marlin's the one running the meth lab. That's what the thefts have been about." He arched a brow. "He had you stealing supplies for him."

One look at Dan's hard features told Jayce there was no use denying it. He sat back against the couch cushions. "So you going to arrest me?"

"No!"

The anger in that one word brought Jayce's head snapping up. He knew where anger like that led. He'd faced it often enough with Marlin.

Oddly, though, Dan's hand wasn't forming a fist. It wasn't coming at him. Instead, he seemed to be dragging in deep breaths. Trying to keep his cool. When he finally spoke, his tone was controlled again.

"Where is the lab?"

"What makes you think I know?"

"Jayce. Where is it?"

He wanted to tell him. Oh, how he wanted to tell him. But how could he? Marlin would know it was Jayce who gave him away. And he'd make Jayce pay.

No, he'd make Jayce's grandmother pay. And Miss Wilson.

"Why are you protecting that creep? All he does is hurt people."

Jayce turned away from Dan, staring at the wall.

"Look, if you're afraid of how this will impact you, don't be. This isn't about you, son. It's about Marlin. And Shannon and Aaron."

Shock pierced Jayce's chest. "What's Marlin got to do with Shannon?"

"Where is the meth lab?"

Jayce ground his teeth. "*What's Marlin got to do with Shannon?*"

Something flickered in Dan's eyes. Something Jayce hadn't

seen since Shannon's and Aaron's funeral. Pain. Fury. And a warning.

That something was coming. Something Jayce had heard about in one of those westerns he and Dan watched sometimes on TV.

A reckoning.

A reckoning was coming. For Marlin.

Two emotions followed on the heels of that thought. Gladness. That Marlin would finally get his. And a sudden, searing agony. Because there was only one reason Dan would look the way he did right now.

If he'd found the killer. The one who'd taken his children from him.

"Are you saying…?" Dread slipped icy fingers around his throat, tightening, cutting off the words. Jayce cleared his throat. "You think Marlin had something to do with Shannon and Aaron being killed?"

Dan didn't reply. He didn't need to. Jayce saw it in his eyes.

"You think he killed them." The minute the words were out of Jayce's mouth, he was on his feet. Screaming. "No! You're wrong. Marlin's crazy, but he wouldn't…" He couldn't finish. Because he knew Marlin would. He most certainly would.

And he'd enjoy every second of it.

Pain scored Jayce's mind, and he turned and ran to his room, slamming the door, as if that could keep the truth from reaching him. But it couldn't.

No more than it could hold back the realization that was tearing Jayce apart. If Marlin killed Shannon and Aaron, then it wasn't just Marlin's doing.

It was Jayce's, too. Because he'd been helping Marlin. Protecting him. Doing what he was told. That's what kept his grandmother safe.

And got the one person he'd ever really loved killed.

~

Dan stood in the living room, staring down the hallway at Jayce's room. Another door slammed in his face.

He wanted to march down that hallway, jerk the door open, and demand an answer. But he didn't move. Because he had the powerful sense that he wasn't alone in the room. In fact, it was as if he could feel a huge, heavenly hand on his shoulder holding him still.

Telling him to wait.

Lord, I have to have answers.

Trust Me.

I do, but—

Trust Me.

Dan let his breath out and stared at the floor. Then he nodded and went to the kitchen, pulling out the coffee.

It was going to be a long night.

The knock on Jayce's door was soft, but he still jumped about a mile when he heard it.

It seemed so strange, Dan knocking on doors in his own house. But he told Jayce he'd never just barge in. "This is your room. You have a right to your privacy."

Jayce appreciated that. He didn't understand it, but he appreciated it. "Come in."

Dan stuck his head in. "Time for tonight's reading. You want to join me or take a break?"

Jayce slid off the bed. "I'll come listen."

The first time Dan had suggested they read the Bible together before bedtime, Jayce thought he was kidding. "The Bible?"

Dan kind of shrugged. "Hey, if you'd rather not, that's fine. It's just…" He looked away, that sad look coming over his face again. "Aaron and Shannon and I used to do that. Read together."

That was all it took. "Sounds like a good idea."

Dan eyed him. "Really?"

"Really." Jayce grinned at Dan's surprise. "Let's do it."

At first Jayce did it to help Dan, thinking maybe he'd miss Aaron and Shannon just a little less if they read together. But soon he found he really enjoyed it. In part because he liked talking things over with Dan. But also just because he liked hearing what was in the Bible. It was interesting. A little hard to understand, sometimes, but it said good things. Things that made him think. And things that made him feel good.

The last part made him follow Dan to the living room. He needed to feel better tonight. He was tired of feeling like a hypocritical crud.

Dan settled into his chair, and Jayce took his spot on the couch. He closed his eyes, listening as Dan read.

"Okay. We were in 1 John. Chapter four…"

"Verse sixteen." Jayce cracked one eye open and saw Dan's smile.

"Good memory."

He grinned, closed that eye again, and settled back.

"'We know how much God loves us, and we have put our trust in him. God is love, and all who live in love live in God, and God lives in them. And as we live in God, our love grows more perfect. So we will not be afraid on the day of judgment, but we can face him with confidence because we are like Christ here in this world. Such love has no fear because perfect love expels all fear."

Jayce opened his eyes. "All fear?"

Dan stopped. He looked down at the page, read the words again, then gave a slow nod. "Yeah, that's what it says."

Jayce sat on the edge of the couch. "But, I mean, people are afraid all the time."

"Well, he kind of addresses that. Listen. 'If we are afraid, it is for fear of judgment, and this shows that his love has not been perfected in us.'"

Judgment. Jayce understood judgment. Understood it and knew he deserved it.

"You want to talk about this?"

Jayce did, more than anything, but he couldn't. Not yet. He stood. "I think I need to just think for a while. That okay?"

Dan studied him, and Jayce thought he might object. Instead he just said, "Sure. I'll see you in the morning."

"G'night."

Dan's voice followed him down the hallway. "Sleep well, Jayce."

Yeah. As if.

Jayce paced, back and forth, back and forth. The words Dan had read to him kept pounding at him.

"We have put our trust in him…God is love…So we will not be afraid…perfect love expels all fear…"

And then the words that haunted him most of all, words he couldn't escape, no matter how he tried: *"If we are afraid, it is for fear of judgment, and this shows that his love has not been perfected in us."*

Fear of judgment. Was that what he felt? What had him up all night, feeling like some kind of lion trapped in a cage?

Suddenly, Shannon's voice echoed through him. *"You're just like Aslan…you growl loud and show your teeth…you're not a tame lion. But you're good. Down inside."*

Jayce closed his eyes. He could swear he felt her hand on his chest, just over his heart. The memory of that gentle touch broke his heart, and he turned, looking for someplace to run. Escape.

But there was no place for him to go. No haven, no real sanctuary…

Or was there?

Going to the door, he listened. No sounds. Dan had to be asleep by now. Jayce cracked the door open, slipped from his room, and eased down the hall.

To Shannon's room.

Slipping inside, his gaze swept the room. Most of Shannon's things were gone. Still, if he closed his eyes, he could feel her here. Walking around the room, he touched the furniture, trying to see her. Asking her to help him.

"I want to be good. I want to be the way you thought I was…"

He jerked his hand to brush away tears.

How stupid can you be?

Jayce choked out a protest. He couldn't deal with the voice. Not now.

Crying? Over what? So Marlin killed them. Big deal. It's not like you put the gun in his hand.

If the voice had been audible, Jayce could put his hands over his ears, block it out. But there was no way to stop the dark words filling his mind.

"I didn't *have* to give him the gun. If I'd just told Dan about it all, Marlin would be in jail. And Shannon—" his throat was so tight he had to swallow hard to talk—"would still be alive!"

Fine. Have it your way. It's all your fault. So go ahead. Tell ol' Deputy Dan. What do you think he'll do when you confirm what he suspects? That you've been working with the person who killed Shannon and Aaron? That you've been covering for him? Protecting him? You'll be lucky to end up in jail.

Desperation settled into the cracks and crevices of Jayce's spirit. He put his hands over his face. "Help me…"

Who are you talking to? There's no one here. This is just a room. A stupid room. There's no spirit here. No Shannon. It's empty.

Just like his life.

Jayce spun, ready to bolt out the door, and slammed into the lamp on the bedside table. As it bounced and rolled, he froze. Listening. Then letting out a breath when it seemed like

Dan didn't hear. With a hard sigh, he got down on the floor and reached under the bed for the lamp. It was just out of reach.

Flipping onto his back, he wriggled under the bed, managed to get his fingers around the lamp cord—and stopped.

What was that?

He peered at the mattress above him. Something was there. He could see it through the wires of the bed frame. Wriggling out from under the bed, he pulled the lamp out, put it back in place, then lifted the mattress.

Two books lay there. He grabbed them and lowered the mattress back in place. When he looked down at the books, he caught his breath.

Shannon's journal. Her Bible.

No one in the room? Maybe not. But someone led him to these books.

It's a coincidence. Besides, you should give them to the deputy. They're not yours to read...

The voice went on, but Jayce wasn't listening. Heart pounding, clutching the books close, he went back to his own room and settled onto the bed. He held his breath and opened the journal.

It only took a second for the impact to hit him.

Shannon wasn't gone. She was right here, in the pages before him. Jayce saw her joy in the doodles, heard her voice in the prayers she recorded. Months of prayers.

About him.

For him.

August 15. God, be with Jayce. Show him You love him lots, just the way he is. I mean, You know everything about him, inside and out, and You love him. ☺ That's so cool! I read 1 Samuel 16:7, and that made me think of Jayce. And that's cool, too. Thanks, God.

He flipped several pages.

August 27. God, can You somehow show Jayce he belongs to You? Show him You're the true Aslan, and he can trust You with everything. I went back and read two of my favorite verses today. Psalm 56:3–4. I'm gonna pray for that to be true for Jayce. ♥

Page after page showed her persistent care for him.

September 4. Jesus, Jayce is so special. Help him see that about himself. ☺ Help him know You died for him. † Just for him! You set him free, Jesus. Help him know that! Psalm 103:2–4. That's for Jayce!

September 12. God, be Jayce's Daddy. Let him see that he's got the best Daddy in the world in You! Make Romans 8:14–16 really true for him.

September 16. God, it's so much fun to see Jayce smile. 😎 To hear him laugh. He seems happier. He really does. That's because of You, huh? You're loving Jayce through us. Thank You, God. I read Ephesians 2 today, verses 1–10, and I wanted to dance! I just know Jayce is going to meet You soon. I can't wait, God. I just can't wait.

And then, the last entry. Looking at the date, Jayce's heart constricted. She wrote this the night before she was killed:

October 2. God, I'm really, really worried about Jayce. Marlin Murphy is...well, I can't write that kind of word. But he's not a nice person. I think Jayce is afraid of him. But he doesn't need to be. Show him that, God. My reading today was Psalm 62, and I want Jayce to feel that way. Like You're his rock, his fortress. Please make it true for him. And help me know how to help

Jayce best. I want him to be with us in eternity. Because I love him, God. And I know YOU love him. So whatever it takes, I'll do it. And You know what? I think Aaron and I have an idea. It's kind of risky, but I know You're with us. So we'll be okay. No matter what happens. Just help Jayce to be okay, too. Thanks, God!

As Jayce read those last words, he caught back the sobs clawing up his throat. Shannon loved him. More truly than anyone in his life.

He closed his eyes and leaned his head back against the wall. *Why, God? Why did she have to die?*

When he opened his eyes, his gaze fell to her Bible. He'd never read a Bible himself before. Just listened as Dan read from it. He looked at the journal again. The things Shannon listed in her journal—Romans, Psalms, all of that—were Bible verses. Well, if Shannon loved them that much, then he would, too.

Haven't you invaded her privacy enough? She's dead. And it's your fault!

He held her Bible in his trembling hands, feeling the texture of the leather cover.

Do you really think she'd want you reading her stuff like it belongs to you? Bad enough to read her journal. But her Bible? Those things are private!

He studied the gold edges of the thin paper.

You, of all people, have no right!

Anger stiffened Jayce's spine. "Fine! You're probably right. But you know what? I don't care. I don't care what you say. What matters is Shannon, and what she said."

Lips compressed, he hunted out the verses she'd listed. But as he read, something strange happened. It was as though he'd never read anything like this before. As though the words almost came alive on the page.

As though they sang with the same joy he'd always heard

in Shannon's voice—and his heart responded. A strange feeling bloomed inside him, a warmth that grew and spread. When he came to the final passage, he lifted the Bible and read it out loud.

"'I wait quietly before God, for my salvation comes from him. He alone is my rock and my salvation, my fortress where I will never be shaken.'"

Never be shaken. To never again be afraid…oh, how he longed for that!

"'So many enemies against one man—all of them trying to kill me. To them I'm just a broken-down wall or a tottering fence.'"

The image of Marlin and his gang drifted through Jayce's mind.

"'They delight in telling lies about me. They are friendly to my face, but they curse me in their hearts…. My salvation and my honor come from God alone. He is my refuge, a rock where no enemy can reach me.'"

No enemy. Not Marlin. Not the creeps who hung with him. Nobody.

"'O my people, trust in him at all times. Pour out your heart to him, for God is our refuge. From the greatest to the lowliest—all are nothing in his sight. If you weigh them on the scales, they are lighter than a puff of air. Don't try to get rich by extortion or robbery. And if your wealth increases, don't make it the center of your life. God has spoken plainly, and I have heard it many times: Power, O God, belongs to you; unfailing love, O Lord, is yours.'"

Jayce stared down at the next words, and for a heartbeat dread settled over him. "'Surely you judge all people according to what they have done.'"

If that was true, then what would happen to him? He'd done terrible things! If God was going to judge him, then what hope was there?

The answer came in the form of one of the earlier verses

he'd read with equal speed: "'Praise the LORD, I tell myself, and never forget the good things he does for me. He forgives all my sins and heals all my diseases. He ransoms me from death and surrounds me with love and tender mercies.'"

Jayce wanted that. Forgiveness. Tender mercies. He wasn't even completely sure what tender mercies were, but he wanted them. Holding Shannon's Bible to his chest, he looked at the ceiling.

"God, are You there?"

Though no voice answered, Jayce knew He was. He could feel it.

"Listen, I'm no good at this." A rough chuckle escaped him. "I'm no good. That's the truth. But Shannon…God, she was good. And she said I could be, too. That You could make me good. So please, do that. Make me the way Shannon saw me. Okay?"

He looked down at the Bible in his hands and smiled. As he stood and laid the Bible and journal on the stand next to his bed, he realized something.

There was silence inside.

The angry voice wasn't just silent. It was gone.

In its place were all the words he'd read tonight. Shannon's words, from her journal. The words from the Bible. And as he let them echo through him, Jayce felt something strange. Something he'd never felt before. It wasn't until he'd gotten ready for bed and slipped under the covers that it finally occurred to him what the feeling was.

Peace.

He reached up to turn the light off, then laid his head on the pillow. For once, the darkness wasn't imposing. Instead, it seemed quiet. Welcoming. He lay there for a long time, just soaking in the new feelings sweeping over him.

Things were different. No, *he* was different. He wasn't sure how or why, but he was. And that meant he had to do something.

He wasn't looking forward to it. But it had to be done. He rolled to his side and punched his pillow into shape. At least he didn't have to do it alone. Like Shannon wrote, God would be with him. So he'd be okay.

No matter what happened.

THIRTY-THREE

*"You can clutch the past so tightly to your chest
that it leaves your arms too full to embrace the present."*

JAN GLIDEWELL

*"In his kindness God called you to his eternal glory by means
of Jesus Christ. After you have suffered a little while,
he will restore, support, and strengthen you,
and he will place you on a firm foundation."*

1 PETER 5:10

THIS IS SO HARD!

Shelby sat across the booth from Dan, her hands folded in her lap. She'd had them on the table, but several times it took all her willpower not to reach out and take Dan's hand, and ask him to talk to her. Really talk to her. Not just rattle off information about how Jayce was doing. Not sit there, his stiff every move and reserved word screaming out to her how much she'd lost.

Lord, how do I deal with this? With having to be around Dan all the time? I miss him so much...

She studied his features, saw the shadows behind those blue eyes, the weariness that left his features drawn. She'd been so angry with him, with the way he treated her. But lately she realized the anger had faded.

In its place was sorrow. Grief for the death of what might have been. She'd asked God, over and over, to take her feelings away. To change her so that she looked on Dan as a good friend. A brother.

But every time she saw him, every time she heard that deep voice, her traitorous heart shifted into overdrive, and she knew.

She'd never stop wanting to support him, to comfort him, to be a part of his life. She'd never stop wanting to give him her lov—

"I just don't know what to do."

His words pulled her attention back to the conversation.

"It's not that Jayce and I are having problems." He took his napkin and started shredding it into tiny pieces. "We're getting along great. That's what makes it so hard to know he's protecting Marlin Murphy."

"Why do you think that is, Dan? I mean, Jayce doesn't even like Marlin."

"I wish I knew."

Shelby stared down at her plate, at the sandwich she hadn't touched. "There has to be a reason." What would make Jayce protect someone he hated? What motivation…?

She gasped, and before she realized what she was doing, she grabbed Dan's hand. "You don't think—"

Dan's hand tensed under hers. His gaze, which was on their joined hands, lifted to meet hers. Shelby jerked her hand back. "I'm sorry."

He shook his head. "No, it's okay."

She focused on her purse, on pulling out her wallet.

"Shelby, I've got it. I asked you to meet me—"

She tossed the money on the table and jumped up. She had to get out of here before she did something even more stupid. Like burst into tears in the middle of Lou's Diner.

She almost made it to her car when Dan caught up to her. He grabbed her arm. "Shelby, please, wait."

She stopped, but she didn't look at him. Couldn't. Just kept her eyes fixed on the ground. His grip gentled, and he took hold of both her arms, turning her toward him.

"Shelby."

Such tenderness in the way he said her name. Tears jabbed at the backs of her eyes. She hadn't heard him say her name like that for so long.

"Shelby…please."

She bit her lip, staring now at the front of his uniform. One finger slid under her chin, tipped her head up so their eyes met. She saw the surprise—and then the remorse—when he realized she'd been crying.

He cupped her face with one hand, then pulled his handkerchief from his pocket and wiped her tears with the other. "I'm an idiot."

She didn't argue. His lips quirked at that.

"I'm sorry, Shelby. I really am. I just…" He sighed, releasing her. "I don't know how to act around you anymore."

She took his handkerchief. "Yeah, well, welcome to the club, bucko." She blew her nose once, twice, then folded the kerchief and held it out to him.

He looked down at it then at her. "Um. Keep it."

She realized what she'd done, and suddenly she was laughing. Dan's laughter joined hers, and they stood there, hooting like a couple of loons until tears ran down their faces. People walking by stared at them, and a few sidestepped them as though they were contagious.

Which just made them laugh all the harder.

Several minutes went by before they could get themselves under control. Finally, Dan laid a hand on her shoulder, using the other to wipe at his tearing eyes.

"Oh, man!" He clutched at his side. "That hurt!" His grin drew her lips into a smile as well. "And it felt great."

"Yes." She drew in a deep breath. "Yes, it did."

He straightened, sliding his hand down her arm to take her hand. "What do you say, Shelby? Can we start again? Maybe be friends for a while and, I don't know, see where that takes us?"

She squeezed his hand, then let it go. "I'd like that."

His smile was open and relaxed for the first time in a very long time. "Me, too."

"Well, I'd better get back to—"

"Wait. You were going to say something in there, before I got stupid."

She punched his arm. "You didn't get stupid. You've been there for quite some time."

"Ha ha. So do you remember what you wanted to say? About Jayce and Marlin?"

She frowned then her eyes widened. "It was about why Jayce covers for Marlin."

"And?"

"Well, we agree there has to be some reason Jayce won't talk about Marlin, right?"

Dan inclined his head. "Right."

"And we all know how good Marlin is at threatening people."

"Right again."

"So…?"

He arched his brows, holding out his hands. "So? Care to enlighten the poor confused male?"

Shelby chuckled. "Jayce's grandmother." She watched his face and saw the pieces of the puzzle that had been haunting Dan spinning into place.

"Of course. Marlin is threatening Jayce's grandmother."

Shelby nodded. "It makes perfect sense, when you think about it. Jayce covers for someone he hates…"

"…to protect someone he loves." Dan turned and headed for his cruiser.

"Hey!" Shelby trotted after him. "Where are you going?"

"We." Dan took her arm and hustled her along beside him. "The question is, where are *we* going. And the answer is, to see Mrs. Dalton." He gave her a grim smile. "I think it's time for Gramma to take a little vacation."

∾

"I'm done."

Marlin Murphy heard the words. Understood them. He just couldn't believe that Jayce was saying them. Just like that. Like Marlin would smile, pat Jayce on the head, and say, "Okay, see ya."

Yeah. Right.

Marlin pulled the cigarettes from his pocket, choosing one with care. He hopped onto the picnic table, sitting on the edge. Normally the town library wasn't his preference for a meeting, but it was late enough that there wasn't anyone around. When his cigarette was lit, he took a long, satisfying draw, blowing out the smoke and watching it rise into the darkness.

Then, and only then, did he look at Jayce. "Excuse me?"

Jayce didn't flinch at the low threat in Marlin's words, but then Marlin hadn't expected him to. This kid was as fearless as it got. If he could just get past his conscience, he'd be perfect for the business.

"I said I'm done. With all of it. With you."

"That so?" Marlin took another drag on his cigarette, letting the smoke seep deep into his lungs, warming him, shoring him up. "Says who?"

"Says m—"

Marlin cocked his head when Jayce stopped. Maybe he was wising up, changing his mind.

"No. That's not really true. It's not me; it's God."

Oh, please! Marlin flicked the cigarette away. "God."

"Yeah. God."

"So you're tellin' me you got religion."

The punk actually smiled. "No. I'm telling you I got God. And Jesus. And I'm done. Because of them."

Standing, Marlin let out a bark of laughter and slid his hands into his pockets. "So that's why you asked me to meet you here and to come alone." He considered bringing the stupid siblings with him but didn't want them—or anyone else—to think he was afraid of Jayce.

Or of Deputy Dan.

He smirked. "Smart boy."

Jayce dipped his head. "This is between you and me, Marlin."

"You and me and your grandmother, you mean?"

"No."

There was something in the kid's eyes that tensed Marlin's jaw. "No?"

"My gramma's gone." Jayce looked way too pleased when he delivered this tidbit of news. "Left this afternoon. I don't know when she'll be back."

Tentacles of anger slithered through Marlin, wrapping around his gut, his heart, squeezing. "So...Granny's gone, and you figure you're free."

"You can't hurt her, Marlin."

"Maybe not her." He took a step toward Jayce. "But there *are* others."

"You mean Miss Wilson."

Marlin just smiled.

"I don't think so."

His smile faded. "What's that supposed to—"

"She told me what happened that night. About Dan. About what he told you."

The memory still made Marlin seethe. "So?"

Jayce smiled. The little puke actually smiled! "So I think you know as well as I do that he meant every word. And you don't want him comin' down on you."

It wasn't a question. It didn't need to be. He was right.

"So your leverage is gone, Marlin. And that means we're done. Don't call me. Don't contact me at all. You leave me alone, and I—" his gaze pinned Marlin's—"will leave you alone."

"Are you *threatening* me?"

Jayce lifted a shoulder. "Just telling you how it is." With that, he turned and walked away.

Marlin's hand slid into his back pocket, fingered the knife he kept there. He itched to pull it free and plant it right in Jayce's oh-so-straight back.

But he didn't.

No, that would be too fast, too easy.

And, Marlin thought as he watched Jayce disappear around a corner, one thing he would not do was make this easy for good ol' Jayce. Oh no. The kid wanted it over. Well, so be it. Marlin would make that happen. But he'd do it his way. In as slow and painful a way as possible.

Oh, yeah. The time had come to show Jayce just who was really in charge.

Time was running out.

Dan had been waiting, just as God told him to. He hadn't pushed Jayce this morning at breakfast, or when he drove him to school. Later that afternoon, Jayce called, as he always did, to let Dan know he was home from school. As much as Dan wanted to take a little side trip, stopping off at the house for a chat, he hadn't done it. He just went about his work.

Waiting.

But as the day wore on and quitting time drew near, Dan grew more and more restless. He was on the phone to his sisters, asking them to pray. By the time he got home, he could no longer fight off the sense that something was wrong.

He pushed open the front door, calling as he entered. "Jayce?"

He listened for some kind of response, some movement, but heard none. He went to Jayce's bedroom door and knocked. No answer.

Pressing his ear to the door, he listened again.

Nothing.

The apprehension that had been dogging his steps all day ratcheted up a notch, and Dan opened the door, looking into the room. It took a moment for his mind to process what he saw—the bed all but broken in half, pieces of wood lying scattered around on the floor. The bedclothes, torn and tossed about the room. The bed table and lamp on their sides on the floor. Drawers in the dresser pulled out and dumped.

It looked like someone in a rage had torn the room apart.

Jayce.

A sick sensation worked its way through Dan's gut. Almost without thinking, he went to the phone. Dialed the number. And waited.

It seemed like that was all he was doing lately. Waiting.

"Hello?"

Dan cleared his throat at the sound of Shelby's voice. "Hey. It's Dan. I need you to come over here." He glanced down the hallway at the wrecked room.

"Jayce has run away."

Dan opened and slammed cupboard doors in the kitchen, ostensibly to fix a pot of coffee. But in reality, he was trying to vent the anger boiling through him.

He trusted Jayce. *Trusted* him. And this was how he repaid that trust. What a fool he'd been. What a stupid, blind—

The doorbell rang, and Dan slammed another cupboard shut and went to yank the front door open.

Shelby came in, laying a hand on his arm. Before he could stop himself, Dan jerked away. When hurt pinched her features, he cursed himself for being the worst fool possible. But all he said was, "This way."

Spinning on his heel, he led the way down the hallway to Jayce's room.

Shelby followed, then stood in the center of the room, surveying the damage. She walked over to the dresser where clothes and books had been tossed. Slowly, she lifted each item, folding the clothes and stacking the books.

Dan went to grab up the lamp and bed table, dropping them back in place. "I thought Jayce and I were gaining ground. That he was starting to trust me again."

"And now?"

He tried to ignore the curt tone in her voice. He made a sweeping gesture with his hand. "*Look* at this place, Shelby. He's gone. What does that tell you?"

"Nothing."

Women. He ground his teeth. "Then you're not paying attention."

"Maybe *you're* the one not paying attention."

Dan flinched. Was everyone turning on him? "I thought you'd understand."

"Oh, I *understand*, all right." She squared off, arms folded across her chest. "You talk a good game, Deputy Justice, about doing what's right, about believing in people." Her blue eyes glittered. "About second chances. But when it comes right down to it, the minute someone messes up, the axe falls."

"What are you talking about?"

"*You!*" She practically threw the word at him. "I'm talking about you! You're so sure you can't trust anyone, that you can't ever love anyone again, because if you do, they'll leave you."

He stepped back. "You don't know what you're talking about."

"Oh no? What about us, Dan? You say you want to start again. Be friends. But the second I get close, the door shuts. Right in my face."

Her raised hand cut his reply short. "No, don't bother. What was growing between us is in the past. I think I finally get that. But you and I are not what matters most right now." She went back to Jayce's dresser, grabbed something, and held it up for him to see.

What on earth?

Currents of shock ran through him. The Aslan pendant Shannon gave Jayce. The boy would never leave it behind. Dan's gaze met Shelby's. The censure in her eyes was almost more than he could take.

She dangled the pendant on its cord. "Do you really think Jayce left, or was he taken?"

She lowered the pendant into his palm, then he fingered the detail the way he'd seen Jayce do so often. "Taken?"

Shelby stamped her foot on the floor. "Come on, Dan. You're a police officer. *Think!* Does this room look like Jayce ran away?"

Dan had to admit she was right. "Murphy." Of course. Why didn't he realize it sooner? "But why now? What could have made Marlin take this kind of risk?"

Shelby hugged herself. "I don't know, but if Marlin is desperate enough to break into your home and grab Jayce, it can't be good."

"No, it can't." Dan closed a fist around the pendant as certainty filled his soul. If Dan didn't find Jayce soon, it would be too late.

At that thought, terror sliced through Dan. Shaken to the core, he turned and planted his hands on the wall. Closing his eyes, he pled with God for help.

A hand on his shoulder told him Shelby was there, beside him, probably praying as well. He reached up to cover her hand with his.

Dan knew he couldn't deny the truth any longer. Yes, as Shelby said, he was afraid. Afraid to love, to risk losing again. Oh, sure, he'd let Jayce come to stay with him. But the boy wasn't the only one who'd erected barriers. He'd been working hard to hold his love back from Jayce. And from Shelby. Because when you love, you're vulnerable.

And that meant you could be hurt.

But for all his effort, it hadn't worked. The way he felt right now was proof of that. He loved Jayce. Loved him like he was his own son.

And he loved Shelby.

These two meant the world to him. And he was about to lose them. *God, forgive me. Forgive me...and help me.*

"Dan." Shelby's voice washed over him, soaking him in tender concern. "Are you okay?"

He opened his eyes and turned to her, her hand still nestled in his. "I can't do this, Shelby."

The tiny frown puckering her brow before she turned and walked away told him she didn't understand. But how could she? When he hadn't been honest with her.

Well, it was time to change that. Squaring his shoulders, he took the plunge. "I can't lose Jayce." He drew a deep breath. "Or you."

She faced him but didn't move closer. Just stood there, staring at him, as though afraid to believe. Dan understood. He would have to take the first step. And the second. And the third.

He covered the floor between them, gripping Shelby's shoulders with gentle pressure. "I'm sorry." He lifted a hand to cup her face. "I'm so sorry. You were right. I wouldn't let myself admit how much Jayce means to me. How much *you* mean to me."

Tears glistened in her beautiful eyes, and slowly Dan drew her close, folding her in his arms, cradling her against his chest. She pressed her face into his shoulder with a tremulous sigh.

In for a penny, in for a pound, right? Dan spoke the words he'd been holding back for months. "I love Jayce. And I love you. Heaven help me, I love you."

Shelby's laughter was a blend of irony and happiness. She tipped her head to look up at him. "Not exactly the declaration of love a girl dreams of—" she grinned through her tears—"but I'll take it. And I'll take you. Now and always."

He framed her face with his hands, then lowered his head

to kiss her, showing her the only way he knew how that the barriers weren't just down, they were obliterated.

Shelby's arms slid around his neck, holding him close. He didn't argue. When he finally raised his head, he was breathless. And not just because of the effect Shelby had on him.

For rising from deep within him was the warm sound of Sarah's voice. And her words rang through him: *"Live, Dan. Love."*

Moved, shaken, he took Shelby's hands in his. "We've got to find Jayce."

"But where do we look?"

Dan released her hands and went to stare out the window. "I'm betting Marlin took him to the meth lab. That's what I'd do if I had someone I wanted to teach a lesson."

"You think that's what he's going to do?"

Dan started to answer, but the doorbell sounded, cutting him off. Shelby patted his arm. "I'll answer it. You keep looking for some kind of clue."

Dan nodded. Just as well he hadn't been able to answer her questions. He didn't want to tell her that he hoped teaching Jayce a lesson was all Marlin had in mind.

God, please. Help me know where to look. Help me save Jayce… His throat closed. *Because Father, whether he knows it or not, he saved me. Pulled me back from being alone, opened a heart I thought was closed for good.*

As Dan prayed, memories flitted through his mind…images of Marlin and his gang, things Jayce said to Dan…and suddenly, like the mechanism of a lock clicking into place, the answer was remarkably clear.

Dan spun to the door, praying it wasn't too late. "Shelby, I know where to look!"

"Well, then, let's go."

Dan halted, mouth open, staring at Annie and Kyla, who stood with Shelby in the doorway of the bedroom. "Where did you two come from?"

Annie's smile was pure sass. "Same place you did, brother mine. Our dear mummy and daddy."

Kyla nudged her sister. "This is no time for jokes, Annot." She came in to hug Dan. "After you phoned us earlier, Annot and I talked and decided we needed to come do what we could to help."

Dan's heart jumped. "Annie, did you bring Kodi?" His sister's smile was all the answer he needed. "Kyla, you and Shelby stay here, man the phones. Call the sheriff's office and tell them we need some backup out here right away. I'll take my cell phone with me and keep you posted on what's happening."

Kyla and Shelby offered no arguments. No questions. Just a willingness to do what was needed.

No wonder he loved these women so much.

He turned to grab the Aslan pendant and one of Jayce's shirts, then turned to Annie. "You and Kodi, come with me."

"Dan, wait."

He hesitated, turning back to Shelby.

"Where do we send the backup?"

Dan headed for the front door. "To the old lumberyard."

THIRTY-FOUR

*"Noble souls, through dust and heat,
rise from disaster and defeat the stronger."*
HENRY WADSWORTH LONGFELLOW

*"In your majesty, ride out to victory, defending truth, humility,
and justice. Go forth to perform awe-inspiring deeds!"*
PSALM 45:4

"I'M GONNA KILL YOU."

Jayce lifted his aching head to look at Marlin through the one eye that wasn't swollen shut. He knew he was bleeding. Could taste it, see where it splattered on his clothes. The ropes binding his wrists behind the back of the chair burned, cutting into his flesh. The pain from the bruises and cuts on his face, and probably several broken ribs, was intense. But he didn't let any of that show on his face.

No way.

Instead, he just smiled.

Marlin snarled and punched Jayce in the side with a meaty fist. Jayce couldn't hold back a grunt, but that's all he let out.

As much as Marlin enjoyed beating people up—and he did enjoy that a great deal—what he relished most of all was his vic-

344

tims' suffering. "Beat 'em and break 'em." That was his motto, one he carried out with pleasure.

But Jayce was determined. Marlin could beat him to a pulp, which he'd already pretty well done. He could even kill him, which Jayce figured he was going to do. But he wouldn't give the crud the satisfaction of knowing how much it hurt. All he'd give him was silence and smiles.

And prayer.

As crazy as it was, every time Marlin belted him, Jayce found himself praying for the creep. Not pretty prayers, mind you. But they were prayers all the same.

Wham! A fist drove into his face.

God, show Marlin what a crud he is.

Punch! Another hit to the gut.

God, save Marlin, even if he's a puke and doesn't deserve it.

Crunch! An uppercut that slammed Jayce's jaws together so hard he thought his teeth would shatter.

God, stop Marlin before he kills anyone else.

"Come on, jerkface." Marlin snarled in his ear. "Give it up. Go ahead and cry. You know you want to."

Jayce forced his head up. Pried his good eye open.

And smiled.

A string of swearing scorched the air, and Marlin spun and stalked away. Jayce waited until he turned a corner, then let his head fall to his chest as a long, deep groan escaped him.

Oh, man. If he got himself killed, Deputy Dan would never forgive him.

Jayce grinned then winced at the pain that rewarded that action. He only hoped Dan figured out what had happened.

Please, God, I know I don't know You well, but please. Don't let Dan think I left him like that.

He'd been sound asleep when Marlin and his goons jim-mied his bedroom window, slipped in, and grabbed him. They'd gagged him and trussed him up like some kind of turkey surprise, then dragged him out the window and threw him in the back of their truck.

He'd figured they were bringing him here, to the meth lab. And he'd been right. The stupid siblings, Dicky and Jay, jerked him out of the truck bed, dragged him in here, and tied him to the chair. Then they went to sample the lab's product while the fun got started.

All Jayce had to do was survive long enough. Because if Marlin was anything, he was predictable. Jayce had seen it happen too often with others to doubt it. First, came the beating. Then, if the beatee survived, came the gloating.

Just let me make it to the gloating, God. Please…for Shannon.

Marlin actually stopped hitting him sooner than he'd expected. Of course, he could just be taking a break. All that swinging and smashing was probably pretty tiring.

Heavy footsteps drew Jayce's attention. Marlin was coming back.

"You ready for another round, jerkface?"

Jayce didn't reply.

Mock regret painted Marlin's features. "You know, I wanted to take it easy on you. I mean, if you'd cooperated, I would have made it quick. Not so painful."

He shook his head, grabbing a hank of Jayce's hair and jerking his head up. "But no, you gotta sit there playing the strong, silent type. So here's what I wanna know." He stuck his face into Jayce's. "Who you trying to impress, jerkwad? In case you haven't noticed, it's just you 'n' me here."

"No." Jayce wanted the word to come out solid. Confident. Unfortunately, his voice wouldn't cooperate, and it came out ragged. Hoarse. "It's not."

Another tug at his hair almost made him grimace.

"What are you talkin' about?" Fury filled Marlin's face, and his voice dropped to a low, dangerous level. "You told that idiot deputy where we are, didn't you?"

Jayce cleared his throat. "No."

Marlin jolted Jayce's head. "Then what are you talking about?"

Jayce eyed him. *Well, here goes nothing.* "God." He smiled. "God's here, Marlin."

He let Jayce's hair go, disgusted. "God! Give me a break. You really buy that religion crud?"

Jayce shook his head and immediately regretted it. "Not religion. God."

"Oh...I get it." A sneer curled Marlin's lips. "This is because of your little friend. Shannon, wasn't that her name?"

Jayce wanted to swear. To pull out every foul thing he could think of to throw at Marlin to keep her name off his disgusting lips. But that wouldn't help anything.

Stay cool. Just. Stay. Cool. "Yes. That was her name."

Marlin nodded, walking over to a cooler and flipping the lid open. He pulled out a can of beer, popped the top, and took a long drink. He carried the can back to Jayce, holding it out to him.

"Care for a last drink, puke?"

Jayce forced his cracked, bleeding lips into another smile. "Nah. You can have it."

Marlin stared at him for a minute, then a low chuckle escaped him. He took another drink. "I gotta give it to you, Jayce ol' boy. You've got guts. Just like your sweet little Shannon and her brother. They had guts, too. Real guts." He angled another sneer at Jayce. "Too bad it got 'em killed."

Jayce's heart pounded in his chest. This was what he wanted. Marlin talking. Bragging about what he'd done. But Marlin's words did more damage than his fists ever could. They pierced Jayce's heart, shredding it, leaving it bleeding and dying.

The way Shannon and Aaron had been left.

Jayce closed his eyes against the flood of grief that slammed into him.

"Yeah, I couldn't believe it when I figured out what they'd

done." Marlin was really picking up steam now, getting into the story. "There we were, off-loading our supplies from the truck and taking them to the lab behind the old man's place, quiet as you please.

"'Course, we threw some nice, juicy steaks to those mutts of his, first. Kept 'em plenty occupied. We'd just finished bringing stuff in, when I heard this old man's voice tellin' me to stop right there and put my hands up." He snorted. "I turned around, and you know what I saw?"

Jayce forced back the bile that rose in his throat. "No. What?"

Marlin threw back another swallow of beer, swishing it around in his mouth before he swallowed it. "That old man standing there, holding a rifle on us. And your little pals were behind him." Marlin walked to grab a chair and drag it over so he could sit in front of Jayce. "Apparently Deputy Dan's brats snuck into the back of our truck, then slipped out when we reached Brumby's." He arched a brow. "Gutsy but stupid. Almost as stupid as getting Brumby all worked up."

Marlin leaned forward to rest his arms on his knees. "Not real neighborly of them, was it? I mean, getting the old coot killed like that?"

Jayce flinched, and Marlin smiled. "Yeah, wish you coulda been there to see it. That old man actually thought he was in control." Marlin's lip curled. "Thought I'd be afraid of his little rifle. But I haven't been afraid of guns for a long time." The hollow look in Marlin's eyes was chilling. "Not since I took my dad's gun away from him, the gun he always used to threaten me with."

He sat back in his chair, taking another drink. "And you know what I did with it? I used it. On him. Killed him dead. Cops thought it was a suicide." He lifted his beer can in a mock toast. "Here's to the cops, may they always be too stupid to see things aren't what they seem."

"So you killed Brumby." Jayce didn't know how he got the words out past the rage choking him. *God…God, are You there?* "And Aaron."

Marlin's slow smile reminded Jayce of pictures he'd seen of gargoyles. "And your sweet little Shannon? Oh yeah." He rolled the words around in his mouth, savoring them. "I killed them all. Had my own little gun in my pocket, so I took the old man out first. Shannon and Aaron took off running, of course. But it wasn't hard to catch 'em. And thanks to Brumby's gun, it wasn't hard to kill them. Then all I had to do was call the good deputy's office, say I was the old man and that something terrible had happened." This time he toasted himself. "Man. I'm so good it's scary."

Jayce couldn't hold back the sob that tore from deep within him. Nor could he hold back the heated obscenity he spat at Marlin.

"Hey, now." Marlin held his hands up in front of him. "Come on, pal. Let's be fair. After all, it's not my fault your little friends are dead. It's yours."

"You're crazy!"

"Naw, man. I'm not." Marlin ran his finger around the rim of his beer can. "If you'd stuck with the plan instead of trying to be part of some family, this never woulda happened. But you had to go and let outsiders into your life."

Marlin threw the beer can at Jayce, hitting him in the face. He stood, towering over Jayce, and his words came out on a vicious hiss. "You shoulda known better, Jayce." He grabbed Jayce by the chin, forcing him to meet his burning glare. "You never shoulda let Shannon and Aaron into your life. Or that deputy. You gave me no choice, man. You know too much. I couldn't just let you go off and be a happy little family. You shoulda known you'd get them all killed."

He's right. It's your fault they're dead.

Jayce had let himself believe the voice was gone for good. That it was back now, hissing through him, was pure agony. "It's not true!"

Marlin stood back and crossed his arms. "Yeah. It is. But don't worry, Jayce. I figured once you realized you're the one who got your beloved Shannon killed, you couldn't live with yourself." He turned and picked up a piece of wood. "So I'm gonna do you a big favor." He smacked the wood into his palm. "I'm gonna set you free."

Not again.

Dan couldn't believe he was here again. Facing a hostage situation. But this time it wasn't a stranger being held. It was a boy he knew. Cared about.

His fingers curled into a fist. *Jesus, please…don't let this end like—like the last one. Don't let Jayce end up like Sheila. Like her unborn baby. Lord, I'm begging You. Please, save my boy.*

My boy. Dan let those surprising words roll around inside him, and he had no trouble embracing them. Jayce *was* his boy. And Dan didn't just care about him.

He loved him. Like he was his own son.

"We're all set."

Dan turned. Sheriff Grayson had slipped up beside him. "I'll go in the front. That's closest to where Marlin's holding Jayce. You have the others come in from the back and side doors at the same time. That'll give us the element of surprise."

"Where do you want me?"

Dan turned to Annie. Kodi sat at her side, that happy puppy grin on her face. Well, she *should* be happy. She had found the lab for them. The lumberyard was big enough Dan worried it would take too long to find where the lab was located. But when they arrived, Annie held the pendant and Jayce's shirt out to Kodi, letting her gain the scent.

"If he's here, it'll happen fast."

No sooner were the words out of Annie's mouth than Kodi shot forward. Usually, the dog ran free when she searched. But because of the danger of being discovered, Annie had her on the leash. It was all she could do to keep up with the dog. Dan and the officers followed, watching with a mix of amazement and admiration as Kodi honed in on her target.

It had taken ten minutes tops for her to lead them to the lab.

It was located in a large metal building near the back of the lumberyard. Dan climbed on top of some barrels to look in a high window. He could see the meth lab set up at the back of the building.

But what he saw just below the window made his blood boil. A bleeding, beaten Jayce, bound hand and foot to a chair. Murphy sitting in a chair facing Jayce, slugging beer and laughing.

It took every ounce of self-control for Dan to not storm into the building and to wait the ten minutes for everyone to get into position. But now they were ready.

"I want you to stay here with the EMT squad, Annie. Out of danger."

"Kodi and I can help—"

He cut her off. "I'm not kidding. These guys have already taken my children from me. I can't risk letting them take my sister as well."

Dan knew she wanted to say more, but thankfully, she just nodded.

"Let's go, Dan."

He turned and followed the sheriff to the building, taking up his position just outside the front door. He tensed, gun at the ready, waiting for the signal. Prayers flew to heaven with every heartbeat. *God, be with us. Keep us safe. Let me be in time—*

"Go!"

The word shot from the radio on his shoulder, and Dan hit the door full tilt. As it flew open, he charged inside, his gun poised, and drew a bead on a startled Marlin. "Freeze! Police!"

He could hear the command echoing throughout the building as other officers rushed in. Apparently, Marlin heard it, too. As Dan drew within ten feet of them, Marlin reached into the pocket of his pants, then dropped to hide behind Jayce.

Dan barely took two more steps before Marlin stood again, this time with Jayce held in front of him, a knife at the boy's neck, a handgun pointed at Dan.

He'd cut Jayce free only to use him as a shield.

Jesus, please…no! Dan forced his voice to be steady. "Let him go, Murphy."

"Such a dilemma, eh, Deputy? You can't shoot me without going through our boy here. And you know I'll cut him before I die." He pressed the knife against Jayce's neck. "Now outta my way."

Dan could see blood trickle down Jayce's neck. *God…Father…please.* "Not gonna happen. Put the gun down and let him go."

"Freeze!"

Marlin turned his head, and two more deputies came behind the thug, guns drawn. Dan held out a hand. "Don't fire! He's got a hostage."

They stopped in their tracks, guns trained on Marlin.

He stood sideways, looking from the two who'd just arrived to Dan. The knife at Jayce's throat never wavered. Marlin fixed his gaze on Dan. "You think you've won?" He ground the words out. "Well, you're wrong. Just like you were wrong before. Remember? You said one screw up and I was yours? Well, guess what, Sheriff Taylor? Jayce is mine."

Marlin turned the pistol, pressing it into Jayce's temple, smiling when Jayce groaned. "Just like Aaron. And Shannon."

Since the day he found his children dead, Dan had wondered what he'd do if he ever came face-to-face with the one who killed them. Now he knew.

He wanted Marlin dead. Not arrested. Not in jail.

Dead.

His finger tightened on the trigger. One movement. Just a slight squeeze, and it would be over.

"Don't!"

The slurred cry caught at him, and his eyes flickered from Marlin to Jayce. The boy's face was a mass of bruises and cuts, and he could only open one eye. But that was enough. What Dan saw shining in Jayce's eye gripped him, shook him like a Doberman with a rag doll.

Faith.

He saw the light of faith in Jayce's eye. The same light he'd seen every time he looked into his son's or daughter's eyes.

His finger easing on the trigger, Dan focused on Marlin again. The glance at Jayce only took a moment, but it was a moment too long. Dan found himself looking down Marlin's gun barrel.

"I might go down—" there was pure hatred in Marlin's words—"but I'm taking you with me." He smiled. "So I win after all."

As if in slow motion, Dan watched Marlin's finger squeeze the trigger, tensed for the bullet to strike, but two things happened simultaneously.

Jayce gave an agonized cry and threw himself back into Marlin, just as a black blur flew through the air and latched on to Marlin's arm.

Kodi!

As the gun spiraled into the air, Marlin, Jayce, and Kodi all tumbled to the ground. Dan and the other deputies rushed them. Within moments, they had Marlin pinned, his hands cuffed behind his back. Annie was there, too, taking her dog by the collar. "Kodi! Release!"

The dog let Marlin's arm go and dropped into a sit next to Annie.

"I thought I told you to stay outside!"

Annie gave him a demur smile. "You did."

"Well, the next time I give you an order like that…"

Her brows arched. "Yes?"

Dan grinned. "Do me a favor and ignore me again."

She started to laugh, but sudden concern creased her forehead. "Dan, he's hurt!"

He turned to see Jayce lying on the cement floor, not moving. A pool of red was coloring the floor beneath him. Images of Sarah lying there, struggling for air, flashed through his mind. For a moment all he felt was blind panic. He'd lost Sarah. Then Aaron and Shannon.

And now he was losing Jayce.

No.

The word whispered within him, bringing with it a cool wave of calm.

Don't be afraid.

Peace settled over him, bringing with it the undeniable sense of God's presence. His mercy.

Don't be afraid.

As the words echoed again, Dan realized he wasn't. Not any longer. Instead, what he felt was trust. God had Dan in His hands. And Jayce. And there was no better place for either of them.

He dropped beside the boy, taking hold of him and easing him over.

Marlin's knife was buried in Jayce's right shoulder. Dan fought to keep the panic from his voice as he hollered at the other deputies. "Get the EMTs in here!"

Annie knelt beside them, pressing her bandanna to the wound, trying to staunch the flow of blood.

"I'm sorry…I'm so sorry…"

Between Jayce's swollen lips and his sobbing, Dan almost couldn't understand the words. "Sorry?" He forced himself to smile. "Why? Because you just saved my life?"

"It's my fault."

"What is?"

Jayce's ruin face spasmed. "Shannon. Aaron. It's my fault they're dead."

Dan and Annie exchanged a shocked look.

"No." Dan put his hand on the boy's forehead. "No, it's not. Marlin killed them. Not you."

"You don't understand." With a groan, Jayce bent his knee

so he could reach down into his sock. He pulled something out and handed it to Dan.

It was a digital microrecorder.

"It's voice activated."

Dan looked down at Jayce, troubled at the flat, desolate tone in the boy's voice.

"It's all there. Marlin's confession. How he killed Brumby. Aaron." His voice cracked. "Shannon. And why." Tears flowed from his eye. "Listen to it, Dan. Then you'll see. You'll understand."

With that, he turned his face away. Dan slid the recorder into his pocket, then wrapped Jayce in his arms.

"Jayce, look at me." At Dan's firm tone, the boy turned his head, peered out his one good eye. Dan leaned his face close to Jayce's. "Listen to me, son. And I mean listen. I don't care what's on this tape. It doesn't matter. None of it. It wasn't your fault." Emotion clogged Dan's throat, but he forced the words out. "And even if it were, I forgive you."

Jayce's lip trembled. "But Shannon—"

"Shannon loved you." He gripped Jayce's hand. "How can I do any less?"

Jayce stared, his swollen mouth falling open. "Are you saying...do you mean, you love me?"

"Got it in one. I love you. And I want you to stay with me. For good."

"Okay, Deputy, let us in there."

Dan looked up at the EMTs. For a moment, he resisted, loathe to let Jayce go. But Annie put her hand on his arm.

"Let them do their jobs, Danny."

He moved away.

"Dan?"

He glanced over the nearest EMT's shoulder. Jayce's face was so pale. "Yeah, son?"

"You're not...just saying...what you did because...because I'm dying, are you?"

Dan tried to laugh, but it came out on a choked sob. "No. And you're not going to die. You hear me?"

Jayce's lips pulled into a swollen smile. "Yes, sir."

Annie took Dan's arm and led him away. He followed, tears rolling down his face. *Please, Father, for once in his life, please make Jayce do as he's told.*

"Dan!"

At the sound of that voice, Dan jumped up from the waiting room chair and turned. Shelby ran toward him, and he didn't even hesitate.

He opened his arms and drew her into his embrace.

She held him tight, her face buried in his chest. He smoothed her soft hair, savoring her nearness. She tipped her head back to look up at him.

"Is there any word on Jayce?"

"They're moving him to a room. The knife wound was deep, but they were more worried about possible internal injuries from the beating. So they're keeping him here a few days, to watch him."

She touched his face. "He'll be okay, Dan."

He captured his hand in hers, turned his face to press a soft kiss in her palm. "Guess what?"

Her hand trembled in his. "What?"

"I know that." He smiled. "I really do." He drew her to the chairs, and they sat. "It was amazing, Shelby. When I saw Jayce was hurt, I kind of panicked. But only for a second. Then this...wave of calm settled over me. And I just knew. Whatever happened, it was in God's hands. His control." He looked down at their joined hands. "And everything would be right. Regardless. It would be right, because of Him."

She leaned her head against his arm. "I love you, Dan."

It seemed the most natural thing in the world for her to say those words. And for him to cup her face and lower his lips to hers. The waiting room around them, the hospital, it all faded away. There was nothing but the two of them. Dan let that kiss tell her everything that was in his heart: *I love you…I promise we'll have a good life together…I'll cherish you, and every day God lets us be togeth—*

"Uh. 'Scuse me, Deputy?"

Dan and Shelby pulled apart, turning to stare in a daze at the nurse standing in front of them. Dan blinked. Tried to form coherent words. Then tried again. "Y-yeah?"

The nurse's grin brought a sheepish smile to Dan's face, but he didn't let Shelby go. And she didn't seem to mind one bit.

"The boy you came in with, he's settled in his room now. I thought you might like to see him before you headed home."

"I'd like that a lot." Dan stood, then held his hand out to Shelby. "Shall we?"

She slipped her small, strong hand into his. "Absolutely."

THIRTY-FIVE

*"There are things that we never want to let go of,
people we never want to leave behind. But keep in mind that
letting go isn't the end of the world, it's the beginning of a new life."*

ANONYMOUS

*"Your throne, O God, will last for ever and ever;
a scepter of justice will be the scepter of your kingdom."*

PSALM 45:6, NIV

JAYCE WAS COMING HOME.

Dan couldn't wait. In fact, he arrived at the hospital at least two hours early. He sat in Jayce's room, watching as the nurses fussed over the boy, treating him like a young prince. For his part, Jayce took the coddling with surprising good humor.

After yet another young nurse came in to rearrange his pillows, Dan shook his head. "Enjoy it while it lasts, kid. You're not getting this kind of treatment at home."

It was so good to see the healthy color back in Jayce's face. Even his cocky grin was a welcome sight. "Hey, haven't you heard? I'm a hero." He lifted a hand and ticked items off on his fingers. "I saved a deputy's life, got rid of a drug dealer, *and* got the evidence that convicted a killer."

Dan lifted his hand, ticking off his own list. "And got yourself beaten to a pulp, me almost shot, and yourself stabbed…"

358

Jayce leaned back against his strategically placed pillows. "Man! You just don't give a guy a break, do you?"

"Why should he, when he doesn't give a girl a break, either?"

They both turned to the doorway, but all they saw was a huge bouquet of helium balloons and a pair of legs below them.

"Well…" Jayce chortled. "It *sounds* like Shelby."

Dan craned his neck. "And the legs are shapely enough to be Shelby's."

"Ha ha." She came in and tied the balloons to the foot of Jayce's bed. "A regular pair of comedians. That's you two." She leaned over Jayce and planted a kiss on his forehead, then went to give Dan a kiss. He closed his eyes, savoring her nearness.

When the kiss ended, he gave her a slow smile. "Hi."

She touched his face. "Hi back."

"All right, enough of the mushy stuff."

Jayce's goofy grin told Dan he wasn't the least bit serious. Just yesterday Dan told Jayce he had a surprise for him.

"Please tell me it's not more balloons." Jayce grimaced. "There's hardly room in here for me with all these balloons."

"It's not balloons."

"Okay. Good."

"It's actually a ring." Dan watched Jayce's face. "A gold one."

The blank stare Dan got told him he'd have to be less subtle.

"A *wedding* ring."

Jayce almost jumped out of the bed. "You *did* it! You asked Shelby to marry you!"

Dan laughed. "That I did."

"And she said yes?"

Dan delivered a playful punch to Jayce's arm. "She said yes. And, by the way, so did your grandmother."

Jayce's mouth dropped open. "You proposed to my

gramma? Isn't that illegal? Or immoral? Or im*some*thing?"

"Ha ha. She said yes to letting us adopt you, goofball."

"Ooohh." Jayce nodded, his lips doing their best not to grin. "Got it."

"So you'll have a mom one of these days, as well as a dad. You have a problem with that, son?"

"Me? A problem? Not in a million years." The kid's grin almost took up his whole face.

Now Jayce studied the two of them. "So Shelby, if we're such a crazy pair of goons, you sure you want to sign on to this outfit?"

"Oh—" she looked down at Dan, a small smile playing at her lips—"I think I can keep you guys in line."

Dan arched one brow. "Is that so?" He grabbed her around the waist and pulled her onto his lap. He nuzzled her neck. "Don't count on it, woman."

Shelby's laughter surrounded him, and Dan soaked it in. Her laughter was the most beautiful music in the world.

She slid off his lap, then tapped him on the shoulder. "Did you give it to him?"

"Oh." Dan reached into his pocket and stood. "I forgot."

"What?" Jayce's eyes lit up. "Presents? For the hero?"

"Hero?"

Dan shook his head at Shelby. "Don't encourage him."

At his words, the three of them stopped, then Shelby and Jayce said together, "Guys like that don't know when to quit."

"All right," Dan said as their laughter died down. "Very funny." He turned to Jayce. "Hold your hand out, comedian."

Much to Dan's surprise, Jayce did so without question. That simple act of trust warmed his heart more than he could say. He reached out, holding his hand over Jayce's, then dropped the gift into the boy's palm.

Jayce looked down, then up at Dan and Shelby, his eyes glistening. "My Aslan pendant."

Dan took it from his hand and fastened it around Jayce's

neck. He stepped back, his hand on Jayce's shoulder. "There. Back where it belongs."

Jayce gripped Dan's wrist for a moment. "Thanks, Dan."

"Okeydokey, then. Somebody here ready to check out?"

Dan turned to the nurse, holding his hand out for the paperwork she was carrying. "Absolutely."

The paperwork done, they settled in to wait for the nurse with the wheelchair.

"Oh, by the way. There are a couple of visitors waiting back at the house for you."

Jayce looked at him. "Visitors."

Dan knew his grin was wicked. "Your Auntie Kyla and Auntie Annie are there. They've been getting your room all fixed up for you."

"My room?" Jayce frowned. "My room is fixed up."

"Oh, no. It hasn't had the true Justice treatment yet. But now that you're going to be a bona fide member of the family…"

Jayce groaned, leaning back against his pillows. "What'd they do?"

"Let's see, a plaque with your name and its meaning—"

"Which," Shelby joined in, "is actually pretty cool. Did you know your name means 'a healing'?"

Jayce sat up. "Really?"

"Neat, huh?" Shelby took Dan's hand. "Perfect name for someone who was instrumental in helping this guy to heal." Tears sparkling in her eyes. "Kinda makes it seem like God knew we'd all be together."

"Guess He knows what he's doing."

"I'm thinkin' that's a no-brainer."

"Ah ha!" Dan glanced from Jayce to Shelby. "Sarcasm. I recognize it because Aaron was fluent in it."

"Yeah," Jayce said, pulling a face at him, "but I'm a *master*."

"Oh, joy." Dan stood as the nurse came in with a wheelchair. He helped Jayce out of bed and into the chair. "Just keep in mind, dear boy, that my momma named me well."

"Yeah," Jayce snorted as the nurse put the foot rests down for him, "Justice Justice." He rolled his eyes at Shelby. "There's a name that just trips off the tongue."

"That's *Daddy* Justice to you, kid. And don't you forget it."

The nurse stood and surveyed them. "Sure is nice to see a family that has fun together."

Dan's heart swelled. A family. That's what they were. That's what God had given him. And though he'd never stop missing Sarah and the children, he was ready to move forward. To discover what life—and God—held in store.

And there was no one he'd rather discover that with than the two beside him. He took Shelby's hand, then touched Jayce's shoulder and said the words he'd been waiting for days to say. "You ready to go home, son?"

Jayce looked up at Dan. "Absolutely...Dad."

With Shelby at his side, they took the first steps into the future. A future Dan knew would hold blessings and trials. Peace and conflict. Love and learning.

He could hardly wait.

Dear Friends,

I don't know about you, but I don't like suffering. Yes, I understand intellectually that it's a part of life and that being a Christian doesn't give us a get-out-of-suffering-free card. Christ promised us a fellowship in not only His salvation and eternity, but in His suffering as well. But I still don't like it.

Too often when suffering hits, I fall into the trap that captures many of us. I find myself slipping into confusion ("Why is this happening?"), fatigue ("I can't take anything else. I really can't."), and even anger ("Come *on!* Enough is enough!). And more and more, it seems serious trials come one on top of another. In fact, as I write this, we've been dealing with health crises for both friends and family, with friends dying unexpectedly and far too young, and with numerous other stresses and strains. It's just too much.

So here I sit, my head heavy from lost sleep, my chest aching from pressing anxiety, wondering what on earth I can possibly tell you about facing such times with courage and faith…

And then I remember. The answers don't come from me. They come from God. From His Word. His promises. From His call for each of us to be honest about what we're experiencing in life, to be transparent with God and with each other.

So are you struggling? Don't try to hide it. Are you suffering? Share your pain with those who are steeped in God's wisdom and will. Let fellowship with other believers draw you to a place of peace, no matter what the circumstances, until you can at long last say with the suffering Christ, "Even so, not my will, but Thine."

I'm not there yet. Not quite. But I'm comforted by the knowledge that the Lord traveled this treacherous path; that He felt the rocks pressing into His sore, tired feet; that He fell to His knees before His Father, pleading for help…

And that prayer was answered. Gloriously, eternally answered.

No matter what we face, no matter how deep the suffering: God is in control. He is with us, He sees all we face, and He will not let us go. Not now. Not ever.

So lift your voices with me and praise the name of the One who sustains us, who lifts us from the dirt, and who will grant us His strength and endurance at just the right time.

Blessed be the name of the Lord. Forever and ever. Amen.

Karen M. Ball

READER'S GUIDE

1. How were you affected by the following characters?
   Dan
   Shelby
   Shannon
   Jayce
   Marlin

2. How does someone live a life that honors God? In what ways are you honoring God in your life?

3. Why do we have to face trials and pain? And where is God when terrible things happen? Consider Isaiah 53 and Romans 8:15–38, then discuss the insights these readings offer.

4. Is it wrong to doubt God in the face of suffering and loss? Why or why not? What does Psalm 44 say about that?

5. What can we do to prepare for difficulties? Read and discuss the following: Psalm 91:1–2; 119:11; 49–51; Proverbs 4:4; Hebrews 6:17–19.

6. Has something happened in your life that caused you to meet God as you never had before? If so, share your experience.

7. Each of us leaves a legacy by the way we live our lives. Consider the positive and negative legacies demonstrated in the story:
   Dan: a legacy of faith
   Jayce: a legacy of trouble
   Marlin: a legacy of rage and crime
   How would you describe the legacy your parents left you? The legacy you are leaving your own children? Or if you have no children, the legacy you're leaving those who have known you?

8. Jayce's past seemed to predispose him to a certain kind of future. But those who follow Christ should find their identities in Him, not from their pasts or even their families. What gives you a sense of self, of identity? How does the way you see yourself compare with how God sees you? Read Romans 8:1–15 and 1 Peter 1:3–4. What do these Scriptures say about who we really are?

9. Did this story change your perception about God's justice? If so, how?

10. Shelby had to forgive Dan for hurting her. Too often it's those we care about most who hurt us the deepest. If someone you cared for hurt you deeply, how did you reach a place of forgiveness?

11. It's easy to look at a person like Marlin—or even Jayce—and write him off as unredeemable. But what kind of response does God call us to with people like this? Consider 1 Samuel 16:7; Matthew 5:43–45; Luke 6:35–36; and Romans 14:4.

12. God called Dan to reach out to Jayce, and Dan's obedience deeply impacted the boy. Do you know of a troubled teen or adult you can reach out to? If you've already done this, how was your life impacted by doing so? If you've felt the call but haven't followed through, what is holding you back?

13. When our relationship with God slips, so do other areas of our lives. Consider the following emotions Dan felt and discuss how to deal with them:
    Bitterness
    Anger
    Hopelessness

Don't miss Book 2 of KAREN BALL'S
dramatic Family Honor series

Annie sees what few others can...
but is she blind to what matters most?

Annie Justice. Youngest of the Justice clan. Who always saw the world a little bit differently than anyone else. She's finally come into her own as a nationally renowned stained glass artist and, along with her German shepherd, Kodi, one of the most successful K-9 Search and Rescue teams in the Northwest. But all the acclaim in the world can't change Annie's sense that she doesn't really fit in. That feeling is only reinforced when Jed Curry, slick producer of reality TV shows, wants to feature her on his hit show *Everyday Heroes* because she's different. And different sells. Maybe so, but Annie has no interest in that sort of fame. Or the man. At least, that's what she keeps telling herself.

However, everything changes the day Annie and Kodi find themselves in the middle of the Oregon wilderness, struggling against time and the elements to find a lost child. When Annie hears the search is about to be called off, her only ally is Jed. Joined in a race against time—and a battle against the attraction both feel but neither wants—Annie and Jed must find a way to work together and bring the little girl home before it's too late.

Coming spring 2006!

"A story this honest could only come from the deepest, most tender places in a writer's heart. Karen Ball is a highly skilled author who has gifted us with a gripping, heartfelt tale of the times."

—KAREN KINGSBURY, bestselling author of *One Tuesday Morning, Oceans Apart,* and the Redemption series

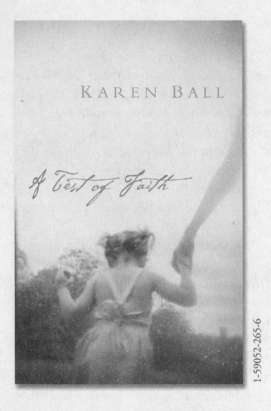

KAREN BALL

A Test of Faith

1-59052-265-6

Anne's daughter Faith is the answer to her lifelong prayer to be a mother. But her dream is shattered when Faith rejects Anne's love and the love of God. After years pass, and God heals their relationship, Anne falls seriously ill. Faith watches her mother weaken, struggling with role reversals and leaning on God as never before. Through all the intricacies of their relationship, all the joys and trials, they learn that God is with them. He brings them peace in the darkness, joy in the midst of sorrow, and hope in the face of death.